SEEDS OF LOVE

Also by Valerie Georgeson

THE TURNING TIDES

The Shadow of the Elephant

SEEDS OF LOVE

VALERIE GEORGESON

Macdonald

British Library Cataloguing in Publication Data

Georgeson, Valerie
The shadow of the elephant.—(The Seeds of love)
I.Title   II.Series
823'.914[F]   PR6057.E5/

ISBN 0-356-12055-4

Typeset in Plantin by Fleet Graphics, Enfield, Middlesex

Printed in Great Britain by
Redwood Burn Limited, Trowbridge, Wiltshire
Bound at the Dorstel Press

Macdonald & Co (Publishers) Ltd
Greater London House
Hampstead Road
London NW1 7QX

A BPCC plc Company

For Chintamani

The author would like to thank the following:

South Shields Central Library, particularly Miss D. Johnson
(Local Studies Librarian, Borough of South Tyneside Libraries)
The pilots of Watch House, South Shields
Mr Gavin H. Brown, for help with Sanskrit excerpts
Mr & Mrs Clapham & Mrs E. Georgeson, for local knowledge

The author also wishes to acknowledge the following
publication:

Blake Complete Writings: ed. Geoffrey Keynes,
Oxford University Press, 1966

PART ONE
Spring 1872

CHAPTER ONE

'Once upon a time . . . ' Bob Ridley paused, and his eyes narrowed, deep in thought. The four young faces round the lamp shone out of the gloom at him, like moons, suspended in wonder as the story began. 'Once upon a time, there was a little baby elephant . . . '

'What's one of them?' Jane's childish face creased into a frown.

'One of what?' her brother asked.

'You know! A little baby thingummy!'

'Thingummy!' Fanny sneered. Jane set her mouth, determined not to be put down by her big sister and tried with all her might to form the word. Her father watched, amused, as the child's memory of the unfamiliar sounds struggled with her tongue.

'Hephalant!' she splurted out at last. Fanny laughed out loud, and Jane looked desperately from her Da to her brother Robert. Robert shook his head.

'I don't know what it is.' The youngest of the four, Josh, kicked rhythmically at his chair refusing even to attempt an answer to the mysterious question of the 'hephalant'.

'Fancy never having heard of one of those!' Their father remonstrated.

'Well I have!' Fanny tossed her hair indignantly, and Bob tried to hide his smile.

'Have you really, Fan?' Jane was all admiration. Fanny turned on the little girl vehemently.

'Of course I have and don't call me Fan!'

'Why shouldn't she call you Fan if she wants to?' Robert rose heatedly to Jane's defence.

'Because, Robert Ridley, you don't use me to cool your porridge with!'

'Shut up the lot of you!' The four children turned startled towards their father. 'Yes.' He nodded slowly. 'That's wiped the smiles off your faces. Always squabbling and going on! Hah! I tell you! I'll be glad to get away to sea and leave you!'

A sudden chill descended on the group and in the silence following her father's explosion, a tiny sob escaped Jane. Neither Robert nor Fanny dared to move a muscle but with a final kick to his chair Josh got up and went out into the back yard to stare up at the stars. His father watched him through the window and shook his head.

'There now.' He sighed. 'See what happens when you start up.' Another tiny sob from Jane. Her father looked lovingly at her, her fair hair silver in the lamplight, her pale face downcast, numb with grief. Robert sat next to her, his arm wrapped protectively round his little sister, heart aching because she wept, the wondering dove-grey of her eyes darkened with pain. It would have touched the heart of any man. And Bob felt a fist tighten in his chest at the sight of them. Jane loved her Da. How could he hurt her? How could he go away for months and months on end and leave her – miss the precious years of her innocence, as he had missed those of his eldest daughter, Fanny? His eyes strayed to her. Fanny looked almost pretty in that light. The amber flame lent a burnish to her brown hair, her eyes shone bright, and her skin looked smooth. Merciful deception; how beautiful she might have been, like her mother before her, if only . . . Bob's eyes fell to her mouth. It was set hard, defiant, and if his eyes were not mistaken in the gloom, it seemed to Bob that her lips had a bitter twist to them. Poor Fanny, her mother's death had come hard to her, after all her sacrifices. To her, he must be specially kind. 'Come on now. What miserable faces!

I'd've done better to have gone down to the Globe.'

'Ah no, Da. Don't go down there!' Jane left her brother's arm and clambered onto her father's knee. 'I don't want you to go away to sea again. None of us does, do we!' Robert shouted a 'No!', Fanny remained stubbornly silent, and outside in the yard, oblivious to them all, little Josh stood and stared at the starry sky.

'Aye well, somebody's got to earn a crust, haven't they? And I don't know any other way of doing it, if I *don't go!*'

'I could get a job.' Robert's chin stuck out defiantly as his Da smiled mockingly. 'I could! I could get a job with the foyboatmen on the river!'

'Huh! Foyboatman! It's all you're fit for!'

'You're a rotten snob, our Fanny! And Robert's better than your la di da Dandy O any day of the week!' Fanny flushed crimson, and another explosion threatened.

'Here now, our Jane, I won't hear a word said against the Tyne pilots.'

'Dandy O's not a proper pilot yet!' Robert objected.

'He soon will be!' Fanny sprang to the defence of her admirer.

'Aye well, like I said, I'll not hear a word against any one of them. So mind now! And you shouldn't tease Fanny, Jane. There'll come a day when you blush at the mention of somebody's name, and then you'll know about it!' Jane squirmed and giggled, exchanging looks with her brother Robert. 'Go on, Fanny, fetch in our Josh. He's been out there long enough.' Fanny drew herself up to her full height and dignity and went out into the yard, escaping the mocking laughter of her siblings.

'Is our Fanny in love, then, Da?' Jane whispered loudly in her father's ear. Hearing every word, Robert burst out laughing, and, in the yard, Fanny turned uneasily to glance in at the window.

'Sh,' their father remonstrated. 'It's a very serious business is love.'

'Tell us about it, Da,' Jane implored.

'You're a bit young for that.' He smiled. 'Best wait till you're older.' Jane's face fell. She looked at Robert who shrugged, then back again at her father.

'I don't see why, Da. I mean, I love you, and Robert and everybody. And our Fanny's only five years older than me.'

11

'An important five years, lass.'

'Is it a different kind of love, then?' The dove grey eyes persisted, dying to know the mysteries that time and her father were hiding from her.

'Aye,' Bob's brow creased. It was at such times that he missed his wife most. How would she deal with questions like this? Why did she have to die and leave him with daughters to bring up? God knows the lads were bad enough!

'Tell's!' the little girl insisted.

But Bob stared out of the window. Fanny was standing behind Josh, talking to him. The boy's back expressed a stubborn refusal to listen, and Fanny gave up in disgust, coming back into the room with an angry expression on her face.

'Men!' Standing at the door with her hands on her hips, Fanny Ridley looked like any fishwife. Her father burst out laughing.

'Come and sit down, Fanny. Never mind Josh. He'll come in when he feels like it.' Catching his mood the younger pair laughed, and Fanny sat, her anger undermined by the general atmosphere of good humour. 'Get on with the story, Dad.' Robert, bored with all the love talk, was determined to get the conversation back to something more interesting.

'I should think you'd be too old for fairy stories, our Robert,' Fanny protested.

'You're never too old! Admit it, Fanny.' Her father smiled at her. 'You still like to listen when I tell my yarns to the little'ns!' Fanny sniffed.

'Yes, but you do grow out of them eventually!' Bob looked seriously at her and Fanny's eyes flinched, looking away as though to hide the thoughts in her mind.

'Why, Fanny? Have you? Have you grown out of them?' Fanny shrugged, and her face was troubled.

'She stands hours up at the Lawe dreaming,' Jane said.

'I like watching the ships!' Fanny explained but still refused to look at her father.

'She likes dreaming about Dandy O!' Bob turned to look at the faces of the younger pair.

'Well, all I can say is, I hope you never *do* grow out of fairy stories. Because, my bairns, if you do, there'll be something wrong!'

12

'Tell's what a hephalant is, eh, Da?'

Bob laughed. 'Now you're asking! Well, it's an animal, a big animal, oh, big as this room, I should think.' The three children gasped. 'Bigger maybe. And it walks on four legs, like a dog, only slow, because it's so big, and weighs so heavy, and it's got a thing that hangs down from its face . . . a great long thing, called a trunk, where its nose should be and it dips it in the water to drink, like.'

'Eeeh, Dad, you're making it up!' Jane laughed at him.

'No I'm not!'

'It sounds very ugly,' Fanny commented.

'Does it now?' Her father gave her long hard look. 'And how would you know. Have you seen one?'

'Well no. I'm only sayin' like.'

'Where does it live?' Robert, no longer bored, interrupted them.

'Oh far away places.'

'What far away places?' Robert wanted to know.

'Oh . . . very far away. They live in jungles and eat trees, or so I'm told.' Jane laughed delightedly.

'Dogs don't eat trees.'

'They might if they were as big as this room,' Robert told her.

'Yes, but Dad's hephalant's only a little baby one, isn't it, Da?'

'That's very true, pet.' And once again, Bob Ridley prepared himself to tell the story.

'Once upon a time, in a place far away on the other side of the world, there lived a little baby elephant. It was a happy elephant, and it had a happy life, with its mother and father and its brothers and sisters, as they roamed about the forests together. When they were hungry there was always the odd tree to eat, and when they were thirsty there were pools and lakes and rivers in which they could dip their trunks and drink to their hearts' content. Our little baby elephant played games like hide and seek with his brothers and sisters, and they always felt safe, because if any danger threatened, their mother and father would raise their trunks into the air and make a loud noise like a trumpet to warn them.'

'Like a trumpet, Da!' Robert laughed out loud.

13

'Aye, that's right, like a trumpet.' Robert and Jane looked at one another, eyes wide with amazement, imagining Mrs Dunn's dog, Gormless, down the street raising its nose and making a sound like a trumpet. It didn't bear thinking about. What would Mrs Dunn say? 'So, all the little elephants were quite safe. But the Mummy elephant warned them to be very careful when they went down to the river to drink, because there dwelt horrible creatures, with great snapping jaws, called crocodiles, that lay in wait to get them.' Jane gasped and crept closer to her brother. 'Now our little baby elephant was always very careful not to go too far into the water and did his best to keep out of the crocodile's way, even though it used to hide in corners, and wait quietly trying to catch him unawares.'

'Horrible thing!' Jane spat.

'Aye well . . . there's a lot of them about, lass,' her father told her. 'Anyway, our baby elephant did alright. He kept out of the crocodile's way, and started to grow up, and so far nothing out of the ordinary had ever happened to him. But the crocodile still lay in wait, biding his time. And the elephant grew bigger and bigger and older and older, till he was almost grown up . . . ' Robert's eye caught that of his eldest daughter, and for a reason she didn't understand, Fanny blushed. 'Well, over the years, our elephant had grown just a bit big for his boots. A bit cocksure like, and he started to get a bit careless.' Jane's face grew pale and serious. 'And one day, when the sun was very hot, and he was big now, you see, so he'd worked up quite a lather rushing round the place enjoying himself, like. Well, he galloped off down to the river for a drink. He had a favourite rock pool, where he often used to go, a secret place, that the others didn't know about, so he could dip his trunk into the water, and have it all to himself. Seeing him, standing there all on his own, the crocodile, a long slithery sort of animal, slid from the river bank into the water and hid himself, behind some reeds. The elephant didn't even see him coming. He was too keen on drinking all he could, and his tummy swelled till he could drink no more. But still he felt all hot and bothered. And the pool looked so inviting. How he would like to plunge into the water and cool himself down! So, in he went, up to his knees, up to his thighs, up to his shoulders, till all you could see of him was his head and his long thin trunk.

'And then the crocodile saw his chance. Quick as a flash he swam out into the pool after him. The elephant saw him. But it was too late. He was too big to move quickly in the water, and soon he felt the crocodile's jaws on him. Well, he fought and he fought with that crocodile, till he was weak and weary. But the crocodile wasn't a land animal like the elephant, he lived in the water all the time, so he didn't get tired at all. And it seemed the game was up for our poor elephant, who had so carelessly fallen prey to the enemy. There was nothing left for him, but to raise his trunk in the air and trumpet out as loudly as he could for help. And the sound of his trumpet broke open the sky. The clouds parted, a great storm started up, and a flash of lightning came down, and hit the crocodile square on the back of its neck, cutting off its head.' Bob slashed at the air with his hand, and Jane flinched as Robert yelled a cry of victory which had the neighbours upstairs banging on the floor in protest.

'Sh,' Fanny warned him. Robert's hand covered his mouth and he and Jane giggled at Fanny's stern look.

'Well,' Bob went on. 'Our elephant somehow managed to get himself out of the water and back to safety on dry land. He was badly wounded, and he had to limp his way through the forest to his family who had been wondering where he'd got to. When they'd heard his story, his Mam and Dad praised the God that looks after elephants for saving their son, and then, tying up his wounds, they warned him not to be so cocksure in future. Because you never know when the enemy might strike, and even a tried and tested warrior like our elephant's Dad, would have a hard time of it fighting off a mighty crocodile like that one! So, with his tail between his legs, our elephant promised to do as he was told in future, and he didn't play too hard, and work himself into a lather and go off on his own to the river again, but he stayed with his brothers and sisters, and his Dad brought him up to be big and strong so that if danger did strike, he would be able to defend himself. And our elephant, growing old and wise, was soon watching over a family of his own, playing happily in the forests unaware of the dangers around them. And when the sun climbed high in the sky and it grew hot in the afternoon, they all rested quietly in the shade, and none of them was allowed to run around so much that they needed to cool off in the river, where they might fall prey to the crocodiles. For you can't always rely on a flash of lightning to save you, can you? Eh?'

A long silence greeted the end of the story.

'That was a funny fairy story,' Jane said at last. 'There was no fairies in it.'

'No. That's true.'

'Could you keep a hephalant for a pet, like Mrs Dunn's dog?'

'Don't be daft,' Robert said. 'There's not enough trees in Trajan Street to feed it!' And Fanny and her Dad burst out laughing.

Josh had disappeared again. He was always going off was Josh. No-one knew why. You could never get a word out of him; a proper little mystery, he was. Fanny was sent off to look for him on the quay, while Bob went round the corner for a fish supper.

'Don't you stray, mind!' Bob warned them as he went. Two serious faces watched him go, then, left to their own devices, and under the watchful eye of Mrs Dunn's dog Gormless who had heard the magic words 'fish supper', they sat on the white step at the front door to discuss the situation.

'How long will Da be at sea this time?' Jane asked.

'You can never tell.' Robert shook his head. 'It all depends. When they get to Africa, they might pick up another cargo, and go on from there to . . . oh . . . Timbuctoo, and then if they got a cargo again, they might have to sail to America, and then . . . '

'But he might be away for ever and ever!'

'Well, a long time anyway.'

'I wish he didn't have to go.'

'He misses our Mam.'

'I know. I heard him crying the other night. I got up and went in, like. But he was asleep.'

'You mean Da was crying in his sleep, our Jane?'

'Aha. He was crying for her. I know he was.' A sob strangled Jane's voice and Robert held her close to him. 'I wish . . . I wish, we could have seen her. I wish we hadn't been sent away to Auntie Eileen's, when she got sick, Robert.'

'They had to send us away, Jane. Look what happened to our Fanny!' A shiver shook the little girl's back.

'I used to like our Fanny.'

16

'Aye. So did I.' Robert agreed.

'Maybe she'll marry Dandy O and then we'll be shot of her.'

'Aye, but who'd look after us when Da was away? We might get sent to Auntie Eileen's for good.'

'Away from the river? Away from the sea? Oh I'd not like that, Robert.'

'No. Neither would I, Jane.'

Gormless shifted restlessly at their side and started a low barking.

'What's wrong?' Robert asked him. In the darkness down the terrace, a figure lurched towards them.

'It's Mrs Dunn. She's back.' Gormless, tail between his legs, eased silently behind them, and crept into the Ridley house, as his mistress, slightly the worse for wear, tottered past them to her own place further along Trajan Street.

'Hallo, Mrs Dunn,' Robert called out to her.

Mrs Dunn stopped, hiccupped, and replied, 'Why hallo there Robert! Jane! Don't do anything I wouldn't, mind!' Then laughing and hiccupping she turned away, to concentrate her mind on the final steps home.

'What did she mean by that?' Jane asked.

Robert shook his head.

The fish supper arrived, but there was no Josh and no Fanny come to that. Bob expressed his disgust by throwing Josh's share to Gormless who thought it was his birthday and yelped with joy before demolishing it in two mouthfuls.

'Not as daft as you look, are you, lad!' Bob laughed at the mongrel, delightedly. But his face dropped as Fanny came into the room. Her face was flushed, and her hair hung loosely round her face.

'Well? Where is he?' Bob asked her.

'I don't know, Da. I couldn't find him,' Fanny replied and dug into her piece of fish hungrily.

'Are you all right, our Fanny?' he asked her.

'Of course I am. Why shouldn't I be?' she retorted a little too quickly.

'Aye well, I'd like a word with you before you go to bed.'

A loud bang on the door sent Robert flying to answer it, and Jane hurrying to clear the table of the debris of their supper. The

Ridleys were a respectable family, and had a reputation to keep up, and it was just as well she'd bothered, for their visitor was none other than Edward Tully, one of the highest paid pilots on the river, and father to Dandy O.

'Why hallo, there, Rattler,' Bob hailed him. 'Park yourself, man!'

'No thanks, Bob. I'm not stopping, like. I thought I'd just return some of your property,' and Mr Tully, known locally by his nickname of Rattler, because he took so many pills for his various ailments that he rattled; Mr Tully turned, and out of the gloom by the door, a slight figure emerged. It was Josh.

'And where have you been?' Fanny shouted at him. 'We've been worried sick. I've searched high and low . . . '

'Aye,' Rattler said quietly. 'Dandy O told me.' There was a short silence. Bob took in Rattler's words but chose to say nothing for the moment. Fanny sank back into the shadows in the corner of the room, thinking to be out of harm's way. 'I found young Josh up by Saint Stephen's.'

'And what were you doing there?' his father asked him. 'I hope you were praying I'd not skelp you one for straying!'

'He was in the churchyard,' Rattler said meaningfully. Bob sighed.

'She's not buried there, son,' he told his wandering son. 'You know that. She's in Saint Hilda's.' Josh kicked at the nearest chair. 'Come on, I'll find you a bit of something to eat.'

'Aye Bob - when is it you're off?'

'Day after tomorrow. First port, Cape Town.'

'Better you than me, man.'

'You can say that again.'

'There's a quoits match tomorrow. Will I see you?'

'Oh aye!' Bob smiled. 'We'll have a pint or two and er . . . I'd like a quiet word about em . . . your Dandy O and . . . ' His look took in the shadowy figure of his daughter hiding in the corner.

'Aye,' Rattler said thoughtfully. 'Aye. I'll see you tomorrow then.'

'Thanks for bringing our Josh home.'

'It's nowt, man. Tarrah!' And off Rattler went back to his house in Pilot Street where the cream of Tyne River life lived,

18

the families of the Tyne pilots, of which Rattler and his family were one.

Jane was almost asleep, head resting on her arms on the table. Her father's face softened as he looked down on the pale hair, shining in the light of the lamp. It was a shame to rouse her. His big, weatherbeaten hand reached out and touched her head gently.

'Come on, pet. Bed time!' Jane stirred and moaned, her bleary eyes looked up at the big figure of her father standing over her.

'Oh, I went to sleep.' She yawned. 'Did I miss anything?' Bob laughed.

'No, pet. Not really. Come on to bed now. Come on our Robert, Josh . . . ' And Josh, relieved to find he wasn't in for a row, meekly followed the other two into the next room. 'I'll be in later!' he called out after them.

'Will you tell's the story about the hephalant again?' Jane asked, yawning loudly.

'You'd not stay awake long enough to hear it!' her Dad told her as he shooed them off to bed.

'Now then, my lass,' he said turning on the figure in the dark corner, 'come into the light where I can see you.' Fanny rose and moved tentatively towards the table in the centre of the room. Then she stopped, just short of the reach of the lamplight. 'Closer,' her father commanded. A moment's pause, and then Fanny came into the full light and her father looked squarely on her pock marked face.

'I think maybe our Fanny's done something she shouldn't,' Jane remarked to her two brothers as all three climbed into the big bed in the next room.

'That's good,' Josh said grinning. 'It'll take his mind off me for a change!'

'You're daft you are!' Robert told him in no uncertain terms.

'Just shows what you know,' Josh retorted, turned his back on them, and started snoring loudly as though he was asleep.

'Stop it!' Jane dug him in the ribs and Josh thrashed his arm back at her, catching her one on her chest.

'Leave her alone!' Robert jumped on him, and the bed springs boinged loudly under the war cries of the two boys.

'I'll take the strap to the lot of you if you don't shut up!' Their father's voice from the next room, rose above the bed and the banging from the people who lived above, and three hands rose to three mouths to stifle giggles.

'Sh,' Jane whispered.

' "Sh" yourself,' Josh answered her, 'Anyway you started it.' And he turned his back again, shutting them out.

'*Is* our Fanny in love, Robert?' Jane asked her elder brother, after a short silence.

'How would I know?'

'I don't know. She's been acting a bit funny, like.' Jane paused and considered Fanny's 'funny' behaviour. 'She moons about a lot, if that means anything.'

'Our Josh moons about.' Josh's leg kicked out behind him to find Robert's shin. 'Ow!' Another pause followed.

'I love Dad.' Jane considered her feelings thoughtfully. 'I loved our Mam as well. I still do.' Beside her, Josh went very still. 'I love you as well.' Josh was shaking, crying quietly beside her. 'And you Josh. I love you.'

'Love's cissy!' He tossed off her comfort and, rejected, Jane turned once again to Robert. 'Do you love me, Robert?'

Robert cleared his throat and shifted restlessly in the bed.

'I suppose so.' He answered her gruffly. A vague uneasiness, a feeling that maybe Josh was right, that love was 'cissy', girls' talk, made him sound cold to her, and Jane, lying between her two brothers suddenly felt all alone, rejected.

'Nobody loves me,' she moaned softly.

'Come on, Jane, let's play a game!' Robert laughed.

Father and daughter sat at opposite ends of the table.

'Have you, Fanny? Have you let him . . . "do" . . . anything? Eh? You've got to tell me!' Fanny Ridley, hair hanging before her face, started to cry, and her father sighed. 'I see,' he said. 'Our Fanny! I thought better of you!' He looked helplessly on the weeping girl in front of him. She was little more than a child, seventeen years old. But old enough all the same. If only . . . if only. 'Why, Fan?'

'Don't call me . . . '

'All right, all right. No need to get on your high horse now. There's many a man'd bray the life out of you for what you've done.'

'I'm sorry, Da.'

'Sorry doesn't change anything, Fan . . . Fanny. Why? Eh? Just tell me that.'

'I thought he was going off me, Da.'

Bob's heart melted. How could he blame the lass? Her and Tully's lad had been sweethearts since Sunday school. She'd been a bonny lass then, his Fanny. And she'd given the lad her heart years ago. Queen of the town end of Shields she'd been. And then, out of the blue, all that had changed. In October 1871, smallpox came to Shields. Bob Ridley was away at sea when his wife, Ida felt the first symptoms of the disease. Immediately she packed her youngest three off to her sister at Hexham, and Fanny, the eldest girl, was left to nurse her at home, because the hospitals were full.

The first Bob Ridley knew of it was when his ship came into port in May of the following summer. The customs officers came on board checking whether there was any illness amongst the crew, and his heart went cold with fear. Freed from quarantine, he ran from the dock up the hill, to his home in Trajan Terrace. The street was empty. Mrs Dunn's dog Gormless, looking thin and uncared for as usual, walked the street all on its own. Bob was grateful for a live creature by his side as it accompanied him to the door of his house. He pushed it open and went inside. Was there anybody there at all? Had they *all* gone? The back room, with its bed against the wall, the room where they ate, and he and Ida slept, was empty. The grate was bare. The table was clean of plates or food. Gormless sniffed the air, and led him into the front room. A figure lay huddled on the bed. It was the figure of a woman. Was it Ida? Softly, Bob went towards her and pulled the shawl from round the face. And then his cry rent the street. His Fanny, his lovely girl, who in his absence had grown into a woman, had been scarred for life.

Mrs Dunn from down the street brought whisky to bring him round. It was hard to take it all in. Ida was gone. There had been mass burials, and no-one knew exactly where she had been laid to rest. Somewhere in Saint Hilda's close by Market Square, Mrs Dunn told him. He should think himself lucky he had a good neighbour like her to nurse his daughter safely through the

21

illness, and his other children out of harm's way in the country. Yes, Bob Ridley was lucky. He had a pocket full of money from the voyage, and he used it to buy food to build up his Fanny and bring her back to health. The epidemic raged on into June, and Fanny gained her strength. Many of her friends had died, many like her were marked. But not all. And Tully's son, Bill, he who they all called Dandy O because he was, after all, a bit of a lad, had his choice of the lasses. And his eye was caught by Eileen Purvis.

It was a blow to poor Fanny. Eileen hadn't been able to hold a candle to her in the old days, when Fanny queened it at the town end, and all the lads called after her. In those days Fanny had had Dandy O on a string and she had played him at her will. But now . . . she had been bested. For his part, Dandy O was sorry for her. He felt some guilt at betraying her, and not liking to hurt her feelings, he kept up the pretence of being sweet on her still. And Fanny, grateful and humbled would do anything to please him . . . anything at all. Bob's hand reached out and touched his daughter's face.

'I didn't want to lose him, Da,' Fanny sobbed.

'I know, pet. I know. Don't worry. We'll sort something out.' Gratefully, Fanny took his hand and kissed it.

'I'm sorry, Da. I am, honest.'

'I daresay, lass. I daresay.' But he couldn't chide her. 'When did he . . . '

'A few weeks back, Da.'

'And tonight?'

'No.' Fanny shook her head. 'I went down to the shed to see him, when I was supposed to be looking for Josh, but he was called out on a job. He went with his brother in the coble.'

'And are you all right?' Bob hardly dared to ask the question.

'I don't know. I expect so. Girls usually are.' Her hard tone shocked Bob. His hand lashed out and caught her across the face. The startled look soon turned sullen.

'Men! You're all the same!'

'You'll be getting a reputation for yourself, my lass! You sound like a . . . '

'A what!' she challenged him. But Bob backed down.

22

'If you don't care about yourself, you might at least care about the rest of us. What about our Jane? Do you want *her* name tainted too?!'

'Huh! I might know it'd come back to her! She's all you care about isn't she? Our Jane! With her little angel face. Butter wouldn't melt, and all that! Hah! Well it's not fair! Why did *I* have to be the one left behind to nurse me Mam! Why did Jane have to get off scot free, eh?'

'Eeh, pet.' Bob's head sank into his hands. 'What am I going to do to help you?'

'I want to marry Dandy O!'

'Aye well. It's maybe the only answer. I'll see what I can do.'

There was a bang in the next room followed by a loud yell and two giggling voices singing,

'There were three in the bed and the little one said
Roll over. Roll over.
So they all rolled over and Josh fell out
And the little one said,
Roll over. Roll over!'

Josh's yell of protest could be heard on the other side of the river!

23

CHAPTER TWO

Next day, two men leaned against the low stone parapet, watching with disbelief, as the interloper from Market Square fairly hammered their own champion from the town end. A stray quoit landed beside them on the wall, almost knocking Rattler's top hat, insignia of his high office as river pilot, into the road. The hat was rescued by a respectful bystander, and given back into the pilot's own hands. He took the courtesy as of right, without so much as a thank you.

'Play quoits? Why man,' Rattler shouted in disgust to the one time 'champion', 'you couldn't play tiddley winks, you!'

'Aye. I reckon we've lost,' Bob remarked. Some of the crowd had begun to disperse, but others stayed on, determined to make up for their disappointment with a stand-up fight.

'Howway,' Bob said. 'Let's get out of it, man.' And the crowd parted to make way for the pilot and his companion, as they wandered down Shadwell Street towards the Lawe.

'Where's your lad?' Bob ventured after a pause.

'Which one?'

'Dandy O.'

'Went out seeking this morning, with our John.'

'Aye, he's going to take after his Dad. No flies on him, eh?'

'We'll be fighting each other for ships this time next year!'

'Oh. Finishes his time then, doesn't he?'

'Talking about buying another coble, taking on an apprentice himself. He's done well. No doubt about it.' Bob felt the awkwardness of his position keenly. What had he to offer this man, who had position, money, and a son who was as good a catch as any in the district. Nothing. Only a lass with a pock-marked skin and no reputation to speak of.

'About our Fanny . . .' he began.

'Oh yes?' Rattler stiffened, knowing what was coming. Bob was putting him in a difficult position. And yet, he owed him something. He couldn't deny it.

'You know her and Dandy O's been knocking about together for a bit now . . .'

'Oh yes?' Rattler repeated.

'Since she was a bairn really. He was a canny lad in them days.'

'What do you mean "in them days"?'

'No offence meant. No offence.'

Rattler reached in his pocket and brought out a couple of bottles of pills. Bob watched in dismay as he chose between them and swallowed a handful. It was a bad sign.

'I only meant how he used to teach the Sunday School and that. Our Fanny thought the world of him. Do anything for him she would.' This last was greeted with a stony silence. 'And him being older than her, like, she's always trusted him, you know.' Another silence. 'If you see what I'm getting at.'

'No, Bob. Tell you the truth. I don't see. I don't see at all.'

They had arrived at the Lawe Top, where groups of old sailors and pilots stood around the old cannon brought back from the Crimea. It stood, as if keeping sentry, looking across the river mouth and out to sea. There sitting at the feet of an old tar, sat Josh Ridley, engrossed in yarns which told of the early days of the American West.

'Hoy Jock! You're not encouraging him, I hope!'

'Get away with you!' the old man snapped. 'I've only just got me audience! You'd not spoil an old man's pleasure, would you?'

'He should be at school, never mind listening to you, you old barsket!' But Josh was up and away, disappearing into the maze of narrow streets that flanked the quayside.

'Spoilsport!' The sailor spat on the ground and went into 'The Crown' behind him to drown his disappointment and find another audience.

Bob was torn. His son, all of ten years old, was running loose round the back streets. But his seventeen year old daughter also had a claim on him, to talk round Rattler Tully into letting her have his son. And Rattler, opportunist as ever, was at that moment walking away from trouble.

'Hoy! Come back, here! You and me's got things to discuss man!' Bob called after him.

'First I knew of it,' Rattler responded resentfully as Bob caught up with him. 'Anyway I'd've thought you'd be after your lad there! He'll be getting himself into trouble if you're not careful.'

'I've already got one bairn in trouble. And I'll deal with her first.' Rattler gave him a sharp look.

'If you mean she's in the family way . . . '

'If she's not it won't be the fault of your son!'

'Hah! Him and who else?'

Bob Ridley reeled at the insult.

'You say that again!' he challenged the pilot.

'Him and who else?' The slow deliberate repetition was too much for Bob. His arm swung out and caught his companion on the side of his head. 'I'm warning you, Bob Ridley.'

'He's not going to get away with spoiling my daughter, Rattler.'

'It's your own fault! You should've watched over her!' The truth of the statement stung Bob to the quick. His fist swung out a second time, but was met by a defending arm, followed by a swift blow to his cheek. 'You great fool, I'll wipe the floor with you!'

'Will you now!' Again Bob aimed, and the old sailors round the cannon gathered closer to watch the fun.

'What's it all about?' one of them asked.

'Bob Ridley's lass. You know . . . always down the pilots' shed.' He winked, and the sound of coarse laughter maddened the father.

'I'll see my lass married yet.'

'Not to a Tully you won't!' the pilot retaliated, and the crowd

26

gasped as the men staggered, swung out and staggered again under the blows they were raining one upon the other.

The old tar had come out of 'The Crown', a whisky in his hand, and he watched the proceedings with some satisfaction.

'I'll take bets on Ridley,' he announced.

'Why he's not a patch on Rattler.'

'Aye but he's got something to fight for.'

'Fanny Ridley! She's not worth it! She's got a face like sandpaper and she's as loose as a bag of rigging in a storm.'

'Aye. But she was canny. I mind when she sat on me knee, listening to the old stories. As sweet a maid as I ever clapped eyes on.'

'Doesn't last long round here!'

Bob fell to the ground, dazed. Through swimming vision he saw the pilot staggering away towards 'The Crown'. He could not let him go. For Fanny's sake; for the sake of his dead Ida, this was one fight he had to win, or she'd be finished, down the hill, like Mrs Dunn, an old soak, who'd do anything for pie and peas and a glass of porter. He forced himself from the ground. Blood dribbled from his nose onto his hands. The figure of the pilot doubled before him. A deep breath, and Bob gathered himself for a final assault. His arms reached out, his limbs forced themselves towards Rattler, and he fell, encircling the legs of his one-time friend, to bring him down onto the cobbles with him. Taken by surprise, Rattler's breath left his body, and the blows came home painfully in the small of his back.

'All right! All right, man! You win!' Bob let the pilot go.

'Told you so,' said the old tar, collecting in the money.

Sprawled under the cannon, the two men commiserated with one another, between mouthfuls of beer and whisky.

'The thing is,' Rattler was explaining, 'it's not really down to me, Bob. I mean there's the lad to consider. He's likely to want some say in the matter.'

'Aye. True,' Bob replied. 'But piloting runs in families. It gets handed down father to son, like, and Dandy O's got a brother. You could lean on him a bit, I daresay.' Rattler thought for a while.

'You're right, Bob, I could.' He thought again. 'I don't like to see a lass of yours going to the bad. You and me's known each other a long time, haven't we?' Slowly Bob nodded in reply.

'Aye and don't forget you owe me one an all.'

'I know, man. I know.'

Could either of them ever forget it? Bob was but a lad at the time, on his first trip. He'd been signed on the *Betsy*, a brig from Littlehampton, and he was on his way home. It was early December. And the master had ideas of another tour round the coast before Christmas. For days it had been blowing a gale, and he could wait no longer. About 9 p.m., when the tide was right, he decided to make a dash for Shields harbour. Determined to avoid the death trap of the rocks on the north side, known as the black middens, he steered a more southerly course, but the wind blew the brig too far, and he fell foul instead of the Herd sands on the other side of the river mouth. At once the sound of three cannon boomed out over the Tyne. And the men of the pilot service ran to man the lifeboat, 'Providence'. Rattler Tully was one of those who struck out for the looming masts of the *Betsy*, drawn on by the cries of sailors in distress. They drew alongside successfully, and made fast the ropes. Or so they thought. But the bow rope was not secure. A strong ebb tide ran round the stern of the vessel, catching the boat's starboard bow, and at that moment a mighty sea swept round to strike the boat under the starboard quarter. 'Providence' capsized, and the volunteer lifeboatmen were thrown into the sea. Bob had thrown a rope from the deck of the *Betsy* which was caught at by one of the volunteers. He hauled him up and knew him to be Rattler Tully. Twenty men had drowned. Twenty brave pilots. Amongst them they had saved almost five hundred souls in the year before. Men, women and children, hurried into the water to fetch in the lifeboat, wailing and keening, as the realisation struck, that their brave men would never return.

It was a night remembered by all the people of Shields, for years to come. But for Bob Ridley and Rattler Tully, it had a special significance. It was the beginning of a long friendship, made across the barrier of class differences.

'I'll tell you what I'll do, Bob. I'll talk to the lad. So help me. I'll talk to him.'

'You can say no more, Rattler. Let's shake hands on it, eh?'

And the two men rose unsteadily to their feet to signal their agreement.

Fanny's hands were sore from the sailmaking, which was now the daily occupation of her life. Sitting at the table in Trajan Street, she stared dolefully at the roughened red of her fingers. A tear fell and stung the sores. Was this all there was? When she'd been little, tough old sailors would stop their frowning, stop their coarse talking, and they would smile on her, as though she had turned up the lamps of joy inside them. Just by being there, she had been able to change them, to soften them. And then she had grown up and all that had changed. Why had it changed? She had become the object of the coarse talk, instead of the one whose very presence prevented it. Yet still they smiled on her, until . . . Fanny's eyes swam with her tears. For in the red scarred skin of her hands, she saw the image of her face. No smiles for her now. Nothing but hard work, and punishment for all the years to come. What sort of a future was that to look forward to? The cold misery of her vision frightened her, and hopelessly she laid her head on her hands to cry. Coming in from school, Jane stood at the door and watched her sister silently. Why did she cry? Was it for their mother? Was it because of Dandy O? The child's heart swelled with pity. Tears started in her own eyes and she couldn't help but rush toward her own dear Fanny, and put her arms round her, to comfort her. And Fanny grasped the child's hand, holding her close, while her aching heart found outlet in a long wail.

'I love you, Fanny. Don't cry,' the little girl said tearfully.

'Do you, pet?'

'Course I do! Oh Fanny, you don't know how horrible it was having to leave you and our Mam when we were sent away. And you were so brave, Fanny. I think you're wonderful, for being as brave as that. I do honest.' Fanny looked at her little sister, and for a second, the marching beat of resentment in her heart stopped. But it was only a second, before it started up again with more vigour than before.

'After everything, did she have to die?' Fanny cried. 'I wouldn't have minded, if there had been some point to it. But it was all for nothing!'

'Poor Fanny. Poor Fanny.' Jane's childish hands stroked soothingly at her sister's face, as though by magic she could smooth the deep wells that pitted the skin. And Fanny felt ashamed before her. The compassion of the child was like a reproach. She knew that at that moment, little Jane would willingly have changed places with her, have taken on all her sorrows, out of love for her. And Fanny knew her own feelings towards the child were dark, full of jealousy and resentment.

'Why couldn't it have been you!' she shouted at her. And immediately she was sorry. Jane's face fell. Misery extinguished the light inside her and she crawled into the corner of the room, helpless with grief for her sister, for her mother and for herself. Fortunately, life decided to intrude on her misery in the most distracting form of hunger. She looked up hopefully as Fanny busied herself to calm her tears.

'What's for me tea?' Jane dared to ask.

'Pig's cheek and like it,' came the smart reply.

For some reason she could not fathom, Jane felt as though she must be to blame for Fanny's misery. She didn't know how, but a question came into her eyes as she watched Fanny, gathering plates, putting the pan on the stove, peeling an onion. She became very still. And Fanny grew uneasy, feeling the watchful eyes on her. Taking the knife to cut the onion, it slipped in her nervous grasp, and she shouted out in fright.

'There now! Look what you've made me do!'

'I didn't do nothing. Honest I didn't.'

Fanny looked at her in exasperation.

'Well then you *should* be doing something!' The pan on the range boiled over, water spluttering onto the coals, dancing onto the grate, dangerously near to where Jane sat. Fanny's rage increased. 'Get out of my way!' She pushed her bewildered sister from her seat. 'Get the bread! Set the table! You great useless lump!'

'Have you cut yourself, our Fan?'

'It wouldn't be my fault if I had!'

'Would it be mine, then?'

'Oh shut up, will you!'

Sadly Jane got the bread from the cold store and set forks and knives on the table. No matter how she tried to work it out, it didn't make sense. But one thing was sure, Jane was in the wrong. Of that there could be no doubt.

On his way home for his tea, Bob called in at the shipping office and was relieved to discover that his sailing time had been delayed a few days, because they were still short of their cargo, and could not go without it. In the circumstances it was a blessed relief. He would like his mind cleared of Fanny's trouble before he left. Otherwise God knew what might happen in his absence and what he would have to look forward to on his return. It was as though fate had, for once, lent him a hand. It didn't happen often, but when it did, by but Bob couldn't half be grateful! So he was smiling broadly as he left the office, and to the man waiting outside, the smile looked a little incongruous on the bruised and battered face.

'You should have seen the other one!' The words were familiar enough. But the accent! Bob turned on his heels, and gasped with surprise as he saw his old friend Chandrika looking quizzically at him from the row of white faces waiting to sign on the *Daisy Queen*.

'Well I never! Is it you, me old mate?' Bob's arms opened in greeting.

'Who else?' And the two men embraced, the white hand grasping the brown, shaking it up and down, squeezing it half to death in his joy and amazement. 'Don't get so excited! You'll break all my bones!' the Indian laughed.

'What're you doing here? In Shields of all places? You're not wanting to sign on old "Daisy" are you?'

'What else would I be doing here?'

'Eeh, I don't know, Chandrika. You take it all so calmly. You'd think you knew we were going to meet up like this! I don't know!'

'I didn't *know* exactly. But . . . '

'Oh you'll be on at me about that blessed destiny of yours next! Is that what it is, eh?'

'Who knows, Bob. Who knows?'

'Well come on. Never mind about all that stuff! Let's get you signed on.' And Bob, ignoring the jealous stares of the waiting men, propelled his old friend into the manager's office.

31

'I'm first mate this trip. So you'll be all right. Howway now.' The door closed on them. And the men folded their arms, muttering belligerently amongst themselves.

Walking home from the office, Bob shook his head with wonder. He was a dark horse that Chandrika. What on earth was he doing in Shields? Wanting to sign on a merchant schooner! Last he'd seen of him he'd been in Bombay, unloading freight for P & O. What a turn up, eh? Mind you, Bob thought to himself, they were all a funny lot them Indians. Canny, but eeh, they had a different way of looking at things. That was for sure. Slowly as he thought about it, his face fell. Maybe it'd been a mistake to ask him round that night. It had been a spur of the moment invitation. If only he'd thought first. What with Fanny being in a state and one thing and another - and what on earth was he going to give him for his tea?

Jane, looking out for him on the front step, was horrified by his dreadful appearance.

'Oh, Da!' she said in dismay.

'What's wrong?' Jane's finger pointed slowly at his face, and then at the tear in his jacket, and Bob laughed. He had forgotten all about the fight of the afternoon. 'Oh that's nothing, lass. Wait till I tell you. I'm not going till the end of the week!'

'Oh, Da! Is it true? Is it really true?'

'Aye!'

'You're not kidding?'

'No!'

'Honest?'

'I said, didn't I!'

'Eeh!' The little girl quickly jumped up to hug her father then rushed indoors, yelling, 'Our Robert, Fanny, Da's not going till the end of the week!' Joy and relief bubbled through the household, bringing a smile even to Fanny's face.

'I'm glad, Da,' she smiled softly.

'Oh aye.' He remembered Chadrika. 'And I've asked this bloke for his tea . . . He's an Indian Hindu. What've we got to eat?'

'Pig's cheek.' And Fanny couldn't understand why her father's jaw hit his boots in horror.

'I don't know why he can't be satisfied with a bit of pig's

32

cheek. It's very nice with sage and onion. Foreigners! Huh!'
Muttering, Fanny set out to the shops with Robert to buy in a bit
of fish, leaving their Jane to tend their father's wounds. Poor
Jane didn't know whether to feel happy because her father was
staying at home for a bit longer, or sad because he'd been hurt.
Her conflicting emotions played comically across her expressive
face, as they competed with one another for supremacy, and Bob
could not help bursting out laughing at her; laughing all the
harder as she tut tutted at him like an old woman for not taking
his injuries seriously enough.

'Why did you have to fight, Da, anyway?' she demanded, as
she soothed lard onto his cuts and bruises, the cool of her hands
healing with their touch.

'In defence of my own,' he answered her.

'What do you mean, Da?'

'Always asking why and what for aren't you?'

'If I don't ask I'll not find out, Da!'

'Cheeky little brat!' He laughed at her. 'Oh well, I don't
suppose it'll harm you to know. I was fighting because of your
sister.'

'Our Fan?'

'Aha. I was fighting for her . . . Well . . . her honour, I
suppose. Her good name.'

'Oh,' came the puzzled reply. 'Why? Isn't Ridley good enough
for her?' Bob looked at her sharply.

'No, lass. In a way it isn't. Not now.' Jane's cool touch paused
and held still on her father's cheek. How could he make her
understand? His rough hand claimed hers, and held it against his
skin.

'You see, she's got to get wed, Jane. She got herself into a spot
of trouble.' Jane looked at her father seriously.

'Is it my fault, Da?' Bob frowned and sat back to look her full
in the face.

'How could that be?'

'I don't know. But somehow I feel as though it must be.'

'Why? Who's been putting daft ideas like that into your head,
eh?'

'Nobody, Da. I thought it all out for myself.'

'You're too deep for me, lass.' He snorted, smiled and touched

33

her cheek. 'How could you be to blame for anything? There's not a dark place in you. Why, you don't even understand what blame is.'

'Fanny thinks I'm to blame.'

The man's face hardened.

'Does she now? Did she say so?'

'She nearly cut herself with the knife and she said it was all my fault.'

'Oh! Is that all!' He laughed with relief. 'I thought you meant . . . ' He tousled her hair, unwilling to finish his sentence.

'Oh I did. I meant the trouble she was in with Dandy O. I meant, that in a way it was all my fault.'

Bob stopped in his tracks.

'You don't know what you're talking about, lass. You don't know what trouble is.'

'I'm in trouble with Fanny.'

'No you're not. She's just a bit bad tempered just now. That's all. You can't take her troubles on your little shoulders. It's got nothing to do with you!'

Jane thought for a while. Fanny's transformation from a playmate into a bad tempered grown up, all within the space of a year or two, had really puzzled her.

'When I'm grown up will I get into trouble like Fanny?' she said at last.

'No, lass.' He looked at the soft lines of her face. Her skin was almost luminous, it was so fair, and the eyes were clear, without any cunning in them. No man would dare to harm her. No man would dare to touch her innocence. 'I'll make sure you don't. No harm will come to you. You'll never see trouble like that. Because I'll watch over you and keep you safe. See if I don't.' Jane smiled, and bent to kiss him. But her face screwed up and she laughed as she showed him the lard on her chin.

'Better go and wipe it off, pet,' he said indulgently.

And Bob was satisfied. His eyes followed her as she went to clean the grease from her face. How had this child come to him? How had he and Ida managed to bring her into the world? She was different from his other children. Different from anyone else on the quayside, come to that. Like a changeling she was, and with a mind as deep as Shields harbour itself. No, he would

34

never fathom her but he would watch over her. He would make up for his carelessness with his eldest girl by taking extra care of the younger.

In the cracked mirror over the range, where her father shaved himself, Jane wiped her pale face clear with the paper from the pig's cheek. The crack split her image in two, and she called her father to look at it.

'Look, Da!' She laughed. 'There's two of me!'

'So there is.' He smiled. 'And one's as pretty as the other.'

Fanny and Jane rushed round dusting and sweeping, before their guest came. Neither of them knew what to expect. Many Arabs had come to Tyneside, but an Indian? And what was a Hindu when he was at home? Josh, found and brought home by Robert, was all excitement.

'Will he have feathers in his hair and that?' he asked his father.

'Why no, lad. He's not a red Indian. He's an . . . Indian Indian, like. You know, from India.'

'Not from America?'

'No! They're two different places altogether.' And immediately Josh lost interest.

'Do they have elephants in India, Da?' Robert asked.

'Aye they do. As a matter of fact, it was Chandrika told me the story of the elephant.'

'The one you told us the other night?' Jane asked, eyes wide with excitement.

'That's the one.'

'Hey!' she shouted. 'He might even have seen one with his own bare eyes!'

So the scene was set for the arrival of the stranger from the other side of the world. Each member of the family had his or her own expectation of what was to come, and each had an attitude all ready to present to him, along with the grilled herring, and the boiled potatoes. But Chandrika expected nothing as he was ushered through the door and into the living room. Neither did he want anything. As though by some sixth sense he felt Fanny's distraction, her resentment because he had intruded on her, created an interval in the play of her life just when she was reaching the most interesting part. He felt too Josh's lack of

35

interest. The youngest boy's eyes wandered, as Chandrika knew his mind must also wander, following the inner world of his imaginings. It would be hard to gain his attention. Only when reality coincided with his dreams, would he sit up and take notice. And Chandrika was not a red Indian. Then there was Robert. Chandrika smiled on him. There was a bright lad, though his eyes were dark and intense. He would want to know everything, while his father stood, awkward, aware of the poverty of the room, afraid that his guest would judge him. And then, there was Jane.

'Have you really seen a hephalant?'

'A what?'

'She means an elephant,' Bob explained with some embarrassment. Chandrika beamed, and everyone relaxed.

'So, Bob, now I know why I had to come to Shields!' And he picked her up, delightedly, throwing her into the air, dancing round and round the little kitchen.

It was an enchanted evening. The early summer sun filtered through the window, softening the hard, sparse line of the room. Its soft glow lent a gentleness even to Fanny's face, and Bob watched with puzzled detachment as his little Jane and the man from the other side of the world chatted away as though they had known one another for lifetimes, while Robert's eyes drained and drank in India from the very pores of the man sitting before him. Mountains rose and fell in his imagination. The snow fell on Mount Kailasa, where the great God Shiva dwelt, encircled by fire, and Nanda Devi, deep in the Himalayas, breathed in the perfume of the Valley of Flowers. Icy waters in deep lakes bathed the rocks where pilgrims trod, and in Kashmir, lotus flowers with thousands of petals grew multicoloured, translucent from the mud. Heat burned the earth in the desert of Rajasthan, and the rains fell, flooding the regions of the earth. Camels pulled carts. Monkeys, parrots, elephants, domes and towers, strange places with stranger names, wove a web of delight around the children. People in bright costumes bought spices in colourful bazaars, and cared more about the Gods than about their own lives. Chandrika drew a map, and showed them his homeland. It was so far away. And yet their father had been there. Chandrika had been born there. So it wasn't just the same as a fairy story. It was real. And one day, one day perhaps, they too would go and see the magic places.

'Tell me about the hephalants, Chandrika,' Jane asked. 'What do they really look like?' Chandrika thought for a while.

'Perhaps it would be easier to draw one for you,' he said at last. 'If you will oblige me with a paper and pencil.' Immediately Robert ran into the next room and fetched his own drawing book.

'What's this?' the Indian asked.

'My lad fancies himself as an artist,' Bob explained. Chandrika turned the pages of the book.

'But he's very good.'

'Now don't encourage him!' Bob objected.

'Why not? Look. Your son is an artist. You should be proud of him!'

Jane smiled at her brother, who had an anxious look on his face.

'Art! What use is art?' Bob wanted to know.

'He has imagination! He has heart. You can see it in his drawings.'

'What use is imagination? He'd do better to stick to real life.'

'What *is* real life, Da?' asked Jane. Bob frowned. How to describe it? He looked to his guest for help and found him observing his dilemma with a twinkle in his eye. Robert, pushing his luck while he had the chance, interrupted.

'My teacher at school says I could go in for drawing.'

'Eh?' Bob's voice boomed across the table. Then he thought for a second. 'Oh like drawing maps and that.'

'No. Pictures, Da. Pictures.'

'Who wants pictures?' he snapped. 'I'll have to have a word with your teacher when I'm next home.'

And Robert smiled to himself, because, with a long voyage ahead, that might just be too late, and Robert's own plans for his future might well have gone too far for even his own Da to prevent.

'I think Robert's pictures are smashing,' Jane said with an encouraging smile to her brother.

'You would!' Fanny snapped. 'You're as daft as he is!'

'He's not daft!'

'Yes he is. You're nothing but a pair of dreamers! I tell you what though, life isn't half going to give you two a shock when you grow up!'

'That's enough, our Fan.' Bob put his hand on her arm.

'What's she mean, Da?' Jane's eyes grew large with fear. 'What kind of a shock?'

'Now see what you've done,' he reproached his elder daughter and she spat like a cat back at him.

'Oh I see! It's my fault again, is it? I might have known it wouldn't be hers!'

'I had a talk with Rattler today.' Fanny stiffened. She could not look at her father. 'I'll tell you about it later.' And two pairs of round eyes looked from father to sister, dying to know what was going on but not daring to ask. 'And if you're on about "dreaming", our Fan, well . . . you need talk! That's all!' His eldest daughter had the grace to flush crimson. 'It seems to me,' Bob looked at his embarrassed guest. 'It seems, my friend, that somehow or other I've spawned a family of dreamers!'

Josh yawned and went through to the next room, ready for bed.

'Oh dear, is it so late?' the guest asked politely.

'No, no. Don't go, Chandrika. It's just time for the littl'n's to turn in. That's all.'

'Not before Chandrika's drawn me an elephant,' Jane insisted. Chandrika obliged, apologising profusely because his drawing did not come up to young Robert's standards, and before they all knew where they were, he had also agreed to tuck the younger ones up in bed, as he retold the story of the elephant in one room, while in the other, Fanny at last heard her father's report of the meeting with Rattler.

When Fanny finally left her father with his guest, the three younger children were already alseep in the big bed. The single candle in the room flickered strange shadows across the walls. She shivered, and took off her dress, laying it across the little fold-up bed she had all to herself. She enjoyed the peace of that time of night. The river noises were dulled, and the fog horns silent. Only the odd drunk on his or her way home echoed on the late night air. Rattler was going to speak to Dandy O. Her heart beat fast; whether with joy or fear she couldn't tell. But she was tired. So tired. Low voices from the next room rose and fell like the murmuring waves on the shore, lulling her brain to thoughtlessness. After all the fighting, all the struggles within, after all the nightmares, perhaps, at last, she would find peace. She stood still, and her eyes followed the flickering shadows as they chased about the room.

And then, her heart stopped. Above her face, facing that of her brothers and her sister, a piece of paper had been pinned to the wall. The slight breeze from the window caught its edges and made it whisper. She moved towards it, and tried, in the faint light, to make out the lines drawn on it. It was Chandrika's elephant. It loomed out of the paper at her, and the flickering light of the flame caught the edge of the trunk which seemed to move as the shadow crossed it, raising itself up at her. She shivered. On the river a sudden blast from a ship made her jump. Suddenly she knew she was cold. She had been standing there for a long time. The voices in the next room had stopped. She looked again at the elephant on the wall. It was only a drawing. And yet, somehow it seemed to threaten her. Jane stirred in her sleep. Fanny woke, as though from a trance, and looked at her. Her arm reached out to touch her brother by her side. She smiled, dreaming sweet dreams of moonlight on deep rivers, flower garlands round her neck, and elephants riding in procession. Watching her, Fanny wondered how long she had been standing there. She could not tell. At last, she blew out the light, huddled under the blanket, and lay listening to the whisper of the breeze as it stirred the drawing over her bed.

CHAPTER THREE

It was one in the morning. Rattler woke Dandy O with a cup of tea.

'Time to be off, me lad,' he said. And by 1.30, the pair of them were moving down river towards the bar. Fire flared from the lamps of schooners, brigs and coasters, laid up along the riversides, lighting up the dangerous path of the pilot's coble, as father and son rowed with the tide out toward the sea. Life swarmed in the darkness, masts intertwined over their heads, voices called, echoing across the river. And for the moment, Rattler held his peace.

The moon was large; looking back over his shoulder, Dandy O glimpsed it, swollen, floating up from the river mouth. He pulled hard on his oars, enjoying the physical strain of muscle against resisting water. He heard his father's breath short and raw in front of him, as he laboured to keep up with the younger man. It was a silent competition, and Dandy O smiled as he pulled harder still, and Rattler shouted out, 'What's the hurry, man? Hold your horses!'

Then the young man stopped, smiled, and allowed the elder to catch his breath before again plunging his oars into the Tyne.

It had been a good day. Dandy O had brought a coaster in, within two hours of seeking. A green captain, nervous of the river bed, had been glad to pay the two Tully lads to guide him into harbour. And then, Dandy O had had an afternoon of it. Fresh from 'The Globe', he had skirted round the back of the sailmaking sheds, avoiding his old flame, and whispered through a loose plank into the ear of Eileen Purvis, herself the daughter of a pilot and well set up in life. His mother smiled on Eileen. She was more than twenty, and therefore nearer to his own age. She knew how to run a household, and though not as pretty as Fanny Ridley had been, she was unmarked by the smallpox. Most important of all, however, was the fact that Eileen was a member of his own kind, born within the fraternity of the Tyne free pilots, and with a bit of money to show for it.

The moon rose like a balloon as they emerged from the river and onto the open sea. It shimmered across the ripple of the water, calm as the pond in Marine Park. Five ships waited at the other side of the bar, all ready supplied with pilots.

'Come on,' Dandy O egged on his Dad. 'Let's go seeking.'

'Which way? North or South?'

'Toss up for it.' The coin shone like silver as it flipped in the air and fell onto Dandy's hand. The other caught it flat against his palm.

'Heads we go south,' said Rattler.

In the moonlight the coin clearly showed 'tails'; so they started out north, looking for a ship in need of a pilot. The bigger the better, for Rattler was a first class pilot and could take on anything you could name. They would pass by the coasters, and make for the big fish tonight.

North past Tynemouth, Blyth and Craster, and the moon rose higher. A fishing boat from Cullercoats, having no luck with the fish, had turned its hand to seeking with them. They let it go for the coaster, at Craster, and drifted a while, watching the performance of pilot climbing onto ship, coble placed in tow, in the eerie light.

'I had a bit of a natter with Bob Ridley the other day,' Rattler said at last.

'Oh aye? How is he, like?' Dandy O asked carelessly.

'Before or after the fight?'

Dandy O burst out laughing. 'Oh I see. Like that was it? I thought you two were great pals and that.'

41

'We are! We are! Doesn't meant to say we can't argue out our differences from time to time.'.

'True. And what were your differences?'

There was a pause. Rattler looked uneasily at the coaster. It was half-a-mile off, but he knew that voices carried over the sea. Especially at night. The men on board would be able to hear every word.

'In a minute, son,' he said. And they waited, while the ship sailed on, swirling the waters, and they themselves drifted farther off.

'It's about young Fanny.' There was total silence behind him. Rattler took his bottle of pills from his pocket and shovelled a handful into his mouth, swallowing hard and almost choking so that Dandy O had to thump him on his back. 'That's better. By them pills is good for you,' Rattler said. And he didn't understand why his son laughed.

'All right, Dad. What about Fanny, eh?'

'She's a canny lass that.'

'Aye. I've got nothing against her.'

'She's sweet on you.'

'Can't help that.' Rattler turned to look at the young man seated behind him. The tone of his voice had sounded hard, but there was a twinkle in his eyes.

'I feel responsible for that lass.'

'All right, Dad. Go on then. Marry her. I'm not stopping you.'

'Your Mam'd have something to say about that!'

'Stop beating about the bush, man!' Dandy grinned at his father, who crouched uneasily on the plank before him.

'Looks don't mean everything, son.' There was a silence. 'I mean, your Mam's not bad for her age, but they all grow old in the end.'

'Dad, I'm fond of Fanny . . . '

'Well then!'

'Well what?'

'Why don't you marry the lass?'

'What about Eileen?'

'First come first served.'

'I'm not a shop, Dad!'

'Aye, and you're not a bloke that fools about with women either.' Now it was Dandy's turn to feel uncomfortable. 'A bit of a lad' was a description he had begun to merit.

'I've gone off her, Dad. I can't help it. It's how she . . . you know . . . her face.'

'It's not her fault. She had courage had that lass, staying behind to nurse her mother. And this is how she gets paid for it.'

'All right. She's got courage. I'll give you that.'

'Like her Dad before her; Dandy, lad, you'd not be here, you know that, if it wasn't for Bob Ridley.' Another silence as the young man considered his situation. 'I owe him, son. We owe him, as a family. I reckon it's time we paid him back.'

'Why's it me's got to pay?'

'Because only you *can* pay. He wants you to marry Fanny.'

Dandy O's voice grew suddenly sharp. 'Why? Is she expecting?'

'Not that I know of.'

'I'll not bring up another man's bairn.'

'Nobody's asking you to.'

'As long as that's clear.'

'Aye.' Rattler paused, waited. Somehow, he didn't know how, the tide in their discussion had turned. It was as though a bargain had been struck. 'So you'll do it, eh?'

'Do what?'

'Marry her?'

'I never said I would.' Another pause. By but the lad was setting up a stiff opposition, harder than the one put up by Bob the day before. 'How do I know she hasn't been with half the lads in Shields?'

'Come on now!'

'No, be fair, Dad. How do I know?'

'Ask her.'

'Hah!'

'When did you . . . '

'I don't know. Couple of months back, I suppose.'

'Why she's hardly had time to go the rounds of the whole town, man!' his father remonstrated.

'All right. How do I know she won't, after we're wed?'

'Eh?'

43

'I mean, if she'll go with me, without the blessing of the vicar, why not go with other blokes, eh? I couldn't stand that, Dad.' Rattler thought for a while, and belched, as his pills hit the juices of his stomach.

'You're just trying to get out of it, son.'

'Aye well, maybe I am and maybe I'm not. I just think Fanny Ridley's changed. That smallpox marked more than her face, I'd swear it. She's not the same lass . . . '

'Think about it, son. With a bit of loving, she'd be as nice as she was before. I bet you.' Then he added. 'Only more grateful, like.'

'Aye well. Like you said. I'll think about it.'

And that was as far as Rattler could get that night.

The moon was setting over Longstone, and the Ridley coble had just found a ship, when Chandrika's eyes opened onto the unfamiliar kitchen in Trajan Street. Silently, he unwrapped his woollen shawl from round his body, and rose from the cold floor, where he had slept, fully clothed. Outside, he heard a barrow rattling over the rough cobbles, and the sound of a bell chimed out at sea. He folded the rug carefully, and threw it round his shoulders, before stooping to retrieve his shoes from under the bed, where Bob still snored.

The sneck made a loud click as he opened the door, and went into the passage. Upstairs, a man was talking in his sleep . . . the Ridley's neighbour. In the front room, the children slept. Chandrika eased open the door and looked in on them. Robert and Jane lay smiling in one another's arms. Josh had his back to them, and lay, arms folded across his chest, in a deep sleep. Chandrika turned his attention to the figure in the other bed. Fanny stirred uneasily. Her eyelids flickered, as though aware of a presence looking down on her. The Indian retreated from the room, crept noiselessly from the house and made his way to the beach.

The salt water felt cold to his face as he rinsed away the sleep of the night. And he pulled his shawl close around him to keep out the damp, misty morning air. On the horizon, a faint light glimmered. He fixed his eyes on it, listening to the sound of the warning bell on the Groyne pier. The light grew, forcing apart the sea and the sky, separating the elements. His lips moved in mantra. And the sun rose. It rose above the sea, red, then pink then gold, till it was clear of the water and its light illumined the beach. Chandrika waded back onto the land, mind clear, heart still, and as he walked along the sand, the sun became a moon at his feet, reflected in the ribbons of water, left stranded on the beach. And suddenly, he felt glad. He lifted up his head and sang,

SumukaschAikadantascha Kapilo Gajakarnakah
Lambodarscha Vikato Vighnanasho Ganadhipa
DhoomraketurGanadyaksho Bhalachandro Gajananah

Dwadshaitani namaniyah pathet shrunu yadapi
Vidyarambhe vivahecha pravese nirgame tatha
Sangrame sankate chaiva vighnastasye na jayate

His voice rose clear over the dunes, catching the ear of the fishermen out at sea, of the sailors, on the quay, and it rose, strange and unfamiliar into the sky, where a seagull caught it up and screeched it high over the town, and the clustered narrow streets.

Fanny ached all over. Her eyes stung even before she opened them to see Jane's face as she offered her her morning tea. She shaded her eyes from the light, and took the cup thankfully. The brew warmed and comforted her.

'It's a smashing day, our Fan. Just like summer!' The child grinned delightedly.

'Don't call me Fan!' was the only response.

'Is she in a bad mood this morning?' Robert whispered as he retreated with his younger sister into the kitchen. And Fanny *was* in a bad mood. She awoke to a turmoil of feelings, as though they had been fermenting in her sleep, and there was fear in her heart. Why? Another sip of tea, and pictures started flowing in her mind, memories of past events, mingled with dreams. Dandy O and Eileen Purvis. Her mother dead in the next room. Mrs Dunn reeking of whisky leaning over her own fever racked body. The first sight of her face in the mirror. Dandy, oh Dandy O, his shock when he caught sight of her at last. And there was some-

45

thing, something, she didn't know what, chasing her . . . No that was the dream. Something in her dreams had been chasing her. The sound of its feet boomed in her ears like the cannon when a ship foundered. What was it? How she longed to see Dandy. To feel his touch on her skin, desiring her again. Inside, she felt cold and lonely. When would God, if God existed, think to put her out of her misery? Why had he picked on her to punish? What had she done to deserve it? Why wouldn't he let her have Dandy O, when she wanted him so much?

A man was singing as he came down the street. Words she couldn't understand. She raised her hands to her ears to shut out the sounds that jarred in her head. She would have to get up. She would have to go to work, as usual, and just hope and pray Dandy O had agreed to marry her. Otherwise . . . otherwise what? A living death without him? No! She could not, would not think about it. He *must* marry her. She, Fanny Ridley, wanted him! Outside the window, Jane's voice shrieked with delight, as Chandrika lifted her high into the air. And trying to sing along with him, she and her Indian friend made their noisy way into the kitchen, past Fanny's door.

Bob was shaving at the broken mirror over the range as they barged in together. And, as Jane shouted her greeting, his hand slipped, so that he cut himself on the cheek, and the blood ran. Jane rushed to stop the flow with a cloth dipped in cold water, while Josh and Robert cut up pieces of bread for their breakfasts, since Fanny had not yet put in an appearance.

'Have some tea, Chandrika,' Bob invited. 'There's a fresh pot.' The Indian's eyes lit up with joy.

'Ah, tea!'

'Like coals to Newcastle, eh?' Bob laughed, submitting to the care of his little girl.

'I know why you cut yourself, Daddy,' she said. 'It's because you can't see properly. It's because the mirror's broken.'

'Oh is that why? I thought it was because I got a shock when you came in, shrieking like a banshee.'

'No, Da. It wasn't that.' Jane was very sure of herself. 'Come and see, Chandrika.' She motioned their guest over to the range. 'Look in the mirror. You can see two of you. Now how could my Dad know which one he was shaving even?' Chandrika smiled.

'Ah yes,' he said. 'A mirror is a very clever thing. It shows you yourself. It can even show you God.'

'There's no such thing.' Everyone turned and saw Fanny standing morosely at the door. 'There is no God.'

'Oh yes there is,' Chandrika said softly. 'God is eternity.'

'What's eternity?' Robert asked.

Chandrika thought for a second. The early sun glinted on the edge of the mirror over the range, its light breaking into a rainbow arc across the wall. He nodded slowly.

'Have you got another mirror anywhere?' He looked round.

'Fan's got one,' Josh said. 'I'll go and get it, shall I?'

'Oh no you won't,' Fanny said sharply, but Josh had already gone, and soon was fetching it in to give to the Indian.

'Thank you,' Chandrika said. Then he took down the cracked mirror from the range and parted the two halves, so that there were three pieces lying on the table. He gave one piece to Robert, one to Josh, and held one himself. 'Be careful you don't cut yourself,' he instructed them. 'Now, I'll stand in the middle holding my piece of mirror, and you Bob must stand beside me, holding your mirror alongside, but pointing inward a little. That's it. And you Josh, you do the same on the other side. Now, Bob, stand inside the three mirrors.' Bob moved forward and bent to look into the glass. He turned his head from side to side. 'What do you see?'

'A man with a cut on his cheek.'

'Only one man?'

'No. Now you come to mention it. There's a canny few of me!' And he burst out laughing.

'Try to count how many Bobs you can see.' Bob shook his head. 'You can't! They go on forever. That wound on your chin goes on forever too. So you see,' he said to the children, 'how careful we have to be, for our errors, once made, cannot be wiped out. They too are reflected back at us forever and forever.'

'Stop bamboozling me, Chandrika, with all your eastern mysteries!' Bob laughed at him. 'You're frightening the bairns!' Chandrika smiled, and made Jane take her father's place. Jane bubbled up with delight, her hands reaching to her face a million million times, her smile flashing round eternity as she stood in the centre of the three mirrors.

47

'So, it isn't just our wounds, and our mistakes that are reflected back on us, it's also our good points. Our smiles and laughter.' He nodded, pleased, at the little girl.

'All you're doing is playing tricks with mirrors,' Fanny objected. 'Like some cheap entertainer at the music hall.'

Her father frowned, embarrassed by her lack of politeness. 'There's no such thing as eternity.'

'You can see it with your own eyes. Look.' And Jane stood aside, while Fanny, suddenly caught in the reflection, saw with horror her own disfigurement coming back at her, again and again on to infinity. She burst out crying and ran from the house.

'That is God's judgement on us,' Chandrika said quietly. 'He merely holds the mirror up so we can see what we are.'

There was a moment of stunned silence. Then Jane ran out after her sister.

'By God, Chandrika, but that was cruel,' said the father.

'Truth often seems so, Bob. But isn't it worse to founder in illusion?'

'No, I don't think so. Sometimes, illusions can be kinder.'

'Poor Bob.' Chandrika sighed. 'In that case, you will not take my word for it. You and yours will have to learn by experience.' The sun went in, and the rainbow on the wall melted away into the grey mist that came in from the sea.

Fanny had run without knowing where she was going. All she knew was that she had to get away, and Jane pursued her through the narrow streets, as though a thread tied the two sisters, and she was drawn on, compelled to follow her in her distress. The little girl's heart burst with the effort of running, and her breath was harsh in her throat. But still she ran on till they had left the house, and were running down the steep slope from the hill they called 'The Lawe', helter-skelter, towards the beach and the sea. Stones tumbled after their feet, and jumped up into their faces. And Jane strove to keep up with her sister, who dived across the sands, straight into a flock of seagulls, whose hysterical cries shrieked at her as they broke the air and fled. And still she ran on, on into the sea, and the weight of the water slowed her, pulling at her thighs. Shaking with fright and exhaustion, Fanny fell into the water, swallowing the salt, arms thrashing, without

48

control. And Jane was with her. She caught at the flailing arms, and commanded her.

'Be still, Fanny! Be still, will you!' And Fanny obeyed, allowing her sister to guide her to her feet. Gently, Jane tried to turn her back towards the sand. But Fanny's eyes searched for the horizon where sea and sky joined. There was no horizon. Only a pallid greyness going on forever, and the sun was hidden in the mist. A fog horn startled her. She shivered, remembering the shadow of the elephant on her wall.

'Come on home,' Jane persuaded her. 'You'll catch cold, Fan.' And Fanny turned her back on the sea, silently allowing herself to be led over the painful stones, back up the hill home.

The stone bottle warmed her, as she lay in bed, and Jane drew the curtain, telling her to sleep. It would all be better when she woke. The Indian man had gone, and the mirrors were back in their places. Fanny's hand reached out from under the blanket and grasped her sister's wrist. Jane, surprised at the grip, was compelled to fight back an urge to pull away, as the hand tightened on her.

'Don't desert me, Jane,' Fanny pleaded. 'Don't desert me.'

'What do you mean? Why ever should I?' So Jane reassured her, and Fanny's hand dropped, releasing her at last.

It was as though a cloud had fallen over Jane's mind. It was Fanny's cloud, but she shared it now, and she couldn't see her way any more. Everything seemed confused to her. The vague feeling that everything was her fault pursued her still. Her mother's death, Fanny's disfigurement, Dandy O's desertion of her sister, Jane took it all on her shoulders like a great weight, and she knew Fanny's pain and longing. It seeped into her like the mist from the sea, and became her own. Her sympathetic heart had drunk it in. But what could she do about it?

She found Robert on the Herd Sands, playing at ducks and drakes. Jane watched him from the Groyne pier, as the flat stones bounced across the water, once, twice, three times. Then she clapped her hands, and Robert, looking up, saw her and smiled. At once, Jane felt better. Her heart lightened and she scrambled down the pier side to be with him.

'What are you doing here?' she asked.

49

'Huh! Our Fanny gives me the jitters,' he said, as though that explained everything. Again he threw, and again a stone bounced.

'Fancy our Dad having to fight for her, eh?'

'Aye well, blokes are *supposed* to fight for their women.'

'Why?'

'To protect them like.'

'Who from?'

'Other blokes.'

'Oh.' Jane frowned. It didn't make sense somehow. But if that was the case, then no wonder men were always fighting each other. 'Men're daft,' she said decisively.

'I'm a man. Well nearly.' Jane looked at her brother, head on one side.

'I hadn't thought about that. I suppose you are really. Would you fight for me?' Robert put his fists up. 'Just show me the man!' he said bravely, and the knots in the thready muscles of his arms hardened for her.

'That's nice,' Jane said, pleased. Robert stopped, a stone in his hand, ready for throwing, and looked up as a schooner sailed across the bar, the pilot's flag flying from its mast.

'Would you like to be a pilot, Robert?' Jane asked him, watching the ship, as it came gracefully out of the mist over the surface of the treacherous waters.

'I wouldn't mind. It'd be better than going to sea, like Dad.'

'I'd like to go to sea.'

'Why?'

'I'd like to see India, and places like that.'

'Huh! All you'd see'd *be* the sea!'

'No, but I would.'

'Why?'

'Because there's got to be another world than this one,' she said, her eyes grey as the horizon, as they peered out beyond it to the sky.

'I expect it'd be just the same once you got there. Once you'd got used to it, like.'

'Do you think so?'

'Aha.' Robert aimed and the stone flew, cutting across the water, to splatter against the stone wall of the pier.

'I wouldn't like to end up like our Fanny, or Mam . . . '

'Why should you?' Robert looked at his sister, sensing her unease.

'I don't know. Why should I be any different?' There was no answer to that. Bob turned his back and looked towards the town. After a pause, Jane asked, 'Who was Dad fighting yesterday?'

'Rattler Tully.'

And Jane thought, shifting her foot over the sand, watching it give way under the pressure from her foot.

'Doesn't he want our Fanny to marry Dandy O, then?'

'I don't think Dandy O wants to marry her!'

'But that isn't fair! She loves him!'

The dovelike eyes flashed fire at her brother, and she turned on her heel to march back up into the town, her voice echoing behind her, 'It isn't fair!'

'Hey, come back!' he called after her. But Jane did not hear him.

She didn't stop to think. She half ran, half walked towards Pilot Street. The old sailors by the cannon hailed her, but she did not hear them. Usually so free and easy, she now had a business-like, determined look about her as she turned away from the street and made her way to the coble landing, where sixty or seventy craft of all shapes and sizes stood in various stages of repair. She looked amongst the men and boys gathered there, but could not see her quarry. The pilot's shed stood to one side, and she made her way towards it.

'Have you seen Dandy O?' she asked an old pilot leaning against the wall. He looked at her for a while, then looked away, chewing a piece of tobacco, thoughtfully. Jane began to think he had forgotten her and was about to move on, when he raised his hand and pointed over the river. Jane looked, and saw a coble making its way from the other side towards the landing stage. In it were two men. She went down to the edge and waited, her eyes fixed on the forms of the two men, her mind idly remembering the verses they had been taught at Sunday School.

At the coble landing and breezy Lawe
The brave pilots then did dwell,

51

And cracked their jokes and spun long yarns,
During winter storms and summer calms
On the seat by the Roman well.

It sounded good that. Like the pilots were heroes. And in a way,
she supposed, they were!

Wisps of mist came up river from the sea, and wrapped about
the boats lining the riverside. There was a chill in the air, and she
wished she had brought something to wrap about her. She
shivered, the flesh on her arms turning to goose pimples. Was it
the cold from the river? Or was it the cold that lay about her
heart, that made her sick with apprehension? What was she
doing there? What could she hope to say that would make things
right for Fanny? The little boat drew nearer, her breath stuck in
her throat, as the grinning Dandy O jumped out to pull the coble
in, shouting,

'Well if it isn't my little angel, eh?' And Jane managed a smile
for him.

'What are you doing here, pet?' Rattler asked her as father and
son dragged the boat onto the beach.

'Nothing.' Jane felt silly, and the older man gave her a funny
look. 'I came to see Dandy O.' Honesty being the best policy
according to her father, she decided to come clean.

'Howway, then!' Dandy O lifted her high into the air and
smiled into her face. But Jane did not smile back. Her eyes were
dark, and her face pale and serious. 'Is there anything the
matter?' he asked her. Rattler, catching the mood, darted the
question, 'Is your Dad all right?'

'Aha,' Jane replied as Dandy set her down on the little beach.
'It's our Fanny I've come about.' The two men looked at each
other, then at the ground, scuffing their boots uneasily.

'That's grown ups' stuff, pet. Not for you to bother yourself
about.'

'I'm nearly twelve, and our Fanny's in a state. And it's your
fault.' Her eyes accused the young man, and he could not look
back at her. Rattler coughed to cover his embarrassment. 'Why
won't you marry her, Dandy O?'

'I never said I wouldn't.'

'You never said you would, either,' she retorted sharply. There

52

was a pause. Rattler surveyed the young girl, then shook his head.

'Don't grow up too soon, pet,' he said, and walked away, leaving his son to the 'angel's' mercy. 'Do you love her?' She pursued him. Dandy O shrugged. There was a lump in his throat. He could not speak even if he could find the words to say. He felt unmanned somehow. No-one else could have done it, not Bob Ridley, not his father, certainly not Fanny. Each one of them had their own axe to grind. But not so Jane. She spoke from her heart, out of love for her sister. It was as simple as that. How could he tell her his thoughts, his fears about Fanny? She made him feel ashamed of his own selfishness. Jane looked at him, waiting for him to say something.

'Maybe . . . ' His voice came out all wrong and he had to cough to clear his throat. 'Maybe Fanny loves other . . . people.'

'She loves me Dad. And she loves me . . . I think,' Jane said thoughtfully.

'No. Not that sort of love, pet.' Again this other kind of love. The one her father had been on about the other night. What was it? He had said she should wait till she was older before she found out about it, yet here she was, because of their Fanny, having waded in the deep end before her time, floundering about, not knowing the tides and currents of the waters of this mysterious other 'love'. 'I mean, she maybes loves other . . . men, like.'

'What other men? You mean like our Robert?' Robert was a man. He'd said so only this morning.

'No, pet.' Dandy O was beginning to feel some exasperation. 'Men like . . . ' He looked across to the shed where Brassie Joe stood watching them with some amusement. 'Like him over there.' Jane looked at Brassie and then frowned back at Dandy O.

'What do you mean by "love" Dandy?'

Dandy thought for a bit. This was awkward. No doubt about it.

'I mean the sort of love your Mam and your Dad felt for each other when she was alive, pet.'

Jane thought for a while.

'I don't think I understand, Dandy. But I know Mam loved me Dad best. And I know our Fanny loves you best.'

53

'Aye well. That's as maybe,' he sighed. And then, fired by his frustration he shouted suddenly, 'I won't have a wife of mine mucking about with other blokes. That's all.' Jane was quiet. 'Mucking about?' What was it? Was that what Mrs Dunn did that her Dad didn't like? Was that what them couples did under the archway at Tyne Dock? There was something not nice about it. She felt dirtied by the thought, and she shook her head.

'Fanny doesn't muck about,' she stated. Dandy looked at her. She was telling the truth. She couldn't help herself.

'She's not been with anybody else, like?' Again Jane saw the pictures under the archways, and heard the low laughter from Mrs Dunn's rooms. She shook her head. Dandy thought for a minute. 'If she's honest, I suppose I do owe her.' Jane's eyes beseeched him. 'It's just, I want to be sure, Jane, you see. I mean once wed, that's it. There's no turning back, pet.' She said nothing. 'All right. I tell you what, and I can't say fairer like. But I used to really like your sister. She was all right. And maybe me Dad's right and she'd be herself again after we were wed. So, what I'm saying is, I'll take her on trial, like . . . ' Jane was alarmed. She was sure that wasn't right. Nobody took anybody on trial. 'I mean, I'll agree to marry her . . . say in a year's time. And if she behaves herself in the meanwhile, fair enough. We'll get the banns read. But if she doesn't . . . well, that's it. I'll wash me hands of her. Right?'

'You mean you'll get engaged, like?'

'Aha. But she'll have to behave herself, mind!'

'Oh she will, Dandy. I promise. She will! She will!' Jane jumped with joy. How this news would please her sister. 'When will you ask her?'

'Eh?' Dandy was taken aback.

'To marry you!'

'Oh that. Well, it's Sunday tomorrow . . . maybe after church, eh?' Jane smiled. The mist had deepened into fog, but to her the sun shone. 'Only mind . . . there's a promise to keep.' Jane nodded then ran off back home to Trajan Street, dying to tell her news.

'He said what!' Fanny was outraged. 'The very idea! How dare he ask such a thing.'

'But Fanny, I promised. You *won't* muck about will you?'

'Wash your mouth out, child!' she chided her.

'Are you not pleased, eh, our Fanny? I made him say he'd marry you.'

'Huh. I'll show him. Who does he think he is!'

'But Fanny, I promised. You will behave, won't you?' And to her surprise, Jane received a sharp smack on the cheek.

CHAPTER FOUR

Jane couldn't stop crying. Her stomach hurt from the sobbing, and no-one could get out of her what was wrong, though her father had his suspicions, as he watched Fanny going tight lipped about her business that night. And his suspicions were confirmed when what looked to Bob like sulkiness exploded into temper. Jane had been hiding in the bedroom, refusing to go out in the street and play cowboys and Indians with Josh, or go down to the beach with Robert. And Fanny had gone in there for a bit of ribbon to put on her bonnet for church tomorrow. Suddenly the peace of the house was shattered by a loud howl from Jane.

'Get off it! Leave it alone!' she yelled, and Bob rushed in to see what was wrong. Fanny had taken the drawing of the 'hephalant' off the wall above her bed.

'It's my room as well, and this thing gives me the creeps,' she was saying.

'It's my hephalant!' Jane insisted and, eyes blazing she went for her sister, pulling at her dress, kicking, and screaming to get the piece of paper out of her hands. Bob was horrified.

'Our Jane!' he said. 'I'm surprised at you!' And he lifted her bodily away from her big sister, plonking her on the bed and holding her there, while she screamed and kicked and cried, ignoring all his commands to be quiet. Her cries were heard out in the street where Josh and Robert played. They came rushing in and stood at the door watching the scene with round, frightened eyes.

'Tut!' Fanny expressed her disgust, and tearing up the piece of paper, pushed her brothers out of her way and left the room, followed by Jane, beside herself with fury and distress.

'Stop it! Stop it, our Fanny! Please, Fanny! Leave it alone!' Bob was powerless to hold the child. Her anger had lent her power and she had thrown him off to rush after her sister, and now, the elder was at the range, where the flames flickered hungrily. Jane let out a loud wail as the paper, like pieces of confetti fell onto the hot coals, and flared into black wisps.

'There now. That's an end of that.' Fanny rubbed her hands with satisfaction. And Jane was left whimpering by the fireplace. Robert's eyes were black. If Fanny had been a man . . . ! But he had to content himself with looks which could have killed. Josh was grinning. His little angel sister was in disgrace. It made a change from himself.

'I'm surprised at you, our Jane,' said her father. 'What a performance. You'll go and apologise to Fanny this minute.'

'I will not,' Jane said defiantly.

'By God, I'll take the strap to you, so help me, if you don't.' His hand reached for his belt, and Robert sprang towards him, holding on to his wrist.

'Dad! Don't! She's only little! She didn't mean it! Our Fan shouldn't have burned her picture.'

Bob's hand relaxed on his belt. He found he was shaking. The shock of Jane's behaviour had thrown him off balance. It was unlike her to be so sullen, so vicious.

'Look what she's done!' Fanny showed her bare arm. A long red scratch ran from wrist to elbow.

'What's got into you, Jane?' Bob asked more quietly. Jane's face was streaked with dark tears. She shook her head miserably.

'You've spoiled her, Dad. That's her trouble.'

'Aye. You're maybe right, our Fanny.' He sighed. 'Mind, I do think it was a bit much you tearing up her picture like that!'

'It was giving me nightmares!'

'Eeh well . . . ' It was all beyond Bob.

57

'She still didn't have the right to tear up Jane's picture!'

'Now shut up, our Robert. And you, Jane. It's Fanny's room as well. And if she took against it so much, she shouldn't have to suffer it. Now let that be an end of it!' One last loud sob from Jane brought a harsh look from her father, and she pushed back her tears, drawing them into the deepest part of her heart, till it ached. Seagulls were screeching overhead. There must be a storm out at sea driving them inland. And in their calls, she heard her own voice, a ghost from the morning, crying out, 'It isn't fair! It isn't fair!'

Bob was at a loss. This wasn't the little girl he knew and loved so much. Fanny's arm was deeply scored. The whole incident had shaken him. He never knew Jane had it in her. Such passion! Such obstinate defiance of him. He was cut to the quick by that. He must take warning. Was there no peace? He had thought himself to be free from worry about Jane at least. A sudden thought struck him. Maybe there was something wrong with her! Mrs Dunn was called in. She felt Jane's arms and legs, and looked at her tongue.

'Growing pains,' she announced, and Jane's nose wrinkled from the smell of whisky on her breath.

'As long as she's not sickening for something,' Bob said anxiously.

'I doubt it. No. It's just her age.' Bob looked at his youngest girl sadly.

'Pity they have to grow up, isn't it?' But he could have bitten out his tongue, as Fanny abruptly left the room. 'I'll need you to keep an eye on them when I'm gone, Missus,' Bob warned his neighbour.

'Oh aye. Don't you worry, Bob. They'll be right as rain. I'll see to that,' she laughed and her chest caught in a long wheeze which left her short winded.

'I don't like her, Dad,' Jane told him after she had gone.

'Now then. She's got a good heart whatever else is wrong with her. Look how she cared for our Fanny when she was ill. And anyway, you'll likely not have that much to do with her. Fanny'll be looking after you most of the time.' It was the devil and the deep blue sea. Jane stared at the kitchen floor moodily, and Bob sighed impatiently. 'Now I won't have you making trouble, Jane.

58

Fanny's made a lot of sacrifices for you and your brothers. You might be nice to her!'

'I'll try, Dad.'

'Never mind, try, you will! It's give and take in this life. That's something you've got to learn, my lass!'

Sent early to bed, Jane lay staring at the holes in the ceiling. Only this morning everything had been all right. Fanny had been in trouble, but not Jane. Now the boot was on the other foot. How had it happened? She'd only been trying to help. No matter how she racked her brains over the problem, she couldn't work it out.

Outside, Robert and Josh played, squalling and whooping as the palefaces gained ascendance over the Cherokee. Josh was full of beans and Robert let him shoot him dead several times before he got fed up and went in to see how their Jane was getting on. Josh kicked at his heels. It was always the same. He always ended up the odd one out. Well, he'd go down to the coble landing and help one of the blokes down there with his boat. There were interesting folk on the quayside. They came from all over the world, and he was good at listening was Josh Ridley. Yes, that's where he'd go and they could all drown themselves for all he cared. He'd not go home till he was hungry.

Robert pushed the bedroom door open softly. Thinking it was her Da or Fanny, Jane kept her eyes shut tight, pretending to be asleep. She felt the bed give, as Robert sat beside her, and she opened her eyes, finally sensing who it was.

'Hallo.'

'Hallo little'n,' he said gently. At once the tiny smile broke, and the tear stained face twisted with pain.

'Oh Robert!' she whimpered. He took her in his arms and rocked her to and fro, to and fro, till the aching in her heart was soothed. 'It isn't fair. Now Dad doesn't love me any more.'

'Course he does,' Robert reassured her. 'Fanny's just pulled the wool over his eyes, that's all. I expect it was all her fault somehow, wasn't it?' Jane nodded.

'I think so.'

'Did something happen this afternoon between you and her?' Jane said nothing and Robert knew he was right. And if Jane wouldn't tell him, then it had to be something very important;

something that would cast a bad light on their Fanny. 'She's not worth it you know,' he said. Jane sobbed.

'I can't tell, Robert. Honest.'

'All right. Look, I tell you what. I'll draw you another elephant. How about that?'

'Oh, Robert, do you think you could?'

'Why yes! I watched that Indian man doing it. It was easy.' So Robert fetched his drawing book and carefully pencilled in the lines of body, head and trunk.

'Eeeh!' Jane cried delightedly. 'That's even better than *he* drew! Honestly you're going to be a great artist, our Robert.'

He smiled at her, then pinned it to the wall.

'Let her put that in her pipe and smoke it,' he declared. Jane giggled and the conspirators curled up in bed together.

There was a special service at Saint Stephen's the next morning. A new lifeboat had been presented to the Institution by the widow of the man whose name graced the boat, Tom Perry. It was the least the town could do, to offer up a memorial service to the man himself, before the christening service took place and the boat was launched. The church was filled to bursting. Seats had been reserved at the front for the dignitaries of the borough and their families, and behind them were the pews of the Tyne pilots. As they walked down the aisle, the Ridley family were hard put to find a space for themselves, since the pilots had turned out in such force. There were the Burns, the Tinmouths, the Whales, the Leslies, the Marshalls, the Phillips, and Fanny noted Eileen Purvis surrounded by her clan. But the Tully family, small as it was, made way for them, and Fanny proudly made a show of passing down the road toward the seats they had been spared. Eileen craned her neck to see. There was nothing in it, she decided. Rattler Tully was known for his soft heart. They had taken pity on the Ridleys, that was all. Dandy O would suffer Fanny next to him through the service but it would be Eileen he would seek out afterwards and chat to in the churchyard.

The organ struck up the old familiar tune loved by seamen everywhere, and the congregation stood as the Reverend Henry

Morton led His Worship George Beattie, Mayor of Shields, the Aldermen, and all their families to the front of the church.

Eternal Father strong to save,
Whose arm hath bound the restless wave,
Who bidd'st the mighty ocean deep
Its own appointed limits keep:
Oh hear us when we cry to Thee
For those in peril on the sea.

All eyes were on the mayor and his family. George Beattie was a big man. Tall, he had a high domed head, thick eyebrows and a strong beard with a hint of red in it. His very size made him imposing, but he strolled in as though he owned the universe. Behind him walked a woman and a little girl. The woman was pretty. She wore a lace dress, and the biggest hat Jane had ever seen. It was covered with fresh flowers and she had a corsage on her bodice made of hot-house lilies. The perfume of the flowers rose with the warmth of her body into the stagnant air of the church, and left a trail of fragrance behind her. Jane thought she had never seen anyone or anything more beautiful. The little girl, however, was known to Jane. She was Harriet May Lovely, and she went to Jane's school. Jane eyed her dress, long and white with a sash of blue and pink rosebuds, and a matching ribbon in her hair. She looked nice, pretty. For the first time, Jane felt the lowliness of her own position, the dowdiness of her own dress, and she longed for Harriet not to see her. For she knew she would lord it over her. The dignitaries took their seats and the service began.

It was a fresh morning. Chandrika knocked and waited at the door in Trajan Street, but got no reply. Mrs Dunn poked her head out of the window up the terrace.

'They've gone to Saint Stephen's,' she called out. Of course. It was Sunday. He smiled at his stupidity and slowly walked, breathing the early summer air, in the direction of the pilots' church. He heard the singing as he turned into Mile End Road, and not wanting to tread on the dead in the grave yard, he waited outside the gate, leaning against the wall, till the service should be finished. The vicar and the mayor came out first, and stood at the porch ready to greet the rest of the congregation, while their families waited patiently behind them. The Ridleys and the Tullys, being further back in the body of the church, were amongst the first out, and try as she would, Jane could not avoid catching Harriet's eye. The eye looked her up and down disdainfully. Jane felt herself blushing, and wondered why she should feel ashamed before this girl. After all, she'd done nothing wrong. There was therefore nothing to be ashamed of! So, raising her head, Jane bravely went straight towards her school mate and said 'hallo'. At first Harriet made no response, and the woman in the lace dress looked on Jane with some surprise.

'Do you know this little girl?' she asked Harriet.

'Oh! Is it you, Jane?' Harriet said, as though she had just picked up a stone and found Jane lurking beneath.

'I think so,' Jane laughed. 'Who else would I be?'

'No need to get clever.'

'Sorry.'

'Why don't you offer Jane some of your toffee, Harriet?' The woman suggested, and smiled disarmingly at her.

'All right.' Harriet thrust foward the bag of toffee ungraciously. Jane put out her hand and took a piece.

'You didn't have to take such a big one, did you?'

'I'm sorry. It was the first bit I saw.' And she tried to put it back in the bag.

'Don't do that!' Harriet spat. 'Your hands have touched it.' And Jane felt that all the filth from the river Tyne must be on them. 'You'd better eat it now!' Jane put the toffee in her mouth and started chewing.

'It's very nice, Missus,' she said to the lady.

'Missus!' scolded Harriet.

'The name is Mrs Beattie,' the lady told Jane. 'We make the toffee at my husband's shop, you know. The recipe's a trade secret!'

'It's very nice,' Jane told her again.

'Thank you. Perhaps you'll call in and buy some one day. The shop's in Fowler Street. Everyone knows Beattie's shop.'

'Oh,' said Jane, 'we don't often go down there.'

'*They* live at the town end,' Harriet explained, derisively.

'I see,' said the lady. 'But you go to the same school, don't you?' And Harriet scowled, so that everyone listening, including George Beattie, was aware that that was a sore point with Harriet May Lovely.

'As mayor of this borough,' His Worship the Mayor intoned, 'I have great faith in the public schools, and to prove it, my late wife's daughter goes there. Who needs to pay the fees of private schools when we have such a body of able people taking care of all our children?' The bystanders applauded. Jane, head on one side, looked up at him. Catching her look, he smiled down at her, then patted her on the head. 'What a pretty girl!' he said. 'Give her some toffee, Adeline.'

'I already have, dear,' she replied sweetly.

Dandy O stood beside Fanny in the churchyard, while Chandrika was talking to her father. Both parties were deep in conversation, and instinctively Jane knew she could not disturb either of them. Robert was trying to prevent Josh from kicking at the gravestones in full view of the assembled crowd, and Jane decided he needed help.

'Excuse me, Missus . . . Beattie,' she said. 'My brother's being a nuisance.' And she left the 'nobs' thankfully, to make her way back to her own kind.

Fanny's eyes were bright behind her veil and her voice was light.

'I wonder at our Jane talking to big wigs!' She laughed. 'Wonders never cease.'

'Children can get away with anything. There *are* no class barriers where *they're* concerned.'

'Who is she?' Fanny was appraising the lady in the lace dress. 'She's got half a greenhouse on her frock!'

'I don't know.' Dandy shrugged.

'It'll be his new wife, I bet!' Rattler nodded at her, and Adeline Beattie, the shadow of her husband, was surprised and pleased to be acknowledged amongst these strangers, so smiled back.

'She looks nice,' Fanny was forced to admit.

'Aye. She does. Let's hope she lasts longer than the other'n.' Rattler Tully shook his head mysteriously and wandered off to let the young couple alone.

Dandy O shifted awkwardly from foot to foot. When would he

broach the important subject, Fanny wondered. If not today, well . . . perhaps never. She had better lend him a hand.

'I hear you were having a chat with our Jane yesterday, Dandy, lad.'

'Oh aye?' A long silence.

'I heard it concerned me.'

'Oh aye?' Another long silence.

'Will you marry me, Dandy O!' Dandy's mouth gaped in astonishment. And beneath her veil, Fanny laughed up at him, surprised at her own temerity.

'I suppose so. If you like.'

'Good. I'm glad that's settled.' Trying not to whoop for joy, Fanny reached out and took Dandy's hand, fondling it in her own.

'You're not a bad lass, Fanny.'

'Thank you very much!'

'Only, Fanny . . . I told Jane . . . '

'She's but a child.'

'I know, but I told her, I have to have a promise.' Swallowing down her pride Fanny stood stiffly, saying nothing. 'Jane said you wouldn't . . . muck me about, like.' Fanny bit her lip. 'You won't will you, because if you do . . . '

'What a thing to say, Dandy!' she laughed it off. 'Why should I do any such thing? Haven't I got the best man on The Lawe for a husband?'

'Not yet you haven't,' he warned her sharply. Fanny felt his hand limp in hers and she went cold.

'When will I have the honour?' she asked derisively.

'Next year. When your Dad comes back, if . . . '

'Next year. Well I'll have plenty of time to make my wedding dress, won't I?' Out of the corner of her eye, Fanny saw Eileen Purvis, standing by the porch. Quickly grasping Dandy O by the hand, she hauled him off in the direction of her father, smiling and laughing.

'Da! We've got something to tell you!'

Eileen Purvis, stock still with fright, burned holes in Dandy's back. He never felt so uncomfortable in his life. To do right by one woman, he had to wrong another. That was the way of it. Well, he could not help it. He sighed, and smiled gamely as Bob

Ridley slapped him on the back.

The three younger Ridley children homed in on the joy. The business with the mirrors had been forgotten, and Chandrika was part of the family, part of the celebration. As Fanny dragged away her intended to show him off to 'the girls' from the sail-making sheds, the Indian gave Bob a questioning look.

'What happened to make him change his mind?' he asked.

'Someone showed him the error of his ways,' said the proud father.

'I wonder who?' Chandrika's eyes dropped to the young girl at his side. Bob followed his eyes with a puzzled expression, and Jane returned the Indian's look fearfully. But Rattler Tully hailed his friend from the other side of the gate, and Bob went over to him, the two men glad to have settled an old score at last.

'How did you know?' Jane asked Chandrika quietly, when they were alone. He shook his head.

'Was it wise to interfere?'

'He's going to marry her. That's all that matters, isn't it?'

'Dear child, that sympathetic heart of yours is going to get you into all sorts of trouble.' Then he walked away sadly, leaving her by the church gate.

'Jane!' her father called. 'Come on lass. We've got an engagement to celebrate!' And the two families of Tully and Ridley made for the grand home in Pilot Street where Fanny was eventually to live.

When the festivities had reached exhaustion point, the Ridley family made their excuses and went back home.

It was late in the day. Darkness was beginning to fall, and the younger members of the family were yawning loudly.

'Bed time!' their father insisted. Josh, Robert and Jane were forced to give in and go to bed.

At last Fanny and her father were alone.

'I'm pleased for you, pet,' he said. 'It'll give you something to think about when I'm gone.' Fanny sobbed.

'I can't believe it, Da. I'd given up hope. Eeh, I'm the happiest lass in the town end. I am honestly.' Bob smiled, and took her head in his arms, letting her cry out her relief. After a pause, the sobbing grew quieter, and he lifted her head to look her full in the face.

'Beauty's not skin deep, Fan. No matter what they say. And, you know, lass, inside, you can be really lovely.'

'Thanks, Da. I'll try to be. I promise.'

'I'm going to be the proudest man in Shields when I go down the aisle of Saint Stephen's with you on me arm. Eeh, fancy you marrying a Tyne Pilot, eh? Who'd've thought it.' He laughed, shaking his head. 'Your Mam'd be proud of you.' Softened and chastened by her good luck, Fanny's face was sweet with love.

'Don't make it a long trip, Da, eh? Catch a packet home, from the Cape.'

'Aye well. We'll see, lass.' And his face grew dark.

'What's the matter?'

'I didn't want to say before . . . casting a gloom on the celebrations and that, like. But, you see . . . I learnt this morning, that we're to set sail tomorrow. That's what Chandrika came to tell me at the church.' Fanny's jaw dropped.

'Oh, Da! But it's so sudden. D'ye want to wake the kids and tell them?' Bob stopped her.

'No, pet. It'll keep till the morning. I wouldn't spoil this day for all the tea in China.' The wind was fairly taken out of Fanny's sail.

'Nothing's ready, Da.'

'I don't need anything, Fan. Not for meself, like.' Fanny looked at him questioningly. 'But I would like to be sure this family's going to be all right, pet.' Fanny nodded. 'You're a woman now. Going to be married. One day, maybe, you'll have children of your own. So, be a good lass, eh? Take care of them three in there.' He nodded in the direction of the other room.

'Of course I will! Need you ask?'

'They're a packet of trouble. I know that.' He shook his head, anxiously. 'You'll have to make Josh go to school. Tell the teacher to keep an eye on him, let you know if he doesn't turn up. And if in doubt, ask Rattler. The lad's always down there on the landing. He'll know where he's got to if anybody does. Now Robert, he'll be all right, just so long as you keep him occupied. I don't like this drawing business. Make him do errands, that'll maybe take his mind off art!' Fanny laughed. 'But Jane,' the father sighed. 'Well, I'm disappointed in her. I've got to say it. I thought *she* was all right at least.'

66

'Like I said, Da, she's spoiled.'

'Aye. She is that. Well lass, it's woman's work, so I give you free rein to do what you think best with her.' He touched her hand lovingly, and gave her the money put by for them all. 'Mrs Dunn's there if you need any advice, and, of course, there's always Mrs Tully.'

'Huh! She resents me. I know she does. She'd far rather Dandy was marrying that Eileen Purvis!'

'Aye well. Give her time. She'll get used to the idea, pet. Now go on. Get to bed. I've got some thinking to do before morning.'

The next day dawned drizzly but breezy, a good day to set sail. Bob slung his bag over his shoulder and followed by the silent foursome of his family, he made his way down to the landing stage. A foyboatman, one of the lesser breed of mortals who made their living on the Tyne, was hailed, and slowly began to make his way towards them. Taking Robert aside, Bob spoke seriously to him.

'Now lad, I'm relying on you. You've got to look after your sisters. Especially Jane, mind. It's up to you to take good care of her.' Sticking out his chest, Robert wanted to say such strong brave words, but he found he couldn't speak at all, so merely nodded. Then taking his last leave of his tearful children, Bob Ridley was sculled over to the waiting ship on the north shore. Silently, they watched him go, as the rain grew heavier and heavier. They could hardly see for the raindrops, hanging on their lashes, mixing with their tears, and finally, drenching their clothes. It fell on the rooftops of the town, on the sand by the jetty, on the river, and the ships, and it fell steadily, heavily on the cold North Sea.

Bob's departure had been all so sudden. There had been no chance for a proper goodbye. They had thought they had till the end of the week, and there'd been no time to get used to the change of plan. It had been like that with their mother. One minute she'd been there and the next she was gone. Their father was embarking on a long and dangerous journey. He was committing himself to the ocean. They might never set eyes on him again. Sadly they turned from the landing stage and went back up the hill. The house was forlorn and empty. No more

67

fairy stories. Fanny hated them, but at least she hadn't dared to touch Robert's drawing on the wall. Robert's throat ached from suppressed tears. His hand reached out to touch Jane's. She smiled at him, and in spite of himself, Robert burst into tears.

On board the *Daisy Queen*, there was great activity. And no-one noticed a young lad, sculling over to the quay, and climbing a rope onto the ship. And when someone did see him, going down below, they thought nothing of it. Young lads were often taken on, and if this one looked a bit young for his age, well, it wasn't their business. He looked as though he knew his way around. So Josh hid himself below deck, waiting in the darkness for the old, creaking schooner to set sail.

Fanny was furious. No sooner had she turned her back than one of her charges had disappeared. Well, if this was what the next year was going to be like, she really didn't think she could get through it without murdering the lot of them! Jane and Robert fled the house, making their way to the Lawe from which vantage point they would be able to see the *Daisy Queen* as she passed out of the river, over the bar, and on her way. The pilot's flag hung, heavy with rain, from the mast. Rattler was on board, his coble in tow, taking the ship safely past the black middens and the Herd Sands, over the bar. The rain stopped. From the deck, Bob Ridley saw the two lonely figures of his son and daughter, standing on the hill top, and he took off his scarf to wave at them.

'That's him!' Jane yelled. Brother and sister waved back with all their might. 'Oh Da!' Jane cried out. 'Da! Come back safe!' Robert forced back his tears. This time he would not disgrace himself. He had to protect his little sister. He had to be a man, for her sake. He would look after her. His arm reached out to comfort her, as the ship, safely out of harbour, paused at the river mouth to set down the pilot. There was a commotion on deck. The two on the Lawe strained their eyes to see. Was it a fight? Then they saw the pilot being set down from the ship into his coble, and close behind him was someone else. Was it Dandy O? The coble was rowed back into the river mouth. And as it got nearer, they saw clearly, alongside Rattler, a bedraggled and resentful Josh Ridley. Jane and Robert put hand to mouth and burst out laughing. What would their Fanny say? The ship waiting outside the harbour set sail at last, and their laughter faded, as they watched it turn. Then the sun came out, and over the river mouth a rainbow formed, clear and bright from north to south. The two lonely figures on the hill stood within its arch watching their father's ship disappear over the horizon.

PART TWO
Winter 1872

CHAPTER FIVE

'Dear Fanny, and all,
    It was so good to get the letter from Robert last week. I am glad
to hear you are all well, and Fanny is looking after you
properly. Let me know if the money runs out and I'll send
something home for you somehow or other. I am afraid I do
not think it likely I shall be home for Christmas.'

Jane and Josh let out a roar of disappointment.
'He promised!' Josh yelled out furiously.
'Hold your horses, Josh,' Robert calmed him. 'Let's finish the
letter.'

'As I thought, we picked up a fresh cargo at the Cape and are
now bound for New York and from there we expect to go on to
Newfoundland before making tracks once more for home.'

'New York!' Josh's eyes grew wide. 'That's in America, isn't
it?'
'You and America.' Jane dug her young brother in the ribs.
'It's all you can think of. What about our Da?'
'It's all right for him. It'll be all hot and sunny where he is!'
'Do you want me to finish this letter or not?'   Robert, frustra-
ted by constant interruption, was growing fractious.

'Go on, Robert. We're all ears,' Jane smiled at him.

As Robert continued with the letter, Fanny sighed deeply, her mind elsewhere, then finally she got up, threw her shawl around her, and left the house. Jane, listening to Robert, grew increasingly uneasy. Fanny had been more restless than usual. She was often heard to say sharp things of Dandy O, though never in his hearing. Jane began to wonder what was the matter, and as the boys brought out the atlas tracing their father's route across the Atlantic, she decided to follow Fanny, to see what she was up to. Quietly, she took the rug from the big bed, and wrapped it round herself, before stepping out into the dark, frosty street.

The moon was in its first quarter and already high in the sky. The stars sparkled like ice crystals, and the iron on her boots struck sharp and clear against the cobblestones. At the end of the street, Jane paused, and listened to the sound of the night. In the Mission Hall, they were singing. A child, barefoot, tottered home, staggering under the weight of a pot of beer. A woman opened her front door and swept out a pile of cockroaches into the road, and a lone man, already drunk, wandered, shouting, from house to house, having forgotten where he lived. On the river, bells clanged and horns blew, and over everything the sound of the sea, relentlessly pounding against the piers and against the shores. The echo of her footsteps faded. Which way to go? What had Fanny been seeking when she left the house? Why had she not wanted to hear the rest of their father's letter? Jane breathed slowly in the cold air, and her mind calmed. There was no reason for her to worry. None at all. Only her instinct agitated her. Ever since the day Fanny struck her, Jane had been wary of Fanny's moods. And tonight, her mood had warned her, as the bell on the groyne pier warned the ships, of danger lurking close at hand. She would find Dandy O. Perhaps Fanny would be with him? If not, he might at least know where she was. After all, Jane and Dandy had struck a bargain. They were in league to keep Fanny straight. Jane's boots clanged on towards Pilot Street and the Tully House.

Mrs Tully had three chins, and they wobbled alarmingly as Jane asked her the whereabouts of her sister.

'How would I know what a body like that one gets up to, I'm

sure!' she said. Standing on the doorstep feeling very much the unwelcome, uninvited guest, Jane stood her ground.

'I just thought you might be able to tell me where your Dandy O was.'

'Our Bill . . . ' Mrs Tully refused to use the pilot nickname, considering he had been blessed with a proper Christian name and all. 'Our Bill's probably at "The Globe". And no decent sort of woman would be seen dead there! I'll say no more.' The three chins wobbled one more time, and the door was shut firmly against Jane.

'The Globe' was full to bursting. The light shone from the door and the windows, and a fug billowed out onto the street. Jane avoided the public and made for the snug, where the women sat, bleary eyed and vociferous, watching her doubtfully, as she came up to them.

'Have you seen Dandy O?' Jane asked.

'I haven't. Have you, Edna?'

'No.' Edna shook her head. 'Eeh you look starved, pet. Will you have a sip of me porter, eh?' Jane sniffed the proffered liquid, and her nose wrinkled. 'It'll warm you up! Feel how cold her hands are!'

'Eeh! Yes! Mind, cold hands, warm heart.'

'Go on! Have a drop!'

'No thanks. Do you know where else he might be?'

'Aye well, you could try "Bella Booth's".' Jane frowned. What sort of place was that? As though she'd read her thoughts the old woman explained. 'Used to be known as the "Noah's Ark". It's a pub, pet. Down Long Bank.'

Dandy O was surprised to see Fanny. She didn't usually come in search of him, and she steered clear of the places his mother disapproved of so much, trying to keep in her good books. After all, she was hoping to live with her one day!

'Is something wrong?' Dandy asked, his mind turning at once to the three Ridley children. Fanny shook her head.

'No. I just felt a bit lonely, that's all.' Dandy smiled at her. She was sweet tonight, her smile was gentle for him. He liked her that way.

'Fancy a glass while you're here?' Fanny nodded, and took the

75

drink gratefully, warming her hands on the hot glass.

'Da's not coming home for Christmas.'

'Eeh, pet. I'm sorry,' Dandy said.

'He promised.'

'Aye well. Circumstances change like.' Fanny pondered this statement, before she spoke.

'I agree with that,' she said at last. 'So what about us, Dandy? Will our circumstances change as well?'

'Eeh well, we can't very well tie the knot without him, can we? Somebody's got to give you away!' He was trying to make light of it.

'You said we'd get married this Christmas.'

'If your Dad got back. Aye. But he's not.'

'Do you not love me, then Dandy?' The old story. Dandy sighed.

'Of course I do. I'm going to marry you, aren't I?'

'But not yet.'

'No.' Fanny sipped her hot porter. 'What difference does a few more months make, eh?'

'You know!' Dandy looked away. He knew all right. The last six months had been torture to him. Courting Fanny was a cat and mouse affair. But usually the man was the cat and the woman the mouse. The situation with Fanny had turned the tables. She pursued him relentlessly. Her smiles flickered at the corner of her mouth, her laughter teased him. She made him drink more than he should, and then tried to take advantage. And she could be very appealing could Fanny Ridley. What she lacked in looks she more than made up for in other directions. She knew how to please a man, and she knew how to be pleasured herself. She drew him on to the threshold of bearable desire. Her lips taunted him, persuaded him he wanted more. Her touch was deft, like the wings of a butterfly on his skin, or hard, demanding, in response to his own need for her. And she always knew what he wanted. How hard it was for him to have to keep turning down somebody who kept trying to give you what you wanted! Poor Dandy O! Not that Fanny felt the slightest bit sorry for him at this moment. She had strained her powers, trying to persuade him to make love to her again. But, he would not! She knew he wanted to, so why, oh why did he resist her?

76

The truth was, that Dandy O was a stubborn man. He had come to a decision the day he agreed to marry Fanny. He had extracted a promise of her good behaviour. Supposing he gave in to her now and made her pregnant? Then where would he be? He would *have* to marry her, good behaviour or not! There was nothing for it. He just had to resist not only her, but his own desperate inclinations! 'Surely now, Dandy, we could . . . you know . . . ' Dandy stood his ground. His body grew stiff with resistance as her hand searched out those places she knew made him shiver with delight. Tremors ran through his body as her hand moved across his back, slowly, sweetly, and his muscles rippled under her touch. She felt him weaken and quickly, nestled closer into him, resting her head on his shoulder, so that her hair tickled his cheek. Then he had to move his head, and his lips were close to hers. And she would not let him kiss her yet. He had to *want* to kiss her, so her lips teased his, drawing him on . . . The atmosphere in 'Bella Booth's' grew warm, and close, and Fanny's shawl dropped from her shoulders, as Dandy's arm touched the skin and held her close to him.

Jane's heart had sunk as she left 'The Globe'. What sort of a wild goose chase had she embarked on? Still her boots clanged on, down Wapping Street with its Flemish houses, and on to Long Bank. A sailor, standing on the corner under a lamp, waiting for somebody, watched her approach. Her bright hair shone under the moon, and she was deep in thought, oblivious of his presence. A sudden movement made her jump. She stopped. He pushed back his cap, and she saw his eyes were on her. She looked behind her. There was nobody. They were at the top of Long Bank, a twisting narrow street, dark, with many hidden corners. Jane's heart pounded in her throat. The strength drained from her legs. She swallowed hard. She would have to walk on, past him. If she ran, it would only encourage him to come after her.

He shifted his weight, ready for her. She was almost within reach of the lamplight. She could see the carved Noah's Ark above the door of the pub. And then they heard it. It was loud and clear. Inside the pub all talking stopped. Outside, the sailor froze, shouted and ran off in the opposite direction. It began slow

77

and low and then grew more insistent. It sounded like the devil himself hammering at the wall of the building. It grew louder and louder. Men and women hurtled out into the street, leaving their drinks unfinished, in their rush to get away from it. Fanny, terrified, held onto Dandy O who led her away from the resounding wall, and jostled by the crowd, they were almost crushed at the door, till, like a cork out of a bottle, they sprang into the street right into Jane Ridley.

'Was it the bogie man?' Jane cried.

'Oh get us home, Dandy. Get us home,' Fanny pleaded. The hammering had stopped as suddenly as it had started. Jack the Hammer, the old tinker's ghost, which would not rest, had been 'at it' again.

'We'll be getting the lifeboats out again tomorrow,' Dandy sighed.

'Aye. Jack always knows when there's a storm coming,' Fanny agreed. Jane had heard of Jack the Hammer, but she had never been down Long Bank in the dark before, and so had never heard the phenomenon of the hammering on the wall of the pub.

'Jack saved me,' she said simply.

'Aye.' Dandy winked at Fanny. 'He saved me an all, pet!' He laughed, but Fanny scowled. So near and yet so far. 'Best give me up as a bad job, Fan,' he whispered into her ear. 'You'll get nowhere till we're wed.'

It didn't occur to Fanny, for some days, to wonder just what Jane Ridley was doing down at Bella Booth's at that time of night. But since she was responsible for the child's whereabouts, she could hardly make a fuss if her own neglect was to blame for it. And she wasn't such a child now, after all. Just by looking at her, you could see, she was beginning to grow into a woman. Well then, she'd better not say anything to Fanny, if she got up to anything, for it would be the pan calling the kettle black! Down at 'Bella Booth's' so late at night! It could only be for one reason! So Fanny thought. And she didn't have much time to spend pondering Jane's motives. After all, there was so much else for Fanny to think about. Promises, promises! Dandy had promised to marry her, if she 'behaved'. Well she *had* behaved hadn't she? And where was the wedding ring to show for it? Her father had promised to be home for Christmas for the ceremony.

And where was he? Half way round the other side of the world. She had promised to be nice, and to keep herself to herself. Hadn't she tried to keep those promises? Rejected, hurt, and humiliated, Fanny felt that if other people could break promises, then so could she! She would show the lot of them! Her restless spirit pounded, like Jack the Hammer, against the walls of her heart, and her heart gave way under the impact.

Jane confided what she had done, to Robert, in bed, that night, while Josh slept.

'Why did you go, Jane?' he asked her.

'I don't know really. I just had this feeling that something was going to go wrong.'

'It's your imagination.'

'Yes. I expect so.'

'That man . . . the one under the lamp. I saw how he looked at me. He sort of looked . . . he frightened me. He made me feel like I had no clothes on . . . ' Robert shushed her growing distress.

'Don't you dare go anywhere like that without me,' he told her, 'never again.'

'No. I won't.' She felt safe in Robert's arms. Outside, it was a dangerous world. Men and women fought each other. They didn't love. Fanny and Dandy O were involved in a kind of a fight. She knew that. And she knew, somehow, that it was a fight Fanny was losing. And, right or wrong, it made Jane sorry for her. Jane thought it must be better to be a man. The women always seemed to come off worst. The look on the sailor's face under the lamp, came back to her again and again. 'Our Fanny likes men looking at her like that,' she said at last.

'It's a dangerous game she's playing, our Jane. It's time you knew about it. To be on your guard.'

Suddenly Robert seemed so grown up. He spoke to her gently. He warned her to be careful about showing her legs when she walked, to keep her eyes to herself so as not to attract attention, to hold her shawl round her head tight and close so that men would not gaze at her face. And Jane felt the world close around her. Every man became a threat to her. Even the old tars on the Lawe now appeared to her as alien, dangerous beings. It frightened her. She had known how children came into the world in a way. In the town end, life was raw, and children grew up

79

seeing and hearing everything, living as they did in such cramped conditions. But Bob Ridley had kept his children closer than most. And Jane, in any case, had a dreaming kind of mind. She saw what she wanted to see, and heard what she wanted to hear. And the world she wanted to see was sweet, the people trusting and worthy of trust. Now, Robert forced her to see that it wasn't always so. He forced her to look at the darker side of life. Afraid, she held onto him, and his arm wrapped round her.

'Don't worry, Jane. Robert'll look after you.'

'Always?'

'Always.'

'Promise?'

'I promise.'

Jane lay cold beside Robert's warm body. She heard him sigh and wondered what he was thinking. She hadn't thought grown ups played games. Only children. And *their* games didn't seem much fun. Someone always got hurt. She remembered her mother shouting crossly at them when they played too hard.

'It'll end in tears,' she had said. And she had usually been right. The grown up games were the same. And Jane could sense that their Fanny was going to end up in tears.

'Can't you sleep?' Robert said at last.

'No.'

'Shall I tell you a story?' he volunteered.

'Tell me the one about the elephant and the crocodile,' Jane asked him, and as he began the story, Jane watched the candle flame flickering across the drawing on the wall.

A week after the ghostly hammerings of Jack, the children of Trajan Street combined with their schoolmates from Saint Stephen's, to seek for adventure. Their favourite game was, 'Let's spy on courting couples'. It was a bit like looking for blackberries in the autumn. Somebody would see some ripe fruit in a bush and the rest would home in on it. Marine Park, sheltered by its trees and bushes, usually provided a fair number of sightings but this Saturday, the children were disappointed. One hopeful bundle of humanity, lying under some bushes near Watch House, turned out to be a tramp curled up for warmth with his dog. He propelled stones and sticks after them, as they fled his wrath, chanting,

Sticks and stones
May break your bones
But bad words never hurt you!

One sharp stone caught Josh on the back of his heel, and he hurled an amazing kaleidoscope of bad words back at the tramp, which made him look at his dog in astonishment.

'Where did you pick up words like that?' Robert asked him as he hopped after them back up to the Lawe.

'On the quayside, man. You can pick up a lot there if you keep your ears open!' And Josh limped off on his own, back to his favourite haunts, as the group of children split, to go their own ways.

'Let's try the Roman Station,' Jennie Tinmouth suggested. 'My Auntie Mavis used to do a lot of courting there!'

The Roman Station lay between Trajan Street and the riverside. Grassy mounds and foundation stones marked the places where Roman soldiers used to sleep or keep watch. A square of green amongst the houses, it was large enough to hide a multitude of sins. Though you had to be careful of the nettles. Many courting couples ended up with stinging rashes in some very odd places! Jane, Robert and Jenny clambered over the mounds, giggling and shushing each other as they thought to pounce on a couple just on the other side. The two girls had gone on ahead, while Robert hung back. He had begun to feel that perhaps, just perhaps, it wasn't quite fair to disturb lovers. He was fifteen years old. Many a lad was working by his age, and many a lad was married before he was twenty. Jane, being younger, couldn't see that there was anything wrong in it. It was just innocent fun to her. But Robert was waking up, and he could see himself on the other end of this game, one day. One of its victims. Sudden surges of feeling took him unawares, and the teacher at his school, the one who encouraged his drawing, smelt sweet when he drew near to her. He had begun to draw her in his book, when she wasn't looking, when he was supposed to be drawing sailing ships, and he tore those precious portraits out, hoarding them in a box under the bed at home. He would have loved to talk about these new feelings with someone, but he couldn't possibly speak of them to Jane. She just wouldn't understand. She would think he was like the other men he had warned her about, the night after 'Bella Booth's'. 'All after one thing'.

Fanny appeared as if from nowhere. She was obviously furious, and her clothes were all over the place. She struggled to pull herself together.

'What are you doing here, our Jane?' she demanded.

'Nothing.'

'Don't give me nothing! Skulking about the place, secretive as you like.' Jane frowned. She wasn't being secretive. But she thought better of protesting. 'Get yourself off home. It's nearly tea time.' She pulled her skirt round. 'By but this wind, fair tears you to tatters,' she excused herself.

'What are *you* doing here, Fanny, come to that?' Jane dared to ask at last.

'Like you, pet,' Fanny answered tartly, 'nothing.'

In a world of his own, Robert scarcely noticed the man stealthily hurrying from the place, his cap pulled down firmly over his eyes.

Robert had drawn Jane a crocodile, which she took with her to school, and which she showed off proudly to her class mates. Jane was doing well at Saint Stephen's. She had been second in her class, close behind Harriet May Lovely, for the last two years. But now, in the Christmas tests, she had come first. Harriet smiled her congratulations, making a great show of her generosity. And Miss Poulson was all admiration for Harriet's Christian attitude. She was so friendly to Jane, it made her flesh creep, and Miss Poulson noticed what looked like antagonism in Jane's response, and was disappointed in her, as her father had been before her. She made them sit next to one another, to encourage a friendship, and Jane had to suffer Harriet queening it over her like Lady Bountiful, day in, day out. The rest of the class admired Harriet. She wore nice clothes, she had a posher accent than the rest of them, and her Da not only had money but was the Mayor of Shields. He was somebody! Therefore Harriet May Lovely was also somebody! Even the teacher was impressed. And soon, Harriet had drawn a gang of devotees about her, her 'yes' men, girls and boys who fell at her feet ready to do her bidding. Everyone knew Harriet was a cut above them, and they had to be deeply grateful for her presence.

But Harriet did not like coming in second in the tests. Her stepfather would not brook second place. *He* had always come in first. And Harriet had, too, until now. Her show of friendship to Jane was overwhelming. She brought a bunch of flowers weekly for the teacher.

'From me Dad's hothouses,' she said.

And at the beginning of the spring term, she also brought Jane a posy. It was made up of brightly coloured flowers and ferns.

'Them's nice,' she said to Harriet.

'Don't you know what they're called?' Harriet asked. Jane shook her head. She'd never seen flowers like that before. 'They're called anemones,' she informed her from a great height. The whole class laughed. Fancy Jane not knowing what anemones were! Even Miss Poulson laughed. And then, Jane noticed that her drawing of the crocodile had gone missing. She searched and searched her desk, growing frantic with worry. Robert would be so hurt if he thought she'd lost it. He'd think she hadn't cared for it enough to look after it. Her distress grew out of all proportion.

'Oh stop going on about it!' Harriet told her. 'I expect it's somewhere!' And she flounced off with her cronies to the playground, leaving Jane, distraught, and on her own in the classroom.

Her body ached with anxiety. She had searched till her mind was in a whirl. And now she was alone. She sat at her desk, perplexed by what had happened. First it had been there and then it had not. But things didn't just disappear, did they? Only people, like her mother and father. So what had happened to it? Light dawned slowly. She looked at Harriet's desk, the desk linked to her own. She thought for a minute, looked out of the window onto the quadrangle outside, then slid her hand along to raise the lid. Her breath stopped. There, peeping out of one of Harriet's books, was the drawing of the crocodile. Suppressing a desire to cry out loud against the injustice, Jane thought carefully, lowering the lid of the desk. She had always known Harriet

83

was her enemy. She had sensed it first, and then Harriet had always jumped at the opportunity to humiliate, show her up, if she could, in her fancy frocks, lording it over them all, till she realised her instinct had been right. Harriet was jealous. That was it. She couldn't bear coming second to Jane. Well, here was the proof. Even Miss Poulson would have to see that Harriet was her enemy, and she wouldn't make them sit together any more.

So, when class came in after playtime, Jane went up to Miss Poulson's desk and told her she knew Harriet had taken her picture.

'That is a very serious accusation, Jane,' Miss Poulson told her.

'I know, Miss. But it's true. I saw it in her desk.'

'And what were you doing in her desk?' Miss Poulson asked her. And Jane blushed. Knowing she shouldn't have pried.

'I don't know what she's talking about, Miss,' Harriet said. 'I think she's gone mad.'

'Well, we'll soon see, won't we? Harriet lift up your desk lid.' Harriet looked far too sure of herself, and Jane's heart sank. She looked inside the desk. Miss Poulson went through every book, and every bit of paper. The drawing wasn't there. 'Well, unless it's invisible . . . ' The whole class laughed, including Harriet, 'I'd say your drawing wasn't there, Jane.'

'No, Miss.' And Jane sat at her own desk, miserably.

'I think we should check *her* desk now, Miss,' said Harriet.

Oh no! thought Jane. She hasn't, has she? But she had. Jane's drawing was back in her own desk. Harriet had spirited it there when no-one was looking. How stupid Jane had been! She had fallen into a trap and she could kick herself. Miss Poulson was furious. She called Jane some dreadful names, and the whole class hissed at her.

Back home, that night, Jane could not bring herself to tell her brother of her misery. He might think badly of her for having opened Harriet's desk, and she couldn't bear that. Or worse, he might think, like Miss Poulson, that she'd made the whole thing up to spite Harriet. So Jane's secret was hidden in her heart, like Robert's, shut in his little box under the bed. Deep in their own problems, and dreams, neither of them began to guess of their Fanny's secret.

Mrs Dunn had noticed how thin and pale Fanny was growing. She had, as she had promised, kept an eye on Bob's children, in his absence. Not that there was a lot she could do for them. Not till Fanny's predicament had come to her notice. The two women locked themselves away in Mrs Dunn's rooms whispering together, and not Robert, nor Jane, nor Josh took the slightest bit of notice.

'First things first,' Mrs Dunn told Fanny. 'Go and see what *he* says.'

Fanny found *him* down at the usual haunt. He was waiting for her by the lamp opposite 'Bella Booth's'. He smiled as she approached him, shawl tight round her ears to keep out the cold.

'Eeh, I'm starved, Jim. Buy's a drink, eh?'

So they went into the pub with the ark outside, and Fanny warmed herself with the glow of porter. 'I've got some news for you, Jim,' she said nervously.

'Oh aye?' he replied, with the usual wordiness of the Tyne seaman.

'Can you guess what it is?'

He looked at her, then looked away, as pale as she was.

'I hope not.'

'I'm afraid it's true. I'm expecting.'

'Whose is it?' he asked, feeling that attack was always better than defence.

'Whose do you think?' she snapped back at him.

'Now then. Don't show your claws!' He edged away from her seat.

'What am I going to do?'

Jim shrugged. 'Ask Ma Dunn. She'll know.' And he got up and walked out on her.

Fanny gulped down the rest of her drink and ordered another. She was coming to the end of their father's money. She would have to send to him for some more. Perhaps, if she smiled nicely, someone in the pub would buy her one . . . No. Wasn't she in enough trouble? Did she have to descend to that? Supposing the word got round. She looked about her, fearfully. Had anyone noticed? Would they say anything to Dandy O? They'd been careful, her and Jim. Tonight was the first time they'd been in the public together. Usually they met under the bridge at Tyne

Dock, or in his room in Wapping Street, or somewhere else, where no-one could see them in the darkness. Why had she done it? Why, oh why? She wished to God she hadn't. It was all his fault! Dandy O's! Why did he have to treat her like that, as if she was the filth under his feet. 'Behave yourself' if you please? What right had he to ask that of her after what he had done to her? 'Behave yourself'! The words drew fire from her soul. He should behave *him*self! She hated him at that moment. And yet, she knew she needed him. She would have to be careful. She would have to play her cards right. This was a game she could not afford to lose. She got up unsteadily and made her way back to Trajan Street, stopping short of the Ridley house, to knock up Ma Dunn, whose dog, Gormless, roused his mistress from her sleep with his barking.

Jane could not fight against what had happened to her at school. She had to bide her time and behave perfectly, to get back into some sort of favour with her teachers. Her classmates might never forget what had happened, and they ostracised her, more and more of them falling into Harriet's camp as time went on. But Miss Poulson was another matter. With the mayor's step-daughter in school, she thought to raise the 'tone' of the lessons. She introduced a poetry class, and had each child learning a piece of poetry every week, which he or she had to recite to the rest of the class. This week she had chosen Wordsworth's 'The Rainbow', and each child had taken the poem home to learn as best it could. Jane slaved over it, and Robert listened impatiently as she fumbled over the words again and again. 'They aren't just words,' he told her. 'They have feelings. Say it as if you mean it, and then you'll remember it easier.' It was good advice and Jane began to learn more quickly. So that when the time came to recite it to the class, she was more than usually confident. She put her special bow in her hair, just to help her along, and sat on tenterhooks while each child took his turn. 'Lovely' coming before 'Ridley' in the register, Harriet's turn came before Jane's. Jane found herself hating the little girl she was forced to sit beside. She didn't much like hating anybody. It wasn't a nice feeling. But she did, all the same. She couldn't help it. She kept wishing Harriet'd forget the words, or fall over and make a fool of herself somehow, but she didn't. She was word perfect and drew praise from the teacher. After the recitation, Harriet plonked herself back in her seat and smiled a sidelong smile at Jane, which said, 'beat that!' And then, at last, Jane's turn came. She paused before beginning, took a deep breath, and imagined the rainbow she had seen when her father had sailed off into the northern ocean. And she began;

My heart leaps up when I behold
A rainbow in the sky.
So was it when my life began,
So is it now I am a man,
So be it when I shall grow old,
Or let me die!
The child is father of the man,
And I would wish my days to be
Bound each to each by natural piety.

There was total silence as Jane finished the poem. Miss Poulson stared at her for some time, then indicated that she should sit down.

'Well,' she said at last. 'That was beautiful. Really beautiful. I might even believe what that poem says after this!'

From that time on, the rest of the class treated her with more respect and Harriet, sensing the change, grew more wary of her. It was a victory. No doubt about it. And Jane owed it all to Robert.

Robert had not realised what it had all meant to her, and he was taken aback by Jane's tearful exultation at tea time.

'Now don't get too cocky, our Jane,' he warned her, grinning.

'Fat chance of that!' she replied and kicked him under the table. And there *was* a fat chance. They had got their own teas, because Fanny wasn't there and Mrs Dunn came down, before they had finished eating, to summon Jane up to her rooms. There was something up. When she got there, Jane found Fanny lying on Mrs Dunn's bed. She was screaming and moaning in agony.

'Keep that cloth wet and hold that piece of wood in your sister's mouth,' Mrs Dunn told her.

'Why? What's happening?' Jane asked in terror, as Mrs Dunn

took a long knitting needle and wiped it carefully on her apron. The smell of cheap gin hung on the air of the room. Fanny was only half-conscious, in spite of her moans.

'She needs a bit of help,' Mrs Dunn told Jane. 'Hold onto her now.' And Mrs Dunn arranged Fanny's legs, and got her needle ready.

'What are you doing!' Jane tried to stop her. She was attacking their Fanny. God knew what she'd done to her already.

'Get out of me way, you silly cat!' Mrs Dunn shouted at her. Jane drew back, and tried to rouse Fanny.

'Fanny. What's happening? What's happening?'

'Do what she says, pet. Please.' There were tears in Fanny's darkened eyes. 'Help her. For my sake.' And then she fell back, exhausted, onto the mattress. And Mrs Dunn began her work. Jane could not look. She began to cry as she held the wood in Fanny's mouth. Convulsive sobs shook her, and she fixed her eyes on Fanny's shocked face, feeling the pain with her, whenever the needle went wrong. And then Mrs Dunn spoke.

'I think it'll be all right now. You stay with her a while, pet.' Mrs Dunn made Jane drink some whisky, and Jane, cold and numb, felt a flush of fever surge through her.

'What did you do to her, Mrs Dunn?' she asked trembling.

'I got rid of a babby. Now mind. No tell-tale tits, if you please.'

'But why? Didn't she want Dandy O's babby?' she asked. 'They're getting married soon, you know.'

'They will, if you keep your mouth shut.'

And then Jane knew that Fanny had betrayed the promise.

CHAPTER SIX

When it was all over, Jane was sick. It was almost light as Fanny finally slept, relieved of her burden, and Mrs Dunn snored in the chair by the range. Wiping her mouth clean, Jane gathered the rug about her and crept from the house. The dim early light had an ethereal quality. Walking down Trajan Street, past her own, sleeping home, Jane felt as though there were feathers in the air. She felt giddy, what with lack of sleep, a sense of unreality, and the sudden emergence from the heavy atmosphere of Mrs Dunn's rooms. Her feet led her down the hill, towards the beach. Everything was marked by a strange clarity. The frost seemed to draw an extra line round everything. Jane didn't think about what had happened. She could not. It had happened and that was all there was to it. She had been made party to a murder. She stood still, looking out over the ocean. The lines of her face hardened, as the child was left behind and the woman emerged. What was done was done. She remembered Chandrika's words;

'. . . our errors once made, cannot be wiped out. They too are reflected back at us forever and ever.'

The night in Mrs Dunn's room would then return eternally to haunt her. A solitary tear slid down Jane's apparently impassive face. Would she never be free of it? Chandrika had not mentioned God's forgiveness. 'Forgive them, for they know not what they do'. She, Jane had not known. And yet, she had. The memory hung about her heart like a stone. She drew a deep breath, as though to make it lighter, and realised that she had been rubbing her arms with her hands, over and over again. Why? She shivered. She felt unclean. She ached to be free again, to have the filth washed from her. A cry escaped from her throat and found its way across the surface of the water, playing ducks and drakes on the waves, bouncing out to sea. In her agony of mind, she fancied that her father would hear her voice, hear her crying out against the weight that was pulling her down and down.

The *Daisy Queen* was, by this time, making for home. She had left Newfoundland on February 28th, 1873, and had soon been driven along in a thick snow squall from west by south. The squall passed, and the crew set the square topsail and topgallant, but during the following night, the wind began to rise again, shifting southerly, and they were compelled to heave to. The gale turned about again and again and the sea grew high and confused. Bob Ridley estimated their position as Lat 45 degrees two minutes and Long 46 degrees 53 minutes. They were making little progress. The ship was straining, and taking water. Day and night merged into one. Chandrika's eyes, blasted by rain, could not make out where sea stopped or sky began. His hands bled from holding the ropes in his wet hands. His bare feet braced against the sides of the ship were all that prevented him from being heaved overboard as the ship rolled and rolled again. Chaos and confusion was the world of the *Daisy Queen* and the men on board her. Again, she rolled, and down below, where Bob was overseeing the working of the pumps, it felt as though they were being dragged down and down, to the very bottom of the world.

Chandrika lay almost flat, as the boom swung. At the well of the wave, when it could go no further down, it paused, and he saw clearly, in the water, something red, the colour of blood. A shiver travelled up his spine, water gushed over him, and the red thing smeared him, till he cried out, with fear and agony, almost losing his footing, slipping, till his knees were against the sides of the ship. But the bloody thing was wrenched away, as the sea

90

spewed up the *Daisy Queen*, throwing her at the sky. And his flesh, exposed, was raw, burning hot. His head swam. He struggled to remain conscious, to keep his grip on the deck of the ship. All was confusion. All was red, bloody, in the churning sea of his mind. And the roar in his ears gave way to a long low wail, and he saw a lone girl standing on a distant shore. She seemed to be calling him. And then, she was in the water. She was part of the water. Her hands tore at him, as she struggled to be free from something unseen, something alive and dreadful that was attacking her. And then, over all, Chandrika heard the crack, as the main boom broke, close to the jaws, tearing the mainsail, and breaking in the top of the galley. Then Chandrika forced his flesh to raise itself, to work, to fight for the survival of each and every one of them.

Jane emerged from the sea, her naked flesh grey with cold, her lips pale. She dried herself on the rug, and shivering now, pulled on her clothes. Her breath was harsh, rasping. She had washed the blood from her. She felt clean again, and her heart was comforted. In the distance, a roll of thunder sounded over the hills. She looked up at the gathering darkness and a flash of lightning tore down from the sky, singeing the town. Tears sprang into her eyes. Shaking with more than cold, she crawled back to Trajan Street and curled up in bed beside her anxious brother.

Rain washed the narrow streets as Jane slept, and Robert watched over her. His face was dark. He saw the frailty of his sister, and he was afraid for her. His hand reached out and stroked her face. Her eyelids blinked, then opened, and she smiled up at him. Robert was there. He would look after her. He had promised. All was well with her world. As her eyes closed again, Robert looked up out of the window, and caught the faint colours of a rainbow, fading even as he looked at it, over the grey roof tops.

Jane grew thin as she watched her sister through the fever. Dandy O came to sit by her, once his mother had been assured it wasn't catching. Rumours of typhoid had been rife. But Mrs Dunn made Jane tell the world, that her sister had suffered poisoning, from some meat that had been kept too long in the cold store. The world was not convinced, but since it was Jane who told them, no-one in the town end cared to dispute the story.

'Jane.' Dandy O's eyes burned with tiredness from his watch. 'I do care about her, you know.'

'I know.'

There was a silence as Dandy O brooded further.

'Ma's all right really. Deep down, like. She'll change her tune once Fanny and me's wed.'

'I hope so, Dandy, lad. Or our Fan's in for a bad time.'

'She will. She will.' Dandy paused. He didn't like to ask, but felt he had to. 'She's not . . . , I mean, your Fanny, she's not been "up to" anything?'

'Like what?' Jane asked him, her clear eyes looking directly into his.

'No. Course not. How could she, in this sort of a state . . . ' His eyes misted with tears. 'If she gets well, we'll have the fanciest wedding Shields has ever seen, and such bonny bairns . . . ' Jane went cold at the mention of children. Should she tell him? Should she warn him that Fanny might have spoiled her chances of ever conceiving his child? What was the point of it? And, after all, hadn't Jane washed her hands of the whole business?

Schooldays grew brighter as the spring advanced and Fanny got steadily stronger. News had come at last, from the *Daisy Queen*. They had strayed off course as they crossed the Atlantic, and had finally been forced to make for the port of Corunna in northern Spain. There they waited, while repairs were put in hand before the final thrust home to the Tyne. Jane took her father's letter to school to show Miss Poulson, and she shared her relief with Ronnie Wilson, a lad who, though a good six inches shorter than her, had 'fallen in love' with her, when she'd recited 'The Rainbow' and whose eyes now followed her, spaniel-like, wherever she went.

Harriet May Lovely could not understand this infatuation of the despised Ronnie Wilson. For, despised he was. Ronnie was merely the son of a ballast worker. And shovelling ballast surely ranked even lower than foyboatman as a trade on the Tyne. Nevertheless, it was a thorn in her flesh to know that one

92

admirer had escaped her. The thought of it gnawed at her, while she pretended not to care at all. But Jane knew, and because of it, she encouraged little Ronnie in his worship of her. Not that she didn't like him. He was a 'canny' lad as they would say in Shields. And it was nice to be thought so much of by somebody. But the main attraction was that it rankled Jane's arch enemy, and she began to enjoy flaunting her superiority over her in that direction, at least.

Ronnie acted as a catalyst in the class. One friend attracted others, and Harriet began to feel her influence slowly ebb away. She viewed her 'Lovely' self in her mother's triple mirrors in their home over the shop in Fowler Street. And she knew she *was* indeed lovely. Her face reflected that loveliness back at her again and again. She stared into the green depths of her repeating image, and considered she had nothing to be jealous of Jane Ridley for. Her eyebrows arched, and her head tilted proudly as she acknowledged her own superiority.

And it was no good Ronnie trying to defend his loved one from the enemy's supercilious attacks. He was a bright lad, but honest, which was a drawback when fighting against someone as devious as Harriet May. So she continued to jibe at Jane. 'Plain Jane' she called her, and Jane, looking in her turn at her thin, pale face in the mirror, believed her.

'You're not plain! You're beautiful!' Ronnie told her. But, though Ronnie was a bright lad, Jane did not believe him. 'Especially when you smile,' he said. 'You get dimples and that.' But Jane hadn't smiled much lately. Perhaps that was why she had become plain, she thought. 'Go on! Smile,' he urged her. Then Jane burst out laughing, and the lad felt his heart would burst with the joy of it.

In time, the thin face began to fill out again, and the dimples returned along with her confidence. She was good at saying poetry in class. The headmaster had made her say 'The Daffodils' in front of the whole school, and what with Ronnie and Robert too sitting there amongst the rest, watching her, Jane had begun to feel she was 'somebody' herself. But most of the things they had to learn, being a Church of England school, were religious. Harriet held her own in these contests, never disgracing herself. And Jane had begun to wish, that after the long struggles between them, Harriet would once, just once, fall flat on her face and be humiliated as she herself had so often been humiliated by her enemy.

The twenty-third psalm had always meant a great deal to Jane and she had known it by heart for ages. So there was no need to learn it when Miss Poulson set it for their homework. Harriet May, brought up by her stepfather in the methodist faith, knew it also. And when her turn came to recite it, she began to speak so quickly, Miss Poulson had to stop her.

'You are not catching a train, child,' she told her drily. Perhaps this upset Harriet May. She was thrown, and stuttered a few times as the recitation continued. Jane felt her heart pound in her chest. Was this to be her moment? 'Thy rod and Thy staff they comfort me.' Harriet regained her poise and continued, 'Thou preparest a table before me in the presence of my anemones.'

Jane spluttered. Ronnie whooped. The rest of the class followed. Harriet May flushed, shaken by this display of mirth against her, looking from one child to the other, wondering what on earth she had said. Miss Poulson called for order. The loud laughter subsided, but giggles ran in currents underneath.

'Start that verse again, Harriet,' Miss Poulson commanded. ' "Thou preparest . . . " '

'Thou preparest a table for me in the presence of my anemones,' Harriet said again. Now there was no stopping the class. Harriet's perplexity turned to fury. Her eyes blazed at her enemy. They said 'Jane Ridley, am I going to get you!'

Chandrika lay sick in the hospital at Corunna as Bob Ridley set sail again for home. The Indian had a slight paralysis, from the sting, but was getting better daily. He had had a lucky escape from the 'man of war' and Bob, though reluctant to leave his friend, felt the urgent call of his family and a coming wedding. The excitement grew in the town end, and Mrs Tully forced herself to call in at Trajan Street to drink a dish of tea with them.

'I'm showing willing,' she announced, and her three chins wobbled into the kitchen, where she sat, suffering the indignity of the humble Ridley dwelling. 'Mind, I don't know how I'll hold me head up in church with the Purvises,' she said. 'They'll not come to the wedding!' But Fanny didn't care. She was sewing herself a wedding dress. It might be made of poplin, but it had flounces and flowers, and her mother's piece of lace on the front. Wedding fever gripped them all. Mrs Dunn went dewy eyed and romantic at the mention of it. Miss Poulson at school gave an old straw hat to be refurbished, saying wistfully as she parted with it, 'I don't suppose I'll be needing it again. Tell your sister she's a lucky lass.'

Robert mooned over his art teacher, and stopped her in corridors to ask about colleges and prospects, only half hearing what she had to say. Jane smiled a lot, and looked pretty again, and Josh . . . ? Josh kept disappearing.

The quayside had always been his favourite place. He had become skilled in the difficult art of sculling, where a single oar was placed at the stern of a coble, and was wiggled dexterously about, till the little boat turned, and made its way drunkenly across the river. He had been known to take on passengers, and take their money, when the foyboatman proper was in the pub, and passengers were waiting. And he had begun to amass savings, which he kept, alongside Robert's box, under the bed at Trajan Street.

One day, Robert caught him looking under the bed and suspected his brother of interfering with his own secret hoard of drawings. Furiously, without stopping to ask, Robert had hauled the lad out, and told him off, warning him against meddling with other people's property. Josh protested, and fought, punching his elder brother hard in the stomach, and running out. Fanny was courting with Dandy O in the kitchen, and the rumpus taking an edge off the pair's appetite for one another, she too grew angry and came into the bedroom. Robert sheepishly told her what had happened. She slapped him, and told him to go after his brother, to make sure the rascal came to no harm.

Turning to go into the kitchen, Fanny heard snoring, and knew that her lover had fallen asleep. She turned back then, wondering what Robert could be hiding under the bed, for him to get so angry. She smiled to herself. She would be able to tease him rotten. For it had to be something he was ashamed of. Pulling up her skirt, Fanny crawled under the bed, and her hands felt about in the dust. They touched something cold and hard, a tin. She grasped it, and pulled it out into the light. It rattled like a collecting box. The lid was tight, but, taking her skirt in her hand to grip the top, she wrenched it off, and out fell Josh's savings.

Fanny sat in the dust, staring at it for some time. She thought it must be Robert's money. She would tackle him about it later on. Meanwhile, she took it out into the kitchen, and hid it under the shelf in the cold store. She frowned. There was a lot of money in that tin. How had Robert come by it? Had he sold some of his drawings? Who would buy them? He had tried standing on the quay tempting passengers, but so far as she knew, he hadn't managed to sell one of them. Perhaps she'd misjudged his talents. Perhaps her father should think again about sending Robert to sea. After all, if there was money in this drawing business, it might be a good idea to encourage him. He liked drawing, if he could earn a living at it, then why not! For the moment, Fanny would keep the money out of Josh's grasping little hands, and tease Robert, by making him think he had lost it.

Later that night, when Fanny was asleep in his father's bed, and Jane and Robert breathed deeply beside him, Josh slid from under the rug, his feet touching the cold, stone floor, and felt for his tin under the bed. His heart stopped. It wasn't there. Resentment flared in him. They had stolen his money! His own family! They were nothing to him! He would teach them what for! In the silent darkness, Josh pulled on his clothes, tied the laces of his boots together, slung them round his neck, and crept out of the house. He heard the sea falling on the shore. It whispered to him and his heart flew to answer it. Without a backward glance he fled down to the quayside, to the coble landing. He waded into the water, pushing the boat before him, then jumped in, his boots clanking against the side. There was a mist on the river. It came in gusts. A tugboat could be heard chugging in the distance. Josh sculled expertly into the centre, and let the tide take him up to the low lights. The white tower loomed out of the darkness, and then was obliterated by the mist. The chugging was getting nearer. It seemed to come at him from all sides. Which way should he go? Best keep on his course. The tug would surely see him? The chugging became a roar, and the captain, feeling a slight bump, looked over the side, and saw a coble, split in two, drifting away from him. He had hit a foyboatman.

'Man overboard!' he called out. Immediately people appeared out of nowhere. The swirling mists threw their voices so that they seemed to haunt the tug, now here, now there. Torches flared.

'I've got him!' somebody yelled. And a hook was put out, catching up the boots, the child's boots.

'By God. It was but a bairn,' the captain said.

No trace of the owner of those boots could be found. The next day, they were traced to Saint Stephen's School, for they were charity boots doled out by the board of governors. And soon, Robert was identifying Josh's belongings, and wondering what on earth, how on earth he was going to tell his father.

As Bob Ridley on the *Daisy Queen* sailed up the coast towards the Tyne, it passed the *Man of the Sea* on the first leg of its journey to the Americas. Josh Ridley never crossed his father's path again.

Rattler's stomach ached as he climbed up the wet ropes onto the *Daisy Queen*. The sea heaved. He had reached the half-way mark, and he held on, without moving, while the ship rolled away from him, and he swung against its side. His palms gripped the rope, leaving the arthritic fingers sticking out useless. And then the ship rolled again, towards him, and he swung away again, the spray splattering up at him, and his right palm slipped. But it was the moment for climbing higher, and Rattler swung out his arm to heave himself upwards.

'Howway, man! You're like a bairn, enjoying itself on the park swings!' Bob, grinning, jeered down at his old mate, hanging on dangerously as the ship began to roll again.

'Hadaway back to Canada!' was Rattler's heartfelt response. Bob's answering laugh was lost on the wind. The little coble, wave-tossed at the stern, was a bonny sight to Bob Ridley, after all the months and months of travelling the oceans of the world. His eyes stung with tears at the sight of his home town, just over the bar. There'd been times when he'd thought he'd never see it again. By but it was a dog's life at sea. He'd had a bellyful and no mistake. When he'd left Chandrika at Corunna, he'd vowed that this was his last trip. He was getting on. He'd never get his master's ticket. Didn't want to. No, he'd leave that to the younger generation. His lad Robert, now, *he* was a bright lad. He'd go far if he'd get his head out of them artistic clouds of his and apply himself. *He'd* make captain all right. It'd be a proud day for Bob would that. He hoped he'd live to see it. That was all. And there'd be a better chance of that if he stuck to the coasters, touring round Britain with coal, and tallow, avoiding the deep water passages, that entailed long months, even years away from home. He'd made a fair packet this trip too, so he could afford to take a drop in wages for a bit. He sighed with satisfaction at the thought. He'd make the group of old tars, reminiscing on the Lawe top yet. See if he wouldn't!

Rattler swung out again. He was nearly at deck level, when a sudden change in the wind turned the ship about, and as it rolled, Rattler's body twisted and banged against the ship's side.

'Watch your hands!' Bob yelled. Just in time. Rattler let his body drop, so that his fingers missed being crushed against the metal edge of the deck.

'By God! That was a near thing!' Bob laughed at him. That was what it was all about, life at sea. It was all a near thing. Once committed to the waves, every second was lived on the very edge of life. It was what a seaman loved and hated. It was what dared him on again and again. But it was not for Bob. Not any more. He was finished. The sea was not going to tempt him again.

Bob helped Rattler scramble onto the deck, and took him along to the bridge, where the captain was waiting for him.

'By, my stomach's in a state.' Rattler threw some pills into his mouth and swallowed hard.

'*Yours* is!' Bob mocked him. 'I think our cook stole all the sheep's heads from the dogs in Mill Dam, before we set out! We lived on them for weeks!' There was no answer to that, and Rattler kept his silence till he was shaking hands with the captain.

'Think you can take her in in this?' The Captain indicated the weather outside.

'Aye well . . . ' Rattler surveyed the waves, and felt the wind

98

pounding, changing. He took a sidelong glance at Bob. He wanted to go in now. It was written all over his face. He was a sailor crying out for home, when all was said and done. But Rattler carried news that would wipe the smile from his face. His stomach turned at the thought. Why had he volunteered to do the dirty deed and tell him about Josh? He must be crackers! That was all there was to it! Still, no good putting off the evil hour. Best get it over with. 'It'll get worse before it gets better,' Rattler told the captain, who smiled, as though daring him.

'You're the pilot! On your own head be it!'

And so, Rattler put his hand to his stomach, belched loudly, and took the *Daisy Queen* in hand.

Dread and longing filled the Ridley children, as they prepared for their father's homecoming. The whole of the town end took on a share of their grief over the loss of Josh Ridley. Grief held the community of the quayside together. Grief and the sea. The two went hand in hand. Many a man gave up a day's earnings or more, to search up and down the river for the lad's body. But it wasn't to be found. Those boots sat on the kitchen hearth at Trajan Street and accused Fanny of her neglect.

'Eeh, I did me best, Mrs Tully!' she sobbed into the three chins down at Pilot Street.

'Aye well, lass,' Mrs Tully sighed, 'you'd need eyes in your backside to keep watch on them three. They're a packet of trouble!'

'I did me best, Mrs Tully. And I wasn't well, you know,' Fanny excused herself. Mrs Tully gulped down a tear.

'Aye well, pet,' she blurted out, 'I blame myself, like.' Fanny's head emerged from under the chins, and she looked at Dandy's mother in surprise.

'Why's that, Mrs Tully?'

'Why, pet, I should have been more help to you.' She could not bring herself to meet Fanny's eyes. 'I mean, you are going to marry my lad, aren't you?'

'I hope so.'

Mrs Tully nodded, and the chins trembled dangerously.

'Aye well. There you are then. Family's family, when all's said and done.' Resignation and vanquished pride softened Mrs

Tully's pink face into an amiable jelly. 'So, lass,' her voice broke as she spoke, 'what will be will be. You and me's got to live together, and the sooner we get on with it the better.'

'You mean, you don't mind me marrying Dandy O?'

'I never said that!' A sudden sharpness knocked any ideas of an easy passage from Fanny's head, but then the tone softened again. 'All I'm saying is, once you become a Tully, you'll be family, like it or not, and we'll be forced to pull together. And well, we might as well make a start now.' Fanny smiled her thanks, with admirable humility, and coming in from a long night on the river, Dandy was pulled up short by the sight of his mother and his intended, arms locked about one another in a firm embrace. He nearly swallowed his tonsils.

'Are you two wrestling, or cuddling?' he asked them, grinning broadly.

It was the silver lining to the cloud that hung about them all. And Mrs Tully was as good as her word. On the Sunday following, she'd had Fanny sitting next to her in the family pew, so that all could see how the tide flowed. And any ideas Eileen Purvis might have had about clan feeling overriding Dandy's promise to Fanny, were promptly dashed. It was a clear signal to the piloting fraternity. Dandy O was 'marrying out'. The Purvises pointedly turned their backs on the Tullys as Church ended, and a new feud had begun. But the Tullys stuck firm, and Jane and her brother were herded behind the safety of Mrs Tully's ample rear, where no-one could get at them. Holding her breath as they passed the Purvis clan standing by the church door, Jane sang under her breath;

Sticks and stones may break your bones . . .

Mrs Tully turned, glared at her, and hissed a 'shush'. Jane's hand reached out for her brother's, and, so protected, they passed the first hurdle of their journey up the social ladder.

To be accepted as 'family' by the pilots made a difference to the lives of Robert and Jane, more than either of them could have dreamt. News travelled fast. And, next day, at school, it was the talk of playground and teachers' room alike. More ballast had been added to Jane's store, and the ship of favour was weighted a little bit more in her direction. Only two people, in Jane's class, were less than pleased as the news spread. Harriet May Lovely had felt the swing away from her, and could do little to prevent it. The 'anemones' business still rankled with her, and 'getting even' remained a major objective in her life. She would have to bide her time. But 'get even', she would . . . one day. She watched Jane Ridley smiling down on her new admirers like Lady Muck, and her eyes narrowed. Harriet had seen another Ridley smile like that. Fanny, in her day, when she queened it over the town end. Harriet had seen it, and look what had happened to her! Yes, pride came before a fall. Let Jane Ridley grow prouder and prouder. It was all to the good. Because, when she fell, she would fall all the harder! So comforted, Harriet withdrew from the battle, to watch and wait.

Jane had expected a sharp assault from the 'Lovely' quarter, to put her in her place, and was surprised to be left so deliciously alone. But the other person who was less than pleased by the turn of events, was an even greater surprise to her . . . Ronnie Wilson. As Jane floated up the social scale, she floated like a dream from his grasp. Son of a ballast worker, his heart sank as he watched Jane, confidence growing, dimples burgeoning, become the object of another admirer, Jack Purvis himself. The news of his cousin Eileen's betrayal had burned a path of deep resentment through his family, sisters, cousins, aunts, uncles, and all. 'Don't even speak to her!' his mother had warned him, as he set out to the same school as 'That Fanny Ridley's sister'. As it happened, Jack had scarcely spoken a word to Jane in his life. But, suddenly, warned off her, he felt the beginnings of a tremor of interest, and Jane, sitting in front of him in class, felt his eyes on her. Someone was definitely sending shivers up her spine! She turned involuntarily to see who it was, and the first smile between the Ridley girl and the Purvis lad was exchanged. Ronnie, watching, felt his heart tighten in his chest and misery clouded his eyes. But, like Harriet May Lovely, he was helpless to do anything about it . . . yet.

So it was, that a tight little family group awaited Bob Ridley, as Rattler rowed him over to the coble landing. His face was grim, and dark. Looking fearfully at him, even Jane found him hard to approach, and they all stood like bottles of milk, as Bob got out of the boat and climbed up to them.

'It wasn't *my* fault!' said Mrs Tully at once.

'Sh, Ma!' Dandy nudged her, and the three chins were stilled.

'Oh, Da!' Jane suddenly flung herself at her father.

'What's this? Looking a bit peaky, aren't you, pet? Have you been ill?'

'She looked after me, when I had the fever,' Fanny told him. 'Never spared herself. She's been a good girl while you've been away, Da.' Bob looked at his eldest in surprise. This was a turn up for the books! The two girls had formed an alliance. They had obviously become firm friends. How was that? Bob sighed. Thinking hurt his brain. It was enough that they *had* become friends. Be thankful for small mercies, he thought.

'I suppose it's not worth another look on the river?' he asked Dandy O. Dandy shook his head, and the bereaved father sadly put his arm round his daughters for comfort.

'It'll cost you thirty pound.'

The voice came as if from nowhere. Mrs Tully stood aside to reveal the thin form of the foyboatman, whose coble had been stolen by Bob Ridley's son. For a second Bob couldn't work out what he was on about. And then the penny dropped.

'I'll see about it.'

'You'll do more than see about it! It's me livelihood. I've got a wife and bairns to support!'

'Aye, all right, Fred. Give's a chance, eh?' Reluctantly the foyboatman let the seaman pass, followed by his family, up the hill and on to his home in Trajan Street.

The boots sat by the hearth for a long time, and no-one liked to move them. Bob had said little about the business, since his return, and had fallen into a deep depression. Was it his fault that Josh had been taken from them? What could he have done to prevent it? He had to feed his family, and that meant going to sea, and leaving them to their own devices. The devil and the deep blue it was. If he'd stayed home to keep watch over them, they'd have starved. And now there was this business of the thirty pounds. It was a fair price for a coble, and the foyboatman had every right to ask for it. He counted through his savings, and knew, that if he paid the man outright, his family would have to go short. How could he do that? Rattler had offered him a loan, but he couldn't take him up on it. He, Bob Ridley, was responsible.

One day, after a long walk down the beach to Trow rocks and back, Bob came into the kitchen at Trajan Street, picked up Josh's little boots from the hearth, and threw them violently, one by one into the yard. His children stood, breathless, waiting. And then Bob Ridley broke down.

'It's my fault!' he shouted. 'My fault! I should keep better watch over you all!' The children were silent, waiting. 'I hardly knew Josh. My own kid! Hardly knew him! Josh!' he cried out, and the neighbours upstairs, listening, waited with the Ridley children, not daring to bang on the floor to silence him. A father's grief had need of its outlet. Then Bob left the house, and went down to 'The Globe' where beer and whisky drowned the memories of Ida and Josh, that nagged at him and pained him.

When he came back, in the early hours of the morning, Bob found his three children sitting silently by the dead hearth. The boots had been retrieved from the yard and hidden out of sight, with the rest of the Ridley secrets under Jane and Robert's bed. And as she put them there, Fanny remembered the tin of money, that she had hidden under the shelf in the cold store. Tortured by feelings of guilt over Josh, Fanny longed to make up for her shortcomings, to help her father, and her remaining brothers and sisters. It crossed her mind to wonder why it was Robert hadn't complained about the loss of his savings. Perhaps he thought Josh had made off with them? Yes, that must be it, she decided. It would be a pleasant surprise to him, when she told them all she had the tin in her own safe keeping.

'You should all be in bed,' Bob told his children gruffly as he slouched into a chair. Jane and Robert got up ready to obey, and Jane bent to kiss her father's cheek. He held onto her hand and looked into her face. 'Forgive me, lass,' he said. Jane was astonished.

'What for, Da?'

'It's not what I've done. It's what I've not done,' he answered, sobbing. 'I'm a rotten father.'

'No!' Robert and Jane crowded round him, determined to

comfort him. 'It's our fault. We never took enough notice of him!' And it was true. The whole family shared the guilt for Josh's disappearance.

'No. It's mine. It's as much my fault as if I'd killed my child with my own bare hands.'

This last stung Fanny. And a new sadness seemed to fall over Jane's face. But it went unnoticed by her father.

'Well,' Bob sighed, 'there's nothing for it. I've got to go to sea again.' Silence greeted this remark. 'How else can I pay for the coble, and still feed you all?'

'Dad . . . there might be a way . . . ' They all turned and stared at Fanny. Her face had brightened. 'Wait a minute.' Then she went to the scullery, and fetched the tin from the cold store. She grinned at Robert. 'I bet you thought you'd seen the last of this, eh?' Robert looked startled. He frowned and stared at the tin which Fanny was opening. She flung the contents onto the table and they glittered in the lamplight. Jane gasped.

'Where did you get that from, our Fanny?' Fanny laughed, and pointed at her brother.

'Ask him!' Robert stood very still, staring at the money on the table. 'You're a dark horse and no mistake, our Robert,' she teased him. 'I'd've thought you'd be proud to tell the world you'd sold some of your drawings!'

'Eh? What's that?' Bob was all confusion. Drink, if it hadn't cheered him, had fuddled his brain. He couldn't work out what was going on at all.

'Come on, Robert, admit it!' Fanny challenged him, smiling. 'See, Dad, there might be something in this artist business after all, eh?' Bob frowned. He felt a net was being drawn about him. Warily, he kept silent, listening and trying to take it all in. 'Go on, Robert. Say something!'

Robert couldn't think *what* to say. He looked at Jane, a puzzled expression in his eyes. She was smiling radiantly up at him, her face all admiration. Her brother, Robert, the artist had sold some drawings! He'd got money for them! In spite of himself, Robert began to feel proud as she looked at him like that. How could he disappoint her? Somehow, he couldn't bring himself to deny it was his.

'Where did you find it, Fanny?' he asked at last.

'Where do you think? Where you left it! Under your bed, you great nitwit!' Jane giggled, excited at the new turn of events.

'Well, Robert?' his father challenged him. 'You'd better tell us all about it, eh?'

Robert took a deep breath. In the lamplight they could not see the flush that crept over his face, and only Robert felt the heat that rose in his spine and sat on the back of his neck, as the idea came to him. The money had been Josh's. Of that there could be no doubt. That was why he had fought him, when Robert had tried to stop him searching under the bed. But Josh was gone. Dead. And even Fanny thought the money was Robert's. He looked at Jane again. Her face had begun to express doubt. Why did he hesitate? His father's face had a new respect in it. If he could convince him that he could earn money by his drawing, then perhaps Robert would be able to follow his calling as an artist, after all.

'Yes. The money's mine,' he said at last. Jane clapped her hands and whooped with joy. Encouraged, Robert went on. 'I did a few drawings of the passenger ships, like, and well, first I sold one to a captain, a Frenchman, who was retiring, and wanted a picture of his ship. And then I sold a couple to passengers as well, and . . . it went on from there, like . . . ' He finished a little lamely, but the rest of his family took his hesitation for modesty.

'Well!' Bob said proudly. 'I take me hat off to you! You're not such a wet nelly, after all!'

'He never *was* a wet nelly!' Jane objected vociferously.

'Miss Reid wants me to go to art college.' Robert took up his advantage quickly . . . too quickly.

'Art college!' his father sneered. 'Don't be so daft, man! Who'd pay for it!'

'He could go to classes though . . . in the evening, in Newcastle,' Fanny put in.

Both Robert and Jane stared at Fanny in surprise. Why was she taking Robert's side like this? Setting herself against her father, for Robert's sake? It was unlike her! 'Not ours to reason why', Robert thought, but 'cash in on the opportunity'. His father was counting the money.

'There's more than five pound here,' he said in awe.

'Aye,' Robert sounded as though he'd known all along. 'I tell you what, Da, you can keep it towards replacing the foyboatman's coble, if you like.' Touched by the magnanimity, Bob looked gratefully on his son.

'That's good of you, Robert. I take it kindly, lad. But it's hardly enough. I'll still need to go to sea.'

In bed, that night, while Fanny snored, relegated to her fold up couch in the front room, Robert's eyes glistened in the moonlight. Jane had curled herself up against him, cuddling him, holding on. He put his arm round her, and lay his cheek against her soft hair. Why had he done it? Why had he pretended? After all it hadn't got him anywhere. His father still hadn't agreed to his being an artist, had he? Shame gripped him. He would have to own up, go back on it. Tell them all tomorrow. Jane stirred in her sleep, and murmured. In the moonlight, Robert saw her smile, and he knew she was happy because of him. Her brother, the artist, had sold paintings, had made real money! The thread of her love and her dependence tied itself about him like a web. And he knew he could not disillusion her. The breeze from the open window rustled something in the room. It whispered, and he raised his head to see what it was. A ray of moonlight cast a shadow on the edge of the paper on the wall, and Robert knew it was the 'hephalant', Jane's 'hephalant', which he had drawn for her. He laid his head back against the pillow and a tear fell onto his sister's golden hair.

CHAPTER SEVEN

Josh Ridley set foot on the New World, and looked about him. He saw ships and more ships. He saw people pushing, shoving, making their way. He had made his own way over the Atlantic. For once discovered, he had worked his passage, and become popular with the passengers, to whom he told tales of the wild west, gleaned from the old tar on the Lawe Top. Every time he told them, his tales grew longer and more elaborate, and every time, his tip, at the end of it, grew bigger, Huh! His family could keep his savings! He had more now than they'd ever robbed from him. The only thing he really regretted leaving behind, were his boots! Yes! He'd show the lot of them! He, Josh Ridley would become a millionaire, then go back and lord it over the whole of Shields. See if he wouldn't! So, it was not as a beggar that Josh landed in New York. He had money in his pocket, and he had contacts. There was a man from the West Coast who wanted to take him on as an apprentice in his offices. He built railways. A woman asked him to be bell boy at her hotel in Chicago. A man who was something in chemicals in New York itself offered him a job, and there were others. He had a walletful of cards, and his head was high. But before Josh made his million, he had something else to do. He bought a railway ticket, and began his long, solitary journey out west.

★ ★ ★

Back home, there was still the coble to pay for. Dandy O had promised Fanny, theirs would be the 'fanciest wedding in Shields', and Bob Ridley had no intention of missing it, coble or no coble. He'd worked for Roper Bros. for years one way or another, and felt, therefore, that he might call on them to show him some consideration. His son, Robert, had insisted he take the five pounds savings he'd earned, and Bob could spare fifteen pounds from his own pocket. So it was for all of ten pound, that he went, cap in hand to the younger Mr Roper. At first, he was all for getting Bob back on a ship, but Bob explained about his daughter, and losing his youngest son, and the young man understood, Bob wanted money, but not work . . . not yet anyway.

'So it's a loan, you're after,' Mr Roper said with some relief, having tried for the best part of an hour to understand what the seaman wanted.

'Aye, that's about it, sir.' Bob almost stood to attention, in his embarrassment.

'Well, I'll have to ask my brothers, of course . . . '

'Oh, I realise that, sir.'

'But well . . . I don't see why they shouldn't agree to it. So long as you sign on, like for the next ship that's available.'

'Anything'll do me, sir. You know that.'

There was an awkward pause.

'Right well, Bob . . . I'll let you know, eh?' Finally, Bob took the hint, and went home.

A week later, a messenger came looking for him. He had to call in at the shipping office. Young Mr Roper beamed a welcome, and handed him the ten pounds.

'Just sign here, Bob,' Mr Roper told him. And Bob signed on for God knew what ship, that might come his way at his master's will.

But, at that moment, Bob wasn't bothered. He gave the money to the foyboatman, and felt a great weight off his mind. He would send to Corunna, inviting Chandrika to his daughter's wedding, and, turning his mind on the past, Bob put a smile on his face, buried all thoughts of his lost son and encouraged his family to do the same.

'We couldn't have a funeral,' he told them. 'But we *are* going to have a wedding. And what a wedding!' The Tullys were all agreement. Mrs Tully and Fanny put their heads together to sort out the catering.

'You know George Beattie's lass, don't you, Jane?' Mrs Tully asked her one day in the Pilot Street kitchen. Jane looked at her aghast.

'Why?' she managed to ask.

'Well, I just thought if we went to their shop, we might get a discount on the flowers and that, with you being a friend of the family as you might say.' It was all Jane could do not to burst out laughing.

'Stop pulling faces, our Jane!' Fanny yelled at her. 'You might ask them, eh?'

'I should think they'd put their prices *up* if *I* asked them!' she laughed.

'Well, I don't think we can manage everything without some help, Fanny,' Mrs Tully told her. 'Go along there. You can but ask.' So it was that Fanny, dragging Jane along with her, took the horse tram to Fowler Street, where they alighted outside Beattie's shop.

Beattie's Florists, Caterers and Nursery, stood in the centre of Victoria Terrace, at number 18. It was half-way up Fowler Street, at the bottom of the hill which led up to the salubrious delights of Westoe Village. Opposite the shop was the Queen's Hall with its big double doors, set between shops on either side, but leading up to an imposing building above, with its elegant, tall windows. As Fanny scurried forward towards the shop door, Jane hung back, gazing with awe up at the huge windows of the Queen's Hall.

'What are you doing, our Jane?' Fanny asked her. 'Catching flies?'

'Eeh!' Jane gasped. 'It's lovely! Really lovely!'

Fanny followed her eyeline over the road, to the huge dome in the roof and the curious turret at the side.

'They have dances and functions and that in there.'

'What's a function, our Fanny?'

'You know, dinners, and buffets and speeches and that sort of thing.'

'What's a buffet?'

'Shut up.'

109

'Do they wear posh dresses, and flowers in their hair?'

'The women do. I don't know about the men, like!' Fanny laughed wryly.

'Eeh, wouldn't it be nice if you could have your wedding tea in there, eh?'

'Aye! Wouldn't it.' Fanny, laughing at the very idea, put her hand on her sister's back and pushed her towards Beattie's.

Jane's feet dragged. Upstairs, a hand twitched at a net curtain and Jane felt the eyes of her enemy piercing through the folds of net. Jane was in her best frock, a blue serge, with a white pinny over it, and she had a blue ribbon, tied in her pale hair. But it was the boots that shamed her most. They, like Josh's before her, were charity boots, big and strong, black clodhoppers, tied up to the ankles with black laces. However she walked, Jane felt clumsy in them, and crossing the threshold into Beattie's shop, she tripped, deepening the embarrassed colour of her face.

'Our Jane!' Fanny hissed at her, as Adeline Beattie came forward to serve them.

'Can I help you, Madam,' she asked.

To hear their Fanny called 'Madam' was an experience in itself. Jane spluttered, and hid her giggles in her handkerchief.

'Stop showing us up!' Fanny hissed in her ear, and Jane bit back her laughter, so that her lips were pale, and clenched. 'Honestly! You look like you've got no teeth in your head now!' And Jane couldn't help herself, she burst out with a loud laugh, that rippled from the dark oak lined shop, up through the rafters into the house above. In her room, at the front of the house, Harriet May Lovely heard it, and frowned. In the parlour at the back, George Beattie was disturbed from his reading, and came to look down through the railings onto the shop floor below.

He saw a young woman in a hat and veil, perusing the catering catalogue with his wife. He hadn't heard Adeline laugh in ages, so it couldn't've been her. It must have been the woman in the hat. He watched and listened carefully. He had been reading poetry, when he had been disturbed by that laughter. Wordsworth was his favourite. 'Intimations of Immortality', was his study for the day and the appropriateness of the lines struck him.

110

Thou child of joy,
Shout round me, let me hear thy shouts . . .
The heavens laugh with you in your jubilee; . . .
I hear, I hear, with joy I hear!

'Have you anything cheaper?' the young woman asked timidly. George shook his head, disappointed. It could not have been her. 'Whither is fled the visionary gleam?' he thought. The laugh he'd heard had pierced through the gloom of the huge old house, like a shaft of light. It could not have been the woman asking for 'something cheaper'. *Her* voice already had overtones of 'the prison house' that closed upon the growing child. Disappointed, he was turning away, believing he had heard some passing stranger in the street, when something white moved against the dark corner where he kept his drawers of seeds.

Jane had soon grown bored, as Fanny and Mrs Beattie turned the pages of the catalogue. At first, they had seen pictures of cakes, so high, you could jump off the top of them! They were called tier cakes, Mrs Beattie explained. They had horseshoes and flowers and bells on them, and were meant for weddings. But they were expensive. A more modest centrepiece would be required for Fanny's wedding breakfast.

'I can see we'll end up with a bit of Dundee cake and marzipan if we're not careful,' Fanny had sighed, as Jane wandered off, her senses aroused by all the excitements of the shop.

The first thing she had noticed had been the smells. The dark sheen of the oak counters, storage shelves and little drawers, showed the care of polish, but the smell of lavender wax pervaded the whole atmosphere of the shop, penetrating through the heady perfumes of hot house lilies, and narcissi, like the base note of some perfume. For it was early spring, and the riot of yellow flowers burst like sunshine from the tubs in the shop window, reflecting again and again in the polished wood, lifting its gloom. On the counter, a small tub filled with multicoloured bunches of anemones, caught Jane's attention and made her smile.

'Thou preparest a table for me in the presence of mine anemones', she thought. Her spontaneous giggle distracted the two women, who glanced at her for a second, before turning yet another page. And Jane went to explore the little wooden drawers on the other side of the shop.

'Behold the child among his new born blisses,' George thought to himself. How had he not seen her? George smiled. She had had her back to him, and the dark blue had disappeared against the sombre wood. So that, when she had turned, her white pinny made it look as though she had appeared suddenly, by magic. Now you see her. Now you don't. Like a little fairy she was. The big man, with the formidable gait, and the frightening beard, had a sentimental streak. This fairy child, girl, half-way to womanhood, touched him deeply. She had something he had not. It was precious. It was fragile, and he wanted it. Watching her, as her eyes searched the gold lettering on the little drawers, his heart ached to touch her, to be near her, as though a little of the fairy gold dust would rub off on him.

Jane's head turned, startled, as the huge man bore down upon her from the stairs. Where had he sprung from?, she wondered. Then, looking up, she saw the little landing with the railing across it, and the glass door into the room beyond. Jane eyed the big stranger with distrust and fear. But his eyes creased and twinkled at her.

'Can I be of some assistance to you, Madam?' George asked her. Miracle of miracles, this man, this man who was none other than the mayor of the whole of Shields, had called *her*, Jane Ridley, 'Madam'!

'She's with me. Don't mind her!' Fanny's sharp voice startled George. He turned on her and scowled, and Fanny stepped back, visibly quailed.

'I'm sorry if I'm being a nuisance, sir,' Jane said breathlessly. 'I was only looking, like.'

'That's what they *all* say,' George laughed at her. And as her eyes strayed back again to the little drawers and the gold lettering, he let his hand touch the pale strands of hair, like threads of gold, that shone against the blue serge.

'Would you like to see what's inside them drawers?' George asked her gently. Jane nodded enthusiastically. He smiled and came closer to her, till his left arm was round her, and his right reached out to open the magic drawers. Adeline glanced nervously up from time to time, as she and Fanny got down to brass tacks, writing out an estimate for the breakfast. The first drawer said 'Thyme'. And when it opened, it turned out to be filled with little dried leaves.

'Smell them,' George said, taking a pinch between his fingers and holding it up to her nose as if it was snuff. Jane sniffed, coughed, because she had inhaled the dust of the herb, and she and George exchanged eyes, laughing. 'Not such a deep breath this time,' he advised her. So Jane tried again. It smelt sweet and savoury both at once. George opened another drawer, then another, then another. Herbs of all sorts, smoky, sweet, tangy, bitter, or heady like the smell of roses in the pot pourri, made her head swirl with sensation.

'Ooh!' she cried joyfully, 'this is a smashing shop!'

'Do you like it?' George beamed on her. She was a girl after his own heart. 'The glory and freshness of a dream.'

'It's like a dream!' she said, and her eyes were huge with wonder. He watched her twirl round and round in her ecstasy. She was like a cat in a bed of catnip, and the bundles of coloured raffia that hung with the dried flowers from the rafters, were like streamers, celebrating her newly awakened senses.

'Behave yourself, Jane!' Fanny brought her up short, but Adeline touched her arm and said gently,

'She's not doing any harm.'

'Give her some toffee, Adeline.'

'We've run out, George, I need to make some more.' And suddenly George's voice was harsh. She had spoiled his treat. The toffee was to have been the final touch to the scene with the girl.

'Have you not made it yet!' he shouted. 'Eeh, I don't know what you do with your time, I don't really!' Jane stared at him in surprise. He faltered, looked at her, then smiled again. 'Never mind, pet.' He looked over to the counter. 'Here, take these home for your tea.' He handed her two large brown eggs from a basket on the counter. 'Fresh laid this morning from me own hens,' he told her.

'But what about Doctor Mrs Fletcher?' his wife was aghast.

'Tell her they didn't lay today!' And with a final look at Jane, the proprietor of the shop marched back upstairs and through the glass door into the parlour.

'Ah,' he sighed soulfully, as he settled back into his chair, and considered how it was that a man such as himself, a man of vision, could be condemned to 'fade into the common light of day'. 'There has passed away a glory from the earth,' he intoned to the poker on the hearth, and got out his accounts books.

Jane held the eggs in her hands as though they were precious stones.

'Feel them, Fanny,' she said. 'They're still warm!' Fanny felt them and nodded.

'That proves they're new laid, pet. Fresh from the hen's backside,' she told her. 'And look, there's even a feather on that one.' Jane gazed with awe on the feather, and as a gust of wind blew it away into the sky, anguish at its loss mixed with the joy of seeing it fly free in the air.

Those eggs were treated 'like Royalty' as Fanny said at tea time.

'Well they *were* given me by a mayor!' Jane told her.

'Anyway, our Fan,' Robert retaliated, 'you're only jealous because he didn't give them to *you*!'

'I am not! And don't call me "Fan"!' Bob smiled. Things were getting back to normal at last after Josh's disappearance. Mrs Tully came round to inspect the famous eggs, before each member of the family took a spoon to them and ate them.

'By, you can tell they're fresh all right!' Mrs Tully nodded her head slowly as she savoured the yolk. 'Beautiful they are! What an honour for you, Jane, eh? Eeh! The mayor of Shields giving you some of his precious fresh eggs. It's something you'll remember to your dying day!' From that moment on, Mrs Tully would eye Jane Ridley with growing respect.

'Huh!' Fanny put in with some asperity. 'It's a pity he didn't honour us with a discount instead. We might have been able to afford some of his blooming flowers an' all then!' Trust Fanny to put a damper on things, her father thought. Still, it was a pity for the lass not to have some flowers to carry on her wedding day. A real shame.

That night, Jane lay wide awake while Robert breathed deeply beside her. The spring weather was changeable, and rain now spattered against the windows in Trajan Street. The sound lulled Jane's mind. She sighed deeply, and fancied that the air she

114

breathed bore the scent of flowers. Pictures of grand porticos, polished wood, mysterious drawers and fancy gold letters whirled across her imagination with silk dresses, and flowers and . . . anemones. The anemones grew legs, and arms. Their faces bore a resemblance to Harriet May. They pursued her up the stairs from the shop, onto the little balcony, through the glass doors, into the palace of Fowler Street. In her dreams it was gilded, and the many mirrors reflected a life of heady luxury and unimaginable ease and beauty.

As Jane gradually fell asleep, Adeline Beattie descended the cellar stairs, a candle in her hands, and suppressed a cry, as a rat scurried across the pool of light at her feet. Bracing herself, she set the candle down. The flowers glared at her out of the gloom. And the brass syringe by the bucket glistened. She picked it up, and filled it from the bucket of water, and then began to spray. As she sprayed, the perfume of the narcissi was released. Contained within the dank walls, it overwhelmed her. Her head reeled. There was that sick feeling in the pit of her stomach again. Her heart knocked hard and fast in her chest. George knew how long it took to spray the flowers. And he'd know, if she didn't do it, because they'd be wilted by the morning, and their prices would have to be dropped. So she kept on, filling the syringe again and again till the reek of flowers rose up into the kitchen above, and the parlour above that, and the bedrooms that towered on up the house, to where her husband lay in bed, waiting for her.

'It says here, it's a "mystical union",' said Robert, as he perused the wedding service in his school prayer book.

'You must have read it wrong then!' Fanny scorned his dreamy expression, and Mrs Tully laughed at him. But Jane put out her hand to touch his arm comfortingly, as she sat beside him at the kitchen table. Certainly, to her elder sister, and Dandy's Ma, marriage seemed a wholly practical business. It meant scrubbing floors, making curtains, sandwiches, hiring tea urns, counting pennies, above all, counting pennies.

'I think, pet,' Mrs Tully stated as she and Fanny sweated over the Beattie estimate, 'I think, that we'd be better off making our own sandwiches.' For a second, Fanny looked disappointed. 'And then,' her future Ma went on, 'we could maybe afford to get you a proper wedding cake, like.' Jane's eyes sparkled.

'You mean with all them tiers, and icing, and flowers and silver paper and that on!' she said excitedly.

'Well, I don't know about the tiers, but we could have the icing and that.' Mrs Tully's three chins were firm with determination. 'And you ought to have a new frock Jane, if you're going to be bridesmaid, like.'

Oh dream beyond compare! A new frock! One like Harriet May's, with a frilly petticoat showing from underneath, in white lawn, with a pink sash, and rosebuds on it. Oh yes, please! Jane thought. 'We'll go up on to the market and get some cloth to make her one,' Mrs Tully suggested. To Jane's surprise and relief, Fanny agreed.

Such extravagance had never been heard of in Trajan Street. But of course, now the Ridleys were consorting with the cream of river life, a piloting family. The bride and groom were to have a freshly decorated bedroom, all to themselves. The old curtains and nets found their way to Trajan Street, where the Ridleys would be able to make good use of them. After all, it could hardly be called charity when it was 'in the family'! Fanny spent much of her time at Pilot Street now, and Jane became her father's housekeeper. So, the putting up of new curtains fell to her. She washed the nets and the drapes in the yard, pleased with the magic of the carbolic, which rinsed the grime away, and left the lace soft and creamy in her hands. She watched it from the kitchen window, as it flirted in the breeze, on the communal line they shared with their neighbours. The lace grew visibly lighter, more giddy, more ecstatic, as it danced itself dryer and dryer. It filled Jane's head with visions. Weddings were lovely things. How she would like to be a bride, to wear lace and flowers, and for people to smile at her. 'Mystical Union', Robert had said it was. Fanny had laughed at the idea. And yet, it was mystical. Wasn't it a union of two souls? Wasn't the love they felt for one another that mysterious 'other' love, everyone was always on about? Jane sighed with longing. She was fourteen. Wasn't that old enough to be told about it? How much older did she have to be?

It had clouded over, and the rain had begun to spit down. Waking from her dream, Jane rushed out into the yard and

116

fetched in the nets and drapes from the line. She would have to bring down the pulley, and dry the things inside. She hauled at the rope, and the rack came down from the ceiling. Then she arranged the drapes and nets over it, before pulling the cord again and sending her washing up above her head to dry. Tying the cord by the mantelpiece, she caught sight of herself in her father's shaving mirror, the one with the crack. The net hung round her head. She would have to bring the pulley down again and rearrange it. But, she hesitated, staring at her reflection in the glass. She, Jane Ridley would one day be a bride, wear a lace veil, and look like this. The damp from the washing was drawn by the heat of the fire, and the glass began to mist. Jane pulled the cord, rearranged the washing and set it back in its place, high above the range.

The excitement of the banns came first. Fanny burned with fear as the Reverend asked if anyone knew of any just cause or impediment, and hoped to God Eileen Purvis wouldn't jump to her feet to object. But Eileen Purvis had stayed away, leaving the rest of her clan to fill the pew in Saint Stephen's. Jack Purvis sat at the centre of his family, across the aisle from the Tullys. He felt his mother and father stiffen on the seat beside him as Frances Ridley, spinster of this parish, had her name read out by the vicar. He suppressed a smile. Now the cat really was among the pigeons. He looked across at his classmate, Jane. She looked happy, oblivious of any bad feelings that might be flying about the rafters of the church. Her nose had a childlike quality about it, only partly formed, soft. And yet, she was growing into a woman. The pale hair wisped across her face. Her hand lifted to push it away from her eyes, and her head turned, to catch him looking at her. Jack nodded to her and smiled. His parents, curious to know who it was their son was greeting, gasped with horror, and stuck their elbows in his ribs. Jack jumped, and almost burst out laughing. And Jane turned her giggle into a sudden fit of coughing. It was all so silly really. As if what Eileen and Dandy O and Fanny got up to had anything to do with them! The moment was a bond between them, and when their eyes met in school, next day, Jane and Jack immediately smiled at one another.

117

Ronnie Wilson crept round the outskirts of Jane Ridley's life. It was as though an invisible barrier had grown round her, a barrier he could not cross. The other lads noticed him mooning about after her, and teased him for it. And he dreaded the day they might tease him in her presence. He wove dreams around her, and as he grew older, those dreams took on a more practical nature. He, like Jane, was fourteen. He would leave school at the end of the coming term, and be forced to take a job. Chances were he would end up shovelling ballast like his father. Piloting was closed to him, as a trade, because he was not of the pilot families. His father hadn't the money for a coble to be a foyboat-man, or a salmon fisherman. But he could maybe go to sea. He could rise from cabin boy to captain, if he wanted. He could read. He could study. And Ronnie Wilson sweated over his letters and his figures in his mother's kitchen, night in, night out, and all for love of Jane Ridley.

But Ronnie's spaniel eyes had become something of an irritation to Jane. When he looked at her, it was as if he was pressing her, demanding something of her. And it made her feel trapped. She didn't like it. And then, if she looked away, without smiling, he would be crestfallen, so that she would feel sorry, and then, making it up to him by being extra nice, he would turn on his spaniel eyed look again, and so the whole business started up all over again. It was an emotional merry go round, and it drove Jane mad.

Jack Purvis watched this little drama with some amusement, and Jane knew it. It was a blessed relief to her to share the burden with someone who saw it merely as a joke. And so a triangle was formed in the class at Saint Stephen's, and Jane was at the apex of it.

Miss Reid knew just how Jane felt. For she too was suffering from the spaniel eyes of an unrequited lover. Robert's passion grew by the day. In his teacher, Robert saw his dreams combined. She was the one who had taught him how to draw, and she was the one he dreamt of in bed at night. But Robert too had to face the end of his schooldays. Panic grew in him as they drew nearer, and nothing had been decided about his future.

'I can't teach you anything more,' Miss Reid smiled at him.

And Robert's mouth drooped with misery. 'In any case, I expect you'll be leaving us shortly.'

'I could maybe come to you for special tuition, in the evenings,' he suggested hopefully. Miss Reid shook her head and tried not to smile.

'Like I said, pet,' and the 'pet' was meant to put him in his place, 'there's nothing more I can teach you!'

No more Miss Reid, maybe no more drawing. His father would make him go to sea, and then he might never see Miss Reid again. What a future!

The day before the wedding, Robert and Jane took themselves off to Cleadon Hills, to gather the early spring flowers for their Fanny's bouquet. The foyboatman was glad to lend his new coble, bought him by the Ridleys, and Robert took the oars to guide them out of the river.

'I want to row as well!' Jane had insisted.

'Later on, you can. When we're over the bar.' Robert spoke with authority and Jane perched on the seat, gritted her teeth and waited till they were on the rocky sea, and she was allowed to hold an oar at last.

'We've got to get into a rhythm!' Robert admonished her, as her oar swung out too far and scudded across the surface of the water. 'Otherwise we'll just go round and round!'

'All right! Don't go on!' Jane said, wrestling with the oar, and before long, she had got the hang of it, and Robert had slowed his rhythm, making his stroke softer, so she could match it, and they got along fine. They steered well clear of Trow Rocks, where many ships had foundered, and soon were passing the Velvet Beds, and Marsden Rock was in sight. The gulls screeched overhead, a cacophony of sound that was fit to burst their ear drums. The rock stood separate from the main stretch of cliff, like an island. At high tide, the water flooded the caverns beneath it, and you could swim through them, and out the other side with no trouble at all. Only you had to watch the gulls! The cliff was white from them. Jane and Robert dragged the coble to the safety of the shore, and sat on the beach, to eat their lunch.

The river and the quayside seemed a million miles away. The sun shone, sparkling on the sea, and the ships were dark spots on its clear surface. The salt was everywhere. Jane tasted it on her fingers as she ate her bread and cheese. It was good. It was clean. She smelt it on her arms too, as the sun warmed them.

'You're catching the sun!' Robert warned her. 'Mind you don't get burnt!' But Jane didn't mind. She enjoyed the feel of the wind and the sun on her skin. Her hair floated lightly in the currents of air at the base of the cliff. Her muscles ached, and there were blisters on her hands. But it made no difference. She wouldn't swop her life for anyone else's! Not even Harriet May Lovely's! Laughing, she started to climb the cliff, teasing Robert, who was still finishing his lunch.

'Last one there's a cissy!' she called down to him. Hitching up her skirt, her bare feet found the ledges, and she climbed like a young deer up the face of the rock to stand at the top laughing at him.

'Come on, I'll give you a hand!' she called down, and her arm reached out to him to haul him up, but he spurned it, climbing to the top under his own steam.

Rock scabious and ladies' fingers abounded in the clefts of the rock. Buttercup and celandine grew along the cliff top, but deep in the woods of the hills, they found red campion, stitchwort, speedwell, and fern, and wrapping the posy in damp moss, to keep it fresh, they walked back through the fresh spring green of the woods towards the cliff top.

'I don't think I've ever felt so happy in all my life!' Jane's voice sang out her happiness. Robert laughed. She had indeed caught the sun and little freckles were appearing on her face. He liked them. They reminded him of the kid sister who was fast growing up, and disappearing. 'Aren't you happy, Robert?' Robert sighed, and Jane frowned, as she turned to look at him. 'Whatever's wrong?' There was a pause. They were standing on the cliff top, looking down on Marsden Rock and the gulls circling round it. The sea was blue green, and as the tide went out, it left little pools amongst the rocks, and swathes of seaweed along the shore, burnished red like autumn bracken.

'I'm "in love",' he said at last. Jane gasped, then laughed.

'I don't believe you!'

'I am, all the same.' Robert sounded hurt and Jane was immediately sorry.

'What's it like?'

Robert was pulled up short. That wasn't the question he had expected.

'Don't you want to know who with?'

'Yes. I suppose so . . . ' Jane answered reluctantly.

'Can't you guess?'

'No!' Robert thought her voice sharp, resentful and he wondered why. The wind ruffled the surface of the sea, and he shivered.

'Well, it's Miss Reid.'

'Miss Reid at Saint Stephen's!' Jane said in amazement. 'But she's old enough to be your mother!'

'She is not!'

'She is!' Jane knew she was making Robert unhappy, and she couldn't bear to do that. So she added, 'She's very pretty, mind.'

'She's beautiful,' Robert corrected her with feeling.

'If you say so!'

'I wish I could marry her.'

Jane fell silent. She shuffled her feet, longing to dash away, to escape back down the cliff to the beach. But she couldn't leave him like that. She loved him.

'If you did, you'd go away, like Fanny, and I'd not see you.'

'I'll have to go away soon anyway,' Robert said, 'Da wants me to go to sea.'

'You're spoiling the day.'

'I'm sorry.'

'What about your drawing and that?'

'There's not the money to go to college, so I'd have to go to night classes and get a day job.'

'Yes, but you could, couldn't you?'

'Doing what? It'd need to pay good money for the night class fees.' What could Robert do? There wasn't the money for a coble, and if he went to sea, he'd not be able to go to classes at all.

'Maybe our Fanny could get you taken on as a pilot's apprentice.'

'I doubt it. It gets passed on father to son, in the same family. You know that.'

'Yes, but you *are* family, or you will be tomorrow. And if our Fanny never had children . . . '

'Why shouldn't she?'

'Nothing.' Suddenly Jane clammed up. Robert looked at her, sighed, then stared out to sea again.

'I suppose I could always ask,' he said doubtfully.

'Anyway, why don't you just sell some of your pictures?' Jane asked him. Robert drew his breath in sharply.

'It took me ages to earn that five pounds,' he said. 'It wouldn't be enough to live on, let alone pay night classes!'

'All right. No need to snap. I only said.'

'What are you going to do when *you* leave school?' he asked her, to change the subject. Jane frowned. Shades of the sail-making sheds closed round her. Fanny had found a way out of that. She was marrying a pilot, and pilot's wives never worked!

'Ronnie Wilson wants to marry me,' she said without enthusiasm. Now it was Robert's turn to look startled.

'He's very nice of course. But . . . '

'You're not in love with him.'

'Maybe that's what it is.' She looked curiously at her brother. 'What's it like, being in love?' Robert flushed crimson.

'It's . . . horrible,' he said at last.

'In that case,' Jane said with some decision, 'I hope it never happens to me!'

'You'll have to get married one day.'

'Yes. I suppose so. I wish I was a man. And then *I* could go to sea, and see the world, and India and everything.' Regret filled the gap that time was making between them. Their heads turned to look at each other, and their hands reached out and touched. Robert grasped Jane's firmly. 'Would you marry *me* Robert, if we weren't brother and sister?' she asked him.

'Don't be daft!' He laughed at her; crestfallen, and even some-how humiliated, Jane's eyes dropped to the ground. 'I love you, Jane. I'll always look after you. But when you marry some-one . . . '

'Don't tell me!' she snapped, 'It's that "other kind of love", isn't it?' Robert nodded. 'I don't think I'll *ever* get married!' she declared. Robert smiled, as she raised her sister's wedding posy to her nose.

'I bet you will,' he told her, and raced her back down the cliff.

122

Their father was furious when he heard of the loan of the coble.

'The foyboatman didn't mind!' Robert said.

'No! I don't expect he did,' his father retorted, 'if you lost it, he'd only expect me to get him another'n!'

But there wasn't time for a 'proper' row. Fanny was having the jitters, about whether or not Dandy would turn up at the church, or Jane'd fall over her wedding dress, or the cake wouldn't come or God knows what catastrophe might strike. Horror on horrors, if Eileen Purvis was to turn up during the service and be a just cause or impediment! It took all three members of the family to calm her, and a slug of gin from Mrs Dunn to send her off to sleep.

The next day began cloudy. Fanny feared it might rain. But the seaweed in the yard was dry, and boded well. And sure enough, before long, the sun was out, and the sea breezes kicked the clouds away over the hills. Landing at Hull, Chandrika had made his way to the Tyne overland, and, while the clouds were still in the sky, he was walking down Mile End Road towards the quay. He had a wedding present under his arm, and he was looking forward to his reunion with his old friend and his family on their day of happiness.

Calling at Trajan Street, he found Jane lacing her sister into the unaccustomed stays.

'For God's sake pull harder,' Fanny yelled, and the men of the family took over, heaving and straining as Fanny's waist was strangled into the span of her father's hand. Chandrika was horrified.

'You'll damage yourself!' he told her.

'Don't be so old fashioned!' Fanny gasped, her face puce. Chandrika shook his head. The women of his own country would never do a thing like that. But he held his peace. When in Shields . . . he thought, and handed her his present.

'It's like Christmas!' Fanny said gleefully unwrapping it.

'I made it myself,' Chandrika explained, as a little set of elephants emerged, one by one, from the paper. Jane was thrilled, Fanny was surprised, Bob was touched, and Robert admired the carving.

123

'That's the father, the mother, and the smaller elephants are their offspring.' Chandrika showed them, setting them up on the table.

'And that's the baby elephant!' Jane smiled at him, remembering the story. 'Da, you haven't told us that story for ages!'

'Are you not too old for it, yet?' he asked her. Jane shook her head.

'You said, you're never too old for fairy stories,' she reminded him.

'So I did!' he laughed. But Chandrika was reaching into his pocket for something else. He pulled it out and handed it to Jane.

'This is for you,' he told her. It was a four-leafed clover. 'I found it on the road, coming here.' Jane took it in her hand and looked at it.

'I've often searched, but never found one. I'll press it in the big bible and keep it forever.' She smiled up at the Indian, but his eyes searched her, and she looked away. His face clouded. Something had happened. Something had changed in his absence.

'You're growing up,' he told her.

'Yes, aren't I!' she replied, pleased with herself.

Robert had gone ahead to the church with Chandrika, Rattler and George Tully, while Mrs Tully awaited anxiously the arrival of the cake. At last, Adeline Beattie herself turned up in a cab, bearing the precious cake, and a spray of roses.

'Eeh! I'm sorry it's late, but it's that girl! Honestly, she's useless. You can't depend on her, and Harriet wouldn't come. I don't know! You can't get decent help these days for love nor money!' So saying, Adeline bustled into the house, and set the cake at the centre of the Tully table.

'Well, mind,' Mrs Tully told her, 'I can't say it wasn't worth waiting for!'

'And I brought this for the bride,' Adeline sounded apologetic. 'I got the feeling she'd've liked one only I know they're expensive, so I made one up for her . . . don't tell me husband, mind!' The spray of roses lay elegantly against the lace of her blouse. Mrs Tully reached out and took it with tears in her eyes.

'Don't worry, pet,' she whispered in her ear, admitting her to

124

the familiarity of a family friend, 'I won't tell him.' Then she took the roses from her and ran round to Trajan Street, just in time to give them to Fanny. The posy of wild flowers was laid aside, Fanny took the hot house roses in her arms and allowed Jane to arrange the little veil on her bonnet over her face.

'You look really pretty, Fanny,' Jane told her truthfully. For it was Fanny who had the flowers on her dress, and the flounced petticoat, not Jane. Jane was simple in blue poplin, her hair held back by a matching ribbon. But Fanny was the bride. It was her day, and the whole family was bursting with pride for her. Bob held out his arm.

'Come on, lass,' he said and smiled. Then Fanny took his arm, like a real lady, and they walked together, Jane at their heels, up to the waiting church.

Mrs Dunn sat at the back, her hanky already wet with tears. Jane's face clouded as she passed her, and she shivered, as the vicar said,

'It was ordained for the procreation of children, to be brought up in the fear and nurture of the Lord.' Should Jane have said anything to Dandy O? She looked at him, standing there, pale, with a brave expression on his face. Was that night at Mrs Dunn's a just cause or impediment? The weight of her knowledge hung round Jane's neck like a stone. And when they said the Lord's prayer, Jane really thought through the words for the first time. 'Forgive us our trespasses as we forgive them'. She would have to forgive Harriet May Lovely then! Oh horror! She must if she hoped to be forgiven herself! Jane struggled within, as Fanny promised to be true to Dandy and Dandy promised to be true to her. And Jane forgave her enemy as the sun cast a ray through the stained glass, and an arc of colour fell onto the altar of the church. 'Harriet May, I forgive you!' The words echoed round and round Jane's mind. The bride and groom knelt for the blessing, the register was signed, and, at last, it was all over. Smiling broadly, they passed the empty pews of the Purvises and walked out into the sunlight of the spring morning.

Mrs Dunn's dog, Gormless, had followed her up to the church, and was now running wild round the graveyard. Ronnie Wilson, who had been waiting for a view of his beloved at the gate, tried to chase it off. But as the wedding procession emerged from the dark portal of the church, Gormless escaped him, and rushed straight towards the vicar, getting caught up in his skirt. Mrs Dunn screeched at the animal; 'Come here you gormless bleeder!' The vicar's mouth hung open in shock, Dandy O burst out laughing, and Fanny, suddenly charged by the animal from behind, tottered, and as her bridal bouquet flew out of her hand, she shouted out, 'Catch, somebody!'

Jane Ridley caught it in her surprised hands. She bent to smell Adeline Beattie's bridal spray, and found that it had no perfume.

CHAPTER EIGHT

Fanny had been really nice for ages. Too nice! They might have known. Once the wedding was over, she reverted to her old self. The first sign of it was when she started kicking up about the elephants. Mrs Tully had thoughtfully put them on the washstand in the 'bridal chamber', but Fanny would have none of it. She was all for chucking them in the bin.

Her 'Ma', as she'd been told to call Mrs Tully, was astonished.

'Eeh!' she said, 'I *am* surprised! I thought they were rather nice!'

'You have them then!' Fanny almost chucked them at her.

'I wouldn't say no, pet,' and so they found a place in the Tully parlour, on the mantelshelf. Better there than in her own room, Fanny thought. That drawing had been bad enough! An outlandish creature that trumpeted, if you please! It gave her nightmares! She was glad to be shot of it. And she certainly was not going to have a whole herd of the things in her bedroom! Out of sight, out of mind, and the Tullys hardly ever used their parlour, so Fanny could indeed put the ugly things that haunted her dreams, 'out of her mind'.

The second sign of the 'change' came when Bob Ridley, wedding over, finally turned his mind to his son. Robert was fifteen next month. He'd stayed on at school longer than most. He was a bright boy, and Bob was ambitious for him, wanting him to get all the learning he could. But the time had come to consider the lad's future in practical terms.

'Ropers are a good firm,' Bob told him gently. 'They look after you. You could do worse than sign up with them.'

'What as?'

'Well, you couldn't expect too much to start with. I mean, you'd be cook and general dogsbody for a year or so, and then, if you did well, you'd likely go up a peg for the next trip.'

'I hate the sea!' The note of bitterness in Robert's voice, surprised his father. He frowned, puzzled.

'You're just saying that! It's all this arty crafty stuff that teacher of yours has been drumming into your head, isn't it, eh? I've a good mind to go up to that school of yours and tell her what for!' Robert stood abruptly, thrusting back his chair with his legs.

'Don't you dare go near her!' he shouted angrily, eyes blazing. Bob's jaw dropped open. Then his eyes twinkled and his mouth curled into a smile.

'Oh!' he said, knowingly, 'so that's the lie of the land, is it?' Robert said nothing. He had given himself away. He would clam up now, and let his father think what he liked. Bob looked at Jane, who was mending by the fire. She felt his eyes on her, but worked on, refusing to look up, even for a second. So, Bob let the matter rest. He would let the lad think about it, and meanwhile he himself would go along to the shipping office and see what the prospects were.

When their father went down to 'The Globe', and Jane and her brother were left alone in the kitchen, Jane put down her mending, and looked at Robert.

'Cissy Tinmouth saw her down The Bents with an Arab,' she stated. Robert ignored the remark for as long as he could, and then raised his pale face to ask belligerently,

'Who's "her"?'

'You know!'

'No, I don't!'

'Your Miss Reid.'

'She's *not* my Miss Reid.'

'She's not now. She's the Arab's!'

'Shut your mouth!' Robert yelled at her. Jane blanched. Robert had never shouted at her before. She hated him like this, all clenched up and upset.

'I told you before, Robert, she's old enough to be your . . .'

'And I told you to shut up!' he repeated. Jane had the feeling that if she continued in the same vein, she would feel his fist on her face. So, she contented herself with saying,

'Don't say I didn't warn you,' and got back to her mending. Robert sat silently, on the edge of his father's bed, for a while, brooding. The Bents was a huge piece of waste land, south of the Marine Park. There were races, and galas with tents and marquees there sometimes, in the summer. It was wide open, and, he considered, not the place for 'canoodling'. He coughed and asked, nervously, 'What did Cissy say they were . . . er . . . doing?' Jane looked up in faked surprise.

'Walking a dog. Why?' and then she smiled, teasing, as she saw the relief on her brother's face, 'what did you *think* they were doing?' Robert scowled and went out for a look at the sea.

Solitary walks were becoming something of a habit with Robert. He always took his sketching pad with him, but rarely brought back anything worth looking at. Some hastily sketched lines, perhaps, of a seascape or a landscape which could have been anywhere. For Robert had discovered where Miss Reid lived, and more often than not, he ended up somewhere near her house where he hoped he might bump into her. One day, against her better judgement, she had let him carry some things home for her, and she'd given him some tea for his trouble, making it herself in her little kitchen. Miss Reid lived alone, in two rooms above a shop in Saint Aidan's Road. Her rooms were sparse but decent, and they were filled with old books. Robert borrowed one and took it home with him, and when he'd finished it, he asked for another, hoping she'd invite him back to her rooms again. But she didn't. Wise to him, Miss Reid brought two or three books into school for him to choose from. He was humiliated. He knew she didn't want him. She considered him just 'a bit lad'. But Robert had the feelings of a man, and his pride was deeply hurt by her rejection. Still, he could bear it, just

129

so long as there was no-one else. And then, the rumours had started. He had refused to listen at first, but when his own sister reported that his loved one had been seen with another man, Robert could ignore it no longer.

Without a word, Robert got up and walked out of the house. Jane heard the front door bang behind him. She was alone. Anger rose in her. Robert was stupid! She'd thought more of him than to go mooning about like their Fanny! She was disappointed in him! She darned on, and the needle dug deep behind her nail, and she cried out in pain as the blood flowed. She hated Robert; hated him! He was as stupid as the rest of them, stupid as Ronnie Wilson. Hah! Let him get on with it. She was better off on her own! A tear dribbled down her cheek and fell onto her hand. She wiped it away with some irritation, and got on with the darning.

Robert had never known such pain. When he had told Jane that 'being in love' was horrible, he had meant every word of it. The tramping of his feet on the pavement helped numb his feelings, stop his reeling, tortured mind. Pictures of her, lovely and smiling, kept floating to the surface of his consciousness, to be ousted by pictures of the courting couples he'd seen hiding in the bushes of the park. Sordid ugliness on the one hand; pure, unadulterated beauty on the other. He could not believe that she would do anything like that. He shivered as he thought of those couples in the bushes. He could not put her face to the woman, writhing under the man in the undergrowth. She wasn't like that!

He had passed the Lawe Top, and started the climb down the hill. On his right, Robert saw Saint Aidan's Church. He turned the corner, and walked more slowly down the road towards Miss Reid's house. He stopped at the door. Dare he knock? A woman shoved her head out of next door's window.

'Who'd you want?'

'Nobody,' he answered, flustered.

'Silly bugger,' she muttered, and withdrew her head into the house. Taking his courage in his hands, he hammered on the door. And now his heart was like a tight fist in his chest. Why had he done it? Should he run? No, he wasn't a child, playing games, was he? He waited, terrified that the Arab would come to the door, half dressed, having left her behind him in the bed.

There was no answer. Half relieved, half disappointed, his breath came easier, and he began to walk away from the house. What had possessed him? Madness? He would walk down along the beach, recover his senses, and go home to Jane. But as he turned again into Lawe Road, Miss Reid and the Arab walked out of the park together, hand in hand. Robert's heart stopped. They were chatting, lightly, happily, their faces bright. They were obviously so easy and so pleased with each other. They stopped, and she presented her cheek to be kissed. He teased her, then kissed her gently, first on the cheek, then on the lips, and she dropped her head, a smile playing about her mouth, unaware of Robert, up by the church.

Tears stung his eyes. To see her like this, so sweet, so loving, so happy, it drove him into agonies of despair. He turned his back, and ran, ran down the hill to the beach, where he threw stone after stone into the devouring sea.

He would not speak to Jane when he got back in. Their father was asleep, half drunk in the kitchen. She made room for him in the big bed, and he crawled in, cold and numb with grief. Slowly, she put her arms round him, and the warmth comforted him, thawing the pent up emotions, till he was able to cry himself quietly to sleep. The next morning, Robert burned his drawings. There were no more secrets under the big bed in Trajan Street.

Jane dreaded the idea of Robert going to sea. What would she do? He might be drowned or anything! Worse still, he might forget her. She went to their Fanny and Dandy O, hoping to enlist their support.

'You said he could go to night classes in Newcastle, Fan,' Jane reminded her sister.

'Did I?' Fanny said with some surprise. 'I don't remember that!'

'Night classes!' Mrs Tully was astonished, 'what in?'

'Art. Drawing and painting and that.'

'Good God!'

131

'The trouble is,' Jane went on, 'he'd have to pay for them, and he'd need a job, like.'

'He's going to need a job anyway,' Dandy said.

'Bob's got great hopes for him. I know that. Thinks he'll get his master's ticket one of these fine days.' Rattler had a lot of time for Robert, and respected the lad's intelligence. 'And I wouldn't be surprised if he was right,' he added.

'I thought you might take him on as an apprentice, Dandy,' Jane blurted out. There was a sudden silence, broken by Fanny.

'Don't be so daft, our Jane! He's not family!'

Jane looked at her in amazement. 'Yes he is!'

'He's not a Tully! We can't allow just anybody in you know.'

'Ma' put her oar in next. 'I quite agree, pet. We've already flown in the face of tradition with this wedding. Enough's enough. Piloting has to be handed on, father to son.'

'But supposing you don't have any children, Fan!' It was Jane's last weapon. She hadn't wanted to use it. It was like blackmail. But Fanny smiled a slow, smug smile.

'Why, didn't you know, pet?' she said softly, 'I'm pregnant.'

So that was it. Jane walked sadly back to Trajan Street. Fanny had been nice when it suited her, when she feared she might still lose Dandy O. But now she had him! And now, now she was carrying his child, she had no need to be nice. 'Not family' she had said. Her own brother! Fanny had become more of a Tully than the Tullys themselves. And more of a snob too. She wasn't her sister any more.

When Bob broached the subject of Roper Brothers again, he expected a difficult passage. But his son remained silent, for a long time, mulling over the offer of a job on one of the firm's brigs in the autumn. Then, finally, he sighed,

'I've gone off drawing anyway.'

Jane looked up sharply. 'Why?'

'Well . . . you grow out of it, I suppose.' And so the business was settled. In the doldrums of unrequited love, Robert Ridley had dedicated himself to a life at sea.

Bob was thrilled. He took his son down to 'The Globe' and bought him his first whisky.

'That'll make a man of you!' he said, as the lad half-choked on his first mouthful.

'Don't worry, lad,' Rattler reassured him, 'you'll get used to it, in time!' The locals roared with laughter, and the foreign sailors smiled, pretending to understand the joke.

In her heart, Jane knew that Miss Reid was at the bottom of it. If looks could kill, Jane's would have murdered the teacher. Ronnie Wilson had just failed to get taken on by the same company, and sent waves of depression through his spaniel eyes at her. But at least Harriet and Jane seemed to have come to some sort of uneasy truce. After all, Jane had forgiven her! But Harriet was going to be sent to 'Newcarstle', as she called the big city in her posh tones, to be 'finished'! The news of this impending event was crowed over in class, again and again.

'I'll finish her for you, if you like!' Jack Purvis whispered in Jane's ear, and she giggled, then stopped herself with some regret.

In fact, Jane Ridley had far too much on her mind to be bothering herself about Harriet and her boasting. There was her own future to think of. What was *she* going to do? The sailmaking sheds loomed ever nearer, and her heart sank at the prospect. And then, her father had put to sea again. He was only going to Amsterdam and then on to Rouen and Newhaven, local trips, but the house was lonely without him. And Robert had become very moody of late. You'd have thought he'd have tried to make the best of their last times together, but no. The house at Trajan Street had a gloom on it, like a dark cloud that settled round a hilltop and refused to budge.

That night, in bed, while Robert slept, Jane felt a sudden sense of loss. A strange grief had come over her, as though something she had valued very much had suddenly been taken away from her. Her heart ached with a longing for she knew not what. Easing herself away from Robert, she got out of bed and lit the candle. The comforting glow lit up the dark corners of the little room and made a circle of brightness round the drawing on the wall. Shivering suddenly, Jane crept quietly under the blanket and, leaning back against her pillow, she looked at Robert's drawing.

It was funny really. She hadn't looked at it for ages. Yet she loved it. She wondered if elephants were like that, after all. If Chandrika hadn't made off so suddenly after Fanny's wedding, she could, perhaps, have asked him all about it. Suddenly she longed to see the Indian man. Her yearning stretched out to the continent of her imaginings. The Himalayas, so high Gods lived on them, the heat, the snow, the deserts, the elephants . . . above all the real live elephants. She wanted to see them so much, she thought her heart would burst. Such a sense of loss beset her. Why was it? What had she lost? Her whole life was before her! A pain, deep in her belly, distracted her. Her back ached. She wasn't well. That was the trouble. Feeling dry, she got out of bed again to fetch some water from the jug on the washstand. Sipping the cold liquid, her feet on the cold floor, she went back to the bed. She pulled back the blanket to climb in and saw a dark red stain on the sheet.

The shock made her very quiet the next day. Robert had seen the stain when he woke and could not look at her at first. She longed for him to hold her in his arms, to comfort her. But she soon saw that he couldn't. The red stain in the bed had come between them, like the sword a knight placed between himself and his lady in the old stories. Neither brother nor sister spoke of it, and Jane felt more alone than ever. She went, finally, to Mrs Dunn for advice.

'Gin's the best cure for the pain,' she told her. 'Ask your Fanny.' But it was the pain in her heart that Jane couldn't bear. Everything had changed. Robert curled up away from her when she lay beside him, as though afraid her touch would contaminate him.

'Am I dirty now?' she asked the neighbour, feeling vaguely guilty, as she had done when their Fanny had been in trouble. Mrs Dunn shook her head and smiled. She was remembering her first time. She sighed, a tear in her eyes, and looked at the young girl sitting in her kitchen.

'I never knew you were still sharing a bed, mind. Time you had one to yourself, pet. Better start using Fanny's old fold-up, eh?'

That night, when Robert came in from 'The Globe' he was surprised to find Jane already tucked up in the little bed, her eyes shut tight. He knew she wasn't asleep. He looked at her for a

134

minute, then undressed and got into the old bed. Lying still, Jane heard him climb in. She waited. He hadn't yet settled, nor put out the candle. Finally he spoke. 'I know you're awake.'

Jane opened her eyes and looked at him.

'You can have this bed, you know.'

'No. I'm all right here.'

But he insisted. Treating her as though she were made of glass, he helped her into the double bed, and blowing out the candle, he got into Fanny's old fold-up himself. In the darkness, Jane sobbed.

'When will you go to sea?'

'September.'

'What'll become of *me*?' There was no answer.

The brig was rotten through and through. It leaked like a sieve, all the way over to Amsterdam. There was no rest for them. She was heavily laden with a cargo of coal, and drawing more than twelve feet astern. The galley was located in the forecastle, and the only light was from some melted-down fat and cotton, set up in a bully tin. Black soot got everywhere, and stuck fast to the skin with oil. There was no separate room for the mate, and Bob swung uneasily in his hammock, listening to the creaking timber, wondering how much water she'd made while he dozed. Before turning in, he would heat a poker in the stove, and run it over the joints in the timber, so that the pitch would seal it and keep the water out. When at last they reached Amsterdam, Bob refused to go on with her. Slinging his bag over his shoulder, he turned his back on the leaky vessel, and made his rounds of the port, looking for a ship that would take him home. It was a dog's life and that was all there was to say about it. Still, while in Amsterdam, he might as well enjoy himself!

Hitching a lift on a ketch bound for Aberdeen, Bob arrived home unexpectedly. Trajan Street was empty, so he went across to Pilot Street, where his married daughter and her 'Ma' ruled the kitchen together. They sat him down, and fetched him his tea, making a proper fuss of him. Bob enjoyed every minute, and was glad to see the two women getting on so well. He smiled to himself. It wasn't five minutes since they were at each other's throats, and now, well, if they weren't careful, they'd end up

135

looking like each other! Fanny had grown plump with her pregnancy and Bob was glad to see it. His tea set before him, Bob was surprised to find the two women settling, one at each side of him, at the table. He looked from one to the other.

'We thought you ought to know . . . ' Fanny began.

'It's our Jane . . . ' Bob's heart sank. What now, he thought.

'She's grown up.'

'She's a woman.'

Mrs Tully's three chins trembled with deeper meaning. Facts were facts, they said, and that was that.

'Oh aye,' he said at last.

'Men!' they chorused, and Bob Ridley burst out laughing. By, but they were a double act and no mistake.

All the same, when he'd finally got their drift, it made him think. His Jane grown up? A woman? He sighed at the thought. He'd lost his youngest lad, and it was more by good luck than good management that their Fanny hadn't come to grief. That leaky brig'd done him a good turn. He was home again, the women of Amsterdam fresh and green in his memory. He'd better make sure of his other daughter. He'd put Jane on a tight rein. For she needed keeping in order. Or like Gormless at the wedding, Bob had a feeling she'd run riot through her life.

So, Bob Ridley was present for the prizegiving at Saint Stephen's, towards the end of term. It was a big occasion. The school hall was packed. On a dais, at the front, sat the headmaster, the staff, and the dignitaries. George Beattie, with his mayoral chain around his neck, presided as guest of honour, with his wife at his side. In the body of the hall, parents and well-wishers sat on chairs, while the children, boots polished, pinnies starched, and hair combed, sat cross legged on the floor. After all the hymns, and the headmaster's long speech, the younger children began to get restive, and with them, Bob and Fanny, who, proudly displaying her condition, sat next to her father, as the mayor stood for his turn.

'At the end of another year - ' his voice sounded as though he had dug the speech out of mothballs - 'we all look back and take stock of what has been.' He paused for effect. 'Something will have been lost, and something will have been gained.' Another pause. It was most impressive. 'Some of you . . . ' he looked down at the children at his feet, his eye searching them out, 'some of you are leaving this year, and you will not only be leaving your school behind you, when you go, you will be leaving your childhood. You will have become men and women . . . '

'Doesn't he go on,' Fanny whispered to her father.

'He's the mayor. He's entitled.'

'He sounds like he's in the blooming pulpit!'

'Sh,' the woman in the big hat behind them hissed furiously, and father and daughter fell silent.

Everyone had expected Harriet May to get a prize. After all, the mayor was her Dad, wasn't he? She looked smug enough anyway! Jack Purvis got one, for mathematics. Robert got one for his drawing, and the Ridley family clapped their hands sore for him! Ronnie Wilson didn't get a prize, neither did Jane, nor Harriet. She pretended not to notice the delight of her classmates, the digs and nudges and whispers. She pretended not to care. And she didn't care, not much, not so long as Jane didn't get one either. And at least she was spared that. She too had been passed over. But then came the 'turns'. Cissy Tinmouth played a tune on her recorder. The choir sang a song they'd found in 'Christian Endeavour', and Jane Ridley got up to recite a poem.

By this time, the audience was shuffling, coughing, and worrying about whether they'd get home for their teas before Christmas. George Beattie had a glazed expression on his face, and the headmaster had that pained, patient look he put on when he was about to cane you. It said, 'This hurts me more than it hurts you'. Jane, hair brushed till it shone, made her way with difficulty through the hall, and climbed up onto the dais.

'Intimations of Immortality,' she announced, 'by William Wordsworth.' George sat bolt upright. He couldn't believe his ears. His chain rattled with his agitation, as he stared intensely at the bright, shining girl on the dais beside him. Then Jane took a deep breath, paused, and looked around her. Her audience settled, and she began to read the poem.

There was a time, when meadow, grove and stream,
    The earth, and every common sight,

137

To me did seem,
Apparelled in celestial light,
The glory and the freshness of a dream.
It is not now as it hath been of yore; -
Turn whereso'er I may,
By night or day,
The things which I have seen, I now can see no more.

The rainbow comes and goes,
And lovely is the Rose,
The Moon doth with delight
Look round her when the heavens are bare,
Waters on a starry night
Are beautiful and fair;
The sunshine is a glorious birth;
But yet, I know, where'er I go,
That there hath past away a glory from the earth.

The hall was still. After all the long speeches, the impressive words, empty sentiments, Jane's voice rang with truth. It was strong, and clear as the water swirling through the clefts of Marsden Rock. As she went on, and the audience listened, her confidence grew, and Jane lost the slight nervousness of her beginning, forgot about the clodhoppers on her feet, forgot everything, in fact, but what she was saying.

Our birth is but a sleep and a forgetting:
The soul that rises with us, our life's Star
Hath elsewhere its setting,
And cometh from afar:
Not in entire forgetfulness,
And not in utter nakedness,
But trailing clouds of glory do we come
From God who is our home:
Heaven lies about us in our infancy!
Shades of the prison house begin to close
Upon the growing boy . . .

Jack Purvis barely heard the words. He saw how Jane blossomed in the limelight, and recast her in a role of his own creating, costuming her in red dresses, black stockings, and feather boas. George heard the words, and conjured round the girl on the dais a different vision of his own. Ronnie was held captive by the voice. Fanny yawned, and Bob wondered, not for the first time, where on earth this daughter of his had sprung from.

> . . . nothing can bring back the hour
> Of splendour in the grass, of glory in the flower;

Adeline Beattie wiped a tear away with the corner of her handkerchief. The sick feeling in the pit of her stomach troubled her. But she must pretend to be all right; so she sat up straight and struggled to concentrate on the final stanza.

> . . . the meanest flower that blows can give
> Thoughts that do often lie too deep for tears.

There was a long silence. Jane's confidence wavered, but then it began; the clapping, clapping, loud, and joyful, and it was all for her! Her cheeks flushed with the heady pleasure of success, and her admiring school made way for her, as she walked, trembling, back to her seat. And still they clapped. It was as though it would never end. An eternity of applause. She, Jane Ridley, *was* somebody, after all!

CHAPTER NINE

Harriet May Lovely was sick to her boots. Her stepfather could talk of nothing else for days. 'That little angel', as he called Jane, 'shone like a beacon in the wilderness of life'. Adeline hid her smiles; not that she didn't agree with her husband. Jane Ridley was indeed a lovely girl. But, the poor man, who sought for and loved 'spiritual truth', as he called it, with such intensity, nevertheless had a way of putting things which immediately took all the truth out of them. His words and his voice, like his stomach, were overblown, making everything they touched somehow ridiculous. Harriet, however, was less capable of seeing the funny side. The humiliation of having her old enemy held up to her as a model of young womanhood rankled deeply. She had to smile, when George spoke of Jane, agree, when he said how sweet she was, pretend to like her. So her feelings of hatred were suppressed, pushed deep down into her soul. They swelled in her dark, secret places like a tumour that seemed to press against her very heart, an ever-present pain.

There was talk of Jane Ridley becoming an actress after the prizegiving. Whispers of it came to her ears, and Jane's head was giddy with delight. It opened doors for her, and through those doors, she saw freedom. Her heart leapt towards it, like a gull, swooping to its prey in the waves, only to carry it high up into the sky, with the cry of victory, 'Me! Meee! Meeeee!'

Yet there was jealousy and opposition all round! Robert, having given up his own artistic ideas, would have liked to encourage Jane, but he was genuinely concerned for his sister. The very quality which made her shine, which touched the hearts of people, made her vulnerable. There were no walls, no drawbridges around her; she stood naked, the truth of her being shining from her. He had promised to protect her. If someone dared to threaten her with a knife, he would defend her, but how could he defend her from those whose knives were invisible? Like fragile glass, she would shatter in the grip of such a life.

Jane could not understand it. And her disappointment at Robert's lack of support quickly grew to resentment. She was bitterly hurt. In an audience where everyone was applauding, only her brother and her father were silent. And that was the most frustrating part about it. Nothing was said. Her father made no objection, so how could she fight against him? It was like fighting a jelly! But he *did* object and she knew it. He wanted her to work in the sailmaking shed like their Fanny, and she wouldn't! She just wouldn't!

Then, without telling Jane, Bob went to see Miss Poulson. They agreed wholeheartedly that Jane should be protected from herself. One day, no doubt, she would marry, but meanwhile, she had to work, to earn a living. What at? Not acting, it was a profession fraught with danger. And certainly not with the women in the sailmaking sheds! In his heart Bob blamed them, with all their coarse talk, for Fanny's near undoing. Undecided, Bob went home, and kept his silence, while Miss Poulson 'slept on it', and awoke the next morning, wondering why she hadn't seen it before! The answer was obvious! Weren't Jane Ridley and Harriet May Lovely the best of friends? Hadn't the mayor himself spoken highly of Jane? Why not see if he could help? Mr Ridley had said his daughter needed 'keeping in order'. What could be better, than to work under the watchful and fatherly eye of George Beattie? So, Miss Poulson visited the Fowler Street shop, and closeted behind the glass door in the upstairs parlour, she and the mayor talked of the possibilities. She was smiling

141

when she left, and only laughed indulgently as a young girl barged into her in the doorway, a pile of empty boxes in her arms. Looking down on his empire from the balcony, George's fists clenched. 'How often have you been told to use the back entrance?' he barked. The girl dropped the boxes in shock. Adeline shook her head sadly. That girl's days in employment were definitely numbered.

The offer was a generous one. She would be fed and clothed; she would have pocket money, and while working as a messenger girl, she would be trained up to become a proper florist, learning how to make bouquets, sprays and wreaths. She might even find her way to the catering side of the business, to ice wedding cakes, and make swans out of ice cream to grace the tables of the Queen's Hall. It was the height of any girl's ambition, surely? Yet Jane hung back from accepting it.

'Who do you think you are, our Jane? The Grand Duchess?' Fanny snapped. 'I don't know how you can even *think* of turning down such an offer!' And then Jane was forced to admit, even to herself, that the one real fly in the ointment was Harriet May.

'She hates me,' she said, 'she treats me like muck, she does honest. She'll make my life misery, if I go and work there!'

Fanny laughed. 'Her? I wouldn't take any notice of her!'

Jane tried to explain some of the subtleties of the situation to her.

'She's going to a finishing school in "Newcarstle" as she calls it. They're going to make her a lady. There'll be no holding her then!'

'A lady? Her!' Fanny's scornful tone astonished her sister. 'They couldn't do that in a million years! Hah!'

'What do you mean, our Fanny?'

'She's a bastard, that's why.' Jane had heard the word used often enough, softened, sometimes, to 'barsket' by her father so he could pretend he wasn't actually swearing. It usually meant that somebody'd behaved rather badly.

'I know she's not very nice, like, but . . .'

Fanny laughed out loud then.

'No, I mean she's a bastard! I mean she hasn't got a Dad!'

142

Jane frowned. 'Everybody's got a Dad.'

Fanny shook her head. 'Not Harriet Lovely.'

'How?'

'Her mother wasn't married, pet. Harriet May is illegitimate and could never be a lady in her life! She's beneath your contempt.'

Jane frowned. Surely it wasn't Harriet's fault if her mother never got married to her father? Anyway, who was Fanny to call her names?

'You need talk! It's the kettle calling the pot, that's what!'

Fanny was horrified. 'I never brought a bastard into the world, our Jane,' she said quietly.

'All the same,' Jane's voice was firm, 'I don't think you're in a position to cast stones at Harriet!'

'You pious little ninny!' Fanny screeched. Her hand reached out to strike, and then suddenly, her fury gave way to puzzlement. She shook her head, and let her hand drop . . .

'You're a funny'n,' our Jane. You'd think you'd grab at something like that to use against her, if she's such a thorn in your flesh!'

Jane looked at her sister, her eyes dark and serious.

'It wouldn't be fair,' she said, and in her heart she pitied her enemy.

As she lay alone in the big bed at Trajan Street, Jane considered the proposition. Slowly, she realised that her new knowledge gave her strength. After all, pity was power, of a sort. If Harriet knew Jane was aware of the indignity of her birth, she would surely feel less like lording it over her; and, in any case, why should Harriet keep Jane from something she wanted? The obstacle of Harriet May became a spur to acceptance. Harriet was not going to do Jane Ridley out of anything! Like her sister before her, there was an obstinate streak in Jane Ridley. The attractions of the shop grew in her imagination. The ever-present perfume of flowers, serving real ladies from Westoe Village, the curious little drawers full of sweet smelling herbs, kindly Mrs Beattie, good food, perhaps proper shoes, in place of the hated clodhoppers; and she would be independent! She would have pocket money of her own that she could do what she liked with!

Just fancy! The delights of the prospect blazoned into glory, and putting on a face of 'only doing it to please her father', she finally, and with apparent great reluctance, agreed to accept the proposition.

So, it was arranged that Jane would start at Beattie's in September. Bob Ridley breathed a sigh of relief. Satisfied that he had done his fatherly duty, he signed up on a coaster, doing a round trip of the British ports, carrying coal to Yarmouth, and from there, taking its chances to secure fresh cargoes, coming home after a trip of perhaps thirty days. He would soon pay off his debt to his old employer, and with Robert also beginning his career at sea the following autumn, the Ridley family seemed set for fair weather.

Embarking from the Tyne, Bob was surprised to find Ronnie Wilson also of the crew. He had been on board for a few days, getting used to the lay-out of the ship, and helping to stock up on provisions. Since this was his first trip, he was to be general cook and dogsbody. There were seven men to the brig; master, mate and five hands, all prepared to perform any task that might be necessary as the occasion demanded. The work was hard, and the enthusiasm of the crew depended largely on what they had in their bellies. So all eyed the new cook with some apprehension.

'He's got a bit of fat on him, mind.' The skipper thought this boded well, and Ronnie prepared to come up to the challenge. All his studying, all his efforts had been for Jane Ridley. He wanted to prove himself worthy of her. Jane's father was a fair man. He would watch and wait, sizing Ronnie up till he was sure. Then, if he decided he liked him, he would surely back Ronnie all the way. This was his golden chance.

Smiling his nervous smile, Ronnie braced himself for the trial. And there would be one bonus to give him heart! Surely Bob's daughter would come down to the dock to wave her father off? The tide was beginning to turn. They were to go out with it across the bar. There was a light breeze and so the expense of a tug could be avoided, and they could sail out of harbour. Ronnie joined the rest of the men on deck ready for casting off. Now he had to remember everything he had been taught in the previous days. Theories were well enough, but the act of shinning aloft, of going along to the crosstrees and down again was a different matter, and in a small crew, each man had to know just what had to be done, and get on with it at exactly the right moment. A nod from Bob or the master was as much guidance as Ronnie could expect. He would need all his wits about him. The tide was running out. Perhaps Jane would not come down to the quay after all. His heart sank. He had relied on seeing her, on having the memory of her, standing on the shore, to strengthen his resolution through the coming voyage. A nod from the master to the mate, and a word from the mate to the hands, and they were casting off. A pain seared Ronnie's chest. He bit his lip, intent on his work. Sweat dampened his shirt, and a frown creased his brow. Then softly, the brig began to move. Ronnie felt the cool breeze on his face, and looking up, he saw her.

Jane was standing on the edge of the staithes. A ray of light penetrating the dark clouds touched her face. And then it was gone, and Ronnie saw, coming from the shadows to her left and to her right, her brother Robert and Jack Purvis. A cold shaft shot up his spine, and Ronnie shivered, the rope slipping in his grasp.

'Wake up, lad!' Bob screamed at him, and Ronnie started in his panic, falling, picking himself up and grasping tight onto the rope again as Bob came up behind him to help him out.

'Bloody fool!' Jack laughed quietly in Jane's ear. 'Look at his ears flapping now.' Jane grinned. Ronnie did have big ears. It was true. A proper comic turn he was. All the same, she felt sorry for her old admirer, and was surprised how sad she felt, as the ship slipped away. She had grown used to having Ronnie around, following her every movement with his spaniel eyes. She would miss him, like a ship missed its ballast in rough seas. Ballast. Yes. That was Ronnie. There was something sure about him. He had grown to a stocky build, with a full, generous face. She laughed an affectionate laugh, and misunderstanding her, Jack laughed too.

Ronnie managed to assume a confident look, as though he had been sailing all his life. He had a broad grin, which bulged out of his cheeks. He was a tryer. He wanted to be liked, and Bob took to him at once. He knew the lad had a soft spot for his daughter, and he excused his lack of concentration. After all, he could hardly blame the lad. Jane was a lass likely to turn any lad's head.

After a dismal start, the rain began. Ronnie lay on his hammock under the drips from the deckhead above, playing his mouth organ. His first night at sea, wet through and exhausted, found him mentally running through the menus he had planned for the voyage. In calm weather, he would make stews. In rough, it would be puddings, beef in suet, that wouldn't slop over the edges of his pans. He had thought it all out, and, after a supper of mutton and potato, with crisp cabbage, most of the men looked more kindly on him. True, Archie had complained that his gums couldn't cope with his greens. He liked his supper to melt in his mouth, having nothing to chew it with, but he was the only dissatisfied customer. Tomorrow they would have bubble and squeak with the cold meat, and he would fetch out some pickle to sharpen their taste buds. So the men would come to look forward to their meals, knowing that each time there would be something unexpected, tasty. Playing on his mouth organ, Ronnie smiled. He was on a winning streak. No doubt about it.

The summer wind dropped, and they were becalmed overnight. The men, being idle, began to ask what was for their dinner. Ronnie grinned in response.

'He's not letting on,' Bob laughed. 'We'll just have to wait till it's ready, eh?' Already they had begun to revolve around him, drawn by a warm smile, and the promise of food. His Mam had always said that the way to a man's heart was through his stomach. Well, she was right! The clouds parted, the sun shone, and the brig was on her way.

Ronnie opened up the galley, and sharpened his knives. She was making good progress, with a fair wind, and he balanced his frying pan deftly on the flames. The smell of frying cabbage turned his stomach. He was sea sick. His face went pale, and his grin had a strained edge to it, but he wouldn't let on. Passing by, Bob's eye was distracted from the pan to the face of the cook. He smiled to himself. The lad was all right. He was sticking to his post in spite of it. The smell of cooking came and went on the wind, as the crew worked on. They were getting hungry. It was almost dinner time, and Ronnie would soon be dishing out. He went down to the store and fetched up his jar of pickle, and coming back up, he found himself in a different world. They had strayed into a sea fog. Working his way along to the galley, Ronnie was soon back at his post. But as he looked into his frying pan, he wanted desperately to be sick. Swallowing hard, he considered the situation. He had kept his pan half full for fear of it slopping. But the sea was calm enough. Why prolong his agony, by cooking the food in two shifts? Why not put it all in at once, and get it over with? His decision made, he spilled the rest of the onion and the cabbage into the pan, till it was filled to the brim.

Bob was listening in the fog for the gun at Flamboro' Head, and had begun to wonder if they were too far off course to hear it, when suddenly, it sounded right over the masts. Immediately, he brought her to the wind, got the yards forrard, and the mainsheet hauled in. A cry of agony sounded from the galley. The ship was well over on her side, and Ronnie lay sprawled, his legs scalded, bubble and squeak in a mess all around him. Then the next gun sounded. It was astern and they squared away again.

'What's for me dinner?' Archie asked the cook, as he sat, waving knife and fork below deck.

'Cold meat and pickle,' Ronnie said dejectedly.

'Is that all?' Archie spat in disgust. Bob smiled a wry smile as the cook went to fetch more plates.

'By, that's a funny way of walking man!' The crew silently watched as Ronnie gingerly, legs splayed well apart, came back towards them. 'You look like you've been on a horse! What's wrong?' Then he winked, and they all let out a roar of laughter. They knew. The lot of them. And Ronnie accepted their mockery, joining in the laughter. He was one of the lads.

There was the whole of August to get through. Fanny was heavy with child, and made the most of her condition. She had them all running round after her in Pilot Street. There had, after all, been some threat of a miscarriage in the early months, and she had needed looking after. Rattler, dewy eyed at the prospect of a grandchild, and Ma, glad to have somebody to mother, spoiled her rotten. She slept every afternoon, and special little treats were brought her to eat. It was the life of Riley! Dandy O surprised everybody. Dutifully, he fetched Fanny's porter of an

147

evening, 'to build her up', and sat with her, holding her hand on the front, when he took her to get some air. The old tars on the Lawe Top, watching them, shook their heads in disgust.

'She's tamed him!' they said with some regret. 'He's had it now!' With his mother and his wife in league together, Dandy didn't stand a chance. Not that he minded. After all, wasn't it better having it on tap, than having to chase after the lasses? What was more, he was going to be a father. Fanny was providing the heir to carry on the tradition of piloting in the Tully family. For, of course, her child would be a boy. All in all, he was happy as Larry. And deep down, for all his bravado, Dandy liked the women in his life to rule the roost. It was the way he'd been brought up. He knew where he was, and it suited him fine.

His contentment puzzled Robert. How could he bear to watch his wife growing fat, her belly misshapen, her face pink and ugly. Fanny's pregnancy brought the whole business home to him. His feelings, his longings for Miss Reid, came then to that? He was disgusted at his own desires, sensing that somehow they defiled the very object of his affections. When, in the first week of August, he heard that Miss Reid had married her Arab, his mind was thrown into a turmoil of agonised confusion. Why had she done it? Why, oh why did she have to shatter his dreams? He lashed out at the only being he could. He raged and hurled abuse at his sister.

Fanny hardly ever came near them, leaving Robert and Jane to their own devices in Trajan Street. Jane acted as housekeeper, and Robert went out to earn what he could, doing odd jobs, till his ship sailed. Silently, they rubbed along together, the fragments of their artistic dreams floating round them and between them, like wisps of cloud in the summer sky. There was an ache in the heart of each, and lying in bed under the drawing of her 'hephalant' Jane began to get cold feet about the prospect of working in Fowler Street and longed for her brother to comfort her.

'Are you awake, our Robert?' she whispered in the darkness. Robert seemed to sigh. Perhaps he felt lonely too, only, being a man, he didn't want to admit it. Yes, Jane thought; he needed comfort just as she did. So she quietly got out of bed, and crept under the covers beside her brother. Waking suddenly, Robert shouted, 'What are you doing?'

'Nothing,' Jane said in dismay. 'I just wanted a cuddle.'

'Why don't you grow up, and leave me alone!'

Jane quickly scrambled out of his bed and back into her own, to lie there shivering in the cold. What had gone wrong? In her misery she remembered how Robert had loved her and promised to take care of her, how he used to cuddle her when she felt lonely, and Fanny had hurt her. Tears ran down her cheeks, wetting the sheet. Oh how she hated him now! He had grown heartless and cold, and she no longer knew him as her brother! She was alone. No-one cared for her. No-one but her father, who was away at sea, and, perhaps, Ronnie.

They were getting close to Yarmouth. The moon was up. It glanced across the ripples of the calm sea. Normally, on such a night, Bob's heart would fill with nostalgia as he kept his lonely watch. Memories of Ida, homesickness, all would crowd in on him. But not tonight. Bob laughed quietly to himself. No, not tonight, not with Ronnie playing on his mouth organ.

He'll come back and marry me,
Bonny Bobby Shaftoe.

Bob found himself joining in. The strain of music from below decks chased the shadows away. They didn't dare come near him. Ronnie's music, like his broad grin, was definitely catching. A flare, some distance off, caught Bob's attention. He frowned. Dark shapes loomed ahead. Was that a bell he heard?

'Hold your wind down there!' he shouted below. But no-one took any notice. All their voices were raised in singing. 'Damn it!' Bob ran quickly down. 'Hold your noise!' he commanded. Six faces turned towards him, and Ronnie's mouth organ dropped from his lips. Immediately, a bell sounded, quite close. Bob sped back upstairs, closely followed by the captain. Another flare, and they knew that they had sailed straight into a herring fleet. The fishing boats followed the herring down from the Shetland as the summer wore on, and were a constant hazard to other shipping. Not only was there a danger of collision, but of becoming

149

entangled in the nets. The decision was made to wait until morning, before attempting to make further headway, and Bob, once more alone, sat at his watch, as the flares went off around him, and the bells sounded.

'Was it my fault?' Ronnie's voice came at him from behind and Bob jumped.

'Don't do that again, man! You nearly gave me heart failure!'

'Sorry.' Ronnie perched beside him, and stared out into the darkness. The moon had gone down, and Bob's job was difficult enough, as he stared into the blackness for the shapes of the herring fleet. 'Was it, though?'

'What, man?' Bob asked, irritably.

'My fault. That we got stuck in this lot.'

'No. How could it be, eh?'

'I don't know, like. I just thought.'

'You think too much, lad. That's your trouble.'

'Aye. That's what me Mam tells me, as well.'

'Our Jane's like that. Her mind's as deep as the Atlantic. You never know what you're going to find at the bottom of it.' A long silence greeted this remark. Bob turned his head, and his eyes glistened in the darkness. 'Got a soft spot for her, haven't you?'

'Eeh, I'm sorry, Mr Ridley. I hope I don't offend, like.'

'Why no, man! How could you?'

'Well, she's a bit above's like . . . '

Bob thought for a moment as another flare lit up the water.

'I don't know. There's times that I think I understand her. And then . . . it's like when that flare goes out. After the light, it seems to be darker than it was before.' He laughed. 'Am I talking rubbish?'

'I don't think so, Mr Ridley,' Ronnie said doubtfully.

'It's like this, son . . . ' Ronnie smiled at the 'son'. 'In some ways, I'd say she was a cut above all of us. Including me.' Ronnie silently considered this statement.

'Aye. I'd second that.' He bit his tongue. He'd surely put his foot in it now! But Bob went on, 'But looking at it logically . . . I don't see how that can be.'

'No. Not logically, Mr Ridley. No.'

'So . . . she can't be, can she?' Both silently agreed to this. 'And there again, she is.'

'I don't understand, Mr Ridley.'

'No. Nor do I.' A bright light flared. Both men watched it, as suddenly it was extinguished, and the darkness of the night intensified. 'Aye. You're a canny lad, Ronnie Wilson.'

'Oh, thank you, Mr Ridley.'

'Don't thank me. I didn't have anything to do with it.'

'Not much of a catch, though, am I?'

'Why do you say that?'

'Well, I'm not that bright . . . I mean, I try hard . . . Miss Poulson said that on me last report. "Ronnie tries hard" she said.'

'Aye. You do. You try hard.'

'But look at Jack Purvis. He runs away with the prizes, and doesn't have to do a stroke of work, either. I've got to half kill meself just to keep up.' Ronnie sighed. 'Aye, he'd be a better catch for her than me.'

'Jack Purvis? For our Jane? Hah!'

'Why? What's wrong with him?'

'Nowt, man, apart from his name.'

'Oh I forgot about the feud and that.' There was a pause as both men considered the quarrel between the piloting family and the Ridleys. Bob had been glad when their Fanny had married a pilot. But he was no snob. Folk were folk whatever their jobs. And them that stuck their noses in the air were asking to be brought down a peg.

'You know, Ronnie, you're a fool.'

'Eh?'

'You are. You're a . . . a sort of innocent, you. You'll plead the other man's case rather than your own.' Ronnie sighed. There now. He'd done it again. He'd been stupid. Bob Ridley was right. He was a fool. 'You don't think enough of yourself. That's your trouble. You're all right.' His hand touched the lad's shoulder comfortingly. Ronnie was grateful, but 'all right'! What did it mean? Was he 'all right' enough for Jane Ridley? That's what bothered him. 'So you fancy yourself in love with my Jane, eh?'

'I worship her. I do honest.'

'Now don't go too far.'

'Sorry, Mr Ridley.'

'There you go again, apologising. It's annoying. It is, honest.'

'Sorry, Mr Ridley. I mean . . . sorry I said I'm sorry . . . Oh heck!'

In the darkness, Bob smiled as the lad struggled to make sense of his thoughts and feelings. It was a painful spectacle. It was like witnessing an elephant trying to thread a needle. He ought to take pity on him and help him out.

'No. It's all right, Ronnie. No need to explain.' A stone dropped from Ronnie's heart. 'I know how you feel. I tell you what . . . our Jane could do worse.' He nodded sagely.

'Eeh! Mr Ridley! Is that a fact?'

'It is.' A sudden flare lit up Ronnie's face. Bob found his heart melting. You'd think he'd just told the lad he was King of England. 'I trust you,' he added after some consideration.

'Eeh!' was the only response. Ronnie's chest swelled with joy. 'I'll show your trust's not misplaced, Mr Ridley. If it kills me! I promise you that.' And, picking up his mouth organ, he vented his feelings in a loud rendering of 'The Blaydon Races'.

Jane's cold feet got colder as August wore on. And there was no-one in whom she could confide her fears. She spent a lot of time at her sister's house, fetching and carrying. The three chins told her to scrub the shirts. The two chins told her to scrub the steps. And before they were finished, the three chins would be at her again. Jane was reminded of the ugly sisters in the fairy story. Well, if they were the ugly sisters, and she was Cinderella, where on earth was Prince Charming? Where, come to that, had Buttons got to? All *she* had were the mice! Sent off to do some shopping, Jane found herself walking down Long Bank. She hadn't been near the place since the night Jack the Hammer'd drummed them all out of the pub. She shivered, as she approached the lamp on the corner opposite the 'Noah's Ark'. There was no-one there. No-one at all. Women and children scurried about the streets, bogies rattled up and down, the wheels bouncing along the cobbles. Jane held her basket close to her, put down her head, and passed the pub door.

Inside, Jack Purvis was downing a pint. He'd had a good night with his uncle out in the coble, and now he was ready for sleep. His eyes were bleary with exhaustion and beer, and yet something would not let him go home. There was an itch inside him, and the more he scratched at it, the worse it got. What was wrong? He sighed, and looked round the pub. There they all were, the men and the women of his childhood, become the comrades of his manhood. There was nothing new. He had money now. So what? He could spend it. On what? Beer? End up like the rest of them? He eyed their faces. One old woman, deep in her porter, turned her face away. He laughed to himself. What had she to hide? What was she protecting from his gaze? She had nothing he wanted. What did he want? The itch intensified into anger. Jack bit his lip, and it went white till he tasted the blood, then he let go his teeth, and felt the pain, and it was a kind of pleasure. It stabbed through the misery of his boredom. Yes. That was what it was. Boredom. Jack Purvis was bored, bored, bored. It had all come so easy! Son of a pilot, the best job on the river had dropped into his lap. And as last night on the coble had proved to him, he knew more about the job than his uncle already! Jack's tankard fell with a loud bang onto the table. A ripple of shock ran through the saloon. Heads turned, eyes looked, Jack smiled. They hadn't seen anything yet! Renouncing the smug world of his inheritance, Jack left the pub.

She was disappearing round the corner. But he was sure it was her. Her boots clattered briskly on the cobbles and the fair hair swung with the movement of her body. It was Jane Ridley! Jack's tiredness fled, his eye sparkled, and his steps echoed hers down the hill into Wapping Street, where Jane disappeared into a general store. She had a long list. But Jack didn't mind waiting. He stood outside the window, watching the girls go by. He was beginning to yawn, when the bell clanged on the door, and Jane came out, her basket laden to the brim, with flour, potatoes, washing soda, all heavy things, that, of course, required his immediate assistance.

Jane's first reaction was to pull the basket away.

'I'm not trying to pinch it, pet!' Jack laughed. Jane looked up and smiled with relief.

'Oh it's you! How are you getting on? I've not seen you in ages!'

'Oh all right, you know. Working with me uncle just now.'

'Oh yes. You're going to be a pilot, aren't you? No flies on you!'

'None at all, pet.' He grinned and taking the basket from her, began walking her back to Pilot Street. 'I hope you're flattered.' Jane glanced at him questioningly. 'I'm taking me life in me hands, talking to you. You know that.'

'Oh?'

'If my mother, or any of the aunties saw us now, they'd skin me alive!'

'Oh that! I think all this feud business is silly,' Jane said decisively.

'So do I. All the same, like I say, I'm taking me life in me hands.'

'I hope you think I'm worth it then!' Jane laughed.

'Oh aye. You are.' Then he winked; Jane's mouth dropped open, she flushed crimson. 'How's that sister of yours, eh?'

'Oh she's not due till November. Mind, the way she carries on, you'd think she was going to drop it any minute! She's got me run off me feet!'

'Ah!' he smiled, and she smiled back.

'Not that I mind, only there's no fun, like.'

'None at all?'

'Na!'

'Huh! We'll have to see about that.' He handed her back her basket at the end of Pilot Street. 'Don't tell anybody I carried your things, mind. Because . . . '

'You're taking your life in your hands!' she finished for him, laughing. Then he touched his lips with his fingers, and left her to think about it.

And Jane did think. Jack had brightened up her day. He'd always been good fun at school, and he'd helped her to laugh when she would otherwise have cried. She liked him for that. And as she scrubbed away at the doorstep, a glow came to her cheeks. That wink showed he liked her and it was nice to be liked. Later, as Jane walked back to Trajan Street alone, the thought comforted her. The nights were drawing in already. Soon it would be September. She shivered. Fret was coming in from the sea, cold as ice. The house was dark as she approached it. Where was 'Buttons'? Out on his own as usual, no doubt, mooning about the cliff tops hankering after his schoolteacher. The thought hurt

Jane. He had no room in his heart for her any more. She opened the door, and walked into the emptiness. A scurrying in the corner made her jump. Then there was a low growl.

'Gormless!' Jane laughed, and felt her way towards the table where she had left the candle. Lighting it, she saw that Gormless had got one of Robert's socks and was chewing it hungrily. 'Oh you bad dog!' she scolded him. His tail went between his legs, and he disappeared under the table. 'Robert'll go mad!' She went down on all fours and tried to retrieve the sock from him. But he wouldn't let go. 'Give it back!' she demanded. Gormless pulled. Jane pulled. The sock stretched. It was a tug of war and the old dog won, heaving Jane over to lie beside him on the floor, along with the tatters of Robert's sock. 'Oh, Gormless!' Jane cried. The dog, sensing her distress, bent over her and started licking her face. 'I'm glad somebody loves me!' she said tearfully. Putting her arms round the dog's neck, Jane began to cry. The empty house echoed with the sound of her empty heart. There was no-one in the whole of Shields to fill it.

The drips fell on the oilskin Ronnie had arranged like a tent over his hammock. His arms ached. They had finally found a buyer at Yarmouth for their coal, and taken on fish in its place. He had unloaded and loaded with the best of them, scurrying back to his galley to check the supper from time to time. It was tiring work all right. But he couldn't sleep, and he was next on watch, as they made passage for Gravesend. If only Jane could have seen him, heaving baskets of coal, pulling on the ropes, climbing aloft! He remembered her, as she had stood on the staithes, waving goodbye, the shaft of light picking her out. His heart ached for her. He saw her hand raise and the smile for her father. Then he saw the shadows coming out of the gloom to her left and to her right, and a shiver, deep at the base of his spine, curled up his back, and suddenly, swinging his hammock, he jumped down, and ran up on deck.

'What's the marra with you?' Harry asked him. 'You were running like all the bats in hell were after you!'

'Oh . . . ' Ronnie stammered. 'I thought it was time for me watch, like.'

'Keen, aren't you?' Harry took advantage of the situation.

155

There was still three quarters of an hour to go, but if the lad was willing . . . well! Ronnie took over, and Harry went below. Eeh, some folk were born suckers! He picked up Ronnie's mouth organ and played softly as his hammock swung with the motion of the ship.

CHAPTER TEN

Jack Purvis yawned loudly. His mother stiffened beside him in the pew, and in front of him the hairs on the nape of Eileen's neck bristled. Was Jack going to show them all up and yawn again? Or was he going to put his hand in front of his mouth and pretend to cough like any gentleman? Jack considered carefully. Whether to bear the slings and arrows of outrageous family hypocrisy or by yawning end it. Unable to make up his mind for the moment, he merely sighed, and began looking round the church. Not that there was much to see. The old familiar vicar, the old familiar pulpit, the old familiar congregation. Who was here this morning? You could tell the families where the women wore the trousers, because they dragged their men along with them. Like his Ma. Like Ma Tully. Like Fanny Tully. There she was, big as a house end and twice as ugly. And didn't she look proud of herself? If looks could kill, there'd be blood in the aisles between the Tullys and the Purvises. And there was Jane Ridley, on one side of no man's land, and here was he on the other. A proper pair of star crossed lovers! He smiled a secret smile. Seeing it, his mother hoped her Yorkshire pudding would come up to her son's expectations, while he was only hoping he would be able to catch the sweet Jane on her way out. He'd like to see her blush again, like she did when he'd winked at her! She liked him. No doubt about it. There was hope. His smile broadened, as he looked across at her. That would set the cat among the pigeons! He'd like to see their smug faces when they found out about him and Jane! Not that there was anything *to* find out. Not yet. He averted his gaze from his Juliet, and fastened it, instead, on the vicar. Jack's eyes were blank, for he was watching the pictures in his mind, and they were far more interesting than anything the vicar had to say; so interesting, Jack Purvis forgot to yawn.

Miss Poulson caught Jane as she was leaving the churchyard.

'Where's Robert?' she asked. Embarrassed, Jane shrugged. 'His ship sails in a couple of weeks, doesn't it?'

'Yes. I'll miss him,' Jane said simply.

'No you won't! You'll be far too busy learning your new job!'

'Oh. That!'

'What's wrong? Have you gone off the idea?'

Jane sighed. What could she say? Miss Poulson would only be angry if she told her Harriet May was her enemy. She would think she was being spiteful.

'Morning, Miss Poulson!' Jane looked up suddenly to see Jack Purvis standing beside the teacher.

'I heard you yawning during the sermon!' Miss Poulson reprimanded him.

'Come now! You surely wouldn't lecture an ex-pupil!'

'I wouldn't dare!' she laughed. 'You're much bigger than me!'

Jane began to slide away. 'Come back! I hadn't finished talking to you!'

'I'm sorry, Miss Poulson, it's just that . . . ' Jane indicated her sister, one arm under her belly, the other supporting her against the gatepost. She was looking daggers.

'What's wrong with Fanny? Surely she can't mind you talking to me!'

'It's not you, Miss, it's . . . '

'Oh!' The teacher looked at Jack, then feeling eyes on her back, turned her head to see the clan of Purvises assembled behind her. Jack grinned.

' "Two households", Miss Poulson!'

'Oh! You remember your Shakespeare! Well, and there was I thinking all my teaching had fallen on stony ground!'

158

'Do you remember "Romeo and Juliet", Jane?' Jack asked her. Jane looked at him shyly and nodded. Miss Poulson looked from one to the other, and raised her eyebrows.

'I see. Well don't end up stabbing one another, that's all!' Laughing, Jack walked back to his mother, and dutifully asked whether there was any Yorkshire pudding.

Dandy found Robert down at the sheds on the landing, where he'd gone for a breath of fresh air before his dinner.

'By it's good to get out from under their feet!' Robert smiled sympathetically. 'It was bad enough before, but two women in one kitchen . . . !' He shook his head, but his eyes sparkled. Robert felt almost envious. Dandy was happy. You could see that. 'Never get married, lad!' Dandy chuckled, 'never get married.'

'You don't mean that!'

'No.' Dandy stared contentedly across the river, to the High Lights on the north bank. 'No. It's grand. Thoroughly recommend it.'

'Why?'

'If you don't know, I'm not telling you! I'm not your Da!'

'Oh I know about that!' Robert snapped. 'Not that I've . . . you know . . . done it.'

'Even when you have, lad, it's not the same as being married. Take my word for it.'

'That's the trouble.'

Dandy looked the lad full in the face.

'Oh I see! Well, you'll get over it, I expect!'

'I won't! I won't ever get over it!'

'Course you will. We all get out of our romantic notions in the end. It's called growing up.' Robert looked at him seriously.

'What do you mean?'

'I've seen how you've looked at our Fanny.' Robert blushed. Suddenly he felt stripped naked before Dandy. 'Well, let me tell you, there's not a bonnier sight in the whole world, than a pregnant woman!' Robert snorted. 'And if you think otherwise, you want to open your eyes and see.'

'All I can see is a great belly, and a fat face. And then, later on, a squalling kid, dirtying itself, and the woman you fell in love with ends up looking like . . . like your Ma!'

There was a pause. Dandy raised his eyebrows and sighed.

'I see.'

'I mean, I like her and that,' Robert realised he'd gone too far, 'but I wouldn't like to be married to her!'

'Neither would I!' Dandy's joke lightened the tension between them. Robert laughed in spite of himself.

'No, but, I mean, all right, so Fanny's not an oil painting. So what? When I look at her, I don't see her pock marks any more. Do you know, it's the first time I've thought of that. I just don't see them now. To me . . . ' His eyes misted with emotion, 'to me, she's beautiful. Really beautiful.' Robert withdrew his gaze, feeling something like a reverence for Dandy's new found feelings. 'You see, it's what it's all about. Having kids and that. When you get married, you become, well . . . one. Like the vicar says. It's a mystery, you see. Inside her, now, there's a living human being, a child, that's half her and half me, and yet, it's neither one of us. It's itself.' Dandy was amazed at himself. He'd never had such thoughts before. 'Here,' he said, 'I think we should be writing this down!' Robert laughed, and Dandy wiped away a tear with his sleeve. The gesture embarrassed his companion.

'It sounds like the catechism, Father Son and Holy Ghost,' he sneered. But Dandy missed the tone of Robert's voice.

'Aye. Do you know? It is. You're right. Mind, it'd make better sense, if the Holy Ghost was female. I mean, looking at it logically right . . . ?'

'Yes. For God's sake, Dandy, by all means, let's be logical!' Robert pleaded, considering his brother-in-law was getting just a bit carried away with himself.

'Well, logically, if there's a father and a son, there's got to be a mother, eh?' Robert nodded. There was no denying it.

'What about Mary?'

'Oh aye! I'd forgotten about her. I wonder where she fits into it, eh? The Catholics worship her, you know!'

'Well, I'm not a Catholic!'

'Neither am I.' There was a long silence. Robert frowned and kicked at the wooden staithes of the landing.

'I don't see where this is getting us, to be honest, Dandy O.'

'Well . . . ' Dandy took a sidelong look at his companion.

160

Robert was white faced and miserable. Dandy took a leap in the dark. 'Are you in love or something?' Robert's startled response told him he had hit the nail on the head. 'Yes?' Dandy sympathised. 'I know how you feel. I've been there meself, more than once. Horrible, isn't it?'

'You mean you're not in love with our Fanny?'

'Course I'm not. I love her!'

'But . . . '

'They're two different things, lad. Fanny's real. She's having my kid. She cooks me dinner. Bites me head off sometimes. But I love her. And she loves me. Aye she does! Love's what warms your feet in bed, not what keeps you awake night after night dreaming!' Robert was feeling uneasy. He shifted uncomfortably on the wooden landing. He swallowed hard. Best be brave and spit it out.

'And is that why Miss Reid married that Arab? To keep her feet warm in bed, like?'

'Who's Miss Reid when she's at home? Oh I see . . . your lady love, is she?' He laughed.

'Shut up!' Robert's tongue lashed out.

'Sorry I spoke.'

'I can't bear to think of her getting fat like Fanny!'

'Motherhood's a fine thing, lad. Where would you be without it?' Robert said nothing but continued kicking chips out of the wood. 'Women aren't there just for our amusement, you know. I mean sex and babies go together, like.'

'It spoils everything!'

'Only your dreams, son. And who wants them?'

'I do! And don't call me son!'

Dandy sighed. *He* knew what he meant, but he couldn't say it. He'd found fulfilment in his marriage. Robert's love affair of the mind was a sterile thing. It would never give him happiness. Still, if that's how he wanted it . . . ! Dandy gave up and slowly stood.

'Well! Dinner time!' he said. Robert would not, could not look up. He was crying.

Jane was in a flurry. All she'd wanted to do was use the cabbage water to make the gravy. And what a carry on there was! You'd think she'd killed somebody the way they went on! And then they'd got at her about the length of her skirts. As if she could help getting taller? It wasn't something she could control by will power! You'd think she'd made it happen on purpose, because, of course, she was a slut, and *wanted* to show off her ankles!

'You're hardly decent, our Jane!' Fanny had told her. 'I'm ashamed to be seen with you! Well, we'll have to do something about it before you go to work at the Mayor's!'

Their Fanny had said that! Their Fanny of all people! Then the three chins had wobbled dangerously at her, and said, 'Maybe you could pass on some of your dresses, Fanny? I can't see you getting into them again!'

'I will after the baby's born!'

'Huh!' was her only answer, and then of course they'd been at each other's throats, enjoying themselves that way, and Rattler had gone down to 'The Globe' and Dandy O'd gone off somewhere, and she'd just slipped away, sick to the back teeth with the whole lot of them.

Jane wouldn't say no to a new skirt, or frock, even a second hand one of Fanny's'd be nice. And it was true, she'd never get back into her old things, even after the birth. When Ma Tully and Fanny passed each other in the kitchen, you needed a shoe horn between them. Feeling more like Cinderella than ever, Jane got out her three outfits and stared at them mournfully, back at Trajan Street. Now if she was to cut up the skirt, she could add a piece to both of her frocks. That might help. But they'd look horrible. And what about the mayor? As Fanny had said, she couldn't go to work there looking like a scruff. What on earth was she going to do? Harriet May would laugh herself silly! Brown frill on blue serge! Oh no! She couldn't face her arch enemy in that! A pang of envy crept into her heart, as she thought of Harriet's lovely dresses. Jane sighed. What would she give for just one of them? Idly dreaming, she sat on the big bed, staring in front of her.

A gun sounded. Then another. Jane jumped, suddenly alert. Men and women were already running down the street, followed by children, dogs, anything that moved, going in the direction of the lighthouse on the Groyne. A ship was in trouble. It was

162

August! How could it be? Some overconfident skipper saving money by trying to do without a pilot, no doubt. Jumping up, Jane followed the crowd down to the Lawe.

There it was, a three-masted schooner no less, and it had come to grief on the black middens. Men were crowding round the lifeboat. Rattler was there, so were Dandy, Robert, Jack Purvis, the old tars from the Lawe Top. Half of Shields was trying to get in the boat. The Coxwain had chosen his crew, but still they came, climbing over the sides of the boat.

'Will you bugger off!' he shouted to the surplus volunteers and the chosen twenty-two men took her out, rowing towards the middens and the stranded ship. It was a spectacle to be enjoyed. The weather was fine, the men in little danger. The rejected crew stood miserably watching, or shouting suggestions in their cupped hands, across the river. Robert was one of them, and so was Jack Purvis. Not that Jack minded being left out, especially when he saw Jane Ridley amongst the bystanders. She was sitting on the wall, pulling her skirt down, in a futile attempt to cover her ankles. They were nice ankles. They were nice feet too, bare feet.

'What's the matter, hinny?' Mrs Dunn asked her. 'You've not had to pawn your boots, have you?'

'No. I just hate the blooming things. Horrible great clod-hoppers!' Mrs Dunn sniffed.

'You should be grateful you've got a pair to your name, never mind turning up your nose at them!' So saying, she flounced off to 'The Globe', closely followed by Gormless, who deftly evaded the kick aimed at him by his mistress once they were at the pub door. There was food in there, and Gormless was not to be put off.

'Anyway, it'd be a crying shame to hide them!' Jane, intent on the rescue over the river, had not noticed Jack's approach. She jumped.

'Oh hallo!' she said, and then went silent, for once finding nothing to say.

'Hallo,' he said, after a while. This was not how he had imagined the scenario during the morning's sermon! He coughed, and smiled his boyish sideways smile. It never failed! 'Your feet, I mean,' he went on. Jane looked at him blankly. 'It'd

163

be a shame to hide your feet, wearing boots!' He sighed with exasperation. Compliments were inclined to wear thin, if you had to go on repeating them.

'Oh,' she said. 'Have you seen our Robert?' Jack frowned.

'No. Why? You don't need him! You've got me!' Jane looked at Jack as though for the first time. She'd never thought of him as a brother before. He was a classmate, a friend. She liked him. But a brother?

'Brothers are supposed to look after you,' she said seriously.

'Well, I'll look after you.'

'Will you?' He nodded. 'Honest?'

A cry from the lifeboat startled them. They looked up, and saw the first men from the stranded ship being taken aboard. Rumours about the nature of the cargo were flying round. Brandy was favourite.

'Huh.' Jack laughed. 'Probably chalk, or lime, or something like that!'

'Yes. I expect so.'

'Anyway, look at the folk on the other side!' Jane looked. Sure enough the folks of North Shields and Tynemouth were already making their way down to the rocks, in the hopes of 'salvaging' something. 'Come on. This is getting boring,' Jack announced.

'Come on where?'

'I don't know. Where'd you fancy?'

'I'm hungry.'

'Do you like mussels, and whelks and that?'

'Aha.'

'Howway, then.'

Jack stood by the wall, holding out his hands. Jane held back, then, seeing his eyes question her hesitation, she jumped, and fell straight into his arms.

Jack steadied her as she landed. But he held her too long and his grip was too tight. Jane pushed him from her.

'I'm not crippled you know. I can jump off a wall!'

'Sorry, I'm sure!' he laughed at her. 'Only I took you for a lady, like!'

Jane looked uncertainly at him. This was a whole new idea.

'Why? Are ladies incapable or something?' she asked.

164

'No, but they usually accept help from gentlemen. It's good manners.'

'Oh.' This was a painful thought. Good manners, etiquette, Jane'd heard words like that before, but she'd never learnt them. Well, she'd better start, if she was going to work at the mayor's. Again the terrible thought of Harriet May stabbed into her. Her face clouded.

'What's wrong?'

'Nothing.' And Jane was off, laughing, daring him to follow. 'I want me whelks!'

It was a grand day. There was an excitement in the town end, as there always was when the lifeboat had been called out. A light breeze made the grass whisper in the dunes, and the summer sun warmed the air, uninterrupted by the usual sea mists. It was a day on which to forget, on which to live for the moment. Skirts lifted to her thighs, Jane ran through the edge of the water, kicking up the salt spray, laughing till her cheeks ached. Jack splashed her, wrestled with her, trying to get her to fall into the sea, just as Robert used to do. She dared him, then ran from him, and he caught her, then, arms round her, brought her down at last, to sit wailing and laughing in the water.

'You're horrible! I hate you!' But her eyes sparkled. A hint of mischief warned him, and her arms lashed out, catching his feet, to bring him down beside her. Both were soaked to the skin, and dragged themselves away from the water's edge to lie, panting in the dunes, where the sandy hills shaded them from the cool breezes, and the sun could dry them.

'Oh! I haven't enjoyed myself so much for ages!' Jane lay back, her arms thrust above her head, and sighed luxuriously.

'You're a game little piece, I'll say that!'

'Piece of what? Cake? Black pudding?'

'Never mind.'

'No. I want to know.'

'It's just an expression. It means, girl, that's all.'

'Oh.' It was a funny expression, then, Jane thought, but closing her eyes against the sun, she basked in its warmth, and thought no more about it. Her mind drifted, like a balloon, cut free. It soared high over the dunes and the sea, light as a cloud. There was no Fanny, no Robert, no Harriet May nothing; just

Jane, and the blue sky and the warmth of the sun. And now and then she felt the sand, drying on her legs, slide down her skin, shifting, slipping, and she was almost asleep.

'Once upon a time' a memory said to her, 'far away on the other side of the world, there was a little baby elephant . . . ' Whose voice was it? Her father's? Chandrika's? She couldn't tell. It was just a voice, ' . . . and it had a happy life, with its mother and father . . . ' She sighed, and turning over, her chest fell against something hard. A stone. It was hurting her. Her hand moved towards it, to ease it away, but another hand was there before hers, almost under her chest, and she sat up suddenly, eyes wide with shock, not knowing where she was.

'It's the crocodiles!' she cried out. 'Get off! Get off me!'

'Hey! Calm down. Calm down. I'm not touching you!' Her vision cleared, and she saw Jack looking at her with surprise. 'Were you dreaming?' Jane was lost for a moment, not knowing what was real and what was not.

'I don't know. I must have been. I was dreaming . . . ' She stopped, remembering the elephant. 'Jack, have you ever seen an elephant?'

'Course I have.'

'Have you?'

'There was one at the circus. Potter's Circus. It came to Newcastle.'

'Oh.'

'What's wrong, Jane?' She looked at him, wondering what he meant. 'You can tell me, surely. I'm your brother, aren't I?' She smiled. 'Come on,' he encouraged, 'you must be worried about something if you're having nasty dreams, and that.' Jane sighed, and lay back against the sand. The sun had slipped behind a cloud. She shivered, goose pimples bubbling on her arms. 'Cold?' She nodded. Jack took off his jacket. He had been carrying it, when they were playing by the sea, so it was dry, and warm from his body. She welcomed it round her shoulders. 'Better?' Jane nodded. 'Come on. Tell brother Jack. What's up?'

'Well . . . it's Harriet really.'

'Oh the anemone!' he laughed. She smiled.

'Yes. The anemone.'

'What about her?'

166

'You know I've got to go and work at her shop . . . '

'It's not hers. It's her stepfather's.'

'Well, his shop then. I'm dreading it. Honest I am.'

'Huh! You shouldn't let her get you down. She's just jealous, that's all.'

'What for?'

'Well, you're better looking for a start.'

'I am not!'

'Yes you are.' Jane looked at him in surprise. She could see, in her mind, Harriet May in her lovely frocks, dressed up to the nines, and looking gorgeous. She stared doubtfully at Jack. 'Have you looked in the mirror lately?' he asked her. Jane was startled. Her fingers reached into her hair, and pulled at it, as though she was trying to comb it. His hand reached up to stop her. 'I love it like that. All bedraggled. You look like a mermaid . . . long pale tresses, tangled, and blowing round your face, your lovely face.'

'Our Robert never says things like that to me.'

'Familiarity breeds contempt. That's why, Jane. He hasn't really looked at you lately. You're the most beautiful thing ever to hit the town end.' Jane's jaw dropped. Jack had to laugh. 'The nicest thing about you, is that you don't seem to realise it.' He shook his head. 'Eve must've been like you, before she met the snake!'

'That's a blasphemy.'

'No it's not. It's a compliment.'

'I'm not used to compliments.'

'Well, all I can say is, you'd better *get* used to them, because you've not heard the last of them.' Jane felt hot under Jack's coat. She shifted uneasily.

'Come on. That's enough fun for one day,' he said, and held out his hand, ready to pull her to her feet. 'You have had fun, haven't you?'

'Oh yes!'

'And you'd like to do it again, eh?'

'Yes. I would! Only something different next time.'

'Your wish is my command,' he said, bowing. She laughed delightedly.

'I'd like to go to the circus,' she announced. Jack was taken aback.

167

'But they're for children!'

'I don't care. I've never been and I want to see an elephant.'

'All right. Next time the circus comes, I'll take you.'

'Promise?' Jack nodded, and she let him haul her up.

'And now, let's find your whelks for you!'

Pilot Street was in an uproar when Jane got back. Ma Tully was having hysterics in the kitchen, Fanny had taken to her bed, Dandy, Robert and Gormless were generally getting under each other's feet, and Ma Dunn was out in the yard lav, doing unspeakable things to Rattler. No-one took much notice of Jack's presence in the circumstances.

'What's wrong?' Jane asked, astonished.

'There's been an accident!' Dandy wailed mournfully.

'Oh no! The lifeboat?' Dandy shook his head. 'It's Dad.'

'Oh!' Jack got himself ready to catch his swooning lady.

'He was that het up, in all the excitement, that, emptying some pills into his mouth, he swallowed the whole bottle! He says a sudden wave made his hand slip. I don't know. Anyway, there it is. He's out the back now, heaving and straining and trying to pass it.' Jack's lips quivered. Jane caught his eye and had to look away.

'Has the doctor been?' she managed to get out.

'Ma Dunn's given him some opening medicine, and an enema, and I don't know what else.' Dandy shook his head. 'Me Dad thinks he's dying.' A sudden howl from the yard, brought them up short. They stood like statues, listening. Then another howl. Gormless's ears pricked. He snorted, panting, waiting. At the third howl, he joined in. Jane and Jack rushed from the house, muttering about how they'd only get in the way. They ran all the way back to Trajan Street, forgetting about the spies from the Purvis clan, and opening the door of the Ridley house, they fell inside, laughing till their bellies ached, and tears ran down their cheeks.

'Eeh, it's not funny!' Jane said guiltily.

'I know,' Jack replied, and they screamed their mirth till the neighbours banged on the floor in protest.

Late that night, when Robert still hadn't come home, Jane lit the candle, and set it on the mantelpiece beside her father's shaving mirror. The flame and its image flickered back at her in the half dark. She watched it, absently, as it flared taller. Black smoke grew out of the end of it, casting soot over the mirror. And then the flame fell back, burning brightly again. She reached up and took the mirror down, to clean it. As the cloth wiped the blackness from the glass, she saw her own face shining back at her. The pale hair hung lank, matted from the salt water. She was a mess, and yet, with a shock, she realised that Jack had been right. She was also beautiful. The pretty child had grown into a woman, and there was no-one in Shields could hold a candle to her.

To Harriet May, the news of Jane's imminent presence in her father's shop had been like an earthquake in the bedrock of her life. Her security of tenure in Fowler Street had always been under threat. Ever since her mother had died, she had known that her memory, and George Beattie's high sense of moral duty, were the only claims she had on him. She knew he did not like her. No matter how hard she tried to please him, he would not show her favour. There were no prizes for Harriet May. And if life could put Jane Ridley into her own home, a cuckoo in the nest, then what else might it not do to her? From early disdain towards an inferior being, Harriet's feelings towards Jane had turned into fear. Staring into Adeline's mirrors on her dressing table, Harriet saw a stranger looking back at her. The pretty child had grown into a plain woman. The hair curled on the forehead looked odd atop the now heavy features. The nose was strong, and the mouth thin. She pinched her cheeks to bring colour into them, but the downward trend of her lips belied it. She was handsome, Harriet decided, rather than pretty. She had dignity. She lifted her chin into the air to prove it, and promised herself she would always wear long ear rings to show off her slim, aristocratic neck. Yes, Harriet had 'class', which was much more important than mere good looks. So what had she to fear? She told herself that Jane Ridley was to be a mere employee in the establishment, just like Elizabeth. And as he had with Elizabeth, no doubt, her stepfather would soon find fault with Jane, and sack her also! Why, her old classmate would be a mere servant in the house! And she would treat her as such! A sudden smile crossed Harriet's lips. Her decision was reflected into infinity, carried on her smile into the green depths of the reflecting mirrors.

And so September had come, and Jane started at the shop. Robert had been nice to her that first morning, and sent her on her way with a smile and a word of encouragement.

'Don't let the buggers get you down!'

'I won't,' she had replied bravely and her clodhoppers rang out on the cobbles as she began the long walk to Fowler Street. There was a sea fret that morning. You could taste the salt in the air, and the gulls had come into the streets for shelter from rough weather. The brown frill bounced out at her feet, at the bottom of the blue serge. Fanny had not parted with her frock. It was a long walk down Mile End Road, for she would not be able to afford the luxury of the horse tram every day, and she had better start as she meant to go on. This was to be the pattern of her life. She saw the dome of the Queen's first, coming up to her left, and idly wondered what it was like inside. She imagined all kinds of luxury, and brilliance. She sighed, and forced herself to look towards the right, where the shop stood, between a butcher's and a grocer's; 'Beattie's' it said over the door. She took a deep breath and walked in.

'Can I help you?' Adeline looked up in surprise to see the anxious face of her new employee. 'Don't look so frightened. I won't bite you! Not on your first day anyway!' She laughed, and Jane relaxed. She had always liked Adeline Beattie. 'Would you like a cup of tea?'

'Yes, please.'

'So would I. Only don't tell George!' They smiled conspiratorially and went into the kitchen.

Adeline had been wiring in a wreath. Her fingers were pricked from the sharp ends of the wire, and she sucked at one of them, to draw the blood away.

'I bleed easily,' she said. 'George gets annoyed. He thinks I'm a weakling. He's right of course.' She took her finger away from her mouth and as Jane watched, a bright globule of blood grew like a bubble from the end of it. 'I don't clot. That's the trouble.' While the kettle boiled, she ran her finger under the tap. The blood ran through the water, down the drain. 'I daresay you're made of sterner stuff,' she smiled at the newcomer, who smiled back sympathetically. 'The kettle's boiled. I suppose you don't need me to teach you how to make the tea?' Her voice was like honey; it made everything sweet. Jane hurried to oblige her.

Harriet had gone with George into 'Newcarstle' to buy flowers. It was a twice weekly event, one which Harriet enjoyed, in spite of the fact she had to get up before it was light, for the market. Afterwards, there was the treat of staying in town for some tea, and, perhaps, looking at the shops, while George did business elsewhere. She would be out of the way for the whole of the morning. This was an unexpected and blessed relief for Jane, and the relief did not go unnoticed. But Adeline said nothing. She liked to get other people to talk. And that way, she learnt a great deal, storing it away like the herbs in the little drawers of the shop. George might think her a boring, silent companion, but like the wise monkeys, she said, saw and heard no evil. That was her philosophy of life. That was how she got by. She might not have done anything to make the world a better place to live in, but at least she had not made it any worse. Like the desert rose, she would bloom unnoticed, and slowly fade away.

The water ran clear. The flow of blood had stopped. Adeline smiled and drank the sweet tea.

'It's going to be nice to have someone new about the place.'

When Harriet came back with George Beattie, she found Jane already quite at home. She knew where the tea was, where things were kept in the shop, where the lav was, and was now helping Adeline with the wreath for the funeral order.

'I'll do that,' she said, pushing Jane aside. Adeline said nothing, did not even look up, as Jane stood awkwardly by, watching. The red chrysanthemums bled petals everywhere. Jane went out to the back for a brush to sweep them up, and bumped into George. He was heaving his trousers up as he came in, and both stopped in embarrassed shock as they met. George coughed.

'Em . . . what are you doing in here?'

'I came for the brush, Mr Beattie, to sweep up the fallen petals.'

'Ah. Better wait till the wreaths are done. You'll only have it to do again.'

171

'Thank you, Mr Beattie.'

'Has Dr Mrs Fletcher been in for her eggs yet?' Jane shook her head. 'Say "no, Mr Beattie".'

'No, Mr Beattie.'

'Then run next door, and get some.' She followed him out to the till and took the money he offered.

'Have your hens stopped laying, Mr Beattie?' she asked him. Adeline looked up sharply, then glanced at George, who had gone red. Harriet giggled, hiding her laughter by getting on with her work.

'Ask me no questions and I'll tell you no lies,' the mayor said.

'Oh,' Jane turned and left the shop.

She came back, minutes later, with a dozen eggs. George took them from her and inspected them carefully.

'Humph,' he said. Then he sighed, and opened up a drawer, from which he took glue, a few feathers, and some grit. These he pasted onto the eggs carefully, and then he gave four to his wife, four to Harriet and four to Jane. He turned his back, and went upstairs to the parlour. Adeline beckoned to Jane, and all three women went out into the back. Then, Jane watched as Harriet and Adeline ceremoniously lifted their skirts and dropped the eggs into their knickers. Jane couldn't believe her eyes. Harriet snorted with laughter. Adeline's eyes twinkled.

'A trade secret, dear,' she smiled. Jane concealed her eggs about her person, and all three walked back gingerly into the shop. They continued working. Adeline was watching the clock. 'Time,' she said. She picked up a basket from the counter, beckoned again and all three women went, as before, out into the back. They took out their eggs, and put them carefully into the basket, which Adeline then placed back on the counter. Five minutes later, Dr Mrs Fletcher came into the shop. 'Your usual, Modom?' Adeline asked her.

'Let me just check them first,' the lady insisted, picking up the eggs. 'Mmm,' she said, feeling the warmth, 'new laid today.'

'We've just been and collected them,' Adeline said with some semblance of truth. Then she put them in a paper bag, and the satisfied customer left the shop.

Jane was flummoxed. Her mouth hung open in shock. Adeline had to laugh at her, and so, in spite of herself, did Harriet. So those precious eggs the mayor had given her, all those months ago, those eggs that had been treated like royalty, hadn't been new laid at all! They had been bought like any others from the shop next door, and she, like Dr Mrs Fletcher, had been taken in. Jane felt disappointed and cheated, yet, she couldn't help laughing.

'What a performance!' she told Robert later that night. Like her, he could hardly believe it. They decided never to tell Ma Tully. The disappointment would probably kill her!

In fact, Ma Tully had had rather a lot to put up with lately, what with Rattler's accident and all. Bob Ridley came home to an avalanche of news, and could hardly get a word in edgeways as events were rained upon him from all sides. Rattler sat uncomfortably on the one easy chair.

'I'll never be the same again,' he wheezed. 'I've given over all pills and medicaments. They do you no good in the end.'

'They did no good to your end, that's for sure, Rattler!' Jack Purvis laughed at him. Ronnie smiled at the joke. He felt uneasy in the family atmosphere, but saw that Jack did not. He spread himself, and spoke out loud without apology, as though he had the right.

'I'll bet nowt as funny as that happened to you, on your trip, Bob!' Dandy laughed.

'It wasn't funny,' Rattler insisted from his easy chair.

'Oh, I don't know . . . ' Robert smiled.

'Well, as a matter of fact, our Ronnie here kept us in stitches.'

'Oh?' All heads turned to the two sailors.

'Aye. Remember that time in the Downs?' Ronnie squirmed, wishing the earth would open and swallow him up.

'Go on, Bob,' Jack insisted. Ronnie frowned. He hated Jack at that moment. But Bob obliged.

'Well, there was a bit of a summer gale, you know how it is down that way sometimes, and so we brought up, and Ronnie here, was down below, catching up on forty winks, like. Well, I was keeping my eye on this light steamer . . . '

'Damn nuisance them new fangled steamers!' Rattler put in.

'You echo my very sentiments old pal,' Bob agreed. 'Well, it was swinging in to anchor, and in rounding to the wind, it appeared to get hold of him, and he was coming straight for our bows. Well, I shouts below, "Get up on deck!" I says. And they all come up helter skelter like, except our Ronnie here . . . ' They all turned to look at him, amusement waiting to break out on their faces. Ronnie tried to smile, but his face cracked and it ended as a grimace. 'I shouts again. Still no Ronnie!' Ronnie's face was getting redder and redder. 'Well the captain and me ran forward to pay out our cable if we had to, but, to cut a long story short, he managed to go clear. An hour later, Ronnie here comes up on deck, and asks what all the fuss was about!' Everyone burst out laughing, and Ronnie tried to smile. 'And when we told him, he just said, "Oh I thought you were taking the mickey, like!" Taking the mickey! Mind he's a good lad for all that.' Ronnie felt like a dog that had failed to jump through a hoop and then got patted on the head because it licked its master. He was sick at heart. He knew Jane thought him a fool. A nice fool, maybe, but a fool. Ah well. He sighed, and looked at Jack. His grin was as wide as Shields harbour.

CHAPTER ELEVEN

Jane had been at Fowler Street for all of a week, and she was already asking for an afternoon off! She and Harriet had been set to arranging flowers for the Queen's. There was going to be a do there the following night, and Adeline was up to her elbows in the kitchen, cooking for it.

'You'll have to choose your moment!' she had said. 'I wouldn't ask him now. He's bogged down in paperwork. And he hates that!' When *would* be the right moment? Jane thought, as she helped Harriet in the shop. And would she recognise it when it came?

'White chrysanth!' Harriet ordered. Obediently Jane picked one out for her, and presented it carefully, stem first, much as a nurse might hand a scalpel to a surgeon. 'Tut,' Harriet shook her head, disdaining the flower, and Jane picked another, hoping it would meet with approval. Harriet took it, as though doing her a great favour, and added it to her arrangement. 'Pink roses! At least six!' she demanded. And Jane bent to the bucket of roses, choosing them carefully. 'You've got a cheek, I must say!' Harriet said. From her kneeling position by the bucket, Jane looked up to see her workmate looking down on her from a great height. 'Elizabeth never asked for afternoons off!'

'Robert *is* sailing to India!'

'So what!'

'I'll not see him again for ages.' Jane pulled out the required roses, and drained the water from them, before fetching them to the counter where Harriet was working.

'He's only your brother!'

'What do you mean, "only?" ' Harriet snatched the flowers from her and stabbed them into the arrangement. 'You haven't got any brothers or sisters, have you?' The realisation of Harriet's loneliness brought compassion to Jane's voice. It rankled her workmate deeply.

'No! All the more for me!' she said sharply.

'All the more what?'

'Everything!' There was no answer to that. Jane waited for the next order. 'What are you standing there for like a tin of milk!'

'I thought you wanted me to pass you the flowers.'

'Huh! Not much use when you *are* here, are you? You might as well take the afternoon off!'

'I've got to ask Mr Beattie first.'

'I'll ask him for you, if you like.'

'Will you?' Jane was amazed! Such altruism!

'I will if you'll do something for me.'

'What?'

'Scrub the cellar steps.'

Jane frowned. Surely Harriet didn't scrub steps, did she? They had a maid for that sort of thing!

'Does Mr Beattie make you do that?'

'Not usually. But with the do on at the Queen's, we *are* a bit pushed, and Edie's helping Adeline. Of course if you don't want me to ask him for you . . . ?'

'No. It's a good idea. Thank you.' Harriet smiled benignly.

'Wire!' she said. And Jane handed it to her.

Mr Beattie emerged at dinner time and peered over the railings down onto the shop floor where work was in progress. The smell of cooking wafted upstairs making him hungry and bad tempered. It was a headache this do at the Queen's. All the hoi polloi from the village would be there, and George felt not only his business, but he himself, as mayor, was also on trial. He stared moodily at the vases and baskets of flowers, which stood ready lined up on the floor. Was that pork he could smell? Was Adeline making raised pies? His mouth filled with saliva. His stomach rumbled. He pulled in his belt to the second notch, and descended the stair.

Harriet was nervous. She had the look of a dog expecting its master's wrath as George paused on the bottom step and surveyed the arrangements. Jane took a discreet step back, as the mayor reached out to a bundle of support canes and took one. He pointed it at Harriet May and she came out from behind the safety of the counter to stand by her handiwork. It was a tour of inspection. Jane suppressed her laughter, but it twinkled in her eyes. George used the cane like a baton, pointing it at a wilting flower head and propping it, before letting it fall again, as a hiss came through his teeth. So! The roses didn't come up to the mark! His cane parted them, and it was clear he thought them too bunched together. Jane heard the roses shuffle their feet further apart, obedient to the sergeant major. Even the lilies were at fault. They were in the wrong vases. They should have known it was a full dress parade. At the end of the line, George turned on his heel, stood stiffly, and glared at Harriet, who wilted like the flowers. Jane's mirth gave way to pity, for Harriet was twisting up her skirt in her fingers, in her agony. 'Who is responsible for this!?' George barked. Harriet burbled a few words. George pointed the cane at her. Her face was white. She pulled herself together, then said, 'Jane helped me.' George turned his wrath on the assistant. 'Is that so . . . ?' The last word was drawn out slowly like a sword from its scabbard. 'I only handed her the flowers!' Jane objected. Harriet snarled. 'Well I did! It's no use saying otherwise, Harriet May!' 'I see!' George said, and swished the cane over his shoulder. 'Perhaps you would have made a better job of arranging them. Do it!' Marching forward, he stopped at the stairs to dart a glance at the kitchen door, where Adeline and Edie stood trembling. They disappeared like puppets behind the awning when the show is over. And the Mayor stalked back up to his parlour.

'Well!' Harriet flung down a pile of ferns indignantly, and went upstairs to her room. For a moment, Jane stood as if struck by lightning. The vases and baskets of flowers stood in a long line before her. She had them all to do again! And what if she too

177

displeased her employer? She bit her lip, and went out into the kitchen to speak with Adeline.

'He has his own way of doing things, dear. Just don't have any ideas of your own and you'll be all right. Here, look in the catalogue.' She got one out. 'That's one of his favourites . . . autumn colours. He goes on about Harvest Home a lot at this time of year. He's very sentimental.' Armed with the information, Jane set to work. She would have to salvage the flowers already used. The white, she put with dried yellow and brown, wheat, cones, dried grasses of all sorts, even bullrushes, using separate containers inside the baskets, so that the flowers could have water, while the rest of the arrangement stayed dry. The pink roses, she mixed with bronze chrysanthemums. They made a hot arrangement, and the scarlet greenhouse carnations focussed the eye so that you didn't notice any clash of colour. It looked meant. She worked quickly, enjoying the challenge, and Adeline and Edie came out from time to time to peer from behind the door.

'It looks a bit original to me,' Adeline warned her, shaking her head doubtfully. Had Jane overdone it in her enthusiasm? Would he be angry with her? 'Not that I don't like it,' Adeline said, after a moment. The shop door clanged, and George walked in. The maid and the wife disappeared again. Jane stood to one side.

'I've nearly finished, sir,' she said. George frowned, stood back, and looked and looked and went on looking.

'So I see!' he said after a long time. The faces peered out again from behind the door. 'Why didn't you add some sheaves of corn and some baskets of fruit and be done with it?!' Jane's chest tightened in fear. The mayor darted her a look. 'You saw fit to improve on my design I see!'

'I'm sorry!'

'No matter. You'll learn.' Jane thought she was in the dog house, but Adeline beckoned from the kitchen, like a schoolgirl inviting her for a clandestine chocolate.

'He's pleased!' she announced.

'Oh!' Jane was amazed. If that was pleased, then what on earth was displeased? 'Is this a good moment, for you know what?' she asked.

'After his tea.'

Jane's face glowed as she came back into the shop. She stood for a moment, looking at her work with new eyes. She had pleased her employer! His wife had said so. She took in a deep breath, heavy with the scent of chrysanthemums. Then a slight rustle made her look up. Harriet was standing on the balcony looking down at her. Jane flushed.

'It's all right. He's pleased.'

'So I gather.' She came downstairs, swishing out her pink skirt that gathered round her feet like candy floss. Jane watched it longingly. 'A pity your taste doesn't extend to your dress!' Jane glanced down at her own brown flounce. 'Never mind. I suppose you can't help being poor!' Jane swallowed down her anger and humiliation. Harriet's voice carried the edge of a sharp dagger. Jane had made a fatal mistake in pleasing George Beattie, and she knew it.

'I'll still clean the cellar steps for you,' Jane volunteered, hoping by humility to please her.

'I should just say you will! Or I certainly won't ask him about your afternoon off.' Jane's jaw dropped. She knew very well, that after the flower business she would be better off asking her employer herself, but how could she say so to Harriet? She was trapped, and Jane had no option but to let Harriet get on with it.

Adeline had a dizzy spell at tea time, and had to go up to bed, attended by Edie, while Harriet kept the shop. George was over in his nurseries, which lay alongside the Queen's, facing them. He would stay in there for hours on end, lost in his plants and the uninterrupted peace. Jane had never seen them, but she knew there were huge glasshouses with all sorts of rare plants in them. It was the love of George's life. 'Well? What are you waiting for?' Jane frowned, and followed Harriet's look to the back of the shop. She meant that the time had come to scrub the cellar steps. Jane filled a pail of water in the kitchen and dropped a piece of soap into it. Then, gathering up her skirts, she tucked a brush under her arm and went towards the cellar door. She opened it, and stood for a moment looking down into the pitch black. The dark was almost tangible. It had a smell to it, a dank, foetid smell that made her want to retch. Propping open the door, she went for a candle, and lit it, then, turning her back to the cellar she began to scrub the first step. She stepped down, and scrubbed the second, and so on, bringing the candle with her, keeping it close. The chill permeated her clothes as she drew closer to the bottom. She had almost finished. Then the thing scurried, close by her feet, and in spite of herself, she jumped, knocking the candle from the step, and screaming. The candle had gone out. But there was still light coming from the door above. She turned to brave whatever was in the cellar with her. A pair of green eyes blazed at her. Dark things, beetles, spiders, cockroaches scuttled across the slabs of the floor, and the wet pools that lay on it. And then the door above banged shut. All light was gone. Where were they? Where were the horrible things she had seen? Where were those green eyes now? She shuddered, and felt the brown flounce of her skirt move, as something cold and damp touched her bare leg. She screamed and, turning, scrambled up the steps. Coming in from the nurseries, George heard her, and rushed to the cellar door. She fell at his feet as he opened it. He took her elbows and wrenched her up.

'What's the matter with *you*!' he shouted. Jane stopped screaming. Her face was white, and she was trembling.

'The door shut on me. I was scared. The candle went out.'

'The door to the yard's open. The wind must have slammed it. Sit down. Harriet! Some tea!' He sat by her watching as her shivering abated. 'There's nothing I hate more,' he said, 'than hysterical women!' Jane hung her head. George looked at the fair hair, as it fell over her face. 'Still,' he sighed, 'I suppose we've got to make allowances. You're still a child really.' His hand reached out and cupped her chin, raising her face to look at him. He was smiling. 'Still afraid of the dark, are you?' Jane tried to smile back, and nodded. Then she drank her tea, and George paid for a cabbie to take her home.

He had been so kind to her. He was a wonderful man. In some ways she was afraid of him, and yet, she knew, if she wanted to, Jane could wind George Beattie round her little finger. Curled up in her father's arms, Jane felt safe, and warm. She fell asleep, as they sat there by the fire in Trajan Street. The perfume of chrysanthemums filled her dreams, like a vapoury mist. It enticed her up into the house, into the parlour where the Beatties lived. Higher still into the bedrooms, where Adeline slept in white sheets, with lace on her pillows, and always the perfume of chrysanthemums. But something troubled her. Something stirred in her sleep. She jerked, and Bob looked at her, wondering what it was. Deep down in the foundations of the house were dark things, and she had not the light to see them.

The next day, Adeline and Harriet took the flowers over the road to set them up in the foyer and main rooms of the hall. Huge chandeliers hung above them. Gilt gleamed from the ceiling. Red carpets were laid for them. Jane felt like a queen, and was sad when their work was finished and they had to go back to the shop.

'It's all right about your afternoon off,' Harriet whispered in her ear as they crossed the road behind Adeline. Jane looked at her. 'I asked him. He said it's all right.'

'Oh. Thank you, Harriet,' Jane answered. She wasn't so bad after all.

As the time of his departure drew near, the web that tied Robert to his home tightened round him. He still felt the urgent need to escape, yet something held onto him. Jane's distress after the cellar business had shocked him. Deep in his own miseries he had almost forgotten her. He was torn by remorse, and vowed to make up for it in their last days together. They walked by the seashore as they used to, and talked about the old dreams.

'I wish I was going with you,' Jane sighed.

'Why? It's just a leaky old boat, that's all.'

'I've always wanted to go sailing. You know I have. And anyway . . . ' She paused, and her mind filled with the old pictures, and the old imagined delights of the east. 'You're going to India.' Robert laughed.

'Yes. It's funny, isn't it? It's you who always wanted to go there. Not me.'

'You did too!'

'Not as much as you.' He smiled at her sympathetically. 'I wish you could come. I'll miss you.' Jane's heart leapt. She threw her arms round him. He was her own beloved brother again. And she loved him. He hugged her and kissed her a loud smacker on the cheek which almost deafened her. 'What'll I bring you back?' he asked her. Her eyes grew large. He couldn't bring her the

Himalayas. He couldn't bring her a temple. He couldn't bring her an elephant. What could he bring her then?

'I don't want anything. Honest, Robert. All I want's you safe home again. Just as soon as you can.' Her eyes smarted with tears and, when they got home, she pulled out the Family Bible, to give him the pressed four leaved clover, which Chandrika had found for her. 'I wonder what became of him?' she said softly.

'Back working for P & O if he's got any sense,' her father said. 'You might look him up, eh, Robert?'

'I will. Aye. Why not? He was a canny bloke.' All remembered the night of his visit when magic touched Trajan Street. 'I wonder what he'd make of us now?'

Ronnie stood on the Lawe Top with Bob and Jane as Robert's ship sailed over the bar.

'Aye,' Bob said, with tears in his eyes, 'things'll never be the same again.' Jane suppressed a sob, and ran off, on her own, to the beach. There, she splashed through the surf at the water's edge, watching the shadows made by the sun as it dropped behind her. Her shadow lengthened, fading at its edge as the strength ebbed from the light. And then there was no shadow. And she stood alone, looking out over the sea.

Over their pints in 'The Globe', Bob confided in the younger man.

'They're a funny pair, my kids,' he told him, 'I mean, I know where I am with you. You're straightforward like, but them two, they're . . . well, they're a complicated lot. Beyond me!' He sighed. 'I've done me best but . . . ' He shook his head.

'Don't worry, Mr Ridley.' Ronnie touched his arm comfortingly. 'I'll watch over your lass.'

'Aye,' Bob looked at him, 'I wish it was you she fancied.' Both remembered the picture she and Jack had made together, the night Bob had come home. 'I don't know why it is, but my daughters seem to have a liking for pilots!' He laughed, and Ronnie smiled sadly. 'Aye, lad,' he said, his face darkening, 'watch over her.' Then he lifted his glass and drank deeply.

It wasn't fair! Harriet had lied to her! How could she have done it? She hadn't asked Mr Beattie's permission at all! He was

182

furious at Jane for 'skiving off' as he put it. He had a good mind to fire her on the spot. Who did she think she was? Jane trembled as the full impact of his wrath hit her. Her face was pink with the shame of it.

'You're a deceitful little slut!' he spat at her enjoying the words. 'Slut!' he repeated. How was it people wanted to call her that? Fanny loved to say that word. And now, the mayor said it. It wasn't fair! Crying on Adeline's shoulder later, she repeated her protest.

'Life's not fair,' Adeline told her. 'Do you think it's been fair to Harriet? Or me? Or Mr Beattie, come to that?' Jane looked at her mistress, mystified. 'There's not one of us content.'

'Why?'

'Think about it. There's George married twice, and no children of his own. I can't have any, you see. I always lose them.' Her voice was quiet, matter of fact. 'I bleed. There's times our hopes are raised, only to be dashed. Always the bleeding.' She sighed. 'And Harriet . . . ? Well, she's not a happy girl.'

'I know.'

'You see, George is a perfectionist. He expects those outside his family circle to be imperfect, but not those who bear his name. We have to live up to his ideal. And if we don't . . . !'

'What *is* his ideal?' Adeline smiled ironically. 'I think he wants us to be angels, my dear.' She laughed. 'Now, this dress of yours . . . ' Jane looked down at the brown flounce. It had been torn as she scrambled up the cellar steps. 'I wonder if our Harriet's got something that might fit you.'

Twirling in front of Adeline's glass, Jane thought she was in heaven. The simple stripes of blue and white poplin, held in at her waist by pins, flared out. She was the centre of a flower, and the petals revolved around her. Adeline smiled. She knew it would cheer her up. There was nothing like a new frock or a hair do! It always worked a treat for her. And it was working for Jane too.

'I knew you'd like it. It's far too small for Harriet now. I'm sure she's got plenty of new clothes for her new school. She won't miss this one.' Jane hoped so, with all her heart, but deep down, she knew her enemy. Harriet guarded her clothes as a

183

miser guards his treasure. She knew every fold of every dress, and, looking in her wardrobe at night, she drew solace from the racks of garments stored there.

'Are you sure she won't mind?' Jane asked hopefully.

'Too bad if she does. Serves her right for letting you in for it with George!' The wicked gleam came to Adeline's eyes. 'Do have it!' she said. Jane smiled. Such a small thing brought Mrs Beattie joy. How could she deny her? Especially when she wanted the dress herself!

Bob watched his daughter, as they sat by the fire in Trajan Street. She was engrossed in her sewing, the folds of blue and white spread across her knees. She was well provided for. She'd be all right now.

'I'm off again next week,' he told her. Jane looked up in surprise.

'Oh, Da! I shall be all alone!' she cried.

'That's why I went round to Pilot Street this afternoon,' he said. 'They'll be glad to have you!' Jane stared at her father, horrified.

'Do I have to?'

'There's gratitude for you! I thought you'd be pleased!'

'Fanny and me've never seen eye to eye, Da. You know that!'

'Well, you can't stay here on your own.'

'Why not?' Bob's look said, 'Do you need to ask?' And as she tried on the new dress, the soft curve of her waist drew her father's eye.

'Look in the mirror, lass, and you'll see why not,' he said quietly.

The dress had to be worn at work. Adeline expected it and would have been hurt not to see it. So Jane put it on the next day. Walking in from the back, Harriet stopped short on seeing her, and gasped.

'Where did you get that?' she hissed. Not allowing Jane time to reply, she rushed up to her and slapped her hard across her face, sending Jane reeling back, against the counter. 'You're a thief. That's what you are! A thief!' Then she ran upstairs calling out to Mr Beattie, 'Father! Father!' And he emerged from the parlour, in a fury at the disturbance. 'She's been in my room! She's rifled through my things! She's been stealing!' she

184

screamed. George frowned, and looked over the balcony at the girl below. Jane stood silhouetted against the light from the shop windows. Her hair, tied back, shone like a halo round her head. The perfume of roses wafted up from the floor. He looked at the wailing banshee at his side.

'Why don't you just shut up!' he growled. Leaving Harriet close to fainting, George quietly went back inside the parlour and opened his copy of Wordsworth.

Shades of school and stolen drawings closed about Jane. But this time, she had won. Harriet stood paralysed by impotent fury on the balcony above her.

'Mrs Beattie gave the dress to me,' Jane said quietly. 'She said you wouldn't mind.' Biting her lip hard, Harriet turned back up the stair to the upper floors of the house. She entered Adeline's room without knocking, but she wasn't there. Numb with rage, Harriet stumbled forward to sit on the nearest chair, at the dressing table. After a while, she saw her own face looking back at her. Her lip was white. She released her teeth, and there was blood on them. Dark, in the green reflected depths of the triple mirrors, the blood ran down Harriet's chin. And always, from the shop below, came the sweet perfume of chrysanthemums, while, in the midden in the yard, Adeline Beattie was being sick.

CHAPTER TWELVE

Ronnie was becoming something of a hanger on. Unable to get signed on another coaster, he had taken up the burden of his promise to 'watch over' Jane Ridley, as though it was the one purpose of his life. Jane was heartily sick of it. In the mornings, he would meet her at the Tully back door, and, carrying her things for her, would escort her the length of Mile End Road in concentrated silence. Then, Jane safely deposited at the yard gate of the Beattie establishment, Ronnie reluctantly took his leave, only after he had seen her pass through and into safety. In the evening, came the repeat performance. Ronnie would wait in the back lane of Fowler Street, kicking at a dog's bone, till Jane came out, and, dutifully, he saw her home.

With Harriet away at her school during the week, the shop had become an oasis of peace and civilisation; a pleasant change from the raucous atmosphere in Pilot Street, where Ma Tully shouted her commands, Fanny whined her complaints and Rattler moaned about his beam end. What would it be like when the bairn came? Jane shuddered, as she got on blocking in the flowers on the wreaths, sweeping out the shop, warming eggs, and cutting sandwiches for the countless 'teas' they were required to supply for the Boys Brigade, the Church centenaries, the old folks outings and so on and so forth. It wasn't all 'do's' at the Queen's Hall! There were times when crown roast gave way to paste sandwiches, and they were glad of the custom! George took a delight in teaching the new assistant all the tricks of the trade. But still they kept the secret of the toffee from her. Beattie's was famed for it, and all the confectioners in Shields were after the recipe. Even Harriet didn't know it, and if he could have made it himself, George wouldn't even have told Adeline. It had been the creation of the first Mrs Beattie, Harriet's mother.

'She of saintly memory,' Adeline said ruefully, as she prepared an order for Jane to take up to the village. It was Lady Redhead's birthday, and the shipping magnate had ordered a bouquet for the occasion.

'How can she have been so saintly?' Jane asked. 'I heard that Harriet's not got a father.' She blushed even as she spoke the words, and her colour deepened as Adeline looked sharply at her.

'We don't speak of that in this house,' she said. There was a pause. Then Adeline laughed. 'Jane Beattie was no saint, dear. Not until she died, that is.' Jane understood. George had raised his late wife to sainthood after her death, to please himself. 'It's a stick for him to punish me with.' Adeline sighed, put her hand to her back and leaned against the shelves.

'You look tired,' Jane told her, 'why don't you have a lie down?' Mrs Beattie shook her head.

'He'd notice.'

'A glass of porter, then. Ma Dunn swears by it. It puts roses in your cheeks, she says.'

'Why lass!' Adeline chuckled, 'you're bent on leading me to perdition!' Jane frowned, and wondered what she meant.

Jane enjoyed delivering the orders. After blocking, it was her favourite job. She'd never quite taken to warming eggs, especially after she'd forgotten about them and cracked half a dozen of them by sitting down. George had been furious, and Adeline had had to lend her some drawers. But delivering meant getting out of the shop, into the fresh air, and seeing how other people lived. It was a bit of freedom in her day. And there was no Ronnie to shadow her every movement. So her walk was light as she hurried up the hill towards the village, and passing in via the

187

tradesman's entrance, she delivered her flowers. There was no tip. 'Meanies!' Jane clanged the gate behind her and stomped back down the hill towards Fowler Street. It was two o'clock. Her lunch hour. She didn't have to go back just yet. True, she'd left her sandwiches in the back kitchen, but she could do without for once. It would be far nicer just to wander round the shops.

Walking down Ocean Road, she spotted Jack Purvis, coming out of an ironmongers. She stopped short, then wondering why she hesitated, went on again, and caught him up. Jack turned,

'Why hello pet!' he said with obvious pleasure. 'Where have you been hiding yourself?'

'In Pilot Street.' Her nose wrinkled. 'And at work.'

'Oh aye. How's it going, eh? How's the anemone?' Jane giggled, and she held her hand to her stomach.

'Ooh sorry.'

'What's a rumble or two between friends?'

'I've not had me dinner.'

'Well, that's easy mended.' Then he took her arm and guided her over the road, into a small restaurant, where the waitress seemed to know him, and gave them a cosy corner to sit in, well away from the window.

'I can't afford this, Jack!' Jane objected.

'It's my treat, pet.' Jane considered the proposition.

'Well, I suppose I never did get me whelks!' Then they grinned at one another and looked at the menu.

It was a relief to talk to Jack. Her feelings spurted out, and he listened sympathetically.

'It's the same old merry go round we had at school,' she told him. 'Ronnie irritates me, then I'm sharp with him, and then I'm sorry because he looks so hurt, and on it goes, till I'm dizzy!'

'He's a canny lad, mind.' Jack could afford to be generous.

'That only makes it worse! I feel terrible, but I mean I can't help it if I don't . . . ' Suddenly she hesitated, and her colour deepened. The word 'love' could not be spoken, not in front of Jack. Jack noted her stumble; he looked away, considerately, then said softly, 'It's not your fault, Jane. You can't help it if you don't return his feelings. Why, half the men in Shields probably fancy you, and you can't give your love to all of them now, can you?'

188

'The very idea!' Jane's voice squeaked, and heads turned towards them. Jack laughed.

'Sh.' He put his finger to his lips and Jane giggled.

'Sorry.' He looked at her as the waitress put their chops and potatoes in front of them, and then said,

'Do you know, I could fancy you myself.'

'You shouldn't say such things.'

'It's the truth.' Jane looked at him uncertainly then, unable to hold his gaze, she lowered her eyes and concentrated on cutting up her meat. Jack smiled to himself. 'Don't tell anybody about this, will you?' he said. Jane put down her fork and looked up again. 'I mean about our lunch date.'

'Oh no!' Jane reassured him. 'I'd hate you to get into trouble with your family.'

'Thank you. I was thinking . . . if we *could* keep it quiet, just between ourselves, you know, we could maybe do this more often.'

'What? Have lunch and that?'

Jack nodded.

'I don't know. Would it be all right?'

'You've got to eat!'

'That's true.'

'What could be more innocent than to meet up here and have lunch together from time to time?'

Jane considered the matter.

'It'd be nice.'

'Good!' Jack picked up his knife and fork, and ate as though it had all been decided. Slowly, Jane followed suit, and not for the first time in her life, wondered how on earth she'd got into it.

On her return to the shop, she found Adeline looking pale and ill.

'I thought you were never coming back!' she cried. Immediately Jane felt guilty.

'I met a friend. We had a bit of dinner together in the town.'

'Never mind. You're here now. Get me up to me bed.'

Jane took Adeline's arm, and helped her up. On the back of her white skirt was a spreading stain of blood. Jane said nothing. She knew what it meant. She supported her employer up the stair.

189

'Where's Mr Beattie?'

'Over the road. Please God he'll not be back for a bit.'

'Shall I get the doctor?'

'Edie's already gone for him. Now go back down and mind the shop.'

'I can't leave you!'

'Do as you're told!'

Jane ran back down the stairs. There was a lot of work to do, and feverishly she set about it. After half an hour, Edie came back with the doctor. He looked grim and angry as he went up the stairs to his patient. He had been up there for less than ten minutes, when George came home, and finding Edie crying in the kitchen, he immediately demanded what was up. At first she wouldn't tell, but under threat of damnation, she finally gave way and told him;

'The mistress has been taken ill.' George's face sagged. Suddenly he looked older. The fury went from him and he wandered back into the shop, where Jane stood, legs trembling, and pale. After a while, he saw her, and stumbled towards her, holding out his hand. His face crumpled and he began to cry.

'It's God's punishment!' he said. 'God's punishment.' Jane wondered what on earth Adeline had done, that God should punish her. But she said nothing, allowing the mayor to lean against her, and bury his face in her breast, sobbing. 'She was a saint. I was wrong to marry again. Wrong. It's God's punishment for my animal lust!' Jane was shocked. Never had she heard such words in her life.

'Mr Beattie!' she cried out, pushing him from her.

'You see! Even you reject me. Angel, that you are. And you're right. You're far above me. Far above me.' Then he stumbled away and went upstairs to his wife.

Leaving the premises, late that night, Jane was surprised to find Ronnie Wilson still waiting for her by the back gate. It was almost ten o'clock, and he had been there since eight.

'Are you all right?' he said at once. 'I saw the doctor come.'

'It was Mrs Beattie. She's lost another baby.'

'Oh. I'm sorry.' His voice was full of compassion. It touched her heart and suddenly, she found she was crying.

'It's been such a terrible day,' she said, as he gently reached out for her hand and held it warmly, 'such a terrible day!' After a while, Ronnie spoke. His voice was gruff with emotion.

'How is she?' he asked.

'She's still bleeding. She's that pale. The doctor says . . . ' Then she stopped. Ronnie looked at her, and in the dark street, they stood still, as his eyes searched hers. 'He says Mr Beattie's got to leave her alone after this.'

Ronnie nodded. 'Aye. Let's hope he does, then.'

Jane shuddered. 'I wish . . . '

'What do you wish?'

'I don't know really. That's the trouble. I don't know what's what any more.'

'How d'ye mean?'

'Well, love and that. I mean, I don't understand what it is.'

'You will when you feel it,' Ronnie's voice broke, 'like me.' Jane went cold. His tear-filled eyes shone at her out of the darkness. For a moment, there was something in the air, an energy that separated them from the people passing by. It was as though they had been lifted up, and she was giddy with the sensation. Their hands reached out and touched. Then he took hers, and held them tightly.

'If you need me, Jane, I'll be there.'

'I know. Thank you, Ronnie.' Then he kissed her gently on the forehead, and they walked home together.

Adeline lay at death's door for days. Harriet May was called home to help in the shop while Jane and Edie nursed their employer. George was morose, speaking to no-one, and going every morning to the Methodist Church down the road, offered up prayers for his wife's health. His tortured soul gave him no peace, night or day, and he was never to be found when he was needed in the shop. Jane had to go over to the nurseries to get him, when new orders came in. For he had to cost them, and would have wiped the floor with them if they had made up the estimates in their heads. Jane would wait upstairs in the parlour, by his side, as he hummed and haaed over the figures. On one of these occasions, after giving her the written estimate, George stopped her from going, with his hand.

'Stay here with me a while.' Gingerly she sat on the chair

beside him, and he reached for a folder. 'Read to me,' he said. 'Perhaps you have the power to calm the savage breast.' Doubtfully, Jane took a page from him, and began to read;

> . . . thus the Shadowy Female howls in articulate
>   howlings:

> 'I will lament over Milton in the lamentations of the
>   afflicted:
> My garments shall be woven of sighs and heart broken
>   lamentations:
> The misery of unhappy Families shall be drawn out into
>   its border.
> Wrought with the needle with dire sufferings, poverty, pain
>   and woe
> Along the rocky Island & thence throughout the whole
>   Earth;
> There shall be the sick Father and his starving Family,
>   there
> The prisoner in the stone Dungeon & the Slave at the
>   Mill . . . '

Jane's voice faltered. Was this the stuff to assuage a savage breast? George was crying softly. She went to kneel at his side. His hand reached out to hold hers. Finally his strangled voice broke out,
   'And they thought he was mad!'
   'Who, sir?'
   'Blake.'
   'I don't understand it, sir. The poem, I mean.'
   'No. But you can feel what he writes with your heart.' Jane shrugged. George sighed. 'Life is but a vale of tears,' he intoned. He was obviously feeling more like himself again, and Jane rose to her feet.
   'Shall I take this estimate down to Harriet?' she asked him. He nodded, but held onto her hand.
   'I'm going to try, Jane.'
   'Sir?'
   'For her sake, I will try. I will not cease from mental fight, nor shall my sword sleep in my hand, Jane.'

'No, sir.'

'Jerusalem, Jane.'

'Yes, sir.' Then he let her go, and Jane escaped his anguished soul at last.

The ritual of the Tuesday lunch with Jack buoyed Jane up through the weeks of anguish in the shop, and when she came back from them, she was always smiling.

'I think you must be in love!' Adeline laughed at her as she came to sit at her bedside afterwards. Then Jane blushed, denying the charge absolutely. 'Don't think I haven't seen him, hanging about, waiting for you to finish work! Why don't you bring him in some time? I'd love to meet him!' Jane stammered a 'thank you'. Her head was spinning.

'I'm not in love, though,' she insisted, thinking of Ronnie.

'I'll be the judge of that,' Mrs Beattie smiled.

So Ronnie was surprised to find himself invited into the kitchen, when he came to collect Jane that night. He held his hat in his hand, like any workman in the presence of gentry, and watched his p's and q's. Adeline was soft and gentle with him, as she sat, wrapped in a rug by the window; and the next morning, Edie had him in for a cup of tea, before the long walk back to the town end. Everyone liked him. He was 'a canny lad'. Jane, however, was anxious at this display of favour towards him. It was giving him ideas, and it caused her other problems too. George obviously disapproved of Jane's 'follower' as he put it, while Harriet was patently jealous. Nevertheless, the days of Adeline's convalescence were happy ones. The mayor was devoted to his wife. Everyone remarked on it. What a good husband he was! How lucky Adeline was! And, for a time, Jane was less a shop assistant, than a companion to both of her employers. She often read to George, from 'The Christian Endeavour', The Bible, Wordsworth, or Blake, or sat with Adeline, who took a delight in teaching her. 'Je suis, tu es, il/elle est, nous sommes, vous êtes, ils sont,' Jane repeated again and again as she blocked in the flowers, watered the plants, made the cakes, encouraged by both Mr and Mrs Beattie to better herself.

'Education's a fine thing,' the mayor told her. 'You can't get on without it. Look at me! Self taught! Latin, Greek, French, and

193

there's not a man in England who can teach me anything about painting or antiques.' His hand showed off the oils hung on the walls of the parlour, and the pretty furniture he had about the room. 'I was a miner. Did you know that? When I was twelve, I went down the pits, and look at me now! Mayor of Shields!'

Home for the weekends, Harriet watched Jane's progress with dismay. Jane had taken her place. Like an invading cat, she had been kept at first to the kitchen and the ground floor of the house. Then, slowly, the master and mistress had allowed her to infiltrate the upper regions, and then, little by little, she had been accepted. She was one of the family. What more had Harriet to fear? Jane had been given her blue and white dress, and then, later, a dark brown velvet dress, that she had loved two years before. She had stopped bringing sandwiches for her dinner and now joined the family at the table, and her young man also had his foot in the door.

'As a matter of fact,' Harriet said airily, one Saturday as they packed a hamper for the borough firework night, 'as a matter of fact, I've got a young man after me, too.' Jane looked at Harriet with interest.

'What's he like?'

'Rich. Good looking. To tell you the truth, he's a cut above Shields. He has connections in London, you know.'

'Oh I see. I *am* glad for you. Has he asked you to marry him yet?'

'Not yet. But he will.' She smiled smugly. 'Has your young man . . . what's his name . . . Ronnie? Has he asked you?'

'Em . . . no. No he hasn't.'

'Of course, what can you expect from the working classes. I suppose he drinks too.'

'Not much!'

'My father won't let a drop in the house!' Harriet sniffed, and tied the knot of the string too tightly over Jane's finger.

Jane thought no more about Harriet's young man in New-castle. She had enough problems of her own. Fanny went into labour on Guy Fawkes' night. She said a banger had started her off. The entire house was in an uproar by the time Jane got home. Ma Dunn had been sent for, and the men had been shooed out to commiserate in the pub, leaving the women to get on with it. Holding Fanny's hand, Jane was reminded of another night, not so very long ago . . . But the old dame was a good midwife, and Jane prayed that the child would be all right, that God had forgiven them for that other time, and would not punish them now. Fanny held a bottle of gin to her lips, 'to dull the pain' and howled loudly, while Ma Tully and Ma Dunn, at the other end, gave orders to push, and hold still, as the baby worked its way out into the world. Then, finally, it came.

'It's a boy!' Ma Dunn cried victoriously. Later, in 'The Globe', as the Tully family rejoiced, George resigned himself at last to becoming a foyboatman; for Dandy's son would inherit the pilot job, not he, and he put a good face on it, finally carrying his brother home to lie sprawled drunkenly across the hard chairs in the kitchen, while his wife slept with the baby upstairs.

Fanny had been lucky. She had had an easy time of it, and the boy was healthy. He was called Edward after the Prince of Wales.

'What do you mean after the Prince of Wales?' Rattler asked. 'I thought he was called after me!'

'Oh stop moaning, man! And just be grateful you've got a grandson!' his wife told him. If Jane had had her work cut out before, it was doubled now. To top it all, what with the baby crying and Rattler moaning half the night because he couldn't get comfortable on his beam end, she was getting little sleep, and it was beginning to take its toll. So, Ronnie paid for them to take the tram to Fowler Street, on the dark rainy mornings, leaving himself to walk all the way back alone, later, down to the ballast hill, to shovel with his father, earning a few bob, while he waited for a ship.

Adeline was deeply concerned. The travelling to and from the shop was obviously getting too much for Jane. And, in any case, the girl was needed early in the mornings to go to Newscastle. Surely it would be better if she moved into the shop? George said he'd think about it. Think he did. And he liked what he thought. Why, she was like a daughter to them already! He'd be glad to have her about the place.

'She's not having my room!' Harriet stamped her foot in the kitchen as the family discussed the suggestion after Sunday dinner.

'I will not have tantrums in my house on a Sunday!' the mayor boomed at her. And Harriet fled upstairs, to fling herself, crying, onto her bed. Was there no stopping this interloper? Was there no way she could keep that smarmy faced, conniving little bitch out!

The 'little bitch' was, in any case, not allowed to leave the Tully household immediately. She was far too valuable, while Fanny remained 'laid up' after the birth, and for this, Ronnie Wilson breathed a sigh of relief. For, once Jane was ensconced in the Beattie house, what excuse would he have to see her? He had now two weeks' grace, in which to consolidate his relationship to the extent of calling on her, once she was living in Fowler Street. Jane was out the back when he took it on himself to come and see her; and George for once was with Adeline in the shop. They were already taking orders for Christmas and business was getting brisk. He had never done it before, but, if he was going to be a caller at the place, Ronnie felt it was high time he took his courage in his hands and went in through the front door.

The bell clanged, and Adeline looked up. She was very surprised to see the young man she liked so much, and she smiled to him, indicating the whereabouts of the young lady, by nodding her head in the direction of the back. Ronnie nodded, and sat in one of the chairs, till Mrs Beattie should be free. George had also noticed him entering the premises, and he was less pleased. But deep in a financial discussion over a Christmas do at the Queen's, he was not free to question Ronnie's right of entry. Her customer dealt with, Adeline turned her attention on Ronnie.

'Can I help you, sir?' she smiled playfully. Ronnie laughed, his broad grin reached from ear to ear. She was a bonny woman that Mrs Beattie, bonny and kindly. He liked her a lot, and it was good to see her looking lively again.

'Aye, Missus,' he joked, 'you can. I'd like to buy one of them roses.'

'A red one?' Adeline asked, feigning astonishment. 'Now I wonder who that would be for?'

'I wonder,' Ronnie said, laughing, as she picked out the best one for him. 'I only wish I could run to a dozen, pet.'

'It's the thought that counts,' she said, and under the watchful eye of her husband, she had to take the lad's money. It was almost closing time. George's customer left, to consider his estimate, and Adeline left him to lock up, while she escorted Ronnie into the back.

Jane was making Christmas puddings. Her arms ached from stirring the heavy mixture, and there were beads of sweat on her brow.

'Oh hallo, Ronnie,' she said. 'Eeh is it closing time already?'

'It is, dear,' Adeline said. 'My you do look tired. What a shame you have to trek all the way back there. Tut! Never mind. Ronnie's got something to cheer you up.' She stood aside, and Jane, taking off her pinny, looked up to see Ronnie holding a single rose in his hand. She gasped in surprise. He was very bashful, feeling as awkward as he had ever done in his life. Adeline and Edie averted their eyes, and pretended to be doing things to the puddings.

'I'd like you to have this,' Ronnie said. Jane silently held out her hand and took the red flower. She looked at it for some time, then held it to her nose and smelt it. Her eyes lit up.

'It's got a perfume!' She turned to Adeline. 'Here, this one's perfumed. They don't usually have any smell when they come from the hothouses!' Ronnie was pleased, and there was joy in Jane's face. Adeline smiled gently, and began singing in a low voice,

O my Luve is like a red, red rose,
That's newly sprung in June:
O my Luve is like the melodie,
That's sweetly played in tune.

As Fair art thou, my bonny lass,
So deep in luve am I;
And I will luve thee still, my dear,
Till a' the seas gang dry.

As George turned the key in the lock of the shop door, his hand froze. He stood still for some time, listening, then walked slowly

197

into the kitchen. Sensing him, in the room behind her, Adeline's voice grew stronger, filled with emotion.

> Till a' the seas gang dry, my dear,
> And the rocks melt wi' the sun;
> And I will luve thee still, my dear,
> While the sands o' life shall run.

George came closer to Adeline's side, and she turned to him, as though she sang only for him.

> And fare-thee-weel, my only Luve!
> And Fare-thee-weel a while!
> And I will come again, my Luve,
> Tho' it were ten thousand mile.

There were tears on her cheeks. Slowly George bent, and kissed her on the mouth. There might have been no-one else in the room. And then, her hand gently pushed him away, and there was pain in both their eyes. George turned and left the kitchen, and Adeline silently got on with stirring the puddings.

Raising her apron to her face, Edie howled, and ran out to the lav in the back yard, where she could sob in comfort. Ronnie and Jane stood for a while, uncertainly, then putting on her cloak, Jane led him out into the cold night. Standing in the moonlight, she reached out and took his hand. He grasped it firmly, and together, they walked the length of Mile End Road, impervious to the cold, to the passers-by, or to anything the future might hold for them. The red rose was just a bud, but it would bloom for them yet.

The following Tuesday, Jane went as usual to meet Jack at the restaurant. Her heart was troubled, for she knew Jack had hopes of her. And now, with the sound of Adeline's voice ringing in her ears, 'My Luve is like a red, red rose . . . ' she knew she did not, could not, love him. She thought him fun, good natured, she liked him as a brother, and that was all. She would have to tell him so, come out with it, and clear her mind. Waiting for him, at their usual table, she braced herself to break the news.

Jack came in in high spirits. Without waiting for a 'good day' he slapped something on the plate in front of her and sat down.

'Take a look at that!' he said triumphantly. Jane frowned, and looked down at her plate. Two tickets lay there, white, fading to pale yellow, with gold, frilled edges. The tickets said, 'Potter's Circus. Sunday 17th December. 2 p.m. Row A'. Jane stared in disbelief. She was stricken dumb. She looked up at Jack who was silently laughing at her. 'See? I hadn't forgotten.'

'Where's it to be?'

'The Bents. Look, it tells you on the ticket.'

Jane looked, and sure enough it said 'The Bents. South Shields'. It was true. Really true. Jack was going to take her to the circus! Suddenly, she couldn't help herself, she yelped with joy.

'Will there be elephants, and tigers, and horses, and trapeze people and everything?'

'And everything,' Jack took her hand and kissed it, his eyes intent on hers. For a moment, Jane had an impulse to take her hand away. She frowned. 'What's wrong?'

'Nothing. I'm ever so grateful, Jack. You're a good brother to me.' And now it was Jack's turn to frown. 'Do you remember, on the beach that day, you said you'd look after me, be like a brother to me?' Jack smiled and nodded. 'Well, I am grateful. You've helped me such a lot. I don't know how I'd have got through these last months without you.' This was better. Jack was smiling again.

'Good. Now remember . . . don't let on to a soul.' Jane laughed.

'Is your mother such a harridan, then? Would she really turn you out of the house just for being my friend?'

'You don't know my mother. And there's the rest of them. And what about my job? I'm a pilot, pet. One of the clan. The job goes with it.' Jane nodded.

'Yes, of course,' she said. 'I won't let on. I promise.' Then he winked at her, and she winked back, and together, they toasted the circus with lemonade.

The following weekend, Jane moved into Fowler Street. Ronnie helped carry her things, and there wasn't much. But they had to be taken all the way up three flights of stairs to the attics, where Jane had been given a bedroom, next to Edie's. 'The servants' quarters,' Harriet informed her.

'Of course,' Jane said, 'that's what I am. A servant.'

'Now, come on Sundays, for your dinner, after worship, young man. But I don't want you sniffing round here at any other time. Understood?'

'George!' Adeline remonstrated.

'Understood,' Ronnie agreed, and left Jane to settle in, smiling encouragingly at her, as she saw him off down the lane.

'Did you have to speak to him like that!' Adeline whispered.

'I like folk to know their place, wife,' he said dryly, and went into his parlour to read something improving.

Edie had set a fire in the grate, and the flames flickered comfortingly, as Jane set about her unpacking. Her old clothes looked out of place even in this humble room. On the wall was a picture of Jesus. On the bare boards of the floor was a solitary rug. The bedstead was made of iron, and the bed creaked when she sat on it. But it was comfortable. She breathed deeply, trying to settle her nerves. She could smell the pungent perfume of chrysanthemums. It was getting stronger. The perfume crept up the stairs, round the corners, and under the door. Adeline must be spraying them in the cellar, deep under the house. Jane shuddered. A crack in the pane of the dormer window let in a cold draught. She held out her hands and felt it on the palms. Her fingers tingled, then they too felt the breeze. Her brain emptied, and the image of her 'hephalant' came into her mind. Yes, that was what the room needed! She took it out of her bag, and placed it on the wall above the mantelpiece. She looked at it for a long time.

CHAPTER THIRTEEN

There was news of Robert at last! Late on Monday evening, Ronnie ran round to Fowler Street, glad of the excuse to see Jane again before the following Sunday. He ran in the back door, to find the family sitting to their supper.

'What's the meaning of this?' George barked.

'I'm sorry to offend and that, Mr Beattie, sir,' Ronnie panted, 'but there's a letter for Jane from her brother, and there's news of her Dad as well!' Jane almost jumped out of her seat. Restraining her enthusiasm, she looked at George, who gave his permission to leave the table. She took the letter, trembling. It had been opened. Fanny had seen it already.

'Is he all right?' she asked.

'Aha! He's in Bombay, and your Dad says *he'll* be home for Christmas!' Jane squealed with delight. Then she calmed herself.

'Mind, I've heard that before! I'll believe it when I see it!'

'The Tullys've all gone round to "The Globe" to celebrate!' Jane gave Ronnie a warning look.

'What, may I ask, is "The Globe"?'

'Em . . . ' Ronnie looked uncertainly at Jane, who smiled. It was too late. He might as well tell him. 'It's a public house, Mr Beattie, sir.'

'Do you mean to tell me that your family frequents public

houses!' Jane looked at her clodhoppers, shamefaced. 'It seems to me, that your advent in this house was not before time!' George rose from the table, folding his napkin, and went upstairs to his parlour.

'I'm sorry, Jane,' Ronnie said, after he'd gone.

'It's not your fault. And anyway, I can hardly be blamed for my family, can I?' Edie, who took her meal after the family, began clearing away, and Mrs Beattie motioned Ronnie to sit with her.

'You'll take some tea, Ronnie, dear?'

'I don't mind if I do, Mrs Beattie.'

Deep in her letter, Jane did not listen to the conversation between Adeline and Ronnie. Robert was a good letter writer, and interspersed through his paragraphs were little drawings of what he had seen. He had sketched a man carrying five cases on his head. She turned the page, and read;

'Chandrika is once again working for P & O. I found him unloading luggage for the nobs arrived from England. They don't half look funny in their lace and petticoats. Chandrika took me to his home, after he finished work. He's married now, and his little wife's sweet. She's expecting already! Who'd have thought it! He's asked me to stay on with him for a bit, and maybe see a bit of India, while I'm here. I think I might, if Ropers will let me. Chandrika sends his regards. He really likes you, I can tell. But I doubt if he'll ever come to England again, not with a wife and family here. He confided to me that his marriage had been arranged. Can you believe it? I was quite shocked. But he says that it usually works out for the best. And when I asked him about love, he said he loves Shakuntala more every day. She's a shy creature, and worships the ground he walks on, so I'm not entirely surprised! When I asked him how marriages got arranged, he said they look at their horoscopes, to see whether it would work out . . . '

With one eye on Jane, to make sure she wasn't listening, Adeline began to probe Ronnie's suitability.

'When's your birthday?' she asked him.

'April.'

'What date?'

202

'The 23rd, Mrs Beattie.'

'But that's Saint George's Day! Fancy that!'

'Is it? Eeh, well now!'

'So! You're a Taurus are you?' she smiled, watching him eat some leftovers with Edie. He certainly had a Taurean appetite.

'I'm Pisces,' Edie said.

'Don't eat with your mouth full, dear. You'll choke.'

'Sorry, Missus,' Edie suddenly started spluttering and coughing. Her breath came in loud rasps.

'Help! I'm dying!' she gasped.

'I told you, Edie!' Jane looked up from her letter, and Ronnie punched the unfortunate Edie on the back. One last bark, and she was breathing normally again. 'Thank you, Ronnie. Most helpful.' One long hard look to Edie, and Adeline told Ronnie he might sit down again. 'Jane's birthday's in September. She's a Virgo.' Ronnie blushed. Adeline suppressed a smile at his little misunderstanding. 'You certainly ought to be compatible,' she said.

What on earth had they been talking about? Jane wondered. She looked from one to the other. Adeline looked decidedly pleased with herself, and Ronnie was blushing. Dear, sweet Ronnie! She couldn't help feel sorry for him! She smiled at him, and he grinned back. Shovelling potatoes into her mouth, Edie had no interest in the more delicate nuances of the conversation. But Adeline was sensitively tuned, and she could see the lad was slowly winning. She wished him well. He might not be a millionaire. He might not be the brightest brain in the north, but he was 'a canny lad'. He'd take care of Jane, and perhaps, in time, George might see fit to give him an opening in the business. Her mind dreamed on, pink clouds and twinkling stars formed the decor of the play she wrote for the young people. A wistful expression touched her face, and she smiled a little sadly. If only . . . if only . . . she could have rewritten her own love story . . .

Jane saw Ronnie out into the lane. They stood silently for a while, looking up at the stars. The moon was waxing. Its light touched the damp tiles of the roofs, and highlighted the sides of the chimney stacks.

'Shall I see you Sunday, then?' Ronnie asked. Jane shivered.

'No. I've got something on. But I'll be calling in at Pilot Street first thing, for church, if you want to come.'

'Aye. All right. Are you cold?' He was taking off his jacket to give her.

'No. It's all right.' She turned towards him and for a long time, stared up into his face.

'You're the nicest lad I ever met,' she said at last. 'Nicer even than our Robert.'

'I'm flattered!' he grinned.

'You should be.' Her face was serious. His hand reached out to graze her cheek gently. His touch was cool against her skin. 'Cold hands, warm heart,' she said, remembering the old ladies in the pub the night she'd looked for Fanny. 'Ronnie . . .' her tone was urgent. His heart jumped. Then she paused, and her face fell demurely. 'Never mind.'

'No. Tell me, pet.'

'Another time, eh?'

'Whatever you say.'

'Best go now.'

'Aye.'

They stood for a few moments more, savouring the night. Then Ronnie turned.

'Tarrah, then,' he said.

'Tarrah. Be seeing you.' And he disappeared down the dark lane.

The following day, Jane went, as usual, to the little restaurant in Ocean Road. There was a hint of snow in the air. For once she was glad of her clodhoppers on the icy pavements. She felt nervous about this last meeting with Jack, but the sharp ring of her boots on the path told of her determination finally to come clean with him. The waitress was surprised to see her.

'You're early!' she said. 'All the same, pet, I'm sorry, but you've just missed him.' Jane frowned. How could that be? 'He's left a message for you.' Jane took it from her and read;

'Dear Jane,
The tide waits for no man. I've got to go out with my uncle in the coble. There's a big Norwegian ship due in, and being

204

Christmas we could do with the money. See you at a quarter-
to-two on The Bents on Sunday.

　All the best, Jack.'

The waitress watched her curiously as she read. Jane nodded
to her.

'Thank you,' she said, and left the restaurant. He had fore-
stalled her. There was a sick feeling in the pit of Jane's stomach,
a rising panic. She had wanted to tell him today, that her feelings
for Ronnie had changed. It was important. Every instinct told
her so. And now, what could she do? She could not contact Jack
at the Pilot House, or the sheds, or his home, where the rest of
the clan lived and he would not come to Fowler Street. There
was nothing for it. It would have to wait till Sunday. She would
tell him then. If only Robert hadn't gone away. He could have
advised her, perhaps even talked to Jack for her. Rushing on
down the street, Jane seemed to be running away from something. What? She had done nothing wrong! Had she? Jack was a
brother to her. She only needed to make it plain to him, that he
could never be anything else. Her feet raced on. Her mind
chattered. She had no peace. Clattering early into the shop, she
surprised Adeline, who looked up from the pile of holly she was
cutting.

'How was your friend?' she asked, smiling.

'Mrs Beattie. Can I talk to you, please?' Adeline raised her
eyebrows.

'Yes, of course.'

'I'd like to tell you about my Tuesday dinners . . . '

'It's all right dear. I've known for a long time who it was you
were seeing.' Jane was startled. She blushed, and Adeline
laughed. 'Take off your cloak, and help me with this.' So Jane set
herself to make up holly wreaths, pricking her fingers till they
bled, as though she was punishing herself.

Ronnie had found a ship at last. His father had got wind of something, down at the ballast yard, and sent Ronnie round to 'Bella
Booth's' where the captain was known to drink. The cobbles of
the Long Bank were slippery. Ronnie skidded down towards the
door of the pub, and stopped himself, holding onto the doorpost,

to get his breath. Inside, the fug had brewed nicely. A ship had just come in, a Norwegian schooner. Jack Purvis, as its pilot, was standing the round. He saw Ronnie at the door, and invited him in.

'Howway, man! You're just in time!'

'Who's this?' the captain asked.

'Ronnie Wilson. He's a ballast worker.'

'Only till I get another ship,' Ronnie put in.

'Ah,' the captain nodded slowly, 'I'm short of a man or two myself. How are you fixed after Christmas?'

'Oh! I'm available. Wher're you going, like?'

'The Baltic. Mind it's a bit rough this time of year! Gets iced up, ye kna!'

'I don't mind.'

'Good lad.'

'I'm a good cook!'

'Are you now? Why, you can come down and help my missus with the Christmas dinner! By the time she's finished with it, I can never tell whether I'm eating pig or chicken!' Ronnie laughed.

'How's your teeth?' he asked. The captain bared his gums.

'Oh, well you'll like it falling off the bone, eh?' The captain smiled. 'I can cook it so it melts in your mouth, man.'

'That's it! Come and see me, down at the office, Boxing Day. You can get signed on.'

'Great! Ta!' Ronnie downed his pint with relish. It tasted better with the prospect of a ship in view. 'Thanks, Jack,' Ronnie beamed across at the man he considered to be his benefactor.

'For what?' Jack shrugged and ordered another round.

Excitement gave Ronnie the courage to brave Fowler Street once again. Peering in through the shop window, he saw Adeline alone at the counter. It was snowing. Flakes had built up on the panes, and the glass was misted. Looking up, Adeline saw an eye looking in at her. She stared back at the eye and it winked. Then she smiled, and indicated to Ronnie that he could come in.

'Where's his nibs? I mean . . . '

'I know what you mean. He's at a council meeting. They're arranging the children's parties. They have a big one for the poor in the town hall every year.'

206

'Oh. Aye. I went to one of them. It were grand.' He shifted awkwardly from foot to foot, and glanced over to the back of the shop. Adeline's eyes twinkled.

'She's out delivering. I'm sorry.'

'Oh.' Ronnie's disappointment surprised Adeline. 'What's the matter with you? You're surely not missing her already?'

'What do you mean?'

'Why, you only saw her lunchtime!' Ronnie frowned. 'Now come on. I'm not daft. I know all about it.'

'About what, Missus?'

'You and Jane! Your Tuesday rendezvous! Regular as clockwork! Tut! You can't pull the wool over my eyes!'

'Oh. No.' Ronnie was at a loss. What was it all about?

'So what's happened since one o'clock today!'

'I've got a ship!' Ronnie's excitement returned. 'I'm off after Christmas.' Adeline's face fell, then she made a valiant attempt to look pleased.

'Well, now, that's good news, Ronnie,' she said, 'mind, she'll miss you.' And then, she added quietly, 'and so will I.' She bent over the counter and kissed him lightly on the cheek. 'You're a canny lad. She couldn't do better. You'll get on. You'll see.' Not knowing whether to feel happy or sad, Ronnie left the shop. Walking home, he pondered over what Mrs Beattie had said. He couldn't make head nor tail of it. But it had set him worrying. There was something going on that Ronnie definitely did not like.

Sunday 17 December dawned crisp and bright. Jane had permission to join her family at Saint Stephen's for worship, then spend her Sunday with them. Splashing her face in the cold water Edie brought her, she considered the day ahead. A mixture of excitement and apprehension filled her. She wished Robert had been with her. What would he say, if he knew she was going to see a real live elephant at last? She looked over to her mantelpiece where Robert's letter lay, alongside the fading rose Ronnie had given her. Its petals were close to dropping. Yet she had not the heart to take it out of its vase and throw it away. She smiled, as she looked at it. Ronnie and Robert. The two dearest people in her whole life. And both of them sailors! She had

207

grown used to Ronnie. He had always been there, ever since she'd started at Fowler Street. She would miss him terribly when his ship sailed. She sighed. Downstairs, in the kitchen, George Beattie was having his weekly bath before church. He was singing loudly. She could hear him, three flights up.

Everything changes, but God changes not:
The power never changes that lies in His thought:
Splendours three, from God proceeding,
May we ever love them true.
Goodness, Truth and Beauty heeding
Every day, in all we do.

Listening, Jane's eyes passed up from the rose, to Robert's drawing of the elephant. Its edges were curling, and the paper was yellow with age.

Truth never changes,
And Beauty's her dress,
And Good never changes,
Which those two express:
Splendours three, from God proceeding,
May we ever love them true.
Goodness, Truth and beauty heeding
Every day, in all we do.

The draught from the broken pane stirred something over the drawing. Raising her eyes farther, Jane noted a spider's web resting on the picture rail over the elephant. It fluttered in the icy breeze. She fetched a chair and reached up, trying to dislodge it. But, stretch as she would, she could not touch it. She would have to speak to Edie about it tomorrow. Shivering from the cold, she threw her cloak round her, and set out on the long walk to the town end.

Saint Stephen's was full. It was the third Sunday before Christmas, and the strange magic of the approaching festival was already in the air. Arriving late, Jane sat in the back of the church, and knelt briefly to pray. The Reverend Morton was already reading the first lesson.

'O Lord thou art my God: I will exalt thee, I will praise thy name; for thou hast done wonderful things; thy counsels of old are faithfulness and truth . . . '

Peering over the heads in front of her, Jane looked to see where her family were. There were the Purvis clan down near the front, but no Tullys, not so far as she could see. Whatever had happened to them?

Dressed in their Sunday best, Rattler, Ronnie and Dandy sat stiffly in the Tully kitchen, watching Bob Ridley eat. He had come in on the morning tide, and they could hardly leave him, even if it was Sunday morning! For once Saint Stephen's would have to do without them.

'By, we could have done with you on this voyage, Ronnie!' Bob said between mouthfuls. 'We starved to death, man! I thought I'd choke on them dry biscuits. Mind the captain had bread.'

'Aye. He would,' Rattler shifted uneasily on the hard chair and his wife passed him a cushion.

'Eeh it's grand to be back!' Bob looked round him, and his eye rested on the cradle by the range. A tear came into his eye. 'He's a bonny bairn, our Fanny. Aye. You've done us proud. Well done, pet. And you, Dandy O. Eeh aye! What a homecoming, eh?'

'All we need is our Jane!' Dandy said.

'Aye. Where is she? I thought she was coming here, so we could all go on to the church together.'

'She won't know you've got back, Mr Ridley,' Ronnie said. 'She's maybe been kept at the shop. They're busy this time of year. Look, why don't I go and get her, eh?'

'Good idea, son,' Bob nodded, and Ronnie, all decked out in his best clothes, set out on the old journey, along the Mile End Road.

They weren't there. That was for sure. Jane turned her eyes away from the Purvis clan, where Jack stood with his family, and searched the congregation, chattering outside the church porch after the service. No they weren't there! She had better go down to Pilot Street and see what was up. A fine mist was coming in from the sea. The salt stung her nostrils, but at least it kept the frost and the ice away. Quickly, she turned down to Pilot Street, and fell straight into the family gathering. Suddenly all her cares were quite forgotten. Brushed away by the sight of her father, her fears and troubles vanished. As the mist deepened outside the windows, she listened to her father's tales of his voyage, told him the contents of Robert's letter, and the time sped by, till suddenly the dinner was ready, and the whole family sat down to eat it.

Ronnie barged in just as Edie was serving the Sunday roast. The family were upstairs, resting after the service down at The Glebe Chapel.

'What do *you* want?' Edie shrieked. 'You're not expected!'

'Where's Jane?'

'Gone down to see her family. Didn't you know?' Ronnie frowned. So, then, he had come all this way for nothing? How was it he had missed her? Better go back, make sure she was there safe and sound. The salt fret scalded his lungs. He was breathing hard, as he ran back along the Mile End Road. His mind was ringing out alarms. Why did she not turn up at the Tullys? She'd set out from Fowler Street, saying that was where she was going, and she had been expected! So, what had happened to her? The vague feelings of unease that had been troubling him all week now nagged at him painfully. There was something wrong. Like a dog on the scent, he had to follow where his instinct led and track her down.

There was nothing wrong now. Jane left her father, Dandy and Rattler at the door of 'The Globe', and took herself off to The Bents. 'Have a nice time, pet!' her father called after her. 'Mind you don't get eaten by any of the lions!' And Jane had laughed, her feet skipping lightly over the cobbles, as she took the sea road south to the circus. No. There was nothing wrong. She would pay for her ticket at the entrance gate, and she and Jack would have a grand time, and she would tell him about Ronnie, and he'd be pleased for her and everything would be all right. The mist drew about her like a veil, but she hardly noticed it. She was bubbling over in her excitement. And as she approached The Bents, she saw the Big Top looming up out of the mist. She

210

hurried on, lifting her skirt as she ploughed through the wet grass. There were caravans, people, and animals everywhere. Suddenly there was a loud braying noise; it made her jump out of her skin. It was like a cross beetween a fog horn and an ass, only much, much more powerful. What had her father called it? A trumpet? If it was a trumpet, then it was the *last* trumpet and no mistake! It made the hairs stick out on the back of her neck. She turned, and saw a huge grey thing coming towards her out of the mist.

It seemed to roll from side to side. It flapped its huge ears from time to time, and it had a long, long trunk. So, that was an elephant, was it? Jane was rooted to the spot. She watched it coming nearer. Its trunk swung loosely from side to side as it walked, and its huge feet fell softly on the ground. She was not afraid. There was a gentleness about the creature. Drops of mist hung on its lashes, and its eyes were half shut. A man was leading it towards the side of the tent. Suddenly Jane's legs began to move. He was taking the creature away from her. She rushed up to him, and the elephant turned and raised the lids of its eyes to look at her.

'Yes, Miss? Lost your way have you?' The man's accent was strange, southern.

'Is that an elephant?' Jane asked breathlessly.

'Well, it's not a bunch of flowers, that's for sure!' He laughed raucously and Jane forced herself to smile. The elephant was nosing her with its trunk. She giggled.

'It tickles!' she said.

'He likes you. You're honoured.'

'He's very handsome.'

'Wait till you see him in his party frock!'

'Has he got a name?'

'Jumbo. The usual. You know.'

'Can I stroke him?' The man shrugged and Jane reached out her hand to touch the wrinkled, grey skin.

'He won't feel anything. You've got to kick him really hard for it to register, at all!'

'You don't, do you?'

'Only now and then. Just to tell him what to do.' The trunk had slid behind Jane's back, it crept round her waist. She squealed in fright. 'It's all right, he won't hurt you. Gentle as a lamb, he is. He wants to give you a ride.'

'A ride?'

'That's right. He'll lift you onto his back and set you down.'

'Oh!' Jane didn't seem to have much choice in the matter. Jumbo was determined. The trunk tightened. 'He's squeezing me!' Then, as though he'd heard her, the elephant loosened the grip slightly, before lifting Jane up and depositing her on its back. 'Oh my God!' she cried out, and started laughing half with fright, half with excitement.

'Hold onto its ears. You'll be all right.' And then the man led the elephant and Jane, away from the tent, and she held on, rolling precariously, as the animal took her round the perimeter of the Big Top. Then, slipping to one side, Jane let him wind his trunk about her, and set her carefully down on the ground again.

'Oh, that was wonderful!' she cried out, and nestled her face into the elephant's side. The trunk swung from side to side, clonking her gently. It was time for him to go. Jane stood back, tears streaming down her cheeks. 'That was wonderful. Thank you. Thank you very much.' But her eyes were on the elephant, not the man. The elephant, like a ship, swayed away from her, and went on, inside the tent.

Had she really seen it? Had she actually ridden on an elephant? She could not believe it now, as she met Jack at the main entrance. And he certainly did not believe it.

'I did! I did!' she cried. He laughed at her, and took her arm, escorting her to their places inside. Once seated, Jane remembered about the tickets. She fumbled in her bag for the money. 'Oh, Jack, before I forget, I want to give you this.'

'What is it?'

'For my ticket. I can't let you pay for that!'

'Don't be daft!' He pushed the money away. 'A man always pays for his girl.' Jane frowned.

'Yes, but I'm not your girl.' Jack's heart stopped. She was looking at him steadily. 'Am I?' His face was pale, as he started breathing again, then he flushed quite red.

'Of course you are!'

'No, I'm not. Jack . . .'

'If you're not my girl, what are you doing here?'

'You asked me.'

'Yes. Of course. Because you're my girl. And if you're not, then what the hell are you?' Jane went cold. The ringmaster had come into the arena.

The clowns had come on, and were tumbling round and round. They had sparklers in their hands, and in the misty atmosphere inside the tent, the four of them made a sort of Catherine Wheel spinning round and round the central pole. It made her feel dizzy. Jane took a deep breath. She would have to talk to Jack afterwards. They sat stiffly side by side in the best seats, watching, as the show went on. The jugglers came first, and then the clowns again. After them came the horses, and while they set up the cages for the cats, the clowns came and did their slapstick as a fill in. The lions roared. Their trainer cracked his whip. And then it was the interval. Everyone jumped up and started rushing about. But Jane and Jack sat still. She hardly dared look at him. Through the corner of her eye, she saw that his face was pale, and he was biting his lip. There was blood on it. She was sorry for him. It was all her fault. She had misled him. She had not meant to. He had thought more about her than she'd realised.

Jack kept his eyes fixed on the ring. The master came back, and the whip cracked again. He heard it sharp against the air, as he flicked it up and down. It was like gunshot. And then the clowns came, and then the dogs, doing their little tricks, and then, finally, the star turn. 'Jemimah and her team of elephants.' Jemimah was a little girl. She was sitting astride Jumbo as he walked slowly into the ring, followed by another five elephants of all shapes and sizes. At the back, its trunk wound round its mother's tail, trailed the baby of the family. Everyone went 'ah', even Jane, in spite of Jack. She could not help it. The man who had been leading Jumbo when Jane had seen him outside came in last, dressed in a spangled suit. Jumbo himself had red crêpe flowers festooning his bridle. His 'party frock', no doubt. Obediently, the elephants put their front legs on stools, then their back legs, then danced round their stools, then danced round each other, then stood on their hind legs, and trumpeted, their trunks raised high in the air. Jane's happiness ebbed slowly as she watched. The animals did as they were bid, but were merely

213

going through the motions, uninvolved. They were not enjoying what they were doing. Jane tried to imagine them in their native habitat. 'Once upon a time, in a place far away on the other side of the world, there lived a little baby elephant. It was a happy elephant, and it had a happy life, with its mother and father and its brothers and sisters, as they roamed about the forests together . . . ' There were trees, and rivers, and lakes for them to drink at, not just sheaves of hay and buckets of water. They were noble creatures, and she felt ashamed to be watching them perform such demeaning tricks. At the end of the act, Jumbo led his family round the perimeter of the ring, while the audience applauded. As he passed Jane, he swung his trunk towards her, and trumpeted. She reached out, trying to touch him, but Jack pulled back her hand. 'Don't be stupid!' The moment had passed, but one of the crêpe flowers had fallen onto the barrier between them. Jane bent forwards and picked it up. It was shaped like a little red rose. She watched the elephants file out of the ring, and the show was quite over.

The mist had thickened, by the time Ronnie reached Pilot Street.

'She's gone to the circus with a friend,' Ma Tully told him. Ronnie's stiff collar chafed his neck. He loosened it and pulled it away from his skin, which was red and sore. 'Sit down and have a bite to eat, lad. You look all in! She'll be back for her tea!' But he would not wait. He was besieged by a panic. 'Is something wrong?' she asked him. Ronnie shook his head. How could he tell? He had made a promise to Jane's father, to watch over his lass, and something, someone had enticed her from his protection. Who was the friend Jane had gone with? Suddenly, he made the connection. 'Tuesday'! The word rang out in his ears again and again. 'Tuesday', 'Friend'. The words became interchangeable. Well, he would go to The Bents, and see who the friend was. It was his sworn duty. And if the friend was a man? His breath caught in his throat. He quickly thanked Mrs Tully, and left the house, charging off down the coast road south.

If it was a man, well and good, just so long as she was safe. His loss would be the other's gain. But, if Jane should be in any danger . . . ! His pace quickened. It was late. He must hurry, or he'd miss her again. The mist had thickened into a fog. The ships blasted warnings far out at sea. The bell tolled on the Groyne. There were people coming towards him. The circus was out. He was too late! He'd missed her!

'Jack, I've got to talk to you.' Jane held onto Jack's arm as they left the Big Top. He was going too fast for her, dragging her along, as he went, ploughing through the wet grass. 'Where are we going?' He stopped, and she pulled up short beside him, bumping into him. 'I thought you said you would be a brother to me.'

'Hah!' his laugh was a bark, like gunshot to her ears. 'You led me on!'

'I didn't mean to. I didn't realise. Not until it was too late.'

'You knew all right. What's wrong? Found another man, have you? One of the nobs up the village taken a fancy to you, has he? How much did he pay you?' Jane stepped back, speechless with shock. He grabbed her wrist and held it hard. She stared up at him, her lips quivering with fear. She stammered out,

'You don't understand . . . '

'Oh no?' Still holding onto her wrist, he pulled her away.

'Leave go of me, Jack. Leave go. I'm sorry I hurt you. I didn't realise. It was stupid of me, but . . . '

'Shut up.' He hauled her across the road. He was making for the dunes and the beach.

The dunes were engulfed in fog. The sharp grass cut her legs as she was dragged along.

'Let me go, Jack!' Too late. The fog deadened all sound. Her voice came back at her, like a dead echo, shrouded in mist. At last he stopped. In the distance she heard the sea, slithering onto the shore. Still he held onto her wrist. He twisted it round, and her hand opened out to reveal the red flower in its grasp. Suddenly he wrenched her arm behind her back, and the flower fell into the sand. 'Jack. Don't be daft. Don't do anything daft,' she pleaded.

'What's daft about it? I want what I've paid for same as him.'

'Same as who?'

'The nob in the village. The one you've thrown me over for.'

'There *is* no nob in the village. It's nothing like that. You don't understand Jack. Only let me explain.' His grip slackened. She

215

turned, rubbing her twisted arm. 'It's Ronnie,' she said quietly. For a moment, Jack could not believe his ears.

'Say that again!'

'It's Ronnie. Ronnie Wilson. I love him, Jack. I do. Honest.' Jack's laughter doubled back on them, assaulting her ears twice over.

'Pull the other one!'

'It's true, Jack. I didn't realise at first. He's a lovely man, one of the nicest I've ever met. It just sort of grew on me, without me knowing, and then . . . then suddenly . . . I was going to tell you!'

'So, you were courting the pair of us, were you?'

'I never looked on what we did as courting, Jack. Maybe I was stupid, I don't know. But I believed you, you see, when you said that about being like a brother to me, and looking after me. I believed you. Maybe I shouldn't've. I don't know. But I did. I'm just stupid. That's all, I suppose. Stupid. Really stupid!' She was crying now. His hand flashed across her face. She rocked backwards, stumbling against the dunes, and fell into the sharp grass. 'I didn't do it on purpose, Jack. Honest. I'm sorry! I'm sorry!'

'Yes. You will be sorry,' he said. His voice was grim. Jane scrambled in the dunes, trying to get to her feet, but the sand gave under her, and the grass wrapped itself about her legs, and she cried out, as he flung himself upon her.

Ronnie could see nothing. There were people everywhere. It was all confusion. A sudden sound made him turn towards the sea. Was it a scream? Was it human? Then, again, he heard it. This time it seemed to come from the Big Top. It was like a fog horn, loud and furious. His sense of direction had left him. He could not tell where the sound had come from. The fog obscured everything. He looked out to where the sea should have been. Mounds of sand loomed up at him. Then he heard her. Yes. It was Jane. She was screaming. Cursing his heavy boots, throwing his loose collar away from him, Ronnie sprawled up the banks of sand. They gave way under him.

'Oh God help me!' he cried out.

'Help me!' Jane answered him.

Jack looked up and saw Ronnie blundering towards him out of the mist. A fog horn sounded loud and clear. And Ronnie was on

216

him. His fist rang out dully against Jack's jaw, and he reeled back, his leg buckling on the giving sand. Sobbing, Jane crawled out of the grass, her clothes torn, her legs bleeding. She was looking for something, a stone, anything. She must help Ronnie. Jack had struggled to his feet, and was swinging out wildly, while Ronnie watched his chance, grabbed his arm, and brought him down, his head under his arm. Now was Jane's chance. She found a bottle, an old beer bottle left behind by some picnicker. She picked it up and forced herself to her feet, stumbling towards the two struggling men. But then, Jack had Ronnie down; he was on top of him. Or was it Ronnie's head she saw, in the sandstorm they created around them? She raised the bottle, ready to bring it down as soon as she saw Jack's face. And there it was, grinning at her, his sharp teeth grinning at her in his pain, as Ronnie delivered his right hook deep into his stomach. Suddenly Ronnie saw Jane standing above him, the bottle raised in her hand.

'Don't Jane. He's finished. It's all right.'

'I want to!' she screamed out.

'No you don't. You could kill him, pet. Put it down now.' Slowly, and painfully, Jack staggered to his feet and scuttled off, disappearing into the fog.

Ronnie and Jane leaned against one another, panting for some seconds. Pulling himself together, Ronnie turned Jane towards him, and looked her square in the eye.

'Are you all right?' Jane gazed at him bleakly.

'Aha,' Ronnie merely nodded his head.

'Come on. Let's go.' Jane lowered her eyes, and sobbed, 'Ronnie, I've been so stupid . . . !'

'Never mind all that now.' Gently, he nudged her arm. 'Come on. Before you catch your death.'

'I've got a cloak somewhere . . . ' She bent to scour the sand around them. Her hand touched on something small, fragile. It was the flower, the red crêpe flower. She picked it up and began to cry.

'Here it is.' Ronnie picked up the cloak. 'Let's get it round you.' They staggered back to the road, where Ronnie stopped to empty the sand from his shoes, and then they dragged on, away from the sea, up Bent House Lane, towards Fowler Street.

Adeline immediately took charge of Jane. Shocked at her torn,

217

bleeding condition, she demanded to know what had happened. But Jane began to cry, and Ronnie, who was himself in need of first aid, refused to stay, saying, 'I've got to get down to Pilot Street. See her Dad. I'll not rest till I've raised the biggest hue and cry . . . ' And then he was gone.

Edie helped Adeline undress the shocked girl. Jane was shaking. She had something in her hand.

'Let go,' Adeline said. 'What have you got there? Let it go.' But Jane would not open her fist for them to see. After making the patient comfortable, Edie was sent out for the doctor, leaving Adeline to sit by her bed. 'It makes a change this way round,' she joked. Jane lay cold and stiff, trembling spasmodically. The low wail of a distant fog horn sounded.

'I'm all right, hephalant,' she said. Thinking she was delirious, Adeline put her hand to the girl's forehead. It was cool. Then Jane let out a big sigh, and began to move.

'Stay still, dear,' Adeline told her. But Jane would not stay still. 'No. I must . . . I must . . . ' she said. Adeline shook her head. Perhaps it was better to let her have her way. Jane pushed back the coverlet, and got out of bed, padding in her bare feet across to the fireplace. A cold draught touched the back of her head. She looked up at Robert's drawing of the elephant. Then she opened her hand at last, and laid the red flower on the mantel beneath. Far off, on the Groyne, they heard the warning bell toll.

'Your rose has fallen.' Adeline was standing beside her, looking at the red petals which lay scattered over the hearth. Then she too felt the icy breeze. She turned to see where it came from. 'We must get that window mended,' she said.

At first it was only a light drizzle. It seemed to fall out of the very mist, as though the mist had turned to tears. It fell on Ronnie's white face. It soaked into his clothes, and where the wound was red in his side, the blood flowed, through the sand, into the river at the coble landing. Then, when the dawn came up, the mist fled. Ronnie's blood ran thin in the rain.

CHAPTER FOURTEEN

'So, this lad, Ronnie Wilson, tried to rape you . . . '

'No! Not him! It was Jack! Jack Purvis!'

'Really Jane!' Adeline was shocked. It was a wonder George put up with it. And in front of the police as well.

'I'm sorry, Mrs Beattie. I'm sorry but it's just . . . I'm at the end of me tether. I am honest! Why won't any of you believe me?'

'Jane . . . ' George's voice was slow, deliberate. 'A lie's a lie, whether you whisper it, or shout it from the rooftops.'

'I'm not lying!' In the silence that followed Jane's echoing voice, Bob Ridley shifted uncomfortably in his seat. Why did it have to happen to him? Other men had daughters that got married, had bairns . . . Fanny's troubles, in the light of recent events, paled in comparison.

'Aye,' he said at last. 'Ronnie was a canny lad!' Jane snapped at the cue.

'Yes he was. And he'd never've harmed a fly let alone me! It was like I told you. Jack Purvis was the one that attacked me! Ronnie Wilson fought him off, then brought me back here, and then he was going to go and see you, Dad to tell you what had happened, when . . . when . . . oh God!' Helpless fury gave way to distress, and Jane collapsed in a heap into Adeline's arms.

'There now pet. You're overwrought. That's what it is. I think that's enough for now, George.' George sighed, and motioned to the policeman that he should leave.

'Dad! Tell them! Ronnie couldn't have hurt me! He just couldn't! He saved me from Jack Purvis, like I keep telling you. And then Jack killed him!' Bob Ridley shook his head sadly.

'It's beyond me!' he said at last.

'Jane, you simply mustn't keep on saying that Jack Purvis killed Ronnie. How could you know? Were you there?' Jane glared at her employer. 'As far as we know there were no witnesses to the crime. He might have been set on by a gang of thugs. God knows there's plenty of them on the quayside. And serve him right too, if he did what I think he did.' Jane couldn't stand it any longer. Tears streaming down her face, she began screaming.

'But he didn't! He didn't! It was Jack! Why won't you believe me!' Her voice tailed off in a long, desperate wail, ending in helpless sobs.

'Eeh, I'm sorry about this, Mr Mayor, sir . . . ' Bob stood, cap in hand, shaking his head. 'It's all beyond me.'

'If you say that once more . . . !'

'George!' Adeline's voice carried a warning. Bob bit his lip and sat down again. 'I think we should get young Jane back up to bed now. She needs her rest.'

'How can I rest? How will I ever be able to rest again?' Adeline's arms encircled the girl, and she led her gently out of the room.

The icy breeze fanned the spider's web. In the lamplight, Jane watched the delicate fronds wafting to and fro over the drawing of her 'hephalant', and from under the picture rail, the spider emerged to check his snare for prey.

Away in a manger, no crib for a bed,
The little Lord Jesus laid down His sweet head.
The stars in the bright sky looked down where he lay,
The little Lord Jesus asleep on the hay.

220

Carol singers. She had forgotten it was Christmas. Through the dirty glass of her dormer window, Jane looked out onto the stars. The voices were childish and sweet. They knew nothing of her anguish. It did not, could not touch them.

> The cattle are lowing, the baby awakes,
> But little Lord Jesus no crying he makes.
> I love Thee Lord Jesus! Look down from the sky,
> And stay by my bedside till morning is nigh.

It was like another world. Not so long ago, she had been like those children. She had gone carol singing round the town end, round the pubs, round the houses of the shipowners and merchants. It was a different life. It had nothing to do with her. She was cut off from it now. She could never be like those children again.

At the back door of 18 Victoria Terrace, Adeline Beattie stood beaming, with a trayful of mince pies. Smiles answered her and hands reached out, then the children went on their way up to the village, leaving the darkness behind them.

Suddenly flinging back the bedclothes, Jane dashed to the window and looked out. She saw the lantern making off up the back lane. It bobbed, and twinkled, and then was gone. It was like the door closing on her in the cellar, leaving her bereft of light. She wanted to call out to the carol singers to come back. She wrenched open the window, and gasped as the icy draught hit her full on the face. She shivered. The rooftops were black against a navy sky. The stars shone steadily, silently into her darkness. They were deaf to her cries for help, dumb when she needed comfort. Would no-one believe her then? No-one at all?

'What have I done?' Her cry came back to her, echoing. The night before, when she was crying for help in the fog, only Ronnie had heard her. Now he was dead, she would cry in vain. Her voice came back to her, echoing, mocking. 'What have I done?' Perhaps if no-one else would listen, she should listen to herself. Feeling cold, Jane slowly closed the window, and leaned back against the wall, deep in thought.

Why had she said those words? 'What have I done?' After all, she had done nothing. She had not meant to lead Jack on! The flame of the lamp, which had flared in the draught, settled now, and cast a shadow over the room. Jane watched the light flicker across the elephant, and lifting her eyes, she saw that the spider's web had been dislodged in the icy blast, and now hung useless, by a single thread from the rail. As Jane watched, the web moved. There was something inside it, cocooned in the fallen fronds. The movement caught at her attention. She screwed up her eyes to see, in the half dark. The web swung, but still the thread held, and slowly, Jane walked towards it, her eyes intent on it. And now the web convulsed, as the creature trapped inside struggled with all its might against the net, but every movement seemed to draw it tighter round, and slowly, slowly the struggling stopped. Jane watched the stillness. Then, reaching for her chair, she stood on it, and straining upward, touched the fallen web with the tips of her fingers. The web fell into her hands, and she brought it to the lamplight, tearing the tangles apart to see the wretched creature that was inside, desperate to save it. But it was too late. It fell dead onto the table by the lamp, its long legs curled under. The spider had been caught in its own net.

Jane picked up the spider, and laid it, nestling in her palm. She began to cry. No, she had not meant to lead Jack on. And yet she knew that what she had done was wrong. She had lied to her father about the circus, and she had kept her Tuesday dinners with Jack secret. Why had she done so? Because Jack asked her? Or was it because, deep down, she knew there was something wrong, only had not been able to face it. She had needed somebody to lean on, and Robert was not there, so she had used Jack. That was the top and bottom of it. She remembered Chandrika's words to her in the churchyard after Fanny's wedding, 'That sympathetic heart of yours will get you into trouble'. And she would have been in trouble had it not been for Ronnie. Ronnie's name pierced her like an arrow and she gasped with sudden agony, knowing she was at fault and that because of that fault, Ronnie had died. And with him had died her own hopes of happiness. Deservedly. Her face hardened. She would have no mercy on herself. She would punish herself for what she had done.

222

There was a sudden knock on the door. Someone had crept upstairs so silently, she had not heard them.

'Who is it?'

'Me.' The voice was that of Harriet May. Without waiting for an invitation, she walked in, and put a cup of cocoa on the table. 'I thought the poor innocent victim was supposed to be resting!'

'I can't rest.'

'Huh!' Harriet walked slowly round the room, as though inspecting it. 'In that case, I don't see why I should have had to keep shop all day. I've been on my own most of the time. And it's nearly Christmas.'

'I'm sorry.'

'Sorry doesn't mend my hands!' Harriet showed them, raw from holly prickles. 'James is very particular about ladies' hands. It's just as well I'll not be seeing him till I'm back in Newcastle.' For a moment, Jane looked perplexed.

'James? Oh, your admirer.'

'Yes. My admirer.' Harriet had been staring out of the dormer window, and now she turned suddenly to face Jane. 'You see, you're not the only one to have men after you!' Jane coloured. Thrown off her guard, she thought Harriet was referring to Jack. Her heart lurched. She began to stutter.

'What men?'

Harriet stared at her and slowly smiled.

'Have I by any chance stumbled on something?' she asked.

Jane gathered her thoughts. Perhaps somehow Harriet could help her.

'Did you see me and Jack together?'

'Jack?' Immediately, Jane knew she had been wrong.

'If you did, Harriet, I wish you'd say, because they won't believe me.' Harriet's jaw dropped open. For once she was speechless. 'Please, Harriet. I need your help.'

'Why should I help you?!'

'Jack Purvis killed Ronnie. I know he did. You see, Jack had ideas about me. I didn't realise till it was too late, and when I told him about Ronnie, Jack went for me. Ronnie turned up, God knows how, and he chased him off; the next thing, Ronnie's lying dead by the river with a knife in his side. It was Jack killed

223

him! I know it was! So please! Please, Harriet. If you saw us together, tell them!' Harriet May was speechless. Was this Jane Ridley grovelling at her feet? Asking for help? For minutes, the girls stood face to face. The realisation that there were two men involved in the affair hit Harriet like a sledgehammer.

'You little slut!' she spat at her.

'Call me what you like, Harriet. I don't care. Maybe I deserve it. I don't know. Only be my friend now. Please, for Ronnie's sake.'

'Ronnie's dead.'

Jane gulped down a sob, choking on her grief.

'I've got to see justice done!'

'Who for? You or Ronnie? Hah! It's to salve your own guilty conscience, isn't it?'

'Please, Harriet. I've never harmed you, have I?'

'Hah!'

'Why? What have I done?'

'You exist. Isn't that enough?'

'What do you want me to do? Kill myself?' Harriet shrugged. 'Supposing it was your James that had been killed . . . ' A sudden fury stirred in Harriet.

'How dare you so much as mention his name!' she screamed at her. 'You two faced slut!' And Harriet left the room, slamming the door.

Jane stared at the door for a long time. It was true. She wanted justice because she wanted to appease her own conscience. She had told lies. Her punishment would be cruel. For now she was telling the truth, no-one believed her. No-one except Harriet May. Her enemy was, therefore, Jane's only true friend. A pale smile twisted at her mouth. Her eyes fell on the table where the spider lay, and she knew a kinship with it. She too had been caught in her own net. Picking up her cocoa, Jane drank it absently. It was cold, but she finished it all the same.

The next day, the police visited the Purvis house. A little lad saw the bobby knocking on the front door, and the news swept round the town end. It was there at the coble landing waiting for him, when Jack came in from a job.

'What's up?' he asked. 'Has me uncle's past caught up with him at last?' He laughed, and every pilot in the shed laughed

224

with him. They all knew of the 'secret' goings on between Uncle Purvis and the Mission Woman!

'No . . . it's that Ronnie What's his name . . . ye kna. Him that got the chop, like!'

'Oh aye?'

'Bad business that. Found him here on the landing, if you please!' All shook their heads in horror. The very idea!

'I expect they're seeing all the pilots then . . . '

'Aye. Starting with you.' Gordon Tinmouth gave Jack a sidelong look. 'Seems you've been mucking about, eh?'

'Says who?'

'The Ridley girl. That bonny fair haired lass, ye kna . . . her sister's married to Dandy O.'

'Her? Why man! I wouldn't pass the time of day with her!' So saying, Jack left them to their thoughts, and ambled home, as though he hadn't a care in the world.

The policeman was on his fourth cup of tea by the time Jack arrived. The whole clan was seated round about, and the air was thick with pipesmoke. There was total silence and every eye watched, as the policeman reached for yet another spoon of sugar to put in his tea.

'What's this? Christmas already?' Jack asked, smiling.

'Not quite, Mr Purvis. Sit down, will you?'

Seven men went for the one remaining chair. The policeman flushed, visibly thrown. 'I meant him!' he snapped, pointing at Jack. The other Purvises stood aside and let Jack sit, facing the policeman.

'He says you've been seeing Jane Ridley!' Eileen couldn't help herself. She was outraged at the idea.

'I'll ask the questions, Miss!' He turned to Jack. 'Have you?'

'Who says?'

'She does.' Jack's mother had her twopenn'orth.

'Then she's a trollop and a liar.'

'She says that you and her have had the habit of frequenting a little restaurant in Ocean Road of a Tuesday. Is that true?'

'Well, in a manner of speaking yes.' The entire clan gasped.

'What do you mean?'

'I've eaten me dinner there often enough, but I don't know about her!'

225

'Jack? What's all this?' His mother's voice was harsh.

'Well, mother, I've been a naughty lad.' The policeman's eyes narrowed in excitement. 'I've been seeing a canny little waitress that works there.'

'Is that all?' The men laughed and the women sniffed in disapproval.

'Not quite, mother. I'm afraid I've got her in the family way. But I'm going to do the right thing. I've asked her to marry me.' The policeman gaped.

'But why would Miss Ridley say . . . '

'She's trying to make trouble for *us*.' Eileen nodded wisely. 'That's what it is. Her sister stole my man, and now she's trying to get Jack into lumber. What a family!'

'Aye! Why, our Jack wouldn't touch her with a barge pole! There's been a feud between the two families ever since poor Eileen got stood up.' The commotion that followed made further investigation impossible. The policeman left the Purvis house confused and unhappy. He had taken to Jane Ridley, but there could be no doubt - her story was a pack of lies. Perhaps she was covering for someone . . . her father for instance? If Ronnie Wilson had attacked her, then her own family would be the most likely suspects . . .

So it was in Pilot Street the curtains began twitching next. Where were they all the night Ronnie was killed? Dandy was out in the coble. Bob was in 'The Globe', and Rattler was sitting on a cushion by his own kitchen fire with the women folk. They all had alibis. It was a mystery. The policeman left the Tullys in a state of shock.

'Eeh, I'll never lift me head in the street again!' Ma Tully wailed. 'A policeman in the house! Whatever next!'

'Our Jane's got a lot to answer for!' Fanny sank her head into her porter. And Bob Ridley sighed.

'It's all beyond me,' he said.

Jack's wedding took place on the Thursday. The inquest was to be held on the Friday, and the new Mrs Purvis could not be forced to give testimony against her husband.

'Change your story, Jane!' her father urged her. 'I'm saying this for your own good, pet. Because nobody's going to believe you if you stick to this tale about Jack Purvis.'

'It's the truth.'

'Tell the truth and shame the devil!' Harriet's voice lilted mockingly in the shop, where Jane had insisted on working as the week wore on.

'I intend to.' Jane was determined. Nothing would shake her. Harriet smiled secretly. How she would love to be in court to hear her!

That night Adeline gave her a sleeping draught. At first, Jane resisted the waves of drowsiness that stole over her, her eyes obstinately open, fixed on the candle flame beneath her drawing of the elephant. The red crêpe rose lay where she had left it, on the mantelpiece. She could just see it through the iron railings of her bedstead. She shivered, remembering how she had found it in the dunes, remembering the elephant as it suffered itself to be ordered round and round the ring. A fog horn blew. Jane listened, waiting for the answering call. The Last Trumpet. Yes. She would tell the truth and shame the devil. And she would be doing it, not for herself, she would be doing it for Ronnie. A hot tear scalded her cheek. She had not cried for days. Another, pain-relieving tear swelled under her closing eyelids, and the drowsiness grew like a tidal wave, dragging her out into the ocean of sleep, into the great void of her unconscious.

Yet there was to be no rest there. The waves tossed her, and the salt was bitter in her mouth. Weeds tore at her legs and pulled her down, deep down to the ocean bed, and the more she struggled to be free, the more the weeds caught at her, wrapping her round in their deadly embrace. And her chest swelled with the pain of not breathing, and her head pounded, and she heard her father's voice, as if from a great distance;

' . . . over the years our elephant had grown just a bit big for his boots, and he started to get careless. And one day, when the sun was very hot, he galloped off down to the river for a drink. He had a favourite rock pool where he often used to go, a secret place, that the others didn't know about. And seeing him standing there, all on his own, the crocodile slid from the river bank into the water. But the elephant didn't even see him coming. He was too keen on drinking all he could. But he still felt all hot and bothered and the pool looked so inviting. So in he went. And then the crocodile saw his chance. Quick as a flash he swam out into the pool after him. The elephant saw him but it was too late, and soon he felt the crocodile's jaws on him, and it seemed the game was up for our poor elephant, who had so carelessly fallen prey to the enemy. And there was nothing left for him but to raise his trunk in the air and trumpet out as loudly as he could . . .'

She tossed and turned and then her voice was screaming, 'Help me! Help me, Ronnie!'

And Adeline, shaking with fright, was in the room, her hair falling over Jane's face like the weeds of the sea, and Jane was fighting her off.

'It's all right, Jane. It's all right! You're at home. In bed. Look at me!' And Jane looked, and saw Adeline's pale face, creased with pain. 'Let go of me, now. You're hurting me.' And Jane released her grip, falling back against her pillows, while the sweat streamed down her face, and her breath came in loud, desperate rasps.

'I'm sorry.'

'Sh . . . no need to be. No permanent damage done.'

Jane wailed, 'Ronnie's dead!'

'But you've got nothing to be sorry for!' Adeline said.

'Yes. I have. It was my fault. I lied.' Jane sobbed, and her hand reached out to draw Adeline down onto the bed beside her. 'Why won't you tell the police about the Tuesday dinners?'

'What do you mean?'

'You knew I was seeing Jack. You said so.' Adeline frowned. 'That sleeping draught's addled your brain, pet. It was Ronnie you were seeing, remember?' Jane's hand dropped from Adeline's arm.

'There's no escape,' she said dully.

'I don't understand.'

'It doesn't matter. I shall tell the truth tomorrow.'

'I'm glad to hear it.' Adeline rose and went to the wash stand for a towel, then perching on the edge of the bed, she wiped the tears and the sweat from Jane's face. The towel felt cool and smooth.

'You're nice,' Jane said. 'I wish I was as nice as you. You're simple.'

228

'Thank you very much!' Adeline laughed.

'No. I don't mean simple like that. I mean simple like . . . like children.'

'You're but a child yourself.'

'Not any more I'm not.' Adeline drew back, folding the towel in her hands. Her chest was tight with fear.

'You don't mean . . . he didn't . . . Jane, are you still . . . innocent?' Jane snorted.

'I'm still a virgin, if that's what you mean!'

'What else would I mean?' Adeline's eyes searched her out, and Jane was glad it was dark.

'Nothing. Only tomorrow, I shall tell the truth, Adeline.'

'You can do nothing more. And I must say, it's a blessed relief. Go back to sleep now.'

'Good night.'

'Don't let the bed bugs bite.'

Then she was gone, gently closing the door behind her, leaving the scent of chrysanthemums, heavy on the air. For a long time, Jane lay, bathed in a cold sweat, and fell asleep only as the first light was turning the rooftops grey.

The black dress Adeline had laid out for her was made of silk and lace. Jane thought it too grand. She would have preferred something plainer. She stared at herself in Adeline's triple mirrors. Her face was pale and drawn, and the skin had a luminous quality about it, in contrast to the dull black of her gown. Adeline shook her head and sighed.

'You're too young to be wearing black,' she said.

'I'm not. I told you.' What did she mean? Jane's words of last night came back to Adeline. 'Not any more I'm not.' Perhaps it was true. Her voice had changed. It was no longer the voice of a child. It had depths and resonance. It had resolution. Adeline's hand clutched suddenly at her heart. Jane was alarmed.

'What's wrong?'

'Nothing. Just a little palpitation. That's all.'

Looking on the hardened features of Jane Ridley, Adeline's heart had failed her, and Jane knew it. She smiled at the older woman.

'Perhaps you shouldn't come today. George needs you in the

shop anyway. And I'll be all right.'

'Yes. Yes you will. I know you will. Because you are going to tell the truth. You are, aren't you, Jane?' Jane nodded.

'Yes. Yes, I am. You stay here. Have a little lie down, why don't you?'

'But somebody should go with you!'

'Perhaps Harriet May . . . ' Adeline looked at her in disbelief. 'Would you ask her for me?'

'Are you sure?'

'Yes. Please, Adeline. Ask her to come with me. Only don't tell her I said so.'

The inquest was to be held at Waterloo Vale, and George insisted not only on coming along with Harriet May, but also on a cab to take them there. The affair had caused considerable difficulties for George Beattie. All week, people had been coming into the shop merely to gawp at Jane. All week, councillors and electorate alike had looked askance at him, as though somehow he was to blame for his charge's misdemeanours. He would have liked to send Jane home to Pilot Street, to distance himself from her plight. There were times he wished he'd never clapped eyes on her. She was a menace. A positive menace! And then he would look on her face and remember the day he first saw her in his shop. He would remember how she had given of her heart, reading to him, and his would melt. He could not desert her; it was in fact his Christian duty to stand by her. He would there-fore make a big thing out of supporting her through her 'time of trial' as he called it.

She looked calm and sober, beside him, in her black dress and cloak. Whereas Harriet had a distinctly cavalier air about her with the red ribbon in her hat, and the bright paisley shawl which she drew about her shoulders. George frowned. He opened his lips to say something, and then, hearing raindrops on the roof of the cab, was distracted, and fell silent, listening, as the light drizzle scattered its drops over his head.

They were forewarned by the crowd outside the building. Jane's body tensed, and Harriet hung back behind them, as if for shelter, as George took the arm of his employee and guided her in. A hiss was followed by laughter, as they passed through and up the stairs, and Jane felt a cold tremor rise up her spine . . .

The small room set aside for the hearing was full, and people overflowed into the corridor. It was a *cause célèbre*, and George struggled to think just how he might turn it to his advantage.

Mr and Mrs Wilson sat in the front seats, and Jane's heart caught as she passed them. She had thought to keep her composure, but tears kept on coming and her handkerchief was drenched. George leaned across and whispered, 'Better have mine.'

She took it gratefully, blew her nose and settled herself for the ordeal.

When her time came to be called to the witness stand, Jane found she could not stand - her legs were shaking. Harriet, sitting on her other side, turned to her.

'Go on, then!' she said, smiling. 'Tell the truth. I dare you!' It was what Jane needed. Gathering up her strength, she stood and walked to the witness box. She could not look at them. She had to look over their heads, for the room was packed with people she knew. The entire Purvis clan was there, murmuring, and the magistrate brought down his hammer to silence them. Shifting feet replaced the voices, and then all was quiet, and she began her story of the previous Sunday. At first, her voice trembled, but, dropping her eyes for a second, she caught the intense expression in the faces of Ronnie's parents. She would tell it to them, as though there was no-one else in the room. She would vindicate their son and make it known he was a hero. So her voice grew deep and strong, and she told all she remembered of that terrible day.

Sitting in the front seat George's heart lurched. She had not changed her story after all! At first, he was furious. It made *him* look a fool to be protecting such a liar! And the word 'liar' rang out from the back of the room, as though his thought had been heard and voiced. Jane hesitated for a second, but continued with more determination than before. Then the hisses began. She saw her father's face, and Dandy's sitting half way back. They were staring at their boots. Harriet's face expressed surprise and pleasure. She looked behind her, to see the anger of the Purvis clan, and felt a mere frisson of danger on her own account. But George's gaze steadied, as he watched Jane and listened to her. Her voice had the ring of truth in it. She stood straight and still.

231

Her words came out slowly, as though long considered, and calmly she committed herself to a deliberate accusation of Jack Purvis.

When she stood down, it was amidst uproar. George put his arm about her protectively, and shook his head, but his eyes were kind. She almost broke down at the sight of them. At least he believed her now. Mr and Mrs Wilson sat back, satisfied. But it was some time before order could be restored and the proceedings continued. No-one else believed her. There was no evidence, and Jack's wife gave him his alibi. He stood, cocksure in the witness box, and Jane felt sick at the sight of him. His smile twisted at the corner of his mouth, and he played to his family at the back of the room, like an actor, well rehearsed and sure of his lines. George watched the performance critically, and came to his own decision on the matter. He sighed as the proceedings came to an end, and the verdict of the court was given. There had been foul play, by person or persons unknown. That was an end of it. Suddenly, her strength went, and Jane crumpled in her chair. She would have liked to go quietly away, somewhere to hide herself. But George helped her to her feet as Ronnie's parents approached. Mrs Wilson's face was half covered by her shawl, which she had pulled up, as though to hide behind it. But Mr Wilson, bare headed, and frank by nature, held out his hand to Jane.

'Thank you, lass. I know it must have cost you.' Then he nodded slowly and repeated, 'Thank you, lass.' George led Jane, crying, through the menacing crowd and out into a waiting cab.

The rain was heavier now. It came down steadily, washing the town. Jane listened and found it comforting.

'For what it's worth, Jane,' George cleared his throat before continuing, 'I believe you.' She looked at him in amazement. 'I don't condone your behaviour of course. It was a disgrace to any respectable woman; *téte à têtes* in secret places! But I take my hat off to you. I do really. I doubt if many of us could have stood up there and done what you did today! And that, our Harriet, includes you!' Harriet May scowled.

'I don't know!' she snapped. 'I just can't win, can I?'

'And what do you mean by that?' her stepfather barked at her.

'Nothing.' Her voice was sullen, and she retreated into her own thoughts as the rain grew heavier and heavier.

'Mr Beattie, I know this might sound daft . . . ' Jane stammered. 'But I don't want to go back now. I'd really like to go for a walk.'

'Madness! Look at the rain!'

'I don't mind the rain. Honest, I don't. I just need to . . . ' Her voice broke and she sobbed uncontrollably.

'I know how you feel, Jane. There are times when we need a period of deep reflection, in complete privacy, and I daresay this is one of them.' He reached in his pocket, and pressed some coins into her hand. 'All I ask is that you get a cab back. We don't want you catching pneumonia now!' Jane was filled with gratitude. She smiled her thanks and as the cab pulled up on the coast road, she alighted, leaving the grim-faced Harriet behind.

Jane walked along the curve of Sea Road, passing the pier on her left. The sea was calm between the piers, but outside, it was rough and choppy. It tossed spray at the stone walls, scudding across the green rocks, and smattering amongst the pebbles. And the rain fell. Jane's umbrella dripped down her back, soaking into her cloak, but she did not notice it. Her clodhoppers kept her feet dry, and her steps rang out on the paving stones as she made her way south, slackening her pace as the dunes came in sight, and then, stopping, as if she could go no further. The circus had gone. The Bents was empty, and only the tracks and footprints in the mud proved it had ever been there at all. Her chest heaved with emotion. She wanted to run. But where? And she stood, as though paralysed by indecision, watching the rain fall. Why had she come here? If it was to haunt the scene of her misery, far better go away. But if it was to make her peace with Ronnie . . . Slowly she began to walk towards the dunes.

The sand caked in the rain, and crumbled. She wandered through the maze of sand hills and grass, stopping now and then, to look at the changing patterns of light on the sea. The steel grey of the sky was met by the deeper grey of the water. But as the waves swelled up, olive green shaded their underbellies, then, the energy of the ocean surging through them, they paled to a cold jade, before turning into foam. Gulls flapped their wet wings in the downpour and whined softly as they came to rest. And all the time the rain fell, soaking through the back of Jane's cloak, and she wandered on, wondering now if she would know the place again, where she and Jack had fought, and in a way, he had won. And then she saw a piece of glass, sticking out of the sand. Her heart stopped, then lurching forwards she bent to pull it out. It was only a beer bottle. For a moment, Jane looked at it. Anger flared in her, and she knew she hated Jack with all her soul. She pulled her arm back, and hurled the bottle into the air, cursing herself for not having hit him with it.

'You could kill him, pet. Put it down.'

Trust Ronnie to say that! Trust poor, sweet, forgiving Ronnie! Well, she was not sweet! Nor could she forgive! The bottle fell against a stone and broke open, leaving its raw ends jutting up towards the sky. Jane's voice hurled upwards, piercing the clouds.

'Ronnie! Ronnie, forgive me! I love you Ronnie! I love you!' Too late. Much too late. She should have told him the night they had stood, looking at the stars in the back lane. Why had she held back? 'Another time,' she had said, as though time had been in her own hands and she had been master of it. But she was not the master of anything! And Jack had got away scot free! No she was not forgiving! She would hate him with all her heart. She would hate him till kingdom come and beyond. Stumbling forwards, she pulled up short against the jutting glass. The umbrella dropped from her hands, to lie listless in the pouring rain, and her arm reached out towards the shattered shards.

'What have I done?' Her own voice echoed loudly in her head, to be answered by Harriet May's.

'You exist. Isn't that enough?'

'What do you want me to do? Kill myself?' Taking off her glove, Jane knelt and touched the sharp edges of the glass lovingly. And the rain grew heavier, so that water quenched her hand and came between her skin and the glass, as though a cushion had been put between. Staring at the glass, the green glass, she remembered a day in church, when the sun had fallen in through the coloured lights of the window, like a rainbow, and she had forgiven Harriet May. 'Forgive us our trespasses, as we forgive them.' Jane sobbed and snatched back her hand. 'I can't!' she cried out. 'God help me, I can't forgive!' And she left the glass, scrambling through the dunes, running down the long expanse of sand towards the sea. Then, she could run no further. She stopped, in a rivulet of salt water, watching the restless motion of the tide, letting the rain drum down upon her head. And it was bliss. Her brain cooled as the stream of water drenched down, and a deep sigh escaped from her, as her head tilted back, to take the rain on her face. And her breathing slowed, came and went with the rise and fall of the waves, and she felt at peace. Slowly gulping down the rain, she turned her face once more towards the sea. And she knew it was herself she had to forgive at last. Only herself.

Ronnie was buried on the Monday. In spite of the Purvis faction, the Reverend had agreed to inter him in the churchyard of Saint Stephen's. The black silk dress, stained at the hem from the salt sea, had been pressed, and with her father on one side, and George Beattie on the other, Jane made her way to the town end. The crowd closed in on her. Faces she knew, had known from childhood, jeered and threatened her. An arm reached out and tore at her sleeve, leaving lace dangling at her wrist. George Beattie lifted his gold topped cane, and barked, 'Make way, you scum! Make way for the Mayor and his party!'

Many fell back, and moved on, but Jane's head jerked as spittle shot into her eye. Then she looked to see Ma Dunn's face twisted up with hate, reproach written on her face. In that moment, Jane knew, she would never be able to come near the town end again.

The community of the quayside stood, heads bare, round the low walls which marked the boundary of the churchyard, but many mourners stood inside, around the grave that had been dug for Ronnie. Miss Poulson, her eyes red from crying, stood beside Mr and Mrs Wilson, who nodded a greeting to Jane as she came to stand, facing them, on the other side of the grave.

'Man that is born of woman, hath but a short time to live, and is full of misery. He cometh up and is cut down like a flower.' Tears welled in Jane's eyes, so that she could not see as the coffin was lowered slowly into the grave. By her side, her father coughed, overcome by his own emotion.

'Aye,' he muttered under his breath, 'he was a canny lad.' And Jane thought her heart would break.

'Our Father who art in heaven,' the voices came from behind, from before, from the sides, 'forgive us our trespasses . . . ' 'Forgive me Ronnie. Forgive me. Help me to forgive . . . ' And then, the mother threw down the first sod on her son's coffin. 'Raise us from the death of sin into the life of righteousness . . . ' And the father sent earth smattering onto the wood. 'Come ye blessed children of my Father, receive the kingdom prepared for you from the beginning of the world . . . ' And then Jane threw down a single red rose and watched as it was buried under the soil of Ronnie's grave.

CHAPTER FIFTEEN

'And that's another thing!' George Beattie turned on his wife.
'When is Edie going to stop crying into her pail?' Down the
cellar steps, the unfortunate Edie could be heard sobbing her
heart out, as she scrubbed and scrubbed the steps leading down
into the darkness. 'Shut your noise!' he yelled down at her. The
only response was a wail even louder than before, which sent
George, hands raised in prayer to heaven, rushing out of the
house, and over the road to his nurseries. For a second Adeline
stood still watching his retreating back, and then as another wail
issued from the darkness, she uttered a sharp, 'Oh shut up, Edie,'
before walking briskly into the shop.

Down in the gloom, by the light of a single candle, Edie
considered her lot mournfully. What a family they were to work
for! First the missus. Sweet as pie she was to begin with, and
then, just after the Christmas before last, she starts getting
miserable as sin, just like him! And the master? Well now, he was
bad enough before, but he'd got that tetchy of late, always
picking holes, always going on, nag, nag, nag, and flying off
the deep end at the slightest thing. And as for her . . . that Jane
Ridley! Did she have to go round in that old black dress with the
torn sleeve all the time? It's not even as if she'd been engaged to
that lad what'd died! Edie's scrubbing brush halted in mid scrub,

as Ronnie's face smiled at her out of her memory. She'd liked Ronnie. He was always nice to her. She stopped sobbing and sighed. What could she do to cheer herself up? Well, first of all it was Friday, and Miss Harriet was coming home for the weekend. Always full of tales she was, about her posh young man in Newcastle, and she was sworn to secrecy on the subject. After all, the poor lass needed somebody to confide in, didn't she? And if she chose Edie for the honour, well, Miss Harriet showed nowt but sense. She'd never liked the young mistress, 'the young madam' as she used to call her, before, but, and Edie had to admit it, she'd come on since she'd gone to her finishing school, nigh on eighteen months back. She'd got a 'gale in her tail', and had some fun in her, which is more than could be said for the rest of them!

She had reached the bottom step at last. Wiping her nose with her sleeve, Edie looked up the shaft of light that came from the open door above, and saw Miss Jane standing there like an apparition, in her long black dress, and her fair hair scraped back from her face.

'What d'ye want?' Edie shouted up at her.

'The other bucket of narcissi. We've run out in the shop.' Edie picked up her scrubbing brush and her pail and started up the stairs. 'Get it yourself!' she said haughtily, 'I've left you the candle!' Passing Jane at the door, she sniffed, and went into the kitchen to consider what she would cook for supper.

'Ah!' she thought to herself, 'I could just do with a proper old fashioned bit of pan haggerty.' Sniffing at a jar of something on the kitchen table, Edie pulled a face and set it aside to start cutting up onions, potatoes and sausages. Yes. She just fancied a pan haggerty. Well the rest of them would have to like it and lump it. For once she was going to please herself. From the shop, Adeline called. 'Don't forget to use up the left overs, Edie! Make us a nice stew, eh?' Edie put her hand on her hips, sighing. What leftovers was she on about? There was only that half finished jar of bubbly stuff. Like black sago it was really. And without stopping to think, she got a spoon and joyfully scraped the lot in with the sausages and potatoes, before putting it into the oven to cook.

The light was going already. In the shop, a soft pink ray picked out the bowl of anemones on the counter. Looking up from the till, Jane's eye was caught by the gem-like colours of the flowers. She handed her customer her change, and went to the gas mantle to light it.

'I do like the spring,' she said to Adeline, as the customer left the shop. Adeline looked at her, as though from a great distance.

'What did you say?'

'Nothing. Just that I like the spring.'

'Oh. Is that all?' For months, after the inquest into Ronnie's death, Adeline had spoken scarcely a word to her. It had hurt Jane deeply. Already ostracised by her own family, she felt utterly alone. But then, slowly, they had got onto 'polite' terms again. Hardly friendly, but at least it was a working basis.

'Isn't it time you did your lessons?' Adeline asked coldly.

'Can you spare me in the shop?'

'As you can see, Jane, we have no customers.'

So dismissed, Jane went up to her attic room, pulled a bed cover round her, and lighting a candle, buried her head in Latin verbs. 'Amo amas amat, amamus amatis amant. I love, you love, he, she, it loves, we love, you plural love, they love.' A dead language for dead feelings. 'Amabo amabis amabit, amabimus, amabitis amabunt.' 'I will love . . . ' Jane stopped short, and looked at the last pale light at the dormer window. 'Will I?' she whispered. 'Will I?'

Downstairs, Harriet had come home. In her hand, she carried another new hat box. She whispered conspiratorially to Edie.

'Put this in my room. There's a good girl.'

'What's he going to say? He thinks you're a spendthrift as it is!'

'Sh.' Harriet glanced at the stairs, which led up to the living quarters, 'he won't know.'

'Oh I see,' Edie frowned. 'Who's going to pay for it?' Harriet giggled.

'He is!' Now Edie was really foxed. She sighed and padded quietly up the stairs, to do as she was told. The mistress was resting in *her* room, the master was doing physical jerks in *his*. Edie could hear him heaving and straining and swearing too, which he did when he thought nobody was listening. She laughed to herself and walked into Miss Harriet's bedroom, where she hid the box under the bed.

Edie was just about to leave again, when she heard the master curse more loudly, and open his door abruptly. She held her breath. The floor boards moved under her, as George pounded down the corridor. Then he stopped, and knocked on his wife's door.

'Open up! It's your lord and master!' he said. Then Adeline said something, and George went back to his own room, slamming the door, before taking up his chest expanders as though his very life depended on it. Now it was safe to leave. Edie opened Harriet's door softly, crept past the master's room, and made her way back down the stairs to the kitchen, where Harriet was humming softly to herself, and eating a box of chocolates. Edie eyed them greedily, and Harriet passed one along to her.

'I don't like the soft centres,' she said. 'So, you can have those.' Drooling over a strawberry cream, Edie forgot all about the veg and setting her elbows on the table asked after Harriet's young man.

'And do you really love him?' Edie relished the word 'love' as though it was a chocolate, and her eyes ogled the glamorous Miss in her flashy clothes.

'Well I don't know, Edie . . . he loves *me*, of course . . . '

'Of course.'

'But well . . . '

'Why don't you bring him home to meet the master and the mistress?'

'If I do that, Edie, it'll be like a statement of intent.' Edie looked blank. 'Like I had tacitly agreed to sort of marry him.'

'And don't you want to then?'

Harriet shrugged. 'I'm so young, Edie. Too young to settle down, anyway. I want to see something of the world.' She yawned and lay back, nonchalantly. Edie was impressed. 'Maybe, Edie, one day, you too will have a young man, like mine.' Harriet sighed. 'Of course one gets rather bored with going to the theatre, and out to restaurants, and one has one's reputation to consider.'

'That's why you should maybe tie him down, Miss. Sort of . . . marry him, like.'

'I don't want to sort of anything, Edie,' Harriet snapped

240

suddenly, and then relented as Edie's face fell. 'Shall I tell you where he took me larst week?'

'Oh yes! Do!' Edie was all agog. 'Tell me where you went larst week!' Harriet frowned and stared at Edie.

'Are you, by any chance mocking me?'

'No, Miss Harriet. Honest.' Edie's innocent eyes assured her.

'Well, he took me to a ball!'

'No!'

'He did!'

'Never!'

'I tell you, Edie, he did!' For a second, Edie was silenced. And then her thoughts were on the move again.

'But you'd need a ball gown and everything for that!'

'I've *got* a ball gown and everything!'

'Oooh!' Edie's hand shot up to her mouth, and she giggled. 'What's it like?'

'Pink silk, with deep cream lace flounced across the bodice. It fits me like a glove. When James put his hands around my waist ...'

'I hope you was wearing your corsets!'

'Of course I was, Edie. Don't be silly! When James put his hands around my waist ...'

'Oh there you are, Harriet! I wondered if you'd arrived yet!' Edie stood abruptly, her mouth stuffed with chocolate, and began ferociously cutting up the cabbage.

'I didn't like to disturb you when you were resting, Addy.' Adeline smiled.

'How very considerate of you, dear. What was it you two were discussing so intimately?'

'Nothing Missus!' Edie said, choking on her chocolate. Automatically, Adeline's hand reach out to strike her on the back.

'How often have I told you not to speak with your mouth full!' Edie's face went red, then white, then slowly, she regained her composure and began chopping again. 'How long will supper be?'

'I've just got to put the cabbage on ...'

'How long, Edie?'

'I don't know! Maybe twenty minutes ... or so ...'

'I think we'll eat upstairs tonight, seeing as how Harriet's home. Come along, dear ... come up to my room and tell me your news.'

Looking in his long mirror, George considered his figure. Never had his stomach been so flat. Never had his arms been so strong. Never had he had better wind. He shook his head. Now what? What was it all for anyway? What was the point? He wasn't going to run races, was he? He dropped to the floor and did a hundred press ups. Then he did twenty more. Then he lay back, recovering. Then, flat on his back, blinking up at the ceiling through the beads of sweat, that dripped into his eyes, George Beattie began to cry.

'God, help me!' he sobbed, 'God help me!'

The dinner gong woke Jane as from a trance. She had been looking at the same page for an hour. She frowned with annoyance. Mr Beattie would be angry with her, when, later on in the evening, he asked her to conjugate the future tense. And who could blame him, when he gave his precious time to teaching her? She sighed, closed the book, and smoothed her pale hair, before descending two flights of stairs to join the family at supper.

The soup was cold. Congealed fat stood on the top in tiny globules. Jane and Harriet ate it in the heavy silence that lay between the master and the mistress of the house, till Edie came in, at last, with the main course. She plonked it down in the centre of the table with some defiance.

'And what, pray is that?' Adeline asked.

'Pan haggerty, Ma'am.'

'Pan what?' George bellowed. He turned on his wife. 'What do you take me for? Do you think I still work down the pits, woman? Do you think I've learnt no better?'

'I asked for stew!' Adeline said bitterly, 'Edie, what happened to the stew?'

'Pan haggerty *is* a kind of stew, Missus.' Edie's face showed every sign of imminent weeping. George moaned, one hand on his brow.

'Never mind, Edie. I suppose we must be thankful for what God, and you, provide us with!' Edie sniffed, and she left the room, thinking how well she'd done to get away with it.

Adeline took up the servers, and Harriet held the plate ready.

Jane looked greedily at the brown, crisp tops of the potatoes. She'd always loved pan haggerty, and hadn't realised how much she'd missed the old homely rations, like pig's cheek, the things, in fact, she used to long to get away from. She hoped there'd be a few potatoes from the top left for her. As the first dollop plonked onto the waiting plate, Harriet's lip curled.

'Yerrrrrrk!'

'And what sort of a remark is that for a lady?' George asked. Jane looked at Harriet, and Harriet looked at Jane. Immediately they both burst out laughing. George went pink.

'What on earth . . . !' Adeline was staring at the plate. Suddenly she shouted loudly, 'Edie! Edie come here at once!'

'Yerrrrk!' Harriet said again. George's eye fell on the food.

'What in heaven's name is that?' he gasped. 'It looks like frog spawn.'

Edie came in, in a state of some apprehension.

'You called, Missus?'

'I did, Edie. Come here, please.' Edie came. 'Look at that.' Edie looked, and shifted from foot to foot. 'What is it?'

'I don't know, Missus.'

'You must know! Presumably you put it in there!'

'Are you trying to poison us, girl?' George shouted at her. Edie rose to her own defence.

'The missus told's to put it in. I don't know what it is. I only do as I'm told!'

'*I* told you to put it in?' Adeline asked indignantly.

'Yes, Missus. You said put in the leftovers. So I did. It was all the leftovers I could see anyway.'

'Oh my God!' Adeline went pale; her hand trembled.

'*Now* what's wrong?' George demanded.

'Where did you find these leftovers, Edie?'

'On the kitchen table, Missus. There was this jar, left open, half-used it was. Wasn't that what you meant?'

'That, Edie was caviar!'

'Whatever it was, Missus, it was left over from the Queen's buffet do!'

George went white. He looked frantically at the plate, then at the oven dish, as though wondering how much of it could be saved. Then he flung down his napkin, and roaring with rage left the room. Edie flung her apron over her face, and ran out of the other door, sobbing for all her life's worth.

'Shut up, you silly bitch, before I murder you!' George's voice was heard receding into the distance, and he left the house, in search of solace in his greenhouses.

'Well!' Adeline said, after a while, 'I suppose we ought to save its life!' Harriet giggled, then stopped at a glance from her step-mother, who continued serving the meal. Each waited for the other to start. Finally Adeline showed the courage of her convic-tions, and took a ladylike portion on her fork, dropping it into her mouth as though it was a firework.

'Yerrrrk!' she cried, spitting it out again. Then all three women burst out laughing, and they laughed till their sides ached.

'Eeh, but you've got to see the funny side, haven't you?' Adeline said. It was the first time in the history of Beattie's shop that the three womenfolk had been in full agreement.

Jane missed her lesson that night, and when George came back, he found Edie still sobbing in the corner of the kitchen.

'Get to bed!' he ordered. Once again the apron was thrown over her face as she fled upstairs; and in exasperation, George shouted, 'I don't know why you don't just cut two holes in that for your eyes and be done with it!' Edie stumbled on the stair, George shook his head, and she ran up to the attic, as he, more ponderously, made his way to his own room.

'Amo amas amat,' Jane intoned by the light of her bedside candle. Tonight she had been reprieved, but he would surely hear her verbs tomorrow. She yawned. 'Amo amas amat.' Her eyelids drooped. It was no good. She closed the book. It was a pity about that pan haggerty. She'd really been looking forward to it too! She sighed and put out the candle. The house was silent. Harriet slept soundly. Edie dripped tears onto a sodden pillow and Adeline lay stiff as a board in the big bed of her room. Her sides ached from laughing, but there was no smile on her face now. She heard George moving about in his room.

Alert to every sound, like a rabbit in the forest, Adeline felt the menacing threat of George's restlessness. He had begun to pace the room. Back and forth, back and forth. Then suddenly, his door wrenched open, and he was in the corridor. What should she do? She watched her door knob turn slowly, stop, then, after a long pause, George released the knob, and knocked gently on the door. She did not answer. After all, she was asleep, wasn't she? He tried again. Harder this time. Why had she not locked the door? Then he called out, sharply, 'Adeline, are you asleep?' No use pretending she was asleep now!

'What do you want?'

'We have matters to discuss!'

'At *this* hour?'

'I can't conduct a conversation through the door, Adeline!' The wife said nothing, and suddenly the door burst open and he was in the room, a lighted candle in his hand. Adeline got out of bed and pulled on a dressing gown, motioning him to sit in a chair, like a hostess at a tea party when an unexpected guest arrives. George suddenly felt awkward, and embarrassed. But why should he? She was his wife, wasn't she?

'What was it you wanted to discuss, George?' Adeline asked him, lighting a taper at the embers of her fire. George watched her body arch as she raised her arm high, reaching for the candles on the mantelpiece. She stood poised, as the wick took light.

'You're a beautiful woman,' he said. Adeline turned, startled.

'Really George!'

'Yes. Really.'

'We've been married for too long for all that now!'

'*I* haven't.'

Adeline backed away from him, and found herself against her bed. She shot away as though it had been on fire, and stood for safety by the chest of drawers.

'You promised, George.'

'I know, I did, Addy. But it doesn't get any easier. I thought it would. But it doesn't. Perhaps if I didn't see you every day . . . ' Adeline gasped.

'What are you suggesting?' George shook his head. Suddenly he felt exhausted, defeated.

'I don't know. I don't know.' Adeline's eyes were dark with fear.

'I do love you, George . . . I can't help it, can I? The doctor said . . . '

245

'No. You can't help it. The trouble is, Addy, neither can I.'
There was a long silence.

'What are we going to do?' the wife asked the husband. He laughed sardonically.

'You needn't worry, Adeline. I don't think you're in any danger tonight . . . not now.' Adeline sobbed. He looked at her, wondering whether it was in relief, or sorrow that she cried. She was shaking visibly.

'I feel so cold, George.'

'Come near the fire.' She hesitated. 'Come on. I won't bite you!' She came nearer, holding out her white hands to the dying embers. George looked at them, trembling, and was filled with an overpowering compassion for his wife. 'Addy . . . Addy . . . ' Her eyes glowed in the candlelight as she looked, wondering at him. 'I'm a brute of a man.' A tear oozed from the corner of his eye and she longed to reach out her hand to comfort him. But she resisted the temptation.

'I wish . . . I wish I was different. I despise myself.'

'No, no George. You're a man!'

'Made in God's image. Yes. Not an animal.'

'You're not an animal, George.' Her voice wavered. She had turned towards him. His arms reached out to her waist, pulling her into him, and he buried his head in her belly, crying weakly.

'Oh I am! I am! Forgive me, my love! Forgive me!' Her hands, hanging limply at her sides, slowly rose to softly touch his head, stroking gently, caressingly, and he moaned into her dressing gown, his arms tightening round her. But her hands lifted away from him. Feeling the loss of contact with her, George raised his head, and asked desperately, 'Only tell me you want me as much as I want you!' Adeline's eyes pleaded with him. How could he ask her such a thing? 'Tell me!' he demanded loudly. A moment, a haunting moment, and she was pushing him from her, crying out,

'No! No!' George slumped in his chair, creased with pain, but she staggered back from him as he rose, and screamed at her, 'I wish I'd never married you!'

Upstairs in the attic, Jane lay in darkness, listening to the rising voices, 'I blame you, Adeline. Edie's only half there!'

246

'How did *I* know she would finish off the caviar!' Adeline wailed.

'Do you know how much that stuff cost?'

'Here we go again! Money, money, money! It's all you think about!'

Harriet woke with a start. She frowned. Money? Had he found out then?

'If you had to do the books you'd think a bit more about it, woman!'

'It was only one jar of not very good quality roe, when all's said and done, George!'

Harriet breathed a sigh of relief, and sat up in bed, listening.

'Roe! Roe, she calls it!'

'All right, all right. Don't go on at me. It won't happen again. I'll watch her like a hawk.'

'And for God's sake tell her to stop crying! If she goes on like this, I'll have to think about building a Noah's Ark to save us from the flood!' Adeline's door slammed, and George pounded back to his room, slamming that door too. Jane jumped. Well if that was marriage . . . ! Harriet got out of bed, and pulled a box from underneath. She just wanted a little peep. And there it was, in all its glory. She would just try it on one more time. Smiling, she tied the ribbon under her chin and went to the mirror to give herself her full approval. In the adjoining bedroom, Adeline sat stiff with fright, staring into the ashes of her fire, while George, like Edie, cried into his pillow.

'And what is the past tense of the verb "to love?" ' George twiddled with his pencil, as Jane gathered her thoughts.

'Amabam, amabas, amabat, amabamus, amabatis, ama . . . bant?' she queried.

'Correct. Very good. You're an apt pupil!' He slapped her knee with his hand and smiled at her. 'Jane . . . Isn't it time you wore something a little more cheerful?' The remark surprised her. She looked down at her old black silk.

'I thought you liked a sober dress, sir.'

'Don't call me "sir". We're better friends than that, aren't we?'

'Yes, of course, Mr Beattie.' The hand withdrew, and George sighed.

247

'How long is it since you read to me, Jane?'

'Quite a while, Mr Beattie.'

'Read to me now.' He reached for his well thumbed copy of Wordsworth. 'You choose.' Jane took the book from him. It opened automatically at the Ode George loved so much.

There was a time when meadow grove and stream,
The earth and every common sight,
To me did seem
Apparelled in celestial light.
The glory and the freshness of a dream.
It is not now as it hath been of yore;-
Turn whereso'er I may,
By night or day,
The things which I have seen, I now can see no more.

The rainbow comes and goes,
And lovely is the Rose,
The Moon . . .

'You're a rose, Jane.' Jane looked up from the book, startled.

'What? I mean, pardon, sir?'

He was looking at her strangely. His eyes sent an odd sensation creeping up her back. She shivered. And then he looked away.

'I said, *you* are a rose.'

'Oh.' Jane replied.

'My first wife was called Jane.'

'Was she?'

'I still miss her. Not that I don't love Adeline.'

'No. Of course not.'

'Harriet's not much like her really. Probably takes after her father. Pity.'

'I'm beginning to like Harriet!' Jane was herself surprised at the realisation.

'Are you?'

'Yes.'

'Wear something more cheerful tomorrow.'

'But it's Sunday!'

George smiled. 'You're young! Don't let those "shades of the prison house" close upon you yet, Jane!' She frowned, in some confusion. 'I think it's time you forgave yourself for Ronnie's death.' Jane bit her lip, and looked down. 'I see you still pine for him.'

'Sometimes, I feel as though I'll never love anyone, ever again.'

'Once we've given our hearts . . . I gave mine to my first wife. She wasn't very strong, and I . . . well, I wasn't what I am now. We were poor. I started with a barrow on the street. Stop me if I've told you this before . . . ' Jane tried not to smile. 'She was a willing horse. Worked herself literally, quite literally into the ground. I find it hard to forgive *my*self for that.'

'Shall we make a pact, Mr Beattie?' Jane's eyes, filled with tears, were, even so, smiling at him. 'If you promise me you'll forgive yourself, I'll forgive myself, for Ronnie.' He looked back at her, his large bearded face, soft and vulnerable as a child's. His hand reached out to grasp hers.

'Done!' he said. After a pause, in which each reflected on the great event that had just taken place, they both laughed. 'So! What are you going to wear for me tomorrow, eh?' Jane considered the matter.

'I've not got a lot of choice, to tell you the truth!' she said.

'Then that is something we shall have to put right! I shall speak to Mrs Beattie.' With an unfamiliar sensation of light-heartedness, Jane left her employer to get on with the books.

CHAPTER SIXTEEN

The Methodist Chapel lay on the north side of the junction of Chapel Row and Waterloo Vale. It was within walking distance of Victoria Terrace, and the entire household proceeded along the street, behatted, begloved, and carrying their prayer books in their hands. Today, George was preaching, so there could be no absentees on this occasion. He stalked into the building, followed by Adeline, who took little running steps to keep up with him. Then Harriet lagged behind, and close on her heels, Jane and Edie walked side by side, filing into the pew which was set aside for the Beatties.

Jane had taken to Methodism, immediately. Its stark approach to the Divine suited her mood after Ronnie's death, and it pleased her employer to see her taking to more sober ways. For over a year now, she had beaten her breast, 'wailed and gnashed her teeth' over her sins, and now George had said she should forgive herself. Her hand touched the fading black silk of her dress, as he climbed up to the pulpit to speak. When she thought about it, the black had faded, and there was a grey, shiny sheen to the cloth, as though her mourning itself had diminished. Idly she considered the past. It was strangely distant now, as though the events of that dreadful Sunday had happened to someone else. George coughed, and opened his Bible.

'The first epistle of Paul to the Corinthians, Chapter Seven. "Now concerning the things whereof ye wrote unto me: It is good for a man not to touch a woman.

'Nevertheless, to avoid fornication, let every man have his own wife, and let every woman have her own husband.

Let the husband render unto the wife due benevolence: and likewise also, the wife unto the husband.

Defraud ye not one the other, except it be with consent for a time, that ye may give yourselves to fasting and prayer; and come together again, that Satan tempt you not for your incontinency . . . " '

Adeline had taken off her gloves. The movement caught Jane's eye, sitting beside her, as the white fingers pulled at the gloves, stretching them back into shape, pulling, smoothing, setting them down in her lap, and then, carelessly putting them on again.

' "But I speak this by permission, and not of commandment. For I would that all men were even as I myself. But every man hath his proper gift of God, one after this manner, and another after that. I say therefore to the unmarried and widows, it is good for them if they abide even as I.

But if they cannot contain, let them marry: for it is better to marry than burn." ' With deeply furrowed brow, George left the pulpit and took his seat once again beside his nervous wife.

Neither looked at the other, as the congregation rose to sing the hymn.

Forty days and forty nights
Thou wast fasting in the wild;
Forty days and forty nights
Tempted, and yet undefiled.

Searching in her pocket, Edie found a strawberry cream. Surreptitiously, she plucked the fluff from it, and popped it into her mouth.

Shall not we Thy sorrow share,
And from earthly joys abstain,
Fasting with unceasing prayer,
Glad with Thee to suffer Pain?

A dribble of chocolate coloured saliva, oozed down Edie's chin. She felt it, and flicked her tongue out in an attempt to remove it.

And if Satan vexing sore,
Flesh or spirit should assail,
Thou, his vanquisher before,
Grant we may not faint or fail.

She had not succeeded. The tickle on her chin alerted Edie to the continuing progress of the chocolate coloured dribble. The tongue flashed out again. Had she reached it? Too late. George Beattie was walking to the pulpit to say his piece. In agony, Edie wiggled her chin about, hoping to dislodge the tell tale sign of the misdemeanour.

''Tis better to marry than to burn,' George announced, and gave the congregation the benefit of a long hard look. For a second, George hesitated. It was unlike him. Adeline looked up from her gloves, and was surprised to meet her husband's eyes. 'God, you see, is kind,' he stated. 'He knew how we are tempted in this life by the sins of the flesh. And in his mercy . . . knowing our frailty, he has provided for us an institution within whose bounds man's animal nature might be safely confined.' Adeline looked away.

Coming out onto Chapel Row, Jane felt the refreshing spring air on her face, and with it came a feeling of hope. She longed for a walk on the sea front, and for the first time in months wondered how they were getting on at Pilot Street. It would be so nice to go down there and visit. Her eyes took on a wistful look as a stray gull screeched over the rooftops, making its way towards the Gas Works. George and Adeline were deep in conversation with a woman dressed in deepest mourning.

'Who's that?' Jane asked Harriet.

'Mrs Minto. Her husband died three weeks ago.'

'What a shame! And them children can't be more than five or six years old at most!' They watched as George took some large books from Mrs Minto, and smiling and waving, he and Adeline wished her well, and made their way towards the waiting girls. Quickly, while she had the chance, Edie reached for another chocolate and popped it into her mouth, fluff and all. She immediately began choking. Adeline frowned, and gave her the automatic slap on the back, almost sending the sweet flying from Edie's mouth. But the maid held onto it with her teeth, and sniffed the tears back up her nose.

As George joined them, he was shaking his head.

'That poor woman!' he said, in dramatic tones. 'It's hard. It's hard. Life is indeed but a vale of tears!'

'If you say so, dear,' Adeline rejoined, 'she knows how to get people to do things for her, I'll say that.' George glared at her.

'Do you mean to tell me you begrudge that poor widow woman my assistance over these accounts? Is it *her* fault her husband got them into a mess? Is it her fault, he died? Is it her fault . . . ?'

'All right! All right, George. No need to go on . . . dear.' Members of the congregation passing by, greeted them, and George and Adeline smiled their goodbyes between clenched teeth.

'Let us at least put a good face on things, my dear,' he hissed into Adeline's ear, striding quickly away, then vented his feelings by going for his favourite scapegoat. 'Did I see you put out your tongue at me, in church, Edie?' he demanded. Edie gasped, and tried to open her mouth to speak, but could not. 'Have you nothing to say for yourself!'

'Mmm . . . aggh . . . mmm.' Edie declared.

'I see,' said George. 'What is that in your mouth?'

'Mothing.'

'Mothing? And what is a "mothing", if you please?' Harriet giggled, and hid behind Jane's back, while Adeline sighed and looked the other way. 'Is that a sweet you have in your mouth?' Edie nodded. It seemed the easiest way. 'I see. And were you indulging in the same, in church?' Edie nodded more slowly. 'Not only have you shown total lack of respect to God Almighty, Edie! You have shown total lack of respect to *me*!' He punched his prayer book with his fist, growled, and marched off up the road, his wife running behind him, and the three girls trailing in the rear.

'I thought you said they was all soft centres!' Edie complained bitterly to Harriet, as Jane ran ahead and out of earshot.

'Mr Beattie! Mr Beattie!' Jane called out after him. George

slowed his pace, and looked back, as Jane caught up with him. 'I wondered, if you would mind my visiting my family today.' George frowned.

'But Jane . . . you can't go down there! Not on your own.'

'I've not heard from me Dad or Robert for ages, and I'm worried about them. I thought maybe me sister might have had word.' Jane's eyes pleaded with him. Was it the threatened pleasures of pan haggerty that had made her so homesick? Was it the spring air? Or was it, as she had said, concern for her father and brother that made her want to risk the town end.

'On your own head be it!' he said, like Pontius Pilate, washing his hands of the whole business. 'Women!' he thought. 'There's not a rational thought in their heads!'

Jane felt a tremor of fear as she walked down the Mile End Road. Coming first to the church of Saint Stephen's, she hung back, as the congregation came out of matins. She pulled her shawl down over her face, so that no-one would see her, and hid behind a tree in the far corner of the churchyard. From where she stood, she could see the old faces emerging from the dark porch, quite clearly. Close behind, a dog started barking. She jumped, and looked round at it. It was Gormless. He was standing, baying at her, where everyone could see him.

'Sh, you stupid animal!' Jane hissed, 'it's only me! Remember?' For a moment, Gormless looked more puzzled than usual, then slowly, light dawned, and he yelped joyfully, wagging his tail. 'That's no help! Shoo! I don't want them to see me! Go away!' Sadly, Gormless stood, head cocked to one side, then, he seemed to shrug, and made off galloping toward his mistress.

'Come on ye stupid hound, before I kick your teeth in!' Ma Dunn was heard to shout endearingly. Jane prayed the dog would not rush back to her. Was she looking for trouble, coming down here? Far better go home. 'Home,' she said out loud. Yes. Fowler Street was now her home. Not here. This was all part of the past. Part of someone else's life. Why haunt the old scenes, the old people? Did she want to see Ronnie's grave? She shuddered. No. No, she'd rather remember him as he was, alive! Better get away from this place! For God's sake, supposing she saw Jack! An old man came slowly out of the church, walking

254

painfully, his feet shuffling. Jane frowned. This straggler, this pitiful old man was Rattler Tully. Compassion brought tears to her eyes. As the crowd dispersed, she emerged from her hiding place, and drawing her shawl close, she followed her family down the hill to Pilot Street.

'Look what the wind's blown in!' Fanny shrieked, opening the door.

'Who is it?' Ma Tully's voice rose out of her pots and pans. She was cooking the dinner. Looking to left and right, to make sure no-one was watching, Fanny grabbed Jane by the skirt, and hauled her inside.

'What are you trying to do to us? Get us all lynched?' But Rattler's eyes brightened.

'Why if it's not our little angel, eh?'

'Some angel!' snapped Fanny.

'No need to cast stones, pet,' Dandy said softly, 'Howway and sit down. She's in the club again,' he explained. 'And she gets a bit ratty, like. You know how it is.'

'Oh. I *am* pleased.' Jane felt a real pleasure at this news, and watched wistfully, as Dandy helped his wife into a chair, and rubbed her aching back. 'Mind, Eddie's grown.'

'You didn't expect him to stand still, did you?' Fanny muttered, but Dandy's magic hands were working miracles on her. She began to groan with pleasure and relief. 'Ooh I do love you, Dandy Tully!' she said, laughing up at him.

'I know,' he said wryly, his arms reaching round to her front, to pat her swelling belly. 'And there's the proof of it.'

'Oh you're a disgrace!' But Fanny was beaming. He bent to kiss her. 'He's a disgrace isn't he, Ma?'

'That's not news,' she said, up to her arms in potatoes.

'Speaking of news . . . ' Jane began, 'has there been word from Dad or our Robert lately?'

'Didn't you know?' Dandy asked her, 'Robert's coming home in a couple of weeks, and your Dad'll not be far behind him. He was in Margate last heard of.'

In spite of her excitement at the news, Jane felt like an outsider in the family. They all had their places here. There was an open affection amongst them, and she stood awkwardly, politely by.

255

'Howway, pet!' Jane turned to see Rattler, his thin, sinewy arm outstretched towards her. 'Sit on me knee, eh?' Jane went towards him and took his hand in her own.

'I'd be too heavy for you, Rattler.' Rattler's arm went round her waist. 'Aye but you don't mind a cuddle, do you?' Jane smiled.

'To tell you the truth, Rattler, a cuddle's what I need most!' The ice was broken, and they all laughed.

'I knew it!' he said victoriously. 'Them nobs don't know how to go on with each other, man, they're far too polite!' And he winked at Dandy who grinned back, while Fanny slapped him fondly on the wrist.

'When are you going to get wed, Jane, eh?' Dandy asked her. Jane shook her head.

'I don't know, Dandy. Maybe never.'

'Well that's no good!' Rattler told her. 'You'll turn into a dried up old spinster, Jane, if you don't. You've got proper po faced as it is!' Jane gasped, but had no time to reply, as Fanny threw her son at her.

'Here hang onto him, for me!' she said, 'I've got to relieve meself!'

Three hours later, dishevelled and pink, Jane left the Tully house. Her black silk had baby's sick down the front and her fair hair had fallen down about her shoulders.

'You want to watch you don't get picked up looking like that, pet!' Rattler warned her.

'It's all right, Dad. I'll go with her,' Dandy held out his arm to Jane, and she saw that his hand had one finger missing.

'What's happened to that?' she asked.

'Our Fanny bit it off!' he said seriously. Jane's jaw dropped.

'Never!' They all laughed.

'Don't be daft, man! It got caught behind the rope when I was climbing onto deck, a wave threw's against the side, and chopped it clean off.'

'Ah! Kiss it better, eh?' Fanny mocked him, kissing the stump of his finger.

'Gerroff ye silly bitch!' Dandy shouted affectionately. Then he turned to Jane. 'Howway. Let's get you home!' Fanny put her head outside, and looked both ways, calling a greeting to a passing neighbour, before coming back in and whispering urgently,

'Now bugger off! And don't come back here again, for God's sake. I'll get Dad and our Robert to come down to you.' Then the door closed behind her, and Jane followed Dandy out into the street.

Poised over the tea cups, Adeline dropped two lumps of sugar into her husband's tea, and looked across at him.

'Have you not finished with Mrs Minto's accounts yet?' she demanded. George looked up at her.

'These are the *shop* accounts, Adeline,' he told her. Adeline raised her eyebrows. Something was wrong. He was never that calm when everything was all right. Trembling, she brought his cup to the desk and set it down beside him. He looked at it for a moment, then at her hand, which she withdrew. Then he reached for the silver spoon and began stirring. The china jingled in the silence.

'What did you think of my preaching this morning, Adeline?' he said suddenly. Adeline jumped.

'Excellent, I'm sure. As usual.'

'I see.'

There was a long, uncomfortable pause. Adeline began to shift away, but then George spoke again.

'It seems I have to be as Saint Paul,' he said precisely. Adeline snorted. 'I should have thought you'd be glad.'

'Frankly, my dear,' Adeline said haughtily, 'I never thought that much of him!'

'Saint Paul?' George's voice rose dangerously.

'Yes.'

'But he was a saint, woman. Who are you to . . . '

'Exactly. I'm a woman. And he doesn't seem to have thought much of women, does he? And as for him being a saint, I think he was just a trumped up, overblown, self-important imposter!' George's jaw dropped. He went pale, and his pen fell from his hand.

'Do you know what you are saying?'

'I've thought a good deal about it, in the years since you've been preaching. And it seems to me, that if God had wanted people to be celibate, he would never have created the world in the first place. It simply isn't logical, George!' George considered what she had said. It was true. 'I mean,' Adeline went on, encouraged by his lack of response, 'Does he say much about children? The Virgin Mary got married and had a lot of children according to the Bible! The Catholics worship the Mother of God. Hah! Paul was just a . . . a . . . woman hater!'

George was at a loss. Adeline flounced back to her tray, and poured a great deal of her tea into the saucer, missing the cup, in her excitement.

'I mean, I know things are . . . difficult . . . for us, George. But I don't think you should hate me for it. It isn't my fault, you know.'

'Is it mine?'

'Must there be blame?' she challenged him with her eyes, and he looked away, disarmed by the unusual strength of her outburst. 'I wanted to have children George. You know I did. There are times even now . . . ' Her voice trailed away into a sob. And then she gathered more force as her distress grew upon her. 'I know I never will have a child. But that doesn't mean that I don't feel as other women do. There are times, George, there are times when my womb aches to hold your son, and I could cry with the grief of losing him month after month. My life bleeding away from me until it's too late. Can you imagine how that feels, George? To know that soon, very soon, it will be too late?' He had no answer. He felt her eyes piercing him for long moments before she wailed, 'It isn't fair!'

' " . . . there hath passed away a glory from the earth." '

'Oh, shut up!'

'Don't tell me to shut up, woman!' George's voice became dangerous. 'Why, you can't even add up, can you?' Then he flung the books at her. They hit her on the knee, and her hand reached out to rub the spot.

'What do you mean?' she asked, 'what's wrong?'

'We are ten pound short on last week, according to these figures!' Adeline frowned.

'Ten? Impossible.'

'Ten pounds, Addy. Where is it?'

'What are you suggesting?'

258

'Either you've made a mistake, Addy, in which case far better confess it now, or you've spent the money. Which is it?' Adeline took the books, and opened them. Then she looked over to the money, which George had taken out of the box. 'Count it, if you like.' Adeline sighed.

'I'm sorry, George,' she said quietly, 'I suppose I must have made a mistake.'

'Hah!' he said, picking up his cup of tea. 'It's cold! Get me some more!' he ordered. 'And I bet,' Adeline thought to herself, as she went back downstairs to the kitchen, 'Saint Paul had women running round after him too!'

Jane limped into the kitchen some time later, to find Edie ironing. Harriet had gone back to Newcastle.

'What have you done to yourself, Jane?' Adeline asked her in some alarm.

'They threw stones at me!' Jane was crying. 'Some of the children! Dandy caught it on his cheek as well!'

'Tut! You shouldn't have gone!' Adeline reproved her gently.

'I won't any more. I don't belong there now.' Adeline looked at her, longing in her eyes, and then walked deliberately over to her and took her in her arms. It was hard to know which of them was comforting the other.

It was still dark when Jane dressed and left the shop with George the next morning. It was Monday, the day they took the train to Newcastle, buying flowers. George was strangely distant and Jane thought he had forgotten his promise of a dress. She had cleaned the black silk, but it still smelt peculiar, and she was unpleasantly conscious of it, as they rode along the rails towards the city. But in the flower market it was lost in the overpowering perfume of narcissi. It went to her head, making her feel giddy. Seeing it, George offered her his arm, and she clung onto it as they left the market and went to take breakfast in a little cafe in Grey Street. It was a treat worth getting up in the morning for. Only George was so silent, he made her feel awkward. As they waited for their tea, he cleared his throat, 'I heard about the unpleasantness yesterday, Jane,' he said gruffly. 'You must look on *us* as your family now.' Jane looked at him, gratitude pouring from her eyes.

'Dad always said you'd be like a father to me, Mr Beattie.'

259

'And so I am, Jane,' George nodded slowly, in agreement, 'so I am. And I haven't forgotten that little promise I made.' He smiled, and her eyes shone back at him. 'I see you remember it too!'

'Eeeeh!' she said, 'you mean I can really go and buy a proper dress, all of me own?'

'All of your own, Jane.'

He left her in the hands of the shop assistants, and went off on business. Jane wore the ladies out, as she looked first at one colour then another, first plain dresses, then ones with flounces and frills. Should she get one really posh dress? Or should she be sensible and get three plain ones? What a dilemma!

'Try them on Miss Beattie,' the assistant suggested.

'Oh, I'm not Miss Beattie. I'm Miss Ridley,' Jane said smiling. The expression on the assistant's face made Jane blush. They thought . . . well, no matter what they thought, George Beattie was a father to her, whatever they might imagine. It was their own dirty minds, that's all!

She shook with apprehension as George got out his purse to pay the bill. Would he approve? Would he be angry with her for not being sensible?

'Would you like to see it first?' she asked him.

'No, Jane. I'm sure I can rely on your good taste.' And when she got home, Jane and Adeline disappeared upstairs to have a 'try on', leaving George alone in the shop.

'Oh!' Adeline's hands shot up to her face.

'Oh dear. You don't like it. I daresay they'll take it back,' Jane said.

'Take it back? Don't be silly, dear. You look beautiful! Look in the mirror.' Turning to the dressing table, Jane saw herself, tall and slim in the scarlet velvet, her pale throat rising from the tiny frill at the neck, her cheeks flushed with pleasure. Coming up behind her, Adeline took the pins out of Jane's hair, and twisted it up into a knot on top of her head.

'That's better. Very fetching!' she said.

'Will his nibs approve?' Jane fell back into the old familiarity, the relationship they had had before Ronnie died.

'Let's go down and see,' Adeline challenged her. Jane quaked at the idea, then giggled.

'Well he did say I should wear something a bit more cheerful!' George's eyebrows raised a fraction, then dropped again.

'Very nice. A little gaudy. But tasteful,' he said.

'He likes it,' Adeline told her, and Jane smiled.

Later that night, as Jane was working in the parlour at her French translation, George coughed silently, and she looked up to find him standing before her, a parcel in his hands.

'I er . . . happened to see this while I was doing my business rounds this morning,' he said, 'I hope you like it.'

'For me?' George nodded, and sat to watch her as she opened the parcel. She could hardly believe it. What could it be? First a dress, and now . . . now . . . Oh it was a picture! It was a framed print of . . .

'Like it?' he asked her timidly.

'It's beautiful, Mr Beattie. It'll always remind me of our cosy times reading poetry together. Thank you very much, sir.'

George sat back, satisfied. Her face was blank with amazement, as she looked down on a field of corn, and behind it a dark sky, with the dramatic colours of a rainbow splashed across it.

CHAPTER SEVENTEEN

'The trouble is, pet . . . ' Bob Ridley's eyes searched the horizon, as though the words he was looking for lay just out of sight, and might at any moment appear, like the trawler coming towards them over the curve of the world. His eyes narrowed onto its masts, and he shook his head.

'What, Dad?' Bob could not look his daughter in the face. His eyes had fixed themselves on the trawler and would not be distracted from it. 'Please! I've got to know what's wrong!' Then he turned his head to her at last, and there was a sad expression, in his eyes.

'It's just that you've changed so much. You're not the same little lass I used to know.'

'Everybody grows up, Dad. I can't help that!'

'It's not just growing up, pet. You've grown away.'

'Dad!' Jane's reproachful voice had tears in it.

'I mean, I still love you, and that . . . '

'But . . . ' Jane spoke the word for him.

'But, after Ronnie died, nothing could ever be the same again.'

'No.' Now Jane was quiet, and she too watched the horizon, as though wondering what might be in store, just beyond.

'Not that I'm holding that against you . . . Eeh I don't know how to put it.' He shook his head.

'Try. Please.'

'All right. I'll try.' The trawler sailed closer and closer, till, at last, it was engulfed by the harbour, and it disappeared behind the pier. 'It was a brave thing that, standing up there in court, telling them what for. I was proud of you.' Jane could have burst with gratitude at this one tribute from her father. 'But, for a start, it's meant hardship for your family, pet . . . '

'I know.'

'Rattler's in such a state he couldn't work now if he wanted to, it's only the pigeon sweeps that keeps him going! But there's a proper old conspiracy afoot in the Pilot's office to cheat Dandy of his rightful work. They're finding it hard to make ends meet, what with the kiddie, and another one on the way. And it didn't help, you going down the town end the other day, visiting, you know.' Jane sighed.

'You're right. It was selfish of me. I shouldn't have done it.'

'I mean, in any case, they're not your life any more, are they? Why, Jane, you even speak different now. Posher like. It makes people like us uneasy with you!' Jane's eyes burned with sudden anger.

'That's daft, Dad! I'm still the same Jane Ridley!'

'You're not.'

'I am inside!' Her pain pierced him. It was the first point of real contact between father and daughter since the inquest.

'Why *did* you go down there? Eh? What were you trying to prove?'

'What makes you think I was trying to prove something? I just wanted to see them, that's all! Is that so terrible?' Bob shook his head and looked away. 'No. All right. I admit it. I know what it was I needed. I needed to remind myself how a real family lives! I needed . . . I needed . . . a cuddle!' she threw the word at him, defying him to laugh. 'There's times I feel so lonely, Dad! So lonely! You can't know how lonely it can be, when there's no love in a house!' And Bob understood at last. Hadn't he felt the same emptiness in his own aching heart when Ida died? 'Just a cuddle sometimes. That's all. That's all I need. I'm not asking for the moon!'

'Aren't you? Sometimes, I think, maybe that's just what we are

263

asking for, when we ask to be loved . . . ' He smiled sadly, and she laughed a little through her tears, each reaching out to the other, along a bridge of compassion. 'One thing I have learned in life, Jane, and that is, we can never go back. We can only go forwards. Forgive and forget. They go together. Things won't ever be the same. Get used to the idea. You've got to leave us behind now. Live your own life. Find love where you can.'

'But we can see each other sometimes, can't we, Dad? I mean we can meet like this, on the front, have a cup of tea in a cafe, talk, and walk together.'

'Aye. But we mustn't depend on each other, pet. We must meet on equal terms. You're a big lass now. You always were beyond me. So, don't try to lean. Not any more. And then, maybe, we can become friends, eh?' Jane nodded. She sniffed back the tears.

'I love you, Dad.'

'And I love you. That's why we have to let each other go. Then maybe we can find each other again.'

How could she live without love? She would be barren. She would die. She had so much love to give. All she lacked was someone to give it to. Jane fell to her knees, beneath the picture of the rainbow.

'How, in God's name, am I to get through my life?' she demanded out loud to the empty air of her room. 'What does it all mean? I don't understand!'

Alone in the chapel, George knelt and prayed. What was love? Did he, George Beattie, mayor of Shields, lay preacher, and businessman, did he fall short? He had done his duty. He had taken in his first wife's child. He had fed and clothed her. She never wanted for anything! And he had loved his first wife! Hadn't he? Looking up at the shining cross on the altar, George felt as though a spanner had been thrown into the works of his well-used brain. For a moment, he could not think. A slight pain crossed his brow. Surely he could work this one out? He had started from nothing, a barrow boy . . . self taught, Latin and Greek, connoisseur of the arts, and of antiques . . . the pain grew stronger. What was wrong? How was it he could not work it out?

'What is love?' he asked the empty air of the chapel. And there was no answer.

In the Mahalaxmi Temples in Bombay, Robert sat watching Chandrika's back, breathing in the heavy incense of the stifling air. His legs ached. His back ached. Sweat poured down him. And yet, he was glad he had come.

Ya Devi sarva bhuteshu Vishnumayaiti shabdita, namastasye, namastasye namastasye Namoh namah.

Ya Devi sarva bhuteshu Chetanyaetyabhidhiyate namastasye, namastasye, namastasye, namoh namah.

He began to join in, what he thought of as the chorus, 'Namastasye, namastasye, namastasye, namoh namah.'
He looked down at the piece of string on his wrist, and shook his head, smiling. Why had Shankuntala made him do it? She had given him this funny look, and told him she had found him a sister, a young girl in her own family, called Kunti, and at the annual Rakshabandhan celebration, he had given and received the tie of brother and sister binding him to her for life. He still bore the tie, even now.

Ya Devi sarva bhuteshu Kshaanti rupena samstitha namastasye, namastasye, namastasye, namoh namah.

Shakuntala had said something about him having to learn to forgive his sister for being a woman. As if he *could* hold that against her! It was ridiculous! He loved his sister. It was just . . .

Ya Devi sarva bhuteshu, Smrti rupena samstitha namastasye, namastasye, namastasye, namoh namah.

Robert had seen a great deal of his father's old friend during his time in India. Under his care, he had grown up. He had forgotten Miss Reid, and laughed at his old infatuation. But the rift between himself and his sister still bothered him. When, eventually, news of Jane's situation reached him, Chandrika had urged him to go home to her. But, something had held him back. He knew he had hurt her, had punished her for his own disappointments, and now he could not face her. Chandrika's little wife had frowned and shaken her head at him. And the next thing he'd known, was that he had a dark-skinned sister from a Maharashtran village, presumably to practise on!

Ya Devi sarva bhuteshu Daya rupena samstitha
namastasye, namastasye, namastasye namoh namah.

Or, was it himself he couldn't face . . . ?

Ya Devi sarva bhuteshu, Maatre rupena samstitha
namastasye, namastasye, namastasye namoh namah.

The sweat dribbled down inside his shirt.

Ya Devi sarva bhuteshu Bhraanti rupena samstitha,
namastasye, namastasye, namastasye, namoh
namah.

Yes. It was time he went back, and put things right. Surely the tie of blood was stronger than the string about his wrist! Or was it? Surely he loved his own sister?! Suddenly the need to return had become urgent with him. He would tie a rahki round his sister's wrist, and then nothing would come between them again. Was it time which had altered his perspective? Or was it India? It was not the places he had seen. Nor the people. It was . . . something in the air. It crept into your heart while you slept, and made its home there. And suddenly, you were subtly changed. The ceremony was coming to an end. Robert left the temple with his host, and put on his shoes in the courtyard.

'I shall miss you,' Chandrika said, smiling. 'Give my love to your sister. I think so much about her.'

'Love.' Chandrika used the word with ease, but not indiscriminately. For him, at least, there was no problem.

As the holiday approached, and Harriet May came home again, Jane worked side by side with her in the shop, hardly listening to her prattle as she made up the button holes for the Good Friday Parade. Jane's heart was fluttering with anticipation. Soon he'd be home. She wanted him to come. She wanted to see him, and yet, it had been so long since he'd gone away, and his letters had been so few and far between . . . She and Robert had made it up, before he sailed, but it had been like putting a patch on a worn jacket! Perhaps, the cloth around the patch had worn away in the months since she'd seen him. Perhaps he'd changed. Her father said *she* had changed. How should she behave towards her brother? What could she expect?

Edie plonked down their cups of tea on the counter.

'Thank you, Edie,' Jane said absently. Edie pulled a face at Harriet, who giggled.

'She's well away!' Harriet said, and then began a long, whispering conversation. Jane only half heard what they said. The spring sunshine was pouring in through the shop window, onto the brightly coloured anemones, bunched up and ready for sale. Idly her mind wandered as her eye drank in the crimson, the blue, the purple, the white . . . bright as stained glass in a church window.

'Go on!' Edie whispered, 'I'm dying to see it!'

'Which one?'

'The pink one with the cream lace.'

The colours bled onto the shining white marble of the counter, casting a pink glow about the bowl. Like sunset on a mountain top. Like the tip of a Himalayan mountain in the dying light of the sun . . .

'Yes you do. The one you wore when your James took you to the ball!' The blue carried shades of a clear sky, fading in the heat of the midday sun . . .

'I haven't unpacked it, yet.'

'I'll help you unpack, shall I?'

'No! . . . thank you.'

The purple had the reflected depths of an unknown lake, hidden, secretly far away. A place of mysteries . . . Had Robert seen such things? Did they exist, except in her own imagination? Would he describe them to her?

Jane was called up to George's parlour before closing time, and Harriet was left alone in the shop to cash up. But as soon as Jane had walked into the room, George irritably waved her out again. If *he* didn't understand the poem, how then would *she*, a mere woman? He stared down at the scrap of paper sent him from the south.

I asked a thief to steal me a peach:
He turned up his eyes.
I'd ask'd a lithe lady to lie her down:
Holy & meek she cries -

As soon as I went
An angel came.
He wink'd at the thief
And smil'd at the dame.

And without one word said
Had a peach from the tree
And still as a maid
Enjoy'd the lady.

Why! It was disgraceful! George frowned. Were his friends in the poetry circle teasing him? If this was the sort of thing Blake wrote, he was not surprised his work remained largely unpublished!

Surprised by Jane's sudden reappearance, Harriet started as she walked back into the shop.

'Oh you gave me a fright, Jane Ridley! What do you mean by creeping up on people like that?'

'I'm sorry. I didn't mean . . . ' Jane sighed. She couldn't do right for doing wrong today!

'Go on. Take the flowers down to the cellar. Serves you right for spying!'

'But I wasn't . . . oh never mind.' Jane sighed and bent to pick up a tub of daffodils. She would never understand this family in a million years! She staggered to the top of the cellar steps, set down her burden and opened the door down to the darkness. She would need a light if she was going to brave it down there.

As Mayor, George had to lead the procession on Good Friday. He looked splendid in his Mayoral chain, as the bands blared behind him, and the various bodies and organisations marched through the town. Harriet, in her new hat, stood with Jane and Edie, waving from the pavement. With its silk roses and cornflowers she could have won the prize in the parade. But Harriet had not entered her name.

'Why not?' Edie wanted to know.

'Because,' Harriet told her.

'Tell.'

'Shurrup!' Harriet had forgotten her ladylike manners.

'Na! And anyway, I can guess why!' Edie said knowingly. Jane looked at the maid, puzzled. But Harriet flushed, and Jane looked away again. After all it was none of her business. Adeline, pleading a headache, rested in her room. She lay, with the blinds drawn, on top of the counterpane. The distant thudding of the drums drew nearer. Perhaps she should shut the window? She sighed, and raised herself to sit on the edge of the bed. Adeline Elizabeth Rogers. What would her life have been, if she had never married George? He had swept her off her feet, had said he loved her. She shook her head, and went to the window, to open the blinds. The reek of decaying flowers reached her from the yard below. Mounds and mounds of them. She closed the window with a bang. It was high time George took the lot of them over the road, to put on his precious compost heap!

Late that night, George sat up alone in the parlour, reading. Blake was an undiscovered genius. If he did not understand his work, then he, George Beattie was at fault. Not the poet. His brain buzzed with confusion. No good trying to fathom the morality of the angel, when he was not one! Was there no escape from the torment of his mind?

There is a moment in each day that Satan cannot find,
Nor can his watch fiends find it; but the Industrious find
This moment & it multiply, & when it once is found
It renovates every Moment of the Day . . .

The words shouted from the paper in his hand. He read them again, then closed his eyes. ' . . . a moment in each day . . . ' What moment? He listened to the sounds of the house. There was no such thing as silence. The clock ticked. The pause between the ticks was silence. Was that the moment? He listened to the pauses between the ticks. In those pauses, he could hear creaks, sounds of settling in the building. He could hear noises from outside. But between those noises, there was silence. His breath caught in his throat. Perhaps if he listened hard to that split of a second when there was no noise, he would begin to understand . . . There it was. Silence. He listened, and then hung on to the memory of it as the house creaked again. And in his mind, the silence continued, underneath the clock ticking, the fog horns blowing, the fire settling, the creak on the stair.

> . . . the Industrious find
> This moment & it multiply & when it once is found
> It renovates every Moment of the Day . . .

George held on to his silence. The stair creaked again, the coals settled, there was a knock on the door, and the silence fled as Adeline walked in, tight lipped and determined to have her say.

'George, I've been waiting to speak to you . . . ' George sighed.

'What now?'

'It's about that mess in the yard. When are you going to move it?'

'Tomorrow.'

'It smells to high heaven. Why, this afternoon, when I was trying to rest . . . '

'Must you complain all the time?' George bellowed, 'I was just feeling peaceful, damn you!'

'George! That is no way to speak to your wife!'

'You're not my wife!' Adeline's face visibly paled. 'Nor are you a partner in this shop!'

'What do you mean by that?'

'Why don't you ask me if you want money for anything?'

'I do.'

George shook his head. 'The books are wrong again, Adeline!'

'No!'

'I hold you responsible! Either you're an incompetent fool, or you're stealing from the till!' Adeline ran upstairs to her room, slamming and locking the door behind her. Her sobs could be

270

heard in the next house, where the grocer woke; they could be heard in the attics, where Jane was studying her Latin; they could be heard by Edie who pulled the bedclothes over her head; Harriet turned over and slept; George threw his slippers at the fire. Satan's fiends were working overtime!

On Sunday afternoon, Jane helped George move the piles of decaying vegetation. Rolling up her sleeves, she shovelled the stuff onto the barrow, and George wheeled it over the road, through the gate and into his nurseries. Forking over the heap, George considered his employee. He liked her. She was like a daughter to him. More than Harriet May really. Yes. He loved Jane more than Harriet. His fork hung suspended in mid air. 'Love?' Had he then used the word? Why? Surprised at his discovery, he set down his fork, and sat on a stone beside the heap. Slowly he nodded. It was true. If he loved anybody, it was Jane. He loved her like a father. He felt real affection for her. Was that then love? Was that what Adeline wanted? So, by the decaying flowers on his compost heap, George sat pondering on his wife, till the sun began to drop in the sky, and a chill fell on the spring evening.

Harriet had been to Newcastle that morning with George, to buy flowers, and she stayed on to do some shopping. Jane had given her the money to buy some silk poppies for her dress, and now she was sewing them contentedly in place. It would cheer up the navy nicely. But Adeline was frowning as she bent over the books. George was right. There was something wrong. She had counted the money in the till every day that week, and checked it against the written figures. They tallied on Tuesday. They tallied on Wednesday. But they had not tallied today. She sighed. Five pounds was a lot of money. How could it have gone astray? For the moment she would say nothing. She went to her drawer and took out some of her own dress allowance to make it up. Suddenly she heard whispering on the stairs, and Harriet's door opening, then closing quietly.

'I really must speak to Harriet about Edie,' Adeline observed. 'They're as thick as thieves these days! It isn't right!' But, as she went out into the corridor, Adeline heard George shouting, in the yard.

'Come here you blasted brute! Do as you're told, or I'll give

271

you such a hiding . . . !' Who was he speaking to? Really, the place was turning into a positive madhouse! What would the neighbours think?! She ran on past Harriet's room and down to the kitchen. As the door to the yard opened, a yelping beast leapt in on her, sending her reeling backwards.

'Help! Help!' she shouted.

'Heel!' George commanded, grabbing the dog's lead, 'Heel, I say!'

'Oh my God!' Adeline gasped from the distant corner. 'It's the hound of hell!'

'Don't be so soft!' George snapped, 'just look at it!' The little spaniel sat, head cocked to one side, wagging its tail. Shaking like a leaf, Adeline held out a trembling hand.

'Good dog,' she said doubtfully.

'I don't know about good,' George laughed, 'he's a little rascal!'

'He's a filthy brute!'

'Adeline! It's my surprise.'

'It's a surprise all right!' she snapped.

'I thought . . . I thought . . . it might make it up to you . . . you know . . . for not being able to have a baby . . . something to cuddle.' Adeline looked at her husband for a long moment, then rushed out weeping.

But George's disappointment fled as the girls fussed over the little dog.

'I could just love him to death!' Jane said, grinning.

'I'll have to take him back.'

'Why?' Three voices spoke as one.

'It seems Mrs Beattie doesn't like dogs . . . '

'But you can't send him back now!' Jane pleaded for the dog, as though appealing for a reprieve from the death sentence.

'We'll see.' George was weakening. Jane smiled.

'Look at him. Isn't he a little scallywag!'

'Just what I said,' George laughed.

Standing on the sea front, Jane watched the ships coming in. Her feet itched to take her up to the Lawe, and down to the quayside, to be there when Robert's ship docked. She pulled her shawl tight round her shoulders. The wind was cold coming off the sea, and there was a mist lingering on the horizon. A sharp bark drew her attention, and she frowned as Scallywag ran across the beach towards a stray terrier.

'Scallywag! Scallywag! Come back here! At once!' she ordered. The spaniel hesitated, looked round, and suddenly started galloping back to her. He bounded round her legs.

'Come on home. Come on, now. Come home, boy.' Walking him up Bent House Lane, Jane fretted and fumed. It wasn't fair! She wanted to see her brother! He was now so near, and yet, so far. Well, she would just have to be patient and bide her time. Robert would surely come and see her soon!

That same night, as Jane was helping Edie wash up the supper things, there was a knock at the back door. Jane rushed to answer it, and there stood Robert, golden skinned and smiling. Jane cried out, throwing her arms around him. She held his chilled face close to hers, kissing him, before letting him into the room. 'Eeh!' she repeated, over and over again.

'Eeh!' he mocked her. Then their laughter died. Brother and sister looked at one another shyly. 'By, you've grown, our Jane.'

'So've you!' She patted her hair into place, while he shifted from foot to foot. Then he said,

'Are you not going to invite's to sit down, then?'

'Sorry. Would you like a cup of tea?' It was too much for Edie.

'Honest!' she said, 'you two! Give the lad some bubble and squeak. There's some veg left. Make yourself at home, pet.' With that, Edie left them to it and went up to her room in the garrett.

'Who's that?' Robert asked.

'The maid,' Jane laughed, 'but she's the boss in the kitchen, when the "Missus" is out!' She sat at the other side of the table, her hands clasped in front of her, her cheeks dimpling at him. 'I have missed you, Robert,' she said softly. His hand reached out to her, and slowly, she put out her own. They met in the centre of the table, and gripped tightly. There were tears in Robert's eyes. Suddenly he let her hand go, and fished in his pocket for something. Jane frowned. What was he looking for? A hanky? But instead, he pulled out some string. One piece was yellow with a bobble and sparkly stuff on the end. She was drawing her hand away.

'No. Leave it there,' he commanded. He leaned across the table and slipped the string round Jane's wrist, tying it in a knot. 'There,' he said. 'Now you're my sister again. My Rahki sister.' Jane laughed.

'You're crackers, you are! I was your sister before. And what's all this about anyway?' She tugged at the string on her wrist.

'No! Leave it be! It's a symbol of my brotherly love for you. Wear it, for me. Now you tie this on my right wrist.' He gave her the red, tasselled piece of string. Jane shook her head and laughed.

'All right . . . All right. If you say so!' She leant forward, and tied the string, knotting it as he had shown her.

'That's a symbol of your sisterly love for me. We'll never fall out again, eh?' Jane's smile broadened into a grin.

'Now that's a really good idea!' she said.

The next night, Jane went down to Adeline's room to put on her red velvet dress. She had never worn it, not once! She had been waiting for a special occasion. And tonight, her brother Robert was taking her to the theatre! She would see actresses! She would hear the words of great writers! She would be with Robert all evening! Excitedly, she struggled with the dress, and Adeline shook her head, watching.

'Come here! Let me!' Buttoning up the bodice, Adeline smiled. 'It's a pity it's not some handsome beau that's taking you out. That's all I can say! You're a sight for sore eyes, Jane Ridley.' And she sat Jane in front of the triple mirrors, while she set about arranging the long, fair hair. Jane watched her own reflection, and wondered at what she saw. 'Somebody should paint you looking like that.'

'Robert paints!' Jane told her.

'Well then, perhaps, while he's home, we can prevail on him to paint *you*!' Jane laughed, and raised her hand to put a stray curl back in place. 'What's that?' In the mirror, Jane saw that Adeline was looking at the rahki tied around her wrist.

'Oh, it's just a whim of our Robert's. It's a symbol of his brotherly love for me.'

'How strange! Is it an Eastern custom?'

'Yes. I had to give him one too.'

274

'Curious!' Jane held up her wrist to look at the tie.

'I don't know. I think it's a nice idea.' Jane's eyes were large and wet with tears, as she looked into the mirror. The yellow tie was reflected to left and right, and back again to infinity, in the triple glass. It would last forever. Brotherly love.

CHAPTER EIGHTEEN

Shades of green and mists of blue fused and crossed before her eyes. Wisps of gauze fluttered from above, and a silver moon hung over all, as the two lovers bemoaned their fate. Jane's head reeled, unable to contain the feast of poetry, so that it flew from her grasp and she was given up to the emotions of the play, transporting her from scene to scene, like the wind blows the leaves in the autumn.

Poor Lysander. How could he bear it? To love and yet be kept apart from his Hermia?

Oh hell! To choose love by another's eyes.
Or if there were a sympathy in choice,
War, death, or sickness, did lay siege to it;
Making it momentary as a sound:
Swift as a shadow, short as any dream.

Jane brushed a tear from her cheek, and Robert, distracted by the movement, turned to look at her. What was wrong? Was it Ronnie? Had his sister loved him then?

And ere a man hath power to say, Behold,
The jaws of darkness to devour it up:
So quick bright things come to confusion.

What else was love? Robert thought. Hadn't he dreamt his dreams about Miss Reid? And what was to stop him from

276

making the same mistake again, confused by his own dreams.
The characters might change, but the scene remained the same.
Now Helena spoke;

Love looks not with the eyes, but with the mind,
And therefore is wing'd cupid painted blind.

Harriet's hands moved through the pink organdie of her ball
gown, lovingly. White lace hung delicately from the sleeves.
Wave upon wave of filmy pink swept down towards her feet.
Holding it against herself, Harriet swayed before the glass,
encircled in her own arms, the dark haired beau of her
imagination was whispering words of love into her ear.

'James! Oh James!' she crooned, and her eyelids closing on
reality, she gave herself into the bliss of wished-for love. And as she
wished, James began to take a more material shape in her mind.
His skin was golden, and his hair sun lightened, and he had an
aura of the mysterious east . . .

'Adeline! Adeline! I want you!'

Harriet would close her ears. She would not hear the rows, the
discordant sounds. She would not hear Adeline sobbing,
desperate for comfort. Robert's arms were about her. Harriet
opened her eyes, and in the glass she saw the chandeliers of a
ballroom, a million candles burning brightly, and she and Robert
were dancing, dancing . . .

'I can't, George! And in any case it's *my* money! It's meant to
be my dress allowance! God knows it isn't much!' Yes, Harriet
would close her ears. She didn't want to hear.

The Queen of the fairies had left Oberon with her train, and he
was angry. She had crossed him, would not let him take the little
boy as page. Lord Of Illusions, he would then teach her: He
would play a game with her . . . Puck flew off into the fluttering
gauze which hung over the stage.

Having once this juice,
I'll watch Titania when she is asleep,
And drop the liquor of it in her eyes:
The next thing when she waking looks upon,
(Be it on lion, bear or wolf or bull

277

On meddling monkey, or on busy ape)
She shall pursue it with the soul of love.

Jane was surprised to hear Robert laughing! To her it was sad, to play with someone's feelings. As the lovers wandered, lost through the woods, a mist rose, creeping, gusting up around the characters on stage, and out into the audience. And then the curtain fell, and Jane blinked, to find herself once more in reality.

'Oh it's magic!' she whispered. Robert grinned broadly.

'Thought you'd like it! I saw a bit of theatre when I was in London.'

'When were you in London?'

'Stopped off on my way home.'

'Oh. There's such a lot you haven't told me, Robert.'

'What . . . for instance?'

'What was India like?'

Robert smiled and shrugged. 'How can I tell you? It's so hard to describe. When I try, it all sounds so . . . ordinary somehow.'

'You can be very annoying, our Robert!' Jane's eyes blazed at him, but she was smiling at the same time.

'Come on. I'll buy you an ice cream!' He took her arm, and led her out into the foyer, where all the audience milled about. Jane stood against a wall, watching. It was a different world. There was a world outside. There was a world here in the foyer, and then, when the curtain went up again, she would be transported to a different world again! How many worlds were there? And which one should she live in? She preferred the one on stage. She could hardly wait for the interval to be over. Supposing she had become an actress! Oh, how she wished she had! She could have lived in that other world all the time then, playing the parts of fairy queens, and Grecian lovers, to her heart's delight. Robert thrust a vanilla ice into her hands.

'Mmmm. It's good,' she said. She slurped up the ice cream, laughing, but Robert was looking pale and serious. 'What's wrong?' she asked.

'Nothing.'

'Robert! Tell!'

Robert sighed and shrugged, then looked furtively behind him. 'I'll tell you when we get back to our places,' he said. He was

278

upset. What could have happened? She touched his arm with her hand, and he put his hand on hers, then felt the rahki thread still tied to the wrist. He looked down at it, and twisted the end in his fingers. 'I'm sorry I hurt you.'

Jane suddenly jumped, as the warning bell sounded, and Robert guided her back to their seats.

As the gas lowered and the light faded, Robert leant towards his sister and whispered, 'I saw Miss Reid in the foyer. She was with her husband.' Jane looked anxiously at him in the half dark.

'I'm sorry,' she said.

'No need to be. That's the shocking thing. That's what upset me! I didn't feel anything at all! It's just as though it all happened to somebody else!'

'Sh!' the woman behind them commanded. Robert leant closer in, so that no-one else could hear.

'Perhaps one day, you'll feel the same about Ronnie.'

'I don't think so. I really loved him, you see.'

Robert looked back into Jane's unwavering eyes. They gleamed in the darkness. Then he put his arm round her and squeezed her tight. The curtain rose, and the clowns came on.

'How am I expected to pay this bill?'

'I don't know, George. But I can't lend you it. I've spent most of my allowance.'

'What on?'

'This and that.'

'This and that! What's happened to you, Adeline? Have you become a secret drinker?'

'Don't be so ridiculous!'

'It's you who are ridiculous, my dear!'

'How dare you, George!'

'Oh no. Spare me the tears! Tell me the truth! Have you been taking money from the till?'

'No, George. I have not. In fact, I've been putting money in to make up when it's short. That's where my dress allowance has gone.'

'I don't believe you.'

Adeline's jaw dropped. 'Then there's nothing more to be said.' She turned to leave the room. At the door, she stopped; 'If you wish to communicate with me George, I suggest you do it through Jane. For I have no desire for any further discourse with you.' She almost banged into the edge of the open door, as she left. Why had she married him? Adeline sobbed, resentment welling up inside her, as she ran up the stairs. He was a pig! A monster! In the parlour, George hissed loudly, threw down his books and then went up to his room, where he rived away at his chest expander. Washing up, in the kitchen, Edie was startled to hear a loud noise, followed by a curse, and the sound of something smashing on the floor. She looked up at the ceiling, anxiously. The chest expander was no more.

Jane sighed, wishing life could be like the play. If someone like Oberon could only put everything right for her, and when she woke in the morning, she would find Ronnie there. She sighed. Robert's arm closed about her. She looked at her brother thankfully. She wasn't alone. Someone loved her. It was all that mattered. Oberon removed the spell from his queen, and the curtain came down for the last time. For the characters on stage all had ended happily. Silently, brother and sister left the theatre together. Outside, a sea fret made the air damp and chill. They huddled close together in the cab, as though to fend off the coldness of the outside world, whose mists swirled in at the very windows.

Robert was to stay on in Shields for a month, and then, following his agreement with Roper's, he was to sail to South America. Bob had talked his old employers into taking his son on in a higher capacity. He was no longer just a 'boy' but a proper deck hand, who was expected to use his eyes and his ears, to learn all he could. The immediate target was to get his mate's ticket, to come up to his father's level. But after that, the master's ticket beckoned. And Robert submitted to his father's ambitions, unsure what he wanted for himself. He had not touched a paint brush since he had left Shields eighteen months or more ago. Jane was disappointed. She had expected to see a sketch book full of drawings of the exotic places he had seen.

'Can't you do them from memory?' she asked. So Robert had taken up his pencil again to oblige her. He worked at Jane's side, while she wired in the wreaths and made up the wedding bouquets; for after Lent, there was a rush of weddings, and the shop exchanged the perfume of narcissi for that of freesia, and lilies: exotic bridal perfumes! And in Jane's imagination, they filtered into the white marble of the mausoleum at Agra, the tribute of Shah Jehan to his well loved wife, Mumtaz Mahal.

'It's no good!' Robert sighed and put down his pencil. 'You can't draw the Taj Mahal. I mean, you can't draw how it feels, when you look at it. See . . . ' He held up his sketch book. Adeline and Jane both looked at the beautifully drawn lines of a perfect building. ' . . . all you can see from this, is the building. You can't see the . . . the . . . love.' Adeline looked at Robert in surprise, and he blushed to have revealed himself to someone who was, after all, almost a stranger.

'Perhaps, if you *painted* it . . . ' Adeline suggested tentatively. Robert considered the idea.

'I don't think I could.' But Adeline had taken up the idea with enthusiasm.

'Let me buy you some paints, and a canvas. My husband knows so much about painting and poetry and such like. He keeps up with all the new works from London. I'm sure he'd be pleased to help!' A gleam had come into Robert's eyes. He glanced at Jane. She was grinning from ear to ear, sensing his growing excitement.

'Oh do, Robert!' she encouraged him, 'please do!' Robert shrugged, and thanked Mrs Beattie.

'I don't know what to say.'

'You don't have to say anything. Just start painting!'

The question was, how to ask George for the money. That evening, when Robert was with his father in Pilot Street, Jane reluctantly accompanied Adeline to George's parlour.

'Ask my husband, Jane, if he will, please, let me have the money to buy Robert's painting materials.' Jane sighed.

'Mrs Beattie would like to know, sir, if she could have money for painting materials for my brother.'

'What makes him think *he* can paint?' he asked. Adeline showed him the sketch pad, and he looked down his long eagle nose at it.

'As a portfolio it leaves a great deal to be desired . . . Still,' he sighed, 'I suppose one ought to encourage new artists.'

Adeline suppressed her smile, as he went to the drawer where he kept his money.

'When is your brother setting sail for the Americas?' he asked.

'In a month's time.'

'Perhaps, when he's gone, you'll find the time to resume your lessons with me?' Jane blushed.

'I'm sorry, if you think I've been lax, sir.'

'Don't call me sir!' With that he handed Jane the money, and she handed it to Adeline, who left the room without a word.

'Don't go, Jane.' George stopped her, as she turned to follow her mistress. She gave him an inquiring look.

'Nothing.' George waved her away, and sat at his desk, fiddling with the order book. A strange sensation overwhelmed him. He put the papers down. He could not concentrate. The clock ticked too loudly. The women talked too much in the kitchen below. He was aware of a horse going up the hill, in need of a new shoe. It grated on his ears. He sighed. What was wrong with him? He'd behaved like a silly fool. What would Jane think? Why should it matter? He should be glad she was so happy! What *was* the worm in his breast? He had to root it out. There would be no peace for him until he did. So he dug deep inside himself, and found it. And the worm was jealousy. George Beattie jealous? Could it be? He had never been jealous of any woman in his life? And why? Because someone else had brought the flush of happiness to Jane Ridley's face? Because Robert had her heart and he had not? An uncomfortable feeling stole over him. The mysterious poem stared up at him, from his desk.

I asked a thief to steal me a peach:
He turned up his eyes.
I asked a lithe lady to lie her down:
Holy & meek she cries -

He put the poem aside. He had dug deep enough. The rest had better remain buried.

It was a week before Adeline and Jane had the chance to go to Newcastle, and, after doing the necessary buying at the flower market, they went to the usual café in Grey Street, to meet Robert for breakfast. The strong tea might just as well have been

282

champagne. And the mood of giggly lightheartedness lasted, as Robert took them, one on each arm, round the shops to buy his painting materials.

'Tell Mrs Beattie, I am deeply grateful to her for her gift,' Robert said with mock dignity.

'Mr Ridley wishes me to inform you that he is deeply grateful for your gift, Ma'am,' Jane interpreted. Adeline bowed.

'Please inform Mr Ridley that he is more than welcome,' she said, then burst out laughing. 'Oh dear!' she cried, tears rolling down her cheeks, 'poor George! If he only knew!'

'Poor George', left alone in the shop, had had to warm Dr Mrs Fletcher's eggs himself, and his silent, reproachful eyes greeted them on their return, that afternoon. To his chagrin, all three burst out laughing, as soon as they saw him, although, Jane, relenting, wanted to show him the oils and the brushes they had bought, and share their good humour with him. But he felt shamed by her attention. It patronised him. It made him feel like a small boy, who had been left behind on a school treat, and was now offered a sweetie as consolation, and he left them to it.

'Urgent council business,' he said, 'I expect it to be a long session, so don't keep supper back for me.'

'Mr Beattie said . . .'

'I heard what he said!' Adeline's mood was broken. Absently, she touched the coloured petals of the anemones on the counter. 'Let him do what he likes!'

The Taj Mahal gleamed under a crescent moon. Stars twinkled in the deep blue sky. The white marble was luminescent, reflecting in the long pool, that stretched towards her like a carpet, inviting her to reach out, to touch the perfect shapes of dome and minaret, to speed along the mirrored image towards the reality; to merge with the moving expression of the love Shah Jehan had borne for Mumtaz, a love that lived on in the experience of the Taj Mahal. Depths of emotion stirred in her.

'It's beautiful,' her voice cracked with tears. She flung her arms round her brother's neck. 'Thank you for sharing it with me. Thank you for sharing India. Now I know what it was really like.' Robert smiled, and took her arms from round his neck to look into her eyes.

283

'Oh, Jane! I could paint forever, and you still wouldn't have experienced India, only the fragments.'

'Fragments?'

'Yes. It's like . . . it's like looking at a stained glass window. As the sun shines through the fragments of coloured glass, you see the red light, and the blue light and the green. But the window has fragmented the light, the one light that shines through it. I've shown you a fragment here; one piece of the window, a shaft of coloured light, that's all; but to know India, you have to see beyond the fragments. You have to realise the spirit behind it. The sunlight that's behind the glass.'

'I see,' Jane nodded. 'I wish I could go there. It's changed you. You're deeper than you used to be.'

'So are you. Don't forget, the same sun shines on England, as shines on India.'

They were in the kitchen, and Adeline, alone in the shop, was cashing up. Both looked up as they heard her gasp, and then cry out. They rushed in to her.

'What's wrong?' Robert asked. Adeline was white faced.

'I don't understand it.' She shook her head. 'Last time it was a Saturday. Now it's a Monday. It doesn't make sense.'

'What doesn't?' Jane asked. Adeline shook her head absently.

'It isn't me. I'm sure of that. It isn't me.'

Jane and Robert looked at one another, then went back into the kitchen, feeling anxious and puzzled.

'Don't worry,' Robert told her. 'It's got nothing to do with us.'

'No.' Jane smiled up at him. 'Don't let's spoil your last night.'

The house was quiet. George was still at a meeting of the hospital committee. Adeline had gone to bed, and Edie sat alone, by the kitchen fire, reading her penny dreadfuls. Jane undressed slowly, by the light of her candle. A fog horn was blowing. Perhaps if the fog was very thick the next morning, Robert would not have to go! The little pane was still broken in the dormer window, and the fog seeped in, smoking the air of the room. She coughed, and pulled on her nightdress. Robert's painting stood on the wash stand, against the wall. It called her. 'The same sun shines on England as shines on India.' The fragment which she saw in Robert's painting, in the Taj Mahal, was a clue, leading on to the something she was seeking.

284

Downstairs, Scallywag barked loudly. The master was home.
He patted the dog on its head, called him a 'good boy', then came
upstairs, singing,

Love Divine, all loves excelling,
Joy of Heav'n to earth come down,
Fix in us Thy humble dwelling,
All Thy faithful mercies crown.

CHAPTER NINETEEN

Robert's absence was like an ever present grief. Jane tried to drown her feelings in work. And when the long day in the shop was over, she would sit at her books in the garrett, reading into the early hours of the morning. Then, as the dawn light came over the rooftops, and sent its tentative rays into her room, she would glance up from the page, red-eyed, and exhausted, to see the painting on the wall. But it was no comfort. It only reminded her what she had lost. And she began to cry, rocking to and fro in her chair. If only she had been able to stand on the quay and wave Robert off! For Jane had not even had the advantage of saying goodbye, and still half expected to bump into Robert on the street, or, as the door clanged, see him walk into the shop.

As the light grew stronger, Jane lay on her bed, and tried to come to terms with reality. Robert had thrust an envelope into her hands before he left and she had put it away, thinking it contained some message, too painful to be read. Perhaps, reading it now would help. She lay still, for a while, watching, as the white outline of the Taj became more visible, gleaming as though the painted crescent of the moon itself shone on the white marble. Tears sprang into her eyes again. It was no good. She jumped from the bed, ran across to the chest, and pulled open the drawer containing the envelope. For a moment, she hesitated, then, in one bold gesture, she tore it open, and out fell a note, with five pounds, wrapped inside it. The note read, 'To spend on anything you like, Love Robert.'

And she had expected some moving message! Jane laughed, and immediately felt better. Planning what she might spend her brother's present on, she walked up and down, thinking. She needed another dress. Yes, that would be sensible. Or a new cloak? But what she longed for most was a pair of dainty shoes. Her stockinged feet peeped from under the hem of her dress. She watched them flip the cloth as she walked, first one side, then the other, treading lightly on the floor. Her clodhoppers stood, durable, inevitable, by the hearth, where she had left them the night before. She looked at them with hatred. They would burn well. They would keep her warm one long night. Her eyes narrowed. Yes! Her mind was made up!

The smell of Beattie's famous toffee bubbling on the stove, permeated the house, as Adeline bent, red faced over the pan.

'I hate making toffee!' she muttered resentfully, as Jane came in from shutting up shop.

'Shall I do it for you?' Jane asked.

'What? I'd have to tell you the secret recipe, wouldn't I? More than my life's worth!'

'What the mind doesn't know the heart doesn't grieve over,' Jane answered philosophically.

'Huh!' Adeline snorted.

'Where is Mr Beattie, anyway?'

Adeline shrugged. 'Council meeting.'

'On a Saturday?'

'Emergency meeting of the sanitary department, so he said.'

'Oh.' Jane put the kettle on the stove, next to the simmering pan. 'Harriet won't be long. She's cashing up for me.'

Edie had finished scraping the new potatoes, and brought her filled pan to the stove.

'Mind out, Missus!' She elbowed her mistress out of the way.

'Really, Edie!' Adeline scolded her.

'Do you want your dinner or don't you?!' Edie retorted belligerently, and went back to the washing up.

'I blame Harriet,' Adeline whispered. 'She's been getting far too friendly with Edie. It's given her ideas.' Jane nodded. It was true, Edie had been getting more and more 'uppitty' lately. 'I'm afraid I shall have to put her in her place.'

'Perhaps it would be fairer to speak to Harriet.'

Adeline sighed. 'Oh dear! Poor Harriet!'

Jane looked at her, puzzled. 'Why?'

'Tut! Jane! Hadn't you noticed?'

'Noticed what?'

'Why, she's in love with your brother!' Jane's jaw dropped.

'Never!' she said, aghast. Adeline nodded.

'Hadn't you seen her mooning over him? Tut! And he hardly noticed her at all.' Jane was shaken. It had never occurred to her. When Harriet came into the kitchen, she looked at her with new eyes. She looked tired, her mouth turned down at the ends, her shoulders rounded. She was the image of disappointment. She spoke sharply.

'I've finished in there now. You can brush the floor if you like.' Edie, one chore done, picked up her brush and went to start another. Poor, poor Harriet! How selfish Jane had been! She put her arm round her and made her sit, while she set a cup of tea in front of her.

'What's all this in aid of?' Harriet asked suspiciously.

'I thought you looked tired. That's all.'

'Huh!' Harriet snorted in disbelief.

'Adeline, would you mind if Harriet and I met up in town, next Monday, and did the marketing together?'

'You and Harriet?' Adeline was very surprised.

'Yes. If Harriet likes! I certainly would! We could have a look round the shops afterwards. It's your birthday next week . . . ' Harriet looked at her narrowly.

'You didn't buy me anything last year!'

'I know you better now,' Jane said gently. 'If there's anything particular you want, you must tell me.' She stared at Jane for a moment.

'If you like.'

It was easier to get up for the early train, as the mornings got lighter, and there was an air of holiday about the trip to town this morning. Jane chatted happily, as they rattled along to New-castle, trying to draw Harriet out.

'Have you thought what you want for your birthday?' Harriet gave her a funny look.

'Well, maybe I have, and maybe I haven't,' she said. Jane frowned. What on earth did that mean?

'Tell me what you want, then. If I've got enough money, I'll buy it for you.'

'Will you give me whatever I want?'

'If I can afford it!'

'Oh it won't cost you anything.'

Jane sighed. 'What on earth is it, Harriet May?'

'Your picture,' Harriet said simply. There was a long silence.

'What picture?'

Harriet snorted. 'You know very well. The one Robert painted. The one of that white building. My stepfather paid for the paints anyway!'

'Oh.'

'You said you'd give me whatever I wanted.' Harriet was smiling, but Jane's heart was in her throat.

'You said it wouldn't cost me anything,' she whispered.

'And it won't, will it?' Jane looked at her sadly. 'You promised!'

'Yes.' Jane looked out of the window of the carriage. The joy had gone out of the sunlight, out of the day, out of her heart. 'Yes,' she said again, nodding at Harriet May.

Jane came back from Newcastle alone. It was dinner time, and Edie was hanging out the washing in the back lane.

'Are the missus and the master in?' Jane asked her. Edie's voice answered from behind a sheet.

'Missus is in the shop, master's over at the nurseries. There's some bubble and squeak in the oven for you.'

'Thank you, Edie.' Jane manoeuvred her parcels inside, and went up to her room, without seeing a soul. Then she sat on the edge of her bed, as though the stuffing had been knocked out of her. She looked up at Robert's painting. How could Harriet do this to her? But she had promised. She had to give it up. Harriet's birthday was on Thursday. She would take the painting to Newcastle with her on Wednesday, when she went in for the flower market, and that would be the end of it. Abruptly, she jumped from the bed, and took the painting down, turning it to face the wall, before unpacking her parcels, and going back downstairs to eat her bubble and squeak.

Washing day always had a mournful aspect. Clothes hung about the stove, airing. The food was hashed-up leftovers from Sunday. And being market day, Jane was always tired, when finally, evening came. But tonight, she was more tired than usual, as she rocked herself in the chair by the hearth, drinking her tea, and Edie cooked supper. Adeline was still cashing up and George was out. Hot tea and sunshine! Life wasn't so bad! It was peaceful sitting there, thinking of nothing in particular. Yes. She would shut out all thoughts, all feelings, and just enjoy the moment. Jane closed her eyes, and drifted into a doze.

'I've never!' she woke with a start.

'Don't lie to me!' Adeline's voice was shrill and strong. Edie began to blubber.

'It's no use crying! You won't get round me that way!'

'But I never!' Edie repeated through her sobs.

'What's happened?' Jane asked, startled.

'Miss here, has been pilfering from the till! That's all!'

'I've never! So there!' Jane shook with the shock of sudden waking. Was this a nightmare, or what?

'You might as well confess, Edie!'

'I never . . . ' Edie whimpered.

'Own up, girl!'

'Did you say she's been stealing?' Jane asked in astonishment. Adeline nodded.

'I'm certain of it! It's been going on for ages, hasn't it Edie?' Edie flung her apron over her face, and shook her head. 'At first I thought it was me getting the books wrong! And George thought *I* was spending directly out of the till without accounting for it, if you please! So, I started watching, very, very carefully. And now I know!' Adeline was triumphant. The apron fell from Edie's face. How *could* her mistress know such a thing? Jane asked for her.

'How?'

'You remember I was making toffee on Saturday?' Jane nodded. 'Well, I was so harassed, what with one thing and another, that I never got round to checking the books. Harriet cashed up for me, and then came into the kitchen. You and I were already in here. George was out, if I remember. But Edie went into the shop to do the cleaning . . . on her own!' Jane looked from mistress to servant and back again. 'Tonight, I checked the figures for Saturday, *and* for today separately. Saturday's figures were wrong.'

'It could be pure coincidence!' Jane said.

'Hah! Last week, there was money missing too, but I thought it had happened on Monday, a day Edie *doesn't* go in to clean. But last week, you see, I had put all the cash from Saturday and from Monday in together, and checked through both at once. But, the money *must* have gone missing on the Saturday last week too. *And* it happened the week before! Just how much money have you purloined from this establishment, Edie?'

'What's pearl oyned?' Edie asked, mystified.

'Stolen!'

'I'm no thief, Missus. I've not stolen anything.'

'So!' Adeline sighed. 'You're a liar as well, are you?'

'No, Missus.'

'How can I help you, Edie, if you insist on denying everything?'

'I never did it.'

'Tut! I don't know what Mr Beattie's going to say about all this.' Edie's eyes widened with fear. She'd forgotten about him.

'Does he have to know?' Jane asked.

'Of course he does! He virtually accused me of being the thief! I can hardly take the blame for Edie, now, can I?'

'No, I suppose not,' Jane said sadly.

'I'm not staying where I'm not wanted.' Suddenly Edie got on her high horse.

'I should just say you're not!' Adeline snorted.

'I'm not staying where people accuse me of being a liar, and a thief. I'm not. So there!'

'I'm glad we agree.'

'Don't be hasty, Edie . . . Adeline . . . there must have been some mistake. Edie's been with us for such a long time!'

'Too long!' Edie shouted. 'I never did like this family! You all think you're somebody in this town, don't you? Well, you're not. You're just jumped up flower sellers! That's all you are! Huh! Wait till I tell people about the goings on *I* know about!'

'What goings on?' Adeline asked sharply.

'Miss Harriet for a start!'

Adeline and Jane exchanged bewildered glances.

'Don't say anything you might be sorry for, Edie.' Jane took the maid's arm, but Edie shook her off belligerently.

'Carrying on with young men in Newcastle! Huh! Told me all about it, she did!'

'What young men?' Adeline was pale.

'That James! Her beau!' Adeline looked at Jane for clarification.

'She did mention somebody once, more than a year ago, I should think,' Jane said slowly.

'Well, she's been carrying on on the quiet. I know all about it. Disgusting it is. She's been to balls, and had candle-lit dinners with him in private rooms, late at night. Huh! She's no better than she ought to be, that one!'

'Is this true?' Adeline's voice was cold, and hard.

'I don't know,' Jane shook her head, dismayed, 'I thought you said she was in love with Robert.'

'Robert!' Edie sneered. 'Huh! Anything in trousers if you ask me!'.

'Edie!' Adeline's shocked tone finally put an end to the revelations.

'Well, I'm not stopping here. I can tell you that. I'm going.'

'Edie,' Jane caught at her arm, as Edie made for the door. 'Don't go putting stories like that about! . . . Harriet's reputation could be damaged.'

'I shouldn't think she's got any left to damage, pet.' Edie laughed. 'Not in "Newcarstle", anyway!' With that, the maid went upstairs to her room, and could be heard throwing her few things into her tin box with as much noise as possible.

Adeline sat, shocked, at the kitchen table. Jane shook her head, walked back to her chair, sat down, got up again, then went to stand behind Adeline. She touched her arm soothingly.

'It can't be true!'

'What can't? About Edie? Or about Harriet May?'

'To tell you the truth, I find it hard to believe it about either one of them.'

'Don't be so naive!' Adeline snapped, and Jane's hand retreated from her shoulder. Adeline was shaking, her face was white, and she was gripping her hands so hard together, the knuckles showed white. But there was triumph in her fixed smile.

'By God!' she said, 'this'll floor the old bastard!'

Behind her, Jane stood motionless, feeling the life drain from her. The drama had only just begun.

It was half-past eleven when George finally came home. They heard his sprightly step in the yard, but his jaunty aspect took a severe knocking when it came face to face with Adeline.

'Tell him what has transpired, Jane!' Adeline said. And Jane told George all about Edie, and the pilfering, and Edie walking out on them, and everything. George stared at Adeline, an expression of disbelief on his face. There was a long silence.

'Tell him if he doesn't apologise to me now, for thinking *I* was the thief, I'll . . . I'll . . . I'll cause him the biggest scandal Shields has ever seen.'

'What is she talking about?!'

'Mrs Minto!'

'Mrs Who?' There was a long pause. Adeline and George stared fixedly at one another across the kitchen table. Finally George cleared his throat and spoke.

'Ask my wife not to interfere in my private life.'

'How dare he!' Adeline screamed. 'How dare he!'

'How dare you!' Jane said, then suddenly, she threw her hands in the air and shouted at the pair of them, 'This is bloody ridiculous!'

'Jane! Language!' George objected.

'Oh shut up, you pompous fool!' Jane was furious. Man and wife stared at her in astonishment. They'd never seen her like this before. 'What are you? You're supposed to be the mayor! And look at you! Both of you! Playing games! Using me! You're like children! How dare you do this to me! You've used me! You've used Edie come to that! You use whoever and whatever you like just so long as it suits you! Well I won't stand it any more! I'm going to do what Edie did. I'm going upstairs to pack my bags!'

293

'And where will you go?' George asked her.

'I'll go to Pilot Street.' Jane wavered. She knew she could not go there.

'Don't be silly, dear,' Adeline put out her hand and Jane looked at it, refusing to take it. 'Sit down again.' Jane sat. 'I'm sorry. We've not been fair to you. I'm sorry.' Her voice was gentle and sweet. George was staring down at the table. Above his bushy beard, a faint flush crossed his cheeks and his nose was getting redder and redder. Jane's lips twitched. She began to laugh.

'He looks like a gnome,' she said. George looked up, startled. 'Me?'

'Yes. You, George!' Adeline laughed, 'and she's right!'

'You spoke to me, Adeline!'

'Huh!' Slowly Jane got up from her seat again and went towards the kitchen door. When she looked back, they were sitting silently, looking at one another. She heard George whisper, 'I'm sorry, Addy.'

It was decided to say nothing to Harriet, yet. After all, it was her birthday. Better leave it till the following weekend, when George and Adeline could speak to her privately at home. So, on the Wednesday, Jane took herself to Newcastle as usual. But this time, she was accompanied by George, who carried her offering, Robert's painting, under his arm.

'I don't see why you should give her this. It's far too much,' he told her.

'I said she could have anything she wanted.'

'You mean she trapped you into it.' Jane considered her reply, and then said, 'Nevertheless, I promised. And Jane Ridley always keeps her promises.'

'You're a perverse little madam, aren't you?' Jane flushed with anger.

'I promised,' she repeated.

'All right. Have it your own way,' he shrugged. After a pause, he smiled, a teasing smile; 'Penny for them.'

'Oh! I was only thinking . . . well . . . Harriet's probably done me a good turn, in a way . . . '

'And what's that, pray?'

'I love Robert's picture, but . . . but . . . it upsets me.' She looked out of the carriage window, to hide her face from him. 'It makes me want things . . . it stirs deep feelings I can't satisfy.' George coughed.

'And what might they be?'

'Nothing,' she said quietly, 'only I feel better with my old drawing of the elephant on the wall. It's comforting. It's nice.'

Harriet May came home on Friday night, bedecked in ribbons and lace.

'Where's my supper?' she stood, hands on hips, in the kitchen.

'You look like a trollop!' George hissed.

'Don't be too hard on her!' Adeline pleaded in alarm, as he rolled up his sleeves.

'You want to know what there is for your supper, do you?'

'I'm hungry,' Harriet complained, 'where's Edie?'

'Hah! Well, I'll tell you where Edie is!' Her legs had begun to shake. Harriet, who had had a nice week, with presents and birthday cake and everything, was not prepared for this storm out of the blue. 'Edie has been given the sack!'

'No, she hasn't George. She walked out on us.' George exploded;

'Will you let me get on with this, woman!'

'No, George. I won't. Now just keep calm, and sit down. Shouting won't help anybody.' As Jane came in, George blabbed, 'What about the shop?'

'I've locked the door, Mr Beattie, and I've put up the "closed" sign.'

'Who told you . . . ?'

'Jane and I both agree, George, that it is quite enough that Edie has threatened to tell the world about Harriet's goings on, without the customers hearing all about it in our own establishment!' Harriet looked from one to another open mouthed. She was beginning to get frightened.

'What goings on?' she asked. 'I've not done anything! Why, I'm only here at weekends!'

'It isn't what you've been doing here that's bothering us, Harriet May,' Adeline told her, 'It's what you've been doing in Newcastle!'

295

'But I've not been doing anything in Newcastle!' Harriet said in bewilderment.

'Don't tell lies, girl!' George boomed. Harriet looked at Jane for enlightenment.

'They've found out about James,' she said quietly, 'and before you ask, no it *wasn't* me who told them. It was Edie.' Harriet howled a wordless howl.

'No use crying about it now, Harriet,' Adeline told her gently.

'I don't understand . . . Why would Edie . . . ?'

'Edie has been stealing from the till. When we found her out, she got very nasty, and, I suppose to get her own back, she betrayed your confidence. She told us all about your carrying on with this young man of yours. And a good thing she did!' Harriet was silent. What to say? What to do? She was trapped. Like a wild animal, searching for a way out, she looked around and fixed her eye on Jane.

'I don't believe Edie *did* steal from the till,' she sneered; 'Ask *her*!' George and Adeline looked from Harriet to Jane in surprise. Jane took a step backwards. What was this? 'Ask her, where she got the money to buy her new shoes, and her fancy dress!' Harriet said triumphantly.

'Jane?' George asked. Jane shook her head, frowning.

'Jane, you must tell us. Have you been buying new things on the quiet?'

'Have a look in her room!' Harriet said. 'Huh! I was with her when she bought them!'

'Robert gave me the money.'

'Oh yes?' Harriet sneered, 'and him over on the other side of the universe where he can't be questioned!'

'But he did!'

'Very convenient.' Jane looked beseechingly at George and Adeline, but the seed of suspicion had been sown, and it shone from their eyes.

'Jane. Tell the truth,' George demanded.

'I *have* told the truth.'

'But, I don't understand, if it was all above board, why didn't you show me what you'd bought, Jane? Why hide the things in your room?'

'Because all the joy'd gone from them.'

'Hah!' Harriet laughed.

'Harriet had asked me to give her my painting, the one Robert did. It took all the joy away. I've not looked at the things I bought since I got them.'

'You're lying,' George said.

'You know me better than that, sir.'

'I don't know anything, any more,' George said sadly. Adeline turned her pale face away. But Harriet May's eyes did not waver. Harriet would stare out the devil himself. Suddenly the bell clanged at the shop door. Jane tore herself away to answer it. An angry lady stood behind the glass, demanding entrance. Jane pointed to the sign, and mouthed the word 'closed'. And the lady, scowling went on her way. Jane took a deep breath and turned to go back into the kitchen. But her eye was caught by a ray of late sunshine which fell onto the bowl of anemones placed on the counter. She had forgotten they were there. Familiarity had made them invisible.

'Thou preparest a table for me in the presence of my foes.' Well, if God did that, she could hardly expect her foes to like it!

CHAPTER TWENTY

Fanny's childish hand was unfamiliar. Jane looked at the rounded letters, and awkward sentences in surprise. Little Eddie had put a jammy finger right on the most important part of the message.

'Rattler died four days ago. As you know he had never been himself since the bottle of pills got him. He should have been like the rest of us and stuck to drink. It never harmed me, I'll say that. There was a good turn out at the church. Just thought you would like to know, Jane. Otherwise all is well this end.

Your loving sister,
Fanny Tully. Mrs.'

Poor old Rattler! Jane was deeply shocked. She had liked him. Tears sprang into her eyes as she remembered. She had felt lost and lonely, and he had put his arm out to her, ' . . . you don't mind a cuddle, do you?' She could see him now. Poor Rattler! And she'd not been there to see him off! She wondered if her father'd attended the funeral, or whether he was away on a coaster. She had no idea what her family got up to these days. She sighed. And Fanny? She was worried about Fanny. She'd always liked her tipple. Just so long as she didn't like it too much! Perhaps if she wrote to her, arranged to see her in town some time . . . Yes . . . She went to her desk, took out some paper and a pen, to begin writing. 'Dear Fanny . . . ' She looked at her hand. The skin was rough and chapped. All that scrubbing no doubt. She wasn't used to it any more. Her hands had grown soft and white like a lady's. But she was no longer the lady in the flower shop. Harriet had been brought home, and now *she* worked in the shop, while Jane filled Edie's old role in the kitchen, scrubbing the steps, scrubbing the shirts . . . 'Dear Fanny, I was sorry to hear about Rattler. He was a good man, and will be sorely missed.' Yes he would be sorely missed. He left a gap in all their lives. Everything changes. And yet, in a way, it doesn't, she thought, as she looked at the drawing on the wall. There was a feeling of *déjà vu* about her life. As though the same events came round again and again. They only looked different because the characters wore different wigs and costumes. But when you thought about it . . .

There was a time once before when nobody had believed her. But then, she had dug her own trap. This time, she had been unwary, but it was Harriet who had woven the web of lies about her. Ah well. Jane hoped it made her happy. Meanwhile, she would continue scrubbing and washing and cooking. What did it matter? She missed Edie. She hoped she'd found a better place, somewhere else. Perhaps Jane too could find a better place, if she tried? She shook her head. Mud sticks. Even George no longer believed in her, and he had stuck by her against the rest of Shields, after Ronnie's death. Yes. Mud sticks. Harriet's accusation had no foundation, but it raised doubts, because Jane had a reputation for telling lies. George Beattie was good to let her stay on at all.

'. . . Please give my deepest condolences to Ma and Dandy O, and of course to yourself, Fanny. I do miss you all so much. I've had no news of Dad or any of you for such a long time. Do you think we might meet up in town, for a cup of tea and a natter? If you have the time, I would like it so much. Do say you will. I shall put in a stamp for the return letter. Write soon, and let me know.

Your loving sister,
Jane Ridley'

Jane sealed the envelope and went downstairs to post it, before starting the bed time cocoa for the family. As she passed Harriet's door, she heard a strangled sob. She hesitated, one hand on the knob, then passed on. Why should she care? Harriet had made her own bed. Let her lie on it!

And Harriet's bed was soft. The oil lamps cast a gentle shade on the walls of her room, luxuriously papered with a design of roses. Harriet stared at them with hatred. She detested flowers. Their perfume sickened her. Soon Jane would go down to the cellar to fill the pump and spray the chrysanthemums. The stench would rise up the stairs, and make her want to vomit. She was worth more than this! She had been to finishing school and everything! She was cut out to be a lady, not a shop assistant! Didn't George Beattie know that? How was she ever to find a husband stuck in this prison, under her stepfather's beady eye all the time. It wasn't fair. She hadn't even done anything to deserve it! If only she had! She jumped up, and wrenched open the doors of her wardrobe. The line of clothes rocked under her hand. At least she had her dresses! Harriet touched the velvet longingly. Her fingers followed the delicate line of stitching. She put the dress back, and took out the silk; smooth, and sensuous, it reassured her; touching it made her feel loved. She cherished it, and carefully placed it back on its hanger. And then another dress came out, and then another, then still another, till she reached the pink gauzy ball gown, the gown she had only worn in her dreams . . . She held it up against herself. It wasn't fair! She was plain. She was sharp of tongue and sharp of feature. No-one liked her. Well, that was fine because she, Harriet May Lovely, didn't like anyone else either!

'Oh mirror, mirror on the wall, who is the *loveliest* of us all!' To defend herself against the girls at school, she had begun to invent stories; stories about her beaux, and one of them, the handsome James, became so real to her, she began to believe in him herself. That is, until she saw Robert Ridley. But James had done as she bade him. He was her creation; she controlled all he thought and felt and did. Whereas Robert was real, and therefore beyond her grasp. She was tongue tied before him, forced to take a back seat as his sister chatted, took his arm, claimed him as hers! Jane Ridley! She deserved all she got! Why should Harriet be branded as a trollop when Jane had carried on with two men, and one of them killed because of her! It wasn't fair! No. It *wasn't*! And Harriet May could never forgive Jane for that. On her head, Harriet let fall the blame for everything that was wrong in her life; her mother's death, her stepfather's indifference, her own plain looks, her bad temper, for the fact that she was unloved and very, very lonely. She placed the pink dress carefully back on the rail. Her eyes surveyed the long line of clothes. They were all she had. They reassured her that, after all, she did actually exist.

In the kitchen, Scallywag lay, huddled up against the hearth. He opened one eye as Jane came in, and his tail began to wag in a desultory fashion.

'You'll scorch yourself, you daft dog!' she told him, and bent to fondle the animal, pulling him away to a safe distance from the fire. Scallywag rose to his feet, and shook himself awake. 'Want to come walkies?' A single woof, and a pair of sparkling dark-brown eyes answered her. Jane smiled and took his lead from the mantelpiece. Now there was great excitement. Scallywag began barking. 'Sh! You'll get us both into trouble! And there's been enough of that!' He splayed his legs, and yawned, bracing himself for the night air. 'Come on, then!' Jane said, and dog and mistress left the warm kitchen, to strike out into the frosty air.

In the yard, Scallywag pulled back on his lead. Jane sighed, and waited while he relieved himself against the wall. A shaft of light, from an upstairs window, glanced on the midden roof. Jane looked up. Adeline's arm was raised to draw the curtain, and she was looking back over her shoulder, smiling. And then a hand appeared, touching Adeline's shoulder. She tilted her head, laying it against her husband's hand, then turned to kiss it, before raising her arm, to pull the curtain across. Jane lowered her eyes. Scallywag was standing waiting, looking up at her.

'Come on,' she whispered, and the pair of them left the yard quietly together.

First light struck the racks of clothes revealed by the open door of Harriet's wardrobe. Upstairs, in the garret, Jane flung her hand over her head and sighed. She felt weary, grey. The warm bundle at her feet wriggled and worked its way up the bed to lick her face.

301

'Good morning, little'n,' she said, reaching out to stroke him. Scallywag stretched, and jumped off the bed, to wait for Jane at the door of his room. She smiled. 'You'll have to let me get dressed first!' She pulled on her wool stockings and shivered, as the chill hit her bed-warmed body. Then, she looked back longingly at the crumpled place where she had slept. She sighed. No use wishing! 'Honestly, if it wasn't for you, our Scallywag, there'd be nowt to get up for!' Pulling her thick dress over her head, she roughly did up the buttons, and pulled back her hair. 'Come on. Let's see if we can find you any scraps from last night!' Scallywag jumped to his feet, and followed Jane down the stairs. On the next landing, two trays stood outside the rooms. Jane bent to pick up Harriet May's empty cup, then went on to collect the two outside Adeline's room. The cocoa brimmed in the mugs, cold, untouched. She took the tray downstairs, where the dog enjoyed the milky sweet taste of the forgotten bedtime drinks.

The day wore on, dull and grey. Jane brought the flowers up from the cellar and put them in the shop for Harriet to arrange. She made breakfast and cleared up afterwards. She cleaned upstairs, delivered orders, shopped, washed, cooked lunch, cleared that away, and then for her afternoon entertainment, she was faced with leading the grate, scrubbing the cellar steps, and wheeling barrowloads of debris across the road to George's compost heap.

In the chill November air, Scallywag raced across the lines of brussels sprouts, barking and kicking up the mud. Jane peered in through the steamed glass of the conservatory, at the green fronds, and the huge balls of colour that were George's chrysanthemums. Surely he wouldn't mind if she stepped inside. Just for once. Carefully, Jane checked the entrance to the gardens. She could see no-one. She put up a warning finger to Scallywag, then slowly opened the greenhouse door, so she could slip through without creating a draught.

The air was still. It hung, suspended in the warmth, almost tangible. It made the brain melt, soothing the jangled nerves, comforting the heart like a warm hand holding it. Jane breathed deeply, and her weariness stole over her, forcing her to sit on the stool by the work bench. Green, green leaves drenched her mind;

and the heavy scent of flowers, of moss, of warm earth over-whelmed her senses. Outside, Scallywag sat at the greenhouse door, waiting. His mistress would be out in a minute. She wouldn't be long. It was nearly tea time after all. He would be a good dog and wait for her.

'Harriet, is Jane in there?' Adeline called into the shop.

'She went over the road.'

'Oh. Only George is asking for his tea. Well, I don't suppose she'll be long. Be a dear, and put the kettle on will you?' With that, Adeline turned, singing, as she went back up the stairs to George's parlour. Suddenly, a strange noise caught Harriet's ear.

'Sh!'

Adeline turned angrily, 'Who are *you* shushing, if you please?'

'Shush!' Harriet May insisted. There was a low whining noise, and a scraping at the shop door. 'Oh it's only Scallywag!' She opened the door to let him in, but he stood, yelping at them, refusing to come any further. 'What's the matter! Come inside will you. You're letting in the cold!'

'He's trying to tell you something. What is it, old boy?'

'Where's Jane, Scallywag?' Harriet asked.

'There's something wrong.' Adeline spoke with sudden alarm. 'There's something wrong. I know there is. I can feel it!' A customer came into the shop.

'Shouldn't one of us go and see what's happened to Jane?' Harriet asked.

'Oh dear!' Adeline dithered. 'Better ask George.' And Harriet ran up the stairs to the parlour, leaving Adeline to serve, while the dog waited by the door.

They saw the broken pot of chrysanthemums first. And then they saw the hand. It hung like a limp flag at the end of the arm, protruding through the glass, and the stream of blood drenching the pane led to a red pool in the earth beneath. Scallywag was howling, and George's heart was in his mouth as he pushed open the door of the greenhouse and went inside.

'Give me a piece of your petticoat, Harriet!' he commanded.

'What do you mean, give you a piece?' Harriet May objected.

'Tear off a strip! Now!' George bellowed. Harriet jumped to obey, wrenching at the frill, pulling the stitching till it gave, rending the cloth. George grabbed it from her, and quickly fixed it round Jane's arm in a tourniquet. Harriet stared at the white face. She had never seen anything so white in all her life.

'Is she dead?' she whispered.

'Shut up! Hold her head.' Then he gently tried to extricate the arm from the broken glass, revealing the terrible gash in the flesh.

The blood trickled down his shirt, down his trousers, and left a trail through the flowers, and up the stairs, to Jane's room, where George laid her down. Adeline minded the shop, while Harriet ran for the doctor, leaving George alone with Jane. Was she dead? He bent towards her, listening, and his hair lifted in the slight breath from her half open mouth. Thank God. He touched her temple with his hand. Her eyelids fluttered. Her body jerked, and she was awake. The world was a haze of shadows. George's face mooned over her, and her head was filled with cotton wool. She tried to focus her attention; to hold on to reality. But it drifted from her reach. She felt she was sliding, slowly sliding down a long dark tunnel. A great sadness overwhelmed her. But she was too tired to fight against the sliding, sliding, slipping away, and there was nothing to hold on to. Nothing . . . nothing . . . George had lit a candle. It was on the mantelpiece. The flame scorched the shadows, and a halo of light engulfed the wall behind.

'Elephant,' Jane breathed. George followed her eyes to the drawing on the wall.

'What is it, Jane? Do you want it?'

'Yes.' George softly left her side, to take the drawing from the wall and place it in her hands.

'Elephant.'

'Yes. That's your drawing of the elephant,' George assured her.

'Thank you.' Her lips moved but no sound came from them. And he thought she smiled, as her eyes closed.

Would the doctor never come? Adeline glanced at the kitchen door, willing it to open. She blamed herself. 'We've been working her too hard. That's what it is. After all, she came to help in the shop, not to be a maid of all work!' The dog listened, ears pricked, as she unburdened her guilt. Outside, the rain was drenching down. She had begun to think there had been some accident, that Harriet too had come to grief, when, at last, the doctor arrived, soaked through, his black bag in his hand.

'She's upstairs.' Adeline took the doctor up at once, leaving Harriet to change out of her wet things.

Adeline fussed around Jane's bedside, gently removing the paper from her grasp. It was torn, and there was a blood stain on it. She was going to crumple it up and throw it on the fire, but George stopped her, taking it from her, and smoothing it out with his hands.

'She'll want that,' he said.

'Did she do it on purpose?' the doctor asked, as he began stitching up the wound. Adeline looked at George in horror. He shook his head.

'I'm sure not. No. She'd surely not do a thing like that?'

Jane lay between life and death. Slowly, as Adeline and George took turns nursing her, and feeding her, she began to come back into the world, and the haze cleared from her brain. How had it happened? She had been sitting in the greenhouse, feeling drowsy, tired, so very tired, and she had been leaning on her elbow. But she dropped off, and her elbow gave way, knocking over the chrysanthemum. Then she had reached out to save it, but, half asleep, she hardly knew what she was doing, and caught her arm on the broken glass. And then she fainted. She remembered hearing Scallywag barking. He had seemed so far away . . . that was how it had happened. Yes, but not why.

The incident had repercussions in the Beattie household. To begin with, someone had to do Jane's work. Adeline and Harriet shared it at first, but Harriet objected to soiling her hands with washing up, and Adeline got tireder and tireder, as she struggled to cope. The early mornings were the worst. She was so tired, she felt sick. A nausea crept in the pit of her stomach, and her appetite had gone. Seeing her so pale, and drawn, the doctor, on a visit to Jane, was deeply concerned, and took her to her room for a consultation. Jane was sitting downstairs in the parlour, doing her lessons with George, when they heard Adeline cry out; 'Oh God help me!'

Jane shivered. Her cry held the despair of the dunes, the hopelessness of the mists, and the anger of the elephant, trumpeting out of remembered danger. George frowned, looked up at the ceiling as though trying to see through it, and then went very pale.

'What is it?' Jane asked. George shook his head, and covered his face with his hands. 'Is there anything I can do?'

'Nothing. Absolutely nothing.'

Jane was sent round to Edie's home in Laygate, to ask her to come back. At first, Edie slammed the door in her face, and then followed a ridiculous conversation pursued through the letter box, till Edie's hurt pride was finally satisfied.

'The missus has been confined to bed,' Jane told her, 'she's pregnant again, and the doctor says there's nothing for it. If her and the baby are going to live, his nibs's got to leave her alone, and let her rest up for the next seven months.'

'Eeh!' said Edie. 'He'll not like that, mind!'

'You're telling me!' Jane answered ruefully. 'Now, I can't nurse her, and do the housework and help in the shop all at once, Edie, can I? You've got to come back to us! Won't you? Please?' Edie sniffed, and paused a long, long time before replying.

'I'll want a rise! And an apology from *her*!'

The *her* in question, propped up on her pillows, stared straight over Edie's head.

'I'm very sorry, Edie, if you were falsely accused, I'm sure.'

'That's all right, Missus,' Edie sniffed. 'We'll let bygones be bygones . . . in the circumstances.' So Edie came back to work in the Beattie establishment. There was an uneasy truce between her and Harriet May, which now and then erupted into animated bickering. And a feeling of the prison house closed round the household, as Adeline's pregnancy progressed. Harriet not only had to suffer her betrayer in the kitchen, but had also lost her ascendancy over Jane who, since her accident, had somehow worked her way back into favour and out of the low status of kitchen maid.

Jane was sorry to leave her old room. She had become attached to it over the years. It was hers. It bore her mark. The old drawing of the elephant was still on the wall. As she left, she looked back at it. She could not leave it behind. So she took it down with her, to Adeline's room, where the single bed stood ready in the corner. She smiled at her, and a pair of rosy cheeks beamed back.

'You're blooming, Addy!'

'I'm blooming bored!' the lady objected. Both of them laughed.

'Do you know,' Jane turned to pin her picture to the wall, 'I think you're going to hold on to this one!'

Adeline lay back against her pillows, yawning.

'What's that?'

'Oh only my elephant. I hope you don't mind. It's like a sort of mascot really . . .' As she finished pinning it up, Jane stood back, so that Adeline could see. Her face went white.

'It's got blood on it! Take it down! Take it down!'

Immediately Jane tore the picture from the wall.

'I'm sorry. I didn't mean . . .' Adeline was crying.

'It's all right, Jane. In my condition you get . . . fancies. It's all right.' Trembling, Jane consoled her mistress.

'You're doing so well, Addy! There's no need to worry. I'm sure of it!' It was true. Pregnant women *did* have fancies, and there were plenty of real things to worry about . . .

Miss Harriet was 'turning funny', according to Edie.

'She won't let me in her room to clean! She keeps the door locked, night and day!'

'However do you know?' Jane asked, looking up from her letter at the breakfast table.

'I know. That's all,' was Edie's dark response.

'I see,' Jane returned to her letter.

'Is that from that brother of yours?' she asked.

'Mmmm.' Edie sighed. That was all she was going to get out of her this morning And she could just have done with a chat! What a life! Harriet came down looking pale and tired. She didn't bother to answer the 'good mornings', but poured her tea, and held it cradled in her hands, as she stared at the back of Jane's letter.

'Does he say when he's coming home?'

'Mmmmm?'

'Robert. Does he say when he's coming home?'

'No.' Jane put the letter down, and pasted marmalade onto her toast, sighing. 'He's gone on to Japan now. I wish I was a man, don't you?'

307

'What a stupid thing to say!'

'Sorry.'

Edie was biting back a retort, when the mayor himself walked in.

'Eeh, you're up and about early, Mr Mayor, sir,' she said. Harriet gave him a sidelong look, and he responded in a defensive tone.

'Early constitutional! Does you the power of good, Edie! You should try it!'

'Oh no! Not me! All that air's bad for you!' George stopped for a moment, and looked at her.

'Coffee, Edie!' he commanded, and went upstairs to the parlour.

'Huh! And he never touched his cocoa last night, either!'

That night, when the shop closed, and supper had been eaten, Harriet climbed the stairs up to her room. Adeline saw her from her bed, through the half open door.

'Why don't you come in here, dear? Have some company? You could help me with my knitting.'

'I'm sorry, Adeline. I'm busy.' Harriet May walked on past the door, and into her room. Dropping the half-finished baby jacket in her lap, Adeline pondered on her stepdaughter. She was spending far too much time on her own. It wasn't healthy. But Harriet May sighed with relief as her door closed behind her. She turned the key in the lock, and set her candle down. The soft rays of the moon shone in through the window, and by its light, Harriet saw a trail of white lace which led across the floor, to a heap of tulle. Picking up the end, Harriet followed it to a half finished dress. She lifted it gently, and took it to the long mirror, where she held it against herself. Loose threads fell like confetti about her feet. Her face was radiant, as she looked into the mirror and saw reflected there the white outline of the Taj Mahal. He would surely come home soon, and then, then . . .

CHAPTER TWENTY ONE

At first, Jane hated the idea of helping over the road. But George was busy campaigning. The next elections were to be held in May. And Adeline, now six months pregnant, was still confined to bed, while Harriet had the shop to run. So there was nothing for it. She had braced herself to enter in by the little gate, alongside the Queen's Hall, trudging her old clodhoppers through the mud of George's gardens, to the greenhouses. They had to be watered daily, and the lines of vegetables and flowers outside had to be weeded, and thinned. Jane had never had anything to do with gardening in her life, had never even thought of how the flowers grew out of the soil, to bloom and then be cut in their prime, and sold. Most of the flowers in Beattie's were bought at the flower market in Newcastle, but written over the shop front were the words, 'Seedsman and Nurseryman', and George Beattie took a pride in his own produce. It fell to Jane to keep up his reputation.

Early in the year, George had shown her how to thin out his seedlings, and plant them in the earth. A constant succession of plants were brought on in the greenhouses, then put outside, to prosper and be sold in the shop. Jane became adept at the delicate task of separating the individual tiny seedlings, checking the growth of healthy root, and setting them out in rows in the soil.

It was a job which required all her concentration; but it was peaceful, and her mind became still, as her fingers dug deep into the earth, and the tentative roots of young plants were laid tenderly down. Looking up from the brown clay, she was surprised, sometimes, to see the clarity of the airy sky, for she had become one with the earth, satisfied by it, and the longings of her soul were curbed, contained within herself, so that she became content, asking for nothing. Love? What was it after all? Just the desire to continue on the cycle of creation, seed to plant and back to seed again. Adeline was fulfilling that task. From her bed in the house in Fowler Street, she exuded a new atmosphere. It seeped through the ceilings, down into the kitchen, and the shop below. The growing promise of a child lightened the darkness in the cellar, made the colours of the flowers more vibrant, and, like a half felt tremor, the unborn heart beat out its rhythm, day and night, insinuating itself into the heart of the house, and of those who lived in it, unrecognised, yet known; as much a part of their lives as the dreams they could not remember in the morning.

Thoughtlessly, day followed day in natural succession. The earth and the child ruled Jane, and she lay in her single bed in Adeline's room, knowing that three presences peopled the space in which she slept, and that she was a servant to the cycle which continued on through Adeline and the seedlings, rooted in the nurseries. Silent days of contentment, they were. There was a time when she might have fought against it, when she might have felt trapped, chained to this unending cycle and clamour to be free. A time, not so long ago, when to be one with the natural succession of life would have seemed a threat. Glancing at the mended window in the greenhouse, where she was tending the seedlings, Jane remembered the blood. It had changed everything. An accident, nothing more; it could have killed her, instead it had chastened her. She shivered, as she looked at the glass, seeing the broken shards, and her own arm, skewered upon them. Red, spurting blood. It had spattered on her face, and on her dress, and soaked deep into the earth. And the earth had almost claimed her. Perhaps, in a way, it had. For now she felt she belonged to it. She felt its natural rhythm deep within herself, and was glad. Just to be in the present, and a part of everything, was enough. Like the seedlings, she had become rooted in her reality.

Harriet May, wiring flowers, severed from the earth, into wreaths, dreamt her dreams. The circle of death became the horseshoe of life, hanging from a bride's dress; the dust falling on her bedroom, became confetti; and Robert's letters, tied in a ribbon in Jane's chest of drawers, were love letters, kept from her by her enemy. Jane did not want Harriet to be happy. But Harriet would find a way to outwit her. All's fair in love and war. All's fair, she thought, as her fingers bled from the wire; and the block of spring flowers was finished. The house was still. There were no customers. Edie was out shopping. Jane was over the road at the nurseries. Adeline slept upstairs, and George Beattie was campaigning. Harriet's heart skipped a beat. She glanced at the shop door. All's fair. Quickly, she went over to it, and turned the notice so that it read 'closed'. Then, wiping her hand on her apron, she softly, swiftly, stealthily climbed the stairs, past the parlour, on up to the bedrooms, and then on again, to the attics, to Jane's old room. She opened the door. The air was musty, damp. Only the draught from the broken pane ventilated the neglected room. Soft shoed, Harriet sped across to the chest. The drawers were swollen and stiff with damp. She wrenched at the first. The loud squeak made her heart beat louder. Guiltily, she looked up, listening. Her eye caught the stained drawing of the elephant on the wall. The blood had turned brown, to the colour of the earth. Harriet snorted. A filthy thing to have on one's wall! More carefully, she tried the second drawer, and there, under Jane's stockings and petticoats, Harriet found the letters. She slid them inside her bodice, pushed the drawer silently to, and left the room. Flushed with excitement, she turned back the 'closed' notice on the shop door, and, through the glass, saw Jane, coming wearily across the road from the nurseries, in her clay caked shoes.

Jane was thinking of hot tea, and warm baths, as she turned round the back of Victoria Terrace, and down the lane. Baths? Chance would be a fine thing. When had she last had the luxury of a proper bath? A cold wash upstairs in her old room, or a cat lick in Adeline's when she got up in the morning was all she could usually run to. How she would love to soak in the steam of a real bath! Now she thought about it, her back ached something terrible. Perhaps Adeline would let her off for the evening, to attend the public wash house in Cuthbert Street. She groaned, as she sank into the kitchen chair, and gulped down the scalding tea.

'How's the missus?'

'There's nowt the matter with her if you ask me. I've never seen two such rosy cheeks in me life!'

'That's grand,' Jane said, satisfied. 'And where's his nibs?'

'Hah!' came the enlightening reply.

Adeline complained of a headache, and had no use for Jane that night.

'Only rub me a little, later on,' Addy pleaded.

'Of course I will,' Jane smiled softly. She drew the curtains to shut out the glaring sun of the late afternoon, before leaving her mistress, flushed with sleep, to rest alone. Her step was light as she walked down Claypath Lane, past the colliery and on to the baths. It was good to see Adeline looking so well. Perhaps, once the baby was born, George would also settle down, and be happy at last. He hadn't dared to believe in this child. He hadn't dared to look forward to it. And yet, as time had gone on, the tension had begun to slip from him, and the chains of guilt had loosened. Perhaps all would be well. The house which had no love in it before, now held the promise of love's fulfilment. Jane felt its benefit, and was glad.

She paid the woman at the desk, was given her towel, a bar of soap, and shown into a cubicle. It had wooden slats on the stone floor, and a real bath with a tap, from which water spouted, gurgling and hot from the geyser. Bliss! Jane lay back, listening to the sounds of splashing, the scrubbing, hummings and mutterings, that came from the other cubicles. Someone dropped their soap in the water, and cursed. It didn't bother Jane. Her peace was deep inside her. It could not be touched. Rivulets of sweat poured from her brow. She sighed and sank her head beneath the water. Bubbles glugged past her head, and the geyser drummed in her ears, dark and deep. Then, at last, she heaved herself out of the bath, and slowly dried her body, heavy with heat.

Some of the pitmen had come off shift, and were standing in a queue waiting for the mens' cubicles. In their pit dirt, they all looked alike. Keeping her eyes low, Jane gave in her towel, and took back her deposit from the woman on the desk.

'What are you doin' here, pet?' It was a male voice, husky with coal dust. She tried to ignore it. 'Howway, Jane, don't you know's, eh?' She turned, surprised, and looked at the white eyes, with their red rims, staring hopefully out of the black face.

'Why it's never . . . ?'

'It is, you know!' Dandy laughed. 'If you could see your face!'

'But you're . . . ' She indicated the pit dirt and clothes.

'Aye. Well, it's work. You know how it is.'

'A river pilot! Dandy! Eeh! Eeh, I'm sorry. Eeh, Dandy I am sorry.'

'Nowt to blame yourself for, pet. Hey, have you got a minute? Have a drink with's somewhere, eh?' Jane glanced at his dirt. 'Oh they don't mind round here. And the queue'll have gone down by the time I get back.' She smiled her agreement, and they took off down Cuthbert Street, in search of the nearest public house.

Settled in a corner with his beer, Dandy sighed. The grime had worked itself into the lines of his face, and she could see the misery of disappointed hopes etched there. Jane felt the faint stirring of guilt within her.

'Why, Dandy? Tell me why.' He looked down at his glass. 'Come on, love. I am family, you know. You're not betraying anybody by talking to me . . . I won't let on to a living soul, whatever it is.' Her eyes were steady. Looking up at them, Dandy gained courage.

'Well . . . It's Fanny. Or at least . . . oh I don't know. It's all such a mess!'

'Fanny came to Fowler Street to see me . . . ' Dandy looked surprised. 'She didn't tell you?' He shook his head. 'I'd written to her, asking if she'd meet me in a café somewhere, for a natter . . . I felt sort of cut off from you all. I wanted to know how you were, for one thing. And then . . . then I had this accident. Apparently she came to see me, but I was unconscious. I've not heard from her since.' Jane sighed. 'Dandy, I've been selfish. I've been so caught up! I should've thought she might need me!' He put his hands on hers to comfort her. Jane sniffed back her tears. 'I should've got on to her, as soon as I was better. I should've.

313

But I didn't.' She paused, then looked straight at him. 'It's the drink, isn't it?'

'Aye . . . well, that was the start of it.'

'Then, the Purvis lot kept you from your rightful work, and you were reduced to this!'

'No! No . . . We had a bit of trouble with them, but . . . no . . . the reason I'm not on the river this very minute, is I've got no coble!'

'What?'

'Aye!' He gulped down his beer, and the wet, clean mark round his mouth made his lips stand out, red, against his black face. 'You see, I knew Fanny was drinking . . . but I never knew how much. She ran up bills. We couldn't pay them. In the end, I had to sell the coble. There was nowt for it. So, here I am . . . saving up to buy another'n.'

'I see!' So, Jane was not to blame for Dandy's troubles, after all!

'But that's not all, lass.' Dandy put down his glass and clasped his hands tightly together. His voice was harsh and broken, when he spoke again. 'When I found out what she was up to, I went . . . sort of wild like. And I . . . started to lay about me . . . I . . . Don't look at me, Jane. I can't tell you, if you look at me.' Jane tore her eyes from him, a pain in her heart, sensing the horror, hidden in Dandy's shame. 'I went for her, Jane. I couldn't help myself. I felt this anger . . . it possessed me. I wanted to kill her! I did!' Jane shivered, encircled by Dandy's misery and guilt. He laid back against the wall, eyes clenched tight. 'I remember, I'd just come back from a night's seeking. I'd had a big schooner to bring in and I was feeling pleased with myself. I had a bit of money in my pocket, you see, and I'd gone to "The Globe", for a glass, before turning in. It was a wet, grey day, but I was happy. And then, they refused to serve me in the bar. They said my wife owed them. It was a lot of money, Jane. I don't know how they could let her run up a bill like that! I went home, feeling . . . confused, hoping there'd been some mistake. But, in my heart, knowing, all the time, it was true. I blame myself. I'd turned a blind eye to Fanny's drinking. A lot of women drink. It helped her through childbed twice running. I couldn't grudge her that! Two lovely kids I've got. I love them. I do, Jane. I do.'

'I know, Dandy.'

'Anyway,' he sighed, 'I decided to confront Fanny, hoping she'd deny it, like. But she didn't. She broke down and cried, and she told me there were other bills . . . All over the town end, she owed money for one thing and another. Eddie's boots'd been pawned! He was going round in bare feet! It was winter time, Jane! Our son, our little lad! He was suffering! How could she? Eh?' Jane said nothing. 'I saw red. Suddenly, my hands were at her throat. And I liked it, Jane. I liked it. I liked feeling her white, thin neck under my grip. It made me feel strong. I could've crushed her. It made me feel master of her.'

'Ah . . . ' Jane nodded. 'I see.'

'It was Eddie, pulling at me arm, got me to leave go. And then I went for *him*, poor little beggar! Fanny was screaming. And Ma. And the baby was howling in its cradle. Then the rage left me. Just as suddenly as it had come. My hands dropped, and I cried like a bairn. For days after, there was a funny feeling in the house. Dangerous. You could almost touch it. The kids woke with nightmares. And it's not surprising. There were red marks on Eddie's throat. My own lad! And I'd put them there! He screams if anybody so much as goes near him now. And Fanny . . . she couldn't speak for days. I can still see the outline of my own fingers, purple, on her throat . . . '

Jane looked at Dandy. He was lying back against the wall, silent tears running down his cheeks. She watched him for a while, then lifted her hand and laid it gently over his. He grasped it, thankfully.

'I love them, Jane,' he sobbed.

'I know, Dandy. Perhaps that's why . . . perhaps . . . sometimes, love can drive us to what seems like great cruelty.'

Dandy looked at the pale, young woman at his side. 'I don't understand.'

'I'm not sure I understand it myself, Dandy. I only know it is so. Because, in the end, we don't matter. Only the love itself matters.'

'If you're saying the person you love doesn't matter . . . well, you're wrong. You've got to be!'

Jane shrugged. 'I don't think I mean that, Dandy. They do matter. It's just there's something beyond them. Robert told me once, when he was talking about India, the Taj Mahal was like a fragment, a piece of coloured glass in a church window. Only one piece. And through that glass, the sun sends its light. But when we see it, we can't be satisfied, because it's come between us and the light behind it. Perhaps loving one person's a bit like that, and there are times, when the piece of glass has to be broken, so we can reach the sun . . . the love beyond the person, beyond life and death itself. What Fanny did darkened the glass. You had to do something to break it, so the sun would shine through again.'

'That's terrible!'

'Terrible? Yes. It is. God is terrible, Dandy. And yet He loves us.'

Jane looked out of the window. In the street, daylight was fading and the world trembled on the brink of darkness.

'Perhaps we're not meant to understand. But as long as we truly love one another, God will work it out.'

Dandy suddenly felt very tired. Like a child, caught up in a game played by his elders, it had left him exhausted, and afraid.

'Jane . . .' his voice pleaded, 'all I want to know is that it's not my fault.'

She laughed softly. 'Either way, what does it matter? It's what happens now that matters, isn't it?' He nodded slowly. This was something he could grasp. 'Is Fanny still drinking?'

'Not so much.'

'Send her away! Send her to our auntie's in the country! Away from the pubs and the people that'll tempt her! Give her a sort of . . . holiday!' Dandy nodded. 'Ma can look after the kids, can't she?'

'I expect so . . .'

'Now! About your coble! How much do you still need for it?'

'Just over twenty pound.'

'I've got some savings . . . No don't turn me down, Dandy. I owe you. I should've been there to keep an eye on our Fanny. I've got fifteen pounds twelve shillings. You shall have it. So it won't be too long before you're back on the river!'

'I don't know what to say.'

'Don't bother trying, Dandy. Don't bother. You've got to start all over again, like a new bride and groom. Only, maybe, a little bit wiser, eh?'

316

'Aye. A little bit wiser.'

As she got up to go, Dandy grasped Jane's hand urgently.

'Tell me I'm not a murderer, Jane.'

She shook her head and looked away. Murder? If only Dandy knew. She was the murderer. She had helped kill Fanny's baby. Her deceit had been the cause of Ronnie's blood, spilled by the river.

'No, Dandy. You're not a murderer. You're a good man. Only a little bit soft, like me. To love somebody, really love them, you have to give up being soft, for their sake. I think perhaps love isn't such a soft, sentimental thing as people like to make out. No, Dandy. You'll be all right now.' Dandy looked at Jane for a long time.

'I daren't ask what's happened to *you*,' he said at last, 'I daren't ask.'

As Jane closed the door of Fowler Street behind her, she felt the darkness. A shape sat by the dying fire in the kitchen. Edie, asleep in the rocking chair, had failed to light the lamps. The red glow of the hot coals pressed against the blackness of the house. It was warm, close. As her eyes became used to the darkness, she became aware of a deeper darkness, on the other side of the room. A musty smell issued from it. The cellar door was open; it gaped black at her. But she moved into the darkness, reaching for the tapers on the mantel, to light the lamp. She was not afraid. When she was a child, Ma Dunn used to scare her with her tales of 'bogies' and 'bogeymen', who waited for you in dark places, or hid under the bed. But now she was strong. The flame of the taper flared in her face, blinding her for an instant. Then she turned and set the flame to the wick of the oil lamp, containing its energy within the glass of the funnel, which she slipped quickly over the flame, to tame it. Now she could turn back to the gaping door, and close it firmly, before picking up her lamp, and climbing up to Adeline's room.

The darkness came thickly down the stairs towards her, like a black cloud. It dampened the light, which seemed feeble, unable to resist. And the cloud had a smell to it. The smell was smoke. Jane quickened her steps, past the first landing, and on to the second, and, suddenly, Harriet was screaming. Putting down her lamp, Jane tried the door to her room. It was locked. Adeline shouted from across the passage.

'What's wrong? What's happening?'

'Stay in bed, Adeline,' Jane ordered. Putting her shoulder to the door, she hurled her weight against it, again and again, until finally, it gave, and the door wrenched open, to reveal a pillar of fire in the centre of Harriet's room. The pillar had twenty arms and legs, which flailed out, and Jane was tearing the bridal veil from Harriet's head. Flaming fragments floated round about, and then she thrust Harriet onto the bed, wrapping her head in the counterpane. And still the veil burned on the floor, its flames reflected in the triple mirror of the dressing table, in the long mirror in the corner of the room, in the glass of the pictures on the walls, until it seemed they were encircled by a ring of fire. And Adeline was in the room. She was stamping on the flames, her face white, silent, until there was blackness once again, and all they could hear was Harriet's moaning.

'Get back to bed, Adeline!' Jane took her arm, and guided her out, into the corridor. The oil lamp stood, where she had left it, on the floor, shedding its light about their feet. Edie's eyes, black with fright, came at them from the stair head. 'Go fetch the doctor, Edie. It's an emergency. Miss Harriet's burned herself.' Screaming like a banshee, Edie flung her apron over her head.

'I'm dreamin', I'm dreamin', please God tell's I'm dreamin'!'

'Shut up, Edie and do as you're told!' Jane ordered. Edie turned and ran down the stairs, glad to escape into the chill night air, running, running, down the cobbled lane and on to the doctor's house.

Charred fragments floated in the air of Harriet's room. Soot fell on the white dress, hanging from the end of the bed, and on the dressing table, where a blue ribbon lay beside a bundle of papers. Jane stared at the scorched letters. Watching from the bed, Harriet saw, reflected in the triple mirrors, Jane's hand reach out and pick them up, to recognise her brother's writing. She turned to the burned remnants of the veil, lying on the floor, and picked up a small piece of the cloth. White lace. White dress. Robert's letters. Clues.

'Now you know,' Harriet's voice was harsh from the smoke.

'What do I know?'

318

'How I hate you, Jane Ridley. You've taken everything from me. Everything. Even the man I love.'

'Robert? You don't love Robert! How can you? You don't even know him!' Jane's voice slashed through the clouds of Harriet's mind, cold, sharp and without mercy.

'You turned him against me! I read it in the letters. You want him to yourself. You're a conniving little bitch . . . telling lies about me!'

'I have not told any lies, Harriet. Not about you. It's all in your mind!'

'We were going to get married! I was trying on the veil, when I started to read the letters. Letters from Robert, saying he didn't like me. Lies should be burnt. So I burned them.'

'Yes, Harriet. Lies must be burnt. But it was your veil that got burnt! That was the lie!' Jane looked long and hard at Harriet's white face. She might have brought down the entire house, engulfed in the circling flames.

George still hadn't come home. The doctor administered laudanum, to soothe Harriet's pain and shocked nerves. He would stay till George got back. Meanwhile, Jane sat up with Adeline, who had been sick, and now felt the first grinding pains of yet another miscarriage.

'I'm not bleeding, am I?' she pleaded, as she looked at the white sheet under the counterpane. Dark brown, the colour of earth, the blood smeared the linen beneath the pregnant woman.

'Lie quietly, try not to worry. It'll pass,' Jane calmed her. Cold with fear Adeline lay, flat, without her pillows, willing the child not to reject her, not to leave her before its time. Jane quietly whispered the news into the doctor's ear, and he came, smiling, reassuring, to Adeline's bedside, gently feeling her belly, gently soothing her with his words. He gave her medicine, 'to settle things down again', and told her to sleep. Rest was all she needed. Adeline drifted into a fitful doze. Jane sat rigid at her bedside, watching. Then, at three in the morning, George's white face peeked round the door. He stared at his wife in silence.

The light had gone out. What time was it? Jane felt for the matches and lit a fresh candle, checking the clock on the mantel.

It was five in the morning; even darker now; the darkness before the dawn. She took a candle and looked in on Harriet. Edie sat, nodding, while Harriet slept, a deep frown furrowing her brow. A low moan sent Jane hurrying back to Adeline.

'What is it?'

'My back. I think it's breaking.' Jane put her hand underneath to rub her, and felt the sticky blood, that had soaked into the nightdress. Quickly, she withdrew her hand. But Adeline saw the red, before she could hide it behind her back. 'Blood!' she cried out, 'blood! My baby's dying!'

'Keep calm! I'm going downstairs. I think the doctor might still be here.' Jane fled, and Adeline's cries of despair reached after her as she sped down the stairs to the kitchen, where George and the doctor sat, drinking tea.

'She's losing it!' The men stopped talking, looked blankly at her, then, suddenly, each was at the door, jostling to reach the woman.

The darkness began to lose its strength, and the world teetered on the edge of day. Pale faces, exhausted by the battles of the night, looked in dismay on the boy, drowned in the blood bath of his mother's womb. He lay now, swathed in red, as first light fell on his mother's face, white and silent and still as death. Falling to his knees, George cried out,

'The Lord Thy God is a jealous God!'

The sun, blazing red, rose over the horizon; the same sun that shone on India; unstoppable. And a new day dawned, in which everything was changed.

CHAPTER TWENTY TWO

'Jane!'

Frozen by his cry, she stopped at the head of the stair, listening.

'Jane!' The desperation in his voice commanded her. His need would force her to his side. But she was afraid. She shied from the task. She had nothing to offer him but tea and biscuits. Well, it would have to do. She moved slowly on to the door of Adeline's room.

'I'm here, sir.' George's eyes dragged from the corpse, and looked at her, vacantly. 'I've brought you some hot, sweet tea. It'll do you good.' He was disappointed. 'You can't go on like this, Mr Beattie.' She touched him, and flinched at his coldness. 'You must have something!' Suddenly, George grasped her hand. She suppressed a strong desire to wrench herself free.

'You're warm.' His voice cracked. He was going to cry at last. Panic seized her. She wanted him to cry; but why was it *her* shoulder he had to lean on?

'You'll be glad to know Harriet's all right. She really is amazing, that girl. She's finding new ways to do her hair . . . what there is left of it! Actually, she's quite herself again. She had Edie bawling this morning. Just like old times! You'd think she'd be counting her blessings, not complaining. I mean, she's really very lucky not to be scarred for life!' George frowned. How could she talk about hair styles, and crying maids and such mundanity? Jane offered the cup of tea again. His tears dried up, he took it from her automatically, and silently began to drink it. Why could she not have let the poor man cry? Her eye fell on the body displayed in the coffin. She shivered. Why was she so afraid?

Edie was shouting up the stairs. The cortège had arrived. Jane speeded down to the kitchen, in sudden fury.

'Don't you realise, girl, this is a house of mourning?!'

Edie stared at her. 'Who do you think you are!' she said, open mouthed, 'the Grand Duchess?' Jane almost laughed, and was ashamed of the impulse, which prompted her even as she walked at the widower's side, out of the house and into the waiting carriage. Her mouth twitched, and the more she rebuked herself, the worse it got.

Only family and close friends had been invited to the service, but tributes were stacked against the side of the coffin and the perfume of flowers wreathed the mourners, like incense. Slowly Jane breathed it in, trying to calm herself. What was the matter with her? Why did she want to laugh? She had loved Adeline! Harriet, at George's other side, looked straight ahead, shorn, singed hair swathed in a turban, Adeline's fur round her shoulders; oriental somehow. The exotic suited her, and she knew it! She was actually making eyes at the preacher! Jane's voice wavered dangerously, as she sang,

God is working his purpose out as year succeeds to year,
God is working his purpose out and the time is drawing near;
Nearer and nearer draws the time . . .

George tightened his grip on her arm. Shame swamped her. She bit her lip, and raised her eyes to his. Tears were coursing down his cheeks. And now she knew why she had not wanted him to cry. His eyes met hers. It was done. Her heart went out to him. And she was trapped. Caught. Involved in the drama. As the wooden box was lowered into the earth, she knew she was now the sole pillar of the house, its strength, its power. The burden had been passed on.

A shiver rose up her spine. Her hands went cold. Looking up, she saw a woman and three children making their way across the mud, silhouetted against the afternoon sun. How dare she come here! George picked up a fistful of clay to spatter on his wife. 'Earth to earth.' The drama, which Jane had been watching from the wings, would continue without Adeline. But who now was the star performer? Jane set her face against the woman as she drew her brood alongside the trench. Was she going to stand by and watch her take over Adeline's role? Adeline? Her best friend? A woman she had loved? No! Something which had begun, when she cut her arm, had been working in Jane, changing her, so that now, when everything outside her had also changed, she found she was strong. Deep, dangerous feelings stirred within her. What had she said to Dandy? ' . . . love is not such a soft and sentimental thing as people like to make out?' No. It wasn't. It was something strong, formidable. It could face fire and water. It could stand against hell itself, if need be, and not tremble. Yes. She, Jane Ridley, was now the power in the house, and she stood still and silent as a rock at Adeline's grave, watching the woman and her children.

Eyes exchanged messages. Jane remembered Alice Minto. She had been dressed in black, outside the chapel. George had helped her with her accounts. She had moved to Harton Village, where her children could enjoy the country air, and build a new life, forgetting the past. 'Forgive us our trespasses as we forgive those . . . ' In her heart Jane knew Adeline would have forgiven; well then, shouldn't Jane? The woman picked up a clod of earth and threw it into the trench. It was a challenge. George could not take his eyes from her. Alice did not want to be forgiven. She wanted George. But she would not have him. Jane Ridley had walked onto the stage.

They could not afford to keep the shop closed, so the next day, they opened up as usual. But it was Jane who ordered the lunch and supper; it was she who made decisions about catering; she who wrote down the orders. And Harriet accepted Jane's authority, not wanting responsibility herself, yet she resented it. Like a child, she played games with Jane, breaking eggs and pretending it was an accident, or using cream that had gone off to fill a cake. But, as the days passed, Harriet got bored with her little games, and, glad to get out, volunteered for the job of delivery girl. Grateful for small mercies, Jane was free to turn her attention on George Beattie at last.

Standing at the counter, checking the till, Jane sighed, and fidgeted. George was upstairs, alone with his books. He had withdrawn his candidature, and the elections had passed them by; so, he was no longer Mayor of Shields. He had shrunk. White hairs streaked his beard, and his eyes had a haunted look. Why had she done it? What right had she to drag George away and prevent his meeting with Alice Minto? Perhaps, after all, she was just what he needed! But Jane's spirit revolted at the thought. Adeline had suffered because of her! What about George? Wasn't he suffering now? And she was responsible. Guilt pricked her into action. It was time she coaxed him out of himself. After closing, she turned the notice on the door. Harriet had come home late from delivering and sat chatting with Edie in the kitchen like old times; mindless chatter about young men. Jane sighed. She needed some distraction, after all, and it was harmless enough. Taking the tea tray, Jane went up to George's parlour.

'Your tea, Mr Beattie.' George's eyes lit up.

'Jane, what would I do without you?' She was glad to see him smile, and smiled back as she set the tray on the desk.

'Now make sure you eat *all* the sandwiches, this time,' she said, playfully scolding him, 'or, if you're not careful, I'll sit here, watching you, till you've finished!'

'In that case,' George caught her tone, 'I definitely won't eat them up!'

'You *are* wicked!'

'Well, you'll just have to sit there and watch me, won't you?' Jane hesitated. She hadn't bargained for this. 'Why don't you bring another cup?'

'Oh! Are you sure I won't be disturbing you?'

'If there's one thing I need just now, it's disturbing.' Dutifully, she went for an extra cup, while he separated the sandwiches into two neat piles.

When she came back, Jane found that George had moved the tray to the little table, and he was sitting in his armchair. He obviously meant her to sit in the one opposite.

324

'I feel uneasy . . . ' she said, slipping into the seat.

'Why?'

'You know why. It was *hers*.'

'And now it's yours.' There was a long silence.

'What do you mean?' she stumbled over the words.

'Only that you might as well sit in it.' He was enjoying teasing her. Jane tried hard not to show her confusion.

'You've done well in the shop.' His praise pleased her. 'In the kitchen too!'

'Thank you.'

'In fact you've taken over Adeline's role very nicely. I'm most grateful.' Jane poured the tea carefully, without meeting his eye.

'I feel I'm like an extra daughter to you, sir,' she said.

'I haven't *got* a daughter, so how could you be extra?' he bellowed angrily. Jane looked at him reproachfully. 'And don't give me one of your looks! Harriet May's no daughter of mine!' He struggled to regain his composure. 'Don't spoil things, Jane! You've looked after me so well . . . ' His hand reached out to her. She looked at it. He was expecting her to take it. Then she looked at him, and his face was gentle, kind. So she took the hand, as though to shake it; but he grasped it and held it for too long, so she pulled it back again.

'Mr Beattie,' she said carefully, 'I hope you don't think I would presume to fill Adeline's role in this house.'

'You have done so!'

'Not entirely, sir.' She handed him his tea and her eyes blazed anger at his unspoken suggestion.

'No,' he said, meekly taking the tea. 'Not entirely.'

Deliberately, Jane dropped the lumps, one, two, three, into his cup, then reached for her own cup, and began to drink. 'Do eat up, Jane. We need to put some flesh on you.'

'I'm quite fat enough!'

'We'll see.' They drank the first cup in silence, and Jane got up ready to leave, but George prevented her. 'It's so long since we read poetry together, Jane. Could you spare me a little time now, do you think?' Jane stopped at the door, uncertain. She should go. She should make her feelings clear by going down to the kitchen and leaving him to it. But his eyes pleaded with her, so softly, so gently, she found she could not.

'Just for half an hour, I suppose,' she said, abruptly returning to her seat. George reached for the nearest book.

'I found this one recently. I don't think we've read it . . . ' He passed it, open at the chosen page. Jane coughed, and began,

The world is too much with us; late and soon
Getting and spending, we lay waste our powers:
Little we see in nature that is ours;
We have given our hearts away, a sordid boon!
The sea that bares her bosom to the moon:
The winds that will be howling at all hours,
And are upgathered now, like sleeping flowers;
For this, for everything, we are out of tune:
It moves us not – Great God! I'd rather be
A pagan suckled in a creed outworn . . .

'Mmmm!' George breathed in slowly, lying back, abandoned to the sentiment as she finished the verse. 'Like it?' he asked, his eyes opening suddenly.

'Very much. Sometimes I feel a bit like that myself,' Jane said. Her response pleased George.

'Ah . . . I thought there was a little pagan in there somewhere.'

'Sir!' Jane was aghast. 'I'm as Christian as you are! Well . . . almost.' She blushed, fearing she had trodden on the preacher's toes. George laughed loudly.

'I sometimes feel,' he spoke slowly, as though thinking aloud, 'the church is like a cage, containing the lion of religion. We dare not let it free, or it might get out of control!'

'I don't understand you, sir.'

'Don't call me . . . '

'Sorry, Mr Beattie.'

'George.'

Jane frowned. She did not hold with this familiarity. She felt she was being manoeuvred into a position she did not altogether like. And yet she was powerless to prevent it. 'Wordsworth understood all that. What do you think? I mean, really?' Jane paused, reflecting on her own experience.

'I miss the sea,' she said at last. 'Yes. I felt in tune with the sea. I do miss that. It was like a part of me.'

'And, now, instead of walking on the seashore, you spend all your time working in the shop. Getting and spending, Jane. You're made for better things than that.' Jane was silent. 'Wouldn't you like it to be different?'

'When I worked in the nurseries over the road, that sort of made up for it. I felt part of it . . . it may sound silly, but I felt part of the earth instead.' George's eyes fixed on her, as though they wanted to burrow into her.

'Yes! Because it was real! You were part of life, Jane! Life!' He waved his hand at his account books. 'That isn't life!' His voice rose as though he was addressing a meeting. 'Being a mayor isn't life! Being a shopkeeper isn't life!'

'Then what is . . . George?' Reluctantly she used the name. He smiled slightly as the fact she had done so registered.

'You and I, Jane . . . we are different. We have not given our hearts away to worldly things.'

'No?' Jane was surprised.

'No!' he barked. She jumped. 'I want more than that!'

'Sh.' Jane turned to the door, expecting Harriet and Edie to come in any minute.

'Don't shush me, woman!' he yelled. Jane looked at him, alarmed. He was pacing the room, as if he were a wild animal, in a cage of his own. 'I am not afraid of life!' he declared, suddenly stopping in the centre of the room. 'Just give me the chance!' Jane didn't dare look at him. His presence electrified her. It made her excited and afraid. 'Are *you*?' he demanded. At last, Jane found the courage to meet his eyes. They had power. They held her. Something in her rose to meet him. Was it George's eyes she saw? Fear gripped her once again. His eyes were the mirror of her own. In them she saw her own spirit, her own desires, herself, her real self. But she didn't *want* to see! No! She looked away again.

'Are you afraid? I want to know!'

'Of life?'

'Yes!'

What right had he to demand an answer? Her heart shut its bars against him.

'I have all the life I want, thank you!'

George frowned, and sat edgily in his chair.

327

'Hah!' he said at last. 'Women!' He dismissed her with a wave of his hand. Deeply relieved, Jane gathered up the uneaten sandwiches and turned to leave the room. 'Take this with you!' George almost threw the book of poetry at her.

Back in her garret room, undressing by the light of a single candle, Jane saw the picture George had given her, ages ago; the rainbow. She hadn't really looked at it for a while. Rainbows. When she was a child the world had seemed full of them.

'My heart leaps up . . .'

How long had it been since her heart leapt, as it had done tonight? What right had George to demand anything of her? Wasn't she doing enough for him? Wasn't she running his shop? Hadn't she kept his nurseries going when he'd been electioneering? Hadn't she nursed his wife? What more did he want? Men! Always demanding! What right had he? When she had accepted Adeline's burden, she had not meant to . . . Suddenly Jane, her stocking unrolled half way down her leg, sat on the edge of the bed trembling. Hadn't she? She gasped. If only she hadn't looked at him! He had asked if she was afraid of life! Of herself! Of what she had seen when she had looked into his eyes. Her hands dropped weakly to her side, and she lay back on the bed. Adeline had been afraid. And she had died. Blood. The price she had paid for daring to live, for daring to love. Blood. Ronnie too had paid. And yet, was it not better to have lived like them, than to skim across the surface of life, like Harriet May with her dreams, like Edie with her romantic papers, like Fanny, with her drink? Living was, after all, a dangerous affair. You risked death. But did that matter? Adeline gave her heart to George. Ronnie gave his to Jane. What about Jane's heart? Now? Oh why had she come between George and Alice Minto? She thought she had done it for love of Adeline. But the answer lay in the mirror of George's eyes. And she had looked into them! She had seen the answer. He had made her see it. George Beattie! Feelings surged inside her. Life tingled through her limbs, frightening, exciting. Like it or not, she was beginning to live. She sat up against her pillows, and looked across at the drawing on the wall. Her old elephant, stained with her blood, dirty. She, like the elephant, was grown up now, and equipped to enter into the fray. But who, what, was the crocodile? Shivering, she got

up, and finished undressing. She heard George close the door to
his bedroom downstairs. She stopped and listened, feeling his
presence in the house. It was everywhere. It invaded every room,
everything, it was invading her heart.

Harriet grew more and more irritated as Jane stared vacantly into
the middle distance.

'Are you listening to me?' She stood, hands on hips, glaring.

'What?'

'I want to know whether the Adams lot want button holes as
well. It is usual at a wedding, you know, and you've not marked
it down in the book!'

'What wedding?' Jane started suddenly.

'The Adams' wedding! I just told you!' Harriet looked up to
heaven.

'Did I not mark it down?' Jane asked.

'God give me strength! No you did not!'

'Oh dear. I must've forgotten,' Jane said absently. 'We'd better
go up the hill and check.'

'By "we", I suppose you mean "me",' Harriet said indignantly.

'I thought you liked delivering these days!'

'Not to them!'

'Oh? Who to, then?'

'Never you mind.'

Jane frowned. Harriet was bringing her unpleasantly down to
earth. What was she up to? Suddenly she noticed the chenille
turban wound round her head, and the long silk scarf.

'You look like something out of the Arabian Nights!'

'Good!' Harriet replied. 'I'm going to send Edie up the hill,
this time. So there!'

'As you like,' Jane sighed. Harriet was up to something.
Perhaps she should try to find out what it was, before there was
trouble! She sighed. There always *would* be trouble with Harriet
May! You'd think she'd've got used to the idea by now, but each
time, Harriet managed to catch them all napping. She was like a
bomb, ticking under the house. The only thing was, she kept on
going off! Jane's eyes strayed to the shop window, and the
portico of the Queen's Hall opposite. The light outside was
fading. As she stared at the glass, her own reflection grew ever

more distinct. Suddenly, she saw it, and looked away again. What was the matter with her? She was all churned up! She wanted to cry, and searched for the reason. She was missing Adeline. That was it. She was lonely. Yes. And yet the memory of the dead face eluded her. Always George's image came between, like her own reflected in the shop window . . . She looked back at the glass. It was dark now. She turned up the gas mantle. Suddenly Jane Ridley looked back at Jane Ridley. It was so real . . . like looking at someone else. She could see the rigidity, the tension, of the woman in the glass. She walked towards herself, touched her face, and felt compassion as she saw the great black pupils of the eyes, sparkling with fear. Poor Jane. She told herself not to be afraid. The eyes grew more trusting, black turning to blue, a deep blue, a fiery blue. Her heart jumped. The woman in the glass was . . . Quickly she turned the notice on the door. The shop was closed.

Scallywag had fleas. There was no doubt of it. Edie had been complaining for weeks, and now Harriet had been bitten too. Jane rolled up her sleeves and prepared to do battle. But Scallywag was an able opponent. His howl was like the Cullercoats fog horn! It brought George running from the nurseries.

'What's going on?' he asked, pale with fright, as he stood in the door watching.

'I've got to give him a bath!' Jane, red faced and dishevelled, was hanging on to the dog like grim death. George laughed.

'I'll give you a hand, eh?' Jane was so surprised she lost her grip on the hind legs, and Scallywag ran off, joyfully barking round and round the back yard.

'Come back you bugger!' George yelled. Jane's eyes nearly popped out of her head, as he careered round after the dog, shouting and cursing, till man and beast fell, panting to the ground. 'Got him!' George shouted. He picked him up in his arms, and dunked him into the waiting bath. 'I'll hold on to him,' George insisted. Jane put her hands in the soapy water, and began to rub the dog.

'Look! He likes it!' she laughed.

'Rub him harder! Don't be scared. You're tickling him!' Jane hesitated, abashed. 'Let me show you! Hold on to the scruff of his neck. That's it. Now, you've got to rub hard. Really let him feel it!' She watched his hands, massaging the dog. He knew what he was doing, and the dog growled with pleasure. They were small hands, surprisingly, small and sensitive. She remembered a hand on a shoulder, and she outside, looking in . . . before the curtains were drawn. Scallywag had been there too. A hand on a shoulder. Black hairs covered the back and the fingers were square and strong. They dug into the flesh of the animal, and the flesh rippled as the fingers moved. 'Now you try!' She couldn't look at him. 'Go on.' His hand was pushing her out of the way. Her blood drummed in her ears and his voice, which came at her as if from a great distance, was gentle. Was this why she had stood against Alice Minto? She was a fool. George Beattie? It was ridiculous. A flea jumped onto her arm and bit her. She yelped. Quick as a flash, George shot out his hand, and pincered the insect.

'Thank you.' She looked at him at last. He was grinning. Was he laughing at her?

At supper time, Edie served them in the kitchen. George was full of energy. His face beamed with pleasure. He sat at the table, actually cracking jokes if you please! Jane carefully avoided his eye. She found she was blushing, for somehow, she felt his remarks were addressed to her. Was she imagining it? Probably. Harriet sat ever more silent. And when, at the end of the meal, George invited Jane up to his parlour, for coffee and poetry, Edie nudged Harriet so hard, she choked on an iced fancy.

Covered with shame, Jane took the coffee from Edie when she brought it to the parlour door.

'Will you be wanting anything else, Missus?' she asked pointedly. Jane felt anguish at the maid's indiscretion, but George laughed.

'No thank you, Edie. You can wash up now.'

'It's not funny,' Jane objected when Edie had gone.

'I thought it was!' he grinned at her.

'No-one likes to be laughed at!' Jane was near to tears. She was behaving like a fool. He watched her, and she thought he raised his eyebrows slightly, before saying, 'Will you be mother or will I?'

Jane darted a look at him, then bent carefully over the pot, and

331

did the honours as though she were the queen serving the prime minister. George chuckled.

'What's the matter?' she asked, hurt.

'Nothing.' He shook his head, but was still smiling as she handed him his cup.

'Would you like me to read to you tonight?' she asked, keeping her eyes on her coffee.

'No,' he said, 'not yet. I think it's time I read something to *you*.' He snapped open his folder of poetry, cleared his throat, and began;

THE GATES OF PARADISE

My Eternal Man set in Repose,
The Female from his darkness rose
And She found me beneath a Tree . . .

Again the blood in her ears, and his voice so distant . . . male and female . . . light and dark . . . sensations swelled and over-flowed, drowning her attention . . .

. . . Round me flew the Flaming Sword;
Round her snowy Whirlwinds roar'd . . .

Flaming swords, snowy whirlwinds, hot and cold, the words seeped through the veil of her emotions . . .

When weary Man enters his Cave
He meets his Saviour in the Grave
Some find a Female garment there
And some a Male, woven with care,
Lest the Sexual Garments sweet
Should grow a devouring Winding sheet,
One Dies! Alas! The Living & Dead,
One is slain & One is fled . . .

Jane's mind reeled. But he was surely laughing at her! All this talk of sex! She didn't know what the poem was about, but as George had said, she was able to sense its meaning . . . and it was really rather rude! Sensing Jane's discomfort, George's eyes strayed over the top of the page, watching her reaction, as the poem drew to a close.

. . . Weaving to Dreams the Sexual strife
And weeping over the Web of Life.

There was a long silence. George leaned forwards to pick up his cup of coffee, and began stirring it noisily with his spoon.

'You're very quiet,' he said at last.

There was another silence, even longer than the first.

'I remember once there was a web in my room . . . ' Jane began.

'Ah. Ask Edie to see to it.'

'Oh, it's gone now.'

'Good.'

Dear God. He *was* laughing at her! He *was*! Jane looked up desperately. But he wasn't smiling. She felt his eyes, burning into her. She shivered, feeling the creeping ice burn right through, until her brain swam and her coffee spilt into her lap.

'You've upset your cup,' George told her calmly. Jane bolted out of her seat, as though she had been shot, shaking the beads of coffee from her skirt, mumbling that she would have to go and change, and would George please excuse her. 'No,' he said. His hand was on her shoulder. He reached out to touch her cheek. 'Do you love me?' he asked. Jane froze. Her breath stopped. The clock on the mantel did not tick. The horse, staggering up the hill halted. Suddenly she was calm. She looked back into his eyes. There was no time. There was no space. There was only love.

'Yes,' she said.

'Marry me.'

'Yes.'

CHAPTER TWENTY THREE

'Eeh! Eeh! Eeh!' was the sum total of Edie's reaction to the news. And it was more than Harriet volunteered at that!

'Nice to know when people are pleased for you!' George muttered sardonically, as Harriet went silently about her business. Apparently it was a crime to look happy; so Jane and George played the polite role of a couple united entirely for the good of England, taking no pleasure, of course, in the prospect themselves! Jane called her intended Mr Beattie and he addressed her curtly, as he had done before. Neither dared touch the other, and if eyes met, they looked away at once, knowing that contact would generate such happiness, they would be quite unable to hide it.

It was a game they enjoyed playing. Each bubbled with joy and humour, and in spite of themselves, they were forced to concede little grins of self-satisfied delight. Was such happiness allowed? Standing behind the counter, side by side, George's foot inched over to touch Jane's shoe, and sent a shiver of delight coursing through her, wholly out of proportion to the act. Leaning over, to fetch something from the shelves, he would brush his hand lightly across the back of her neck, and, dazed with sensation, Jane would stop mid sentence, leaving customers bemused, hanging on for more.

'How can I concentrate, when you *will* do such things!' she scolded him. Then they both giggled like a pair of children, and continued just as before.

'It's disgusting,' Harriet complained to Edie. 'And anyway, he's old enough to be her father!'

'Ooh, I think it's ever so romantic,' Edie sighed, as she stared into her bucket.

'*You'd* think a lavatory brush was romantic, if it suited you!' Harriet snapped.

'You've only got to look at him! He's twenty years younger! Eeh! All he needed was the love of a good woman!'

'He's had the love of two already!' Harriet May reminded her. 'What makes you think he'd stop at a third? Huh! My poor mother must be turning in her grave!' Edie sighed, considering Jane's predecessors.

'Mind . . . the missus'd be pleased. Eeh! I wish she was here to see it.'

'Edie, there are times when your stupidity is beyond even *my* imagining.'

'Is it? Eeh, Fancy!'

Some time later, Jane came in to ask where the tea was. Edie, well behind with her work, was upstairs turning down the beds. Jane sighed, and set about making tea herself. The shop bell went. Jane frowned. Wherever was Harriet May? You'd think Jane was the only woman in the place! Did she have to do everything herself? She went into the shop, a smile ready on her face, not the smile she kept for George, but the kind that would not cause gossip, even in a Sunday School!

Justice Mrs Fletcher stood, tapping a parasol impatiently on the floor.

'Sorry to have kept you waiting, Madam,' Jane apologised. 'What can I do for you today? Some roses perhaps?' Jane was reaching for the order book, but the parasol cracked against the floor sharply.

'I've got better roses in my own back garden!' the lady snapped. 'I've not come to buy anything.'

'Then what *have* you come for, Madam?' Jane asked courteously.

'I've come to make a complaint.'

'Oh dear.'

'Oh dear indeed!'

'What about, may I ask?'

Justice Mrs Fletcher shifted awkwardly from foot to foot.

'I think, perhaps, it would be more appropriate were I to speak to the manager.' Jane frowned. George was doing the accounts.

'Be so kind as to inform him I am here!' the lady insisted.

'Mr Beattie is extremely busy . . . '

'Too busy for an old and valued customer?'

Jane sighed, and made her way upstairs to the parlour, watched by the Justice's wife, who muttered something under her breath about trumped-up shop assistants.

George smiled charmingly. Mrs Fletcher melted a little, and when he said, 'How delightful to see you again, dear lady,' she melted a little more.

'And you, Mr Beattie.' Jane looked at George in amazement. His eyebrows were positively waggling at Mrs Fletcher. 'We don't see you nearly often enough.'

'Nor I you, Mrs Fletcher.'

'Your talents are quite wasted in this shop, if I may say so.'

'Oh?'

'We need you back in the town hall! The sooner the better!'

'How kind you are, dear lady. Now what can I do for you today?' Suddenly Mrs Fletcher remembered Jane, standing by the counter. She coughed. 'Ah. No need to worry about Miss Ridley. You can rely on her confidentiality.' Mrs Fletcher turned her back on Jane, as though pretending she wasn't there.

'About your delivery girl.' Jane exchanged a glance with George.

'Oh yes?'

'You'll get another, if you take my advice.'

'Really?' George edged his way towards Jane, and Mrs Fletcher was forced to turn a full hundred and eighty degrees to keep up with him.

'Give them an inch and they'll take a mile. You'll learn that.' She gave Jane a look, as if to warn George of possible danger from that quarter too.

'I see.' He was standing far too close to her. Jane felt the warmth of his leg through her skirt, and his hand knocked against her.

'I don't mind her flirting with my chauffeur. But when it comes to my own son . . . '

'Are you trying to tell me that Harriet May has been flirting with your chauffeur?' George's little finger tentatively explored the space round about, and came up against Jane's.

'*And* with every presentable young man up in Westoe Village!' The two fingers locked together in fond embrace. 'That little madam is getting your establishment a bad name!' Mrs Fletcher began to feel the vibrations of something 'not quite nice' going on and Jane tried to pull her finger away, but it was caught tight in George's stronger grip, and she rocked, as he pulled her back.

'Oh dear,' said George.

'Exactly! She'll be getting herself into trouble, you mark my words, and then you'll be landed!'

'Thank you so much for letting me know. I'm most grateful.' George nodded seriously, then suddenly and openly taking Jane's hand in his own, George pulled her forwards. Mrs Fletcher's mouth dropped open and she stepped back as if to ward off a blow. 'May I introduce my fiancée, Miss Ridley?' Mrs Fletcher looked like a filly about to bolt. 'The other young lady, the delivery girl, is my step-daughter.' Under her dress, Jane's foot reached out to kick George. He really was going too far. Mrs Fletcher drew herself up to her full height.

'Fancy!' she spluttered. Darting George a disapproving look, Jane spoke apologetically.

'We *are* sorry Harriet's been a nuisance, Mrs Fletcher. We will of course be speaking to her.' But, the attempt at smoothing ruffled feathers failed utterly.

'Young lady!' the customer intoned, 'I was speaking to the organ grinder, not the monkey!' One quick stab of the parasol on the unoffending floor, and the lady was gone. Unfortunately it was a false exit. For she had trapped the tail of her gown in the door, and had to open it again to free herself, before haughtily walking off down Fowler Street in the direction of Ocean Road.

'You are wicked!' The pent up anger exploded as Jane threw George's hand away from her and stormed into the kitchen.

Bellowing with laughter, George followed her and grabbed her from behind.

'It's not funny!' But she was laughing too, as he turned her round to kiss her first on forehead, then on cheeks, then on lips. And the world was still again. She laid her head against him and he stroked her hair as if it were something precious. Cradled in one another's love, trouble seemed a universe away. And yet a chill crept through Jane. She shuddered and sighed.

'What's wrong?'

'What are we going to do about Harriet May?'

'Shoot her!' George laughed. Jane touched his shoulder, and he looked down into her serious face.

'It really *isn't* funny, you know.'

George sighed. 'I know.'

'She's a sad girl.' They pulled away from one another, reluctantly.

'Edie will have to do the delivering.'

'She can't, George. She's got the housework to do!'

'Harriet May will have to dirty her hands.'

'It's difficult enough, George. No. I'll go back to the kitchen.'

'I won't have it!'

'Someone's got to do the cooking for us, and for the catering side. And we've not made toffee since . . . '

'No!'

'Shall you trust me with the recipe?' He touched her under the chin. 'Oh I think I might.'

'Well, I *am* in favour!' she mocked.

'But Harriet will have to pull her weight, same as you. What you do, she does. You take turns. Understood?'

'If you say so, George.' George grunted. 'Why does she do it?'

'What?'

'Chase after young men like that?'

'Same reason as I chase after young women!'

'George Beattie! And you a respectable married man!'

'Almost!'

Their laughter cushioned the time between Mrs Fletcher's visit and Harriet's arrival home, which came all too quickly. George beat a hasty retreat to his greenhouses, and left Jane to deal with the matter. It was extremely awkward. It would have

338

been far better if George had spoken to her. With deep mis-
givings, Jane asked Harriet May to come up to the parlour where
she wanted to have a word with her. Harriet sat sulkily in
Adeline's armchair.

'Mr Beattie asked me to speak to you, Harriet . . . '

'Getting a bit high and mighty, aren't you?'

'You're not making this any easier.'

'Why should I, stepmother!?' Jane gasped. She hadn't thought
about it before. But Harriet May was right. She *was* going to be
her stepmother! Jane desperately tried to pull herself together.
'Justice Mrs Fletcher came into the shop today.'

'Fancy.'

'She had a complaint to make. About you.' Harriet May glared
at her. 'Mr Beattie was very upset.'

'I don't care.'

'Harriet!'

'Well, I don't. So there.' Jane took a deep breath.

'All right, if you don't care about him, or about the shop, you
might care a little about yourself.'

'What do you mean?' Jane sat on the stool at Harriet's feet, and
looked up at her. 'You're a fine young woman. You have got . . .
style; you stand out from the common mould.' Harriet wondered
if Jane was laughing at her, and looked at her with some
amazement.

'What are you talking about?'

'You have no need to go about throwing yourself at young
men!'

'Who says I do?'

'Mrs Fletcher.' Harriet was silent. 'She says you've been
making eyes at her son . . . and other young men in the village.'
Harriet refused to meet her eyes. 'Have you?'

'What if I have?'

'Then more shame on you to cheapen yourself.'

'Kettle calling the pot if you ask me!' Jane swallowed the
insult.

'You have a social position, which I never had. Those young
men aren't so far above you! But you've put them out of your
reach by flirting with them!' Harriet shifted uneasily in her
chair. 'Don't you want to fall in love and marry some nice,

339

suitable, young man?' Harriet sniffed back a tear. 'Why throw it all away? I don't understand!'

'Don't you?' The sudden sharp retort startled Jane, and hot, bitter tears sprang from Harriet's eyes.

'Harriet . . . '

'It's all right for you! Wind men round your little finger you can! I've seen you! But I'm plain. I'm ugly. And I don't know how to be nice. I don't know how . . . ' The pain, buried deep inside Harriet May Lovely, was harsh in her voice.

'Harriet, dear . . . ' Jane pulled the girl towards her, and held her in her arms, rocking her, to and fro. 'Dear Harriet . . . I wish . . . I wish . . . ' Harriet hiccupped, and the sobs began to subside. 'I wish you thought a little more of yourself.'

'How can I think anything of myself? Nobody else does!'

'I do!'

'Liar.'

'No. I mean it! I didn't! But I do now! Now this minute! Because, I can see what you might have been, might still be, if you'll . . . '

'What?'

'Only respect yourself! And other people will too!'

'Huh! I can just see the old barsket doing that!'

'George! Do you mean your stepfather?' Harriet nodded, drying her eyes on her handkerchief. 'There you are, you see. Look what you just called him. If you don't respect him, he won't respect you. We aren't children any more, Harriet May. We're grown women! We can't expect to have our own way just because we've done the world the favour of being born! We have to *give* a little!'

'A little what?'

'Love.'

'I don't love him. He doesn't love me either.'

Jane couldn't deny it. 'Then you must earn his respect.' Harriet sniffed. 'He's not going to let you deliver flowers any more, you realise that. He'll make us work side by side now!' Harriet began to laugh.

'My God! You must hate me!'

Jane shook her head, smiling. 'There have been times . . . but no. I'm so happy, Harriet. I love your stepfather so very much.'

340

'I don't understand it, but you do, don't you? You're not pretending?'

'Why would I pretend?'

'Well, admit it! It is all rather sudden, isn't it?'

'Not really,' Jane smiled, 'the moment he asked me, I knew I'd always loved him. Only I didn't realise it . . . didn't know how much! Everything else was just . . . a dream. That's all. I love George. Always have and always will. I love him so much . . . ' Jane was crying, her joy spilling over. 'There never could be another man for me. George is just . . . right. That's all. It's how it's meant to be,' she said simply. Harriet gave Jane a shy look.

'What's it like?'

'What?'

'Being in love . . . being loved. Huh! It's happened to you twice already! It's not happened to me once!'

'No. It was different with Ronnie. I think I wasn't quite grown up then. I didn't feel the way a woman really feels when she loves a man . . . '

'I wish you'd tell me . . . '

'One day, it'll happen to you, then you'll know for yourself.' Suddenly the two women were in one another's arms, crying. Harriet blew her nose and asked shyly, 'Can I be your bridesmaid?'

'Yes! Oh yes! Please!'

And now Edie really did have something to cry over. Even George was moved, when Jane summoned him to inspect the dress she was pinning on her unexpected bridesmaid. The house hummed with happiness. People came and went, paying visits, leaving cards, a wedding list was made, the presents began to arrive, and George took Jane on a special trip into Newcastle, to buy the ring.

Jane had not dared ask for what she wanted, and knowing it, George played a game with her.

'You'd better come with me, dear, to make sure I don't order the wrong size.' Dutifully, Jane acquiesced, going along with him to the jeweller's shop. He laughed to himself, as her eye strayed to the tray of diamonds displayed beside them. One in particular caught her eye . . . a diamond solitaire, on a plain gold band. Simple, pure, the stone had a fire in it, and willy nilly, it caught her attention. But she had expected nothing. She had asked for nothing. And she went home again, content. What was it, after all? Just a thing! A mere thing! The band of gold, the one that really mattered, was in George's breast pocket. What more could she ask?

But that night, at supper, George bubbled with a scarce suppressed glee. Darting him suspicious looks, Jane waited for the revelation, whatever it might be. Then, just as she was rising to leave the table, at the end of the meal, he produced a little box, and passed it to her.

'No! No!' she said. 'I mustn't try it on again. It would be unlucky!'

'Open it,' he insisted. Jane sighed, shaking her head, full of doubt, and opened the little box.

A light, refracted into many colours, burst on her eyes, flashing its rays of brilliant, pure fire. She breathed in sharply. George laughed, delighted.

'Is it the right one?' She nodded, lifting her eyes from the ring, to the man, then back again. 'With this ring, I give my heart into your keeping.'

'And I shall be its faithful guardian, to serve and protect it with my love, strong and clear as this bright diamond.' Its light shone in Jane's eyes as she made her vow. Then, George took back the box, lifted the ring from it, and slipped it on her finger. Edie, apron over face, rushed out to soothe her feelings in the privacy of the backyard midden. Harriet, staring at the ring, from the other side of the table, spoke softly,

'It's the most beautiful thing I've ever seen.' She beamed as she melted away to her own room, leaving the pair together.

'I thought she might have been jealous,' George said. Jane shook her head.

'She really can be quite nice when she likes.'

Jane felt she could have taken the whole world into her heart; the earth, the sky, the sea, the plants, the animals and all the people of the earth; but her own family, especially, touched her heart at this time. The news of her forthcoming marriage exploded like a bomb in the town end. Jane Ridley was now to be reckoned with, and her relatives basked joyfully in her reflected glory. The status of the Tullys was restored overnight. Dandy, with his new coble, was a working Tyne Pilot again, and sent his top hat to be mended for the wedding. Robert, now first mate, and dapper in his shore clothes, was summoned home from the far corners of the earth. Fanny returned from Hexham on probation. There was a flurry of new hats in Pilot Street and Bob bought his first new suit ever, to give this changeling daughter of his away. Fortune did indeed smile on them all. Battle-scarred, older, and wiser, each and every one prepared to celebrate the end of one phase in their lives, and the beginning of the next.

Standing before Adeline's triple mirrors, Jane slipped on her simple white lawn dress, and waited patiently, while Harriet fastened it at the back.

'It's so plain!' Harriet complained.

'Yes.' Jane smiled at her reflection.

'You could have had anything! Silk, and Brussels lace . . . ' Jane shook her head.

'I'm happier in this.'

'At least let me curl your hair. I've put the tongs to heat downstairs!'

'I thought I might just bundle up my hair, at the nape of my neck. I've got a pretty snood to hold it . . ' Harriet's lip curled at the silvery web on the dressing table.

'Oh well!' she sighed, 'it's your wedding!'

'When it's your turn, Harriet, you can really go to town!' Jane laughed, and sat down before the mirrors.

'I will! Don't you worry, Mrs . . . '

'No! Not yet. It's unlucky!' Jane swept back the pale golden hair, dropping it into the silver web, and pinning it in place. 'There now. All I need are the flowers!'

Harriet laughed. 'Coals to Newcastle! You sit there. I'll go down the cellar to fetch them.'

Left alone, Jane folded her hands, and rested them on the table. She saw how the fingers had thickened with work. The nails were short and there were rough patches on the skin. But they were good hands. Soon there would be a ring on one of them, a golden ring which she would never take off. This was the last time she would see the image of her maidenhood mirrored there. She looked up, and behind her own reflection, she saw that of her brother, Robert. He was standing close behind her, head and shoulders taller. Their eyes met in the glass, a moment, silent and still, reflected back to infinity in the triple mirrors. Then, he bent and kissed the top of her head.

'I wanted to see you before the ceremony,' he said. 'I have something for you.' He took a small white case from his pocket. Jane took it and set it on the dressing table to open it. Inside was a bible, whose cover was made of the finest ivory, and when she opened it, she saw the pressed outline of Chandrika's four leaved clover. Jane could not speak. She looked back to her brother's image in the glass, her heart too full for words. Once more, he bent to kiss the top of her head, and quietly left the room.

When Harriet bustled in, piled high with flowers, she found the bride sitting lost in thoughtlessness.

'We've not got all day, madam!' she chided. 'Look! What do you think of this?' She dropped a simple garland over Jane's head. It was made of blowsy roses, pink, and cream and white, and the perfume of them blew round her head like a gentle breeze.

'Oh, Harriet! It's lovely!' Harriet beamed, excitedly.

'I've only got a little one for me . . . look it goes on the back.' Jane looked. It was very pretty. 'And here's your posy . . . ' For one terrible moment, Jane had a vision of a posy of anemones, but when she looked, she saw the same huge garden roses, buds, half blown, overblown, rioting together, in pastel shades. She smiled, tears in her eyes, and looked up at Harriet.

'It's perfect,' she said, 'thank you.' Harriet nodded, and set about pinning the garland in place over the smooth, shining hair of the bride.

In the church, the organ was playing. The congregation was assembled. George sat with his best man, Alderman Fancy, in the front row. But there was consternation in Fowler Street. Ma Tully, Dandy and Fanny arrived, complete with two screaming infants, and a visitor in tow.

'Where's Dad?' Jane asked in alarm.

'His coaster's been held up on the bar.'

'Is he all right?'

'Oh aye . . . the captain tried to bring it in himself, and he's gone aground.'

'What am I going to do?'

'I would be delighted to give you away, Miss Ridley.' The visitor came forward from the shadows and presented himself to the bride. Dropping her flowers to the ground, Jane flung her arms about his neck, as she had done years ago, when she had met him outside the house in Trajan Street.

'Chandrika! Oh I'm glad you came! I'm so glad!'

'Robert wrote and told me.' He fished something out of his pocket. 'I wanted to give you something truly auspicious on your wedding day,' he said, handing her his present. It was a coral necklace, the beads intricately carved, and interspersed amongst them were twelve elephants.

'It's beautiful!'

'Put it on.'

Turning to Harriet, Jane gave her the necklace to fasten round her neck.

'What is the significance of elephants?' Harriet asked. 'I know Jane's always had a thing about them but . . . '

'Sri Ganesha, the elephant-headed God, Lord of Innocence, remover of obstacles, may He bless your marriage, Jane.'

Muttering darkly about pagan rites, Fanny and Ma Tully hustled Dandy along with them to the church, just ahead of the bridal party.

At last, the organ blasted out Mendelssohn's wedding march, and Jane, leaning on Chandrika's arm, walked into the chapel, followed by Harriet. Edie cried openly, and George stood proudly watching as his bride approached. Her eyes met his at the altar. Nervously she touched the coral necklace round her neck, then looked up at the cross hanging over them. Calm and sure, each stood, radiant before the preacher. The joy spread through the congregation, as all stood to sing 'The Lord is My Shepherd.' As they sang, Bob Ridley, dishevelled in his old sea clothes, crept into the back of the church. Turning, Jane saw him, and smiled. Poor Dad. At least he'd got there! Now everything was perfect. Clear and strong, Jane's voice rang out at George's side.

345

Yea though I walk through death's dark vale,
Yet shall I fear no ill.
For Thou art with me,
And Thy rod and staff me comfort still.

George slipped the gold band on her finger. And as they turned, man and wife, to walk out of the chapel, Jane's heart ran over, pouring its love, its radiance, its joy, into all who saw her.

In the hotel room in Whitley Bay, Jane took off the coral necklace and laid it on the dressing table, beside George's cuff links. Suddenly shy, she held her wrap close about her, as she reached for her hair brush. She raised the brush in one hand, and the wrap opened, to reveal the outline of her breasts under the silk nightdress George had bought for her. She bent to close it again, and suddenly George was there. He stood behind her, head and shoulders taller than her, and their eyes met in the glass, as he took the brush from her hand, and began, softly, soothingly, to brush her long, shining hair. Feeling him so close, she began to tremble, and he put the brush down, parting the hair at the nape of the neck, to kiss her. She moaned softly, her head swaying back, to lean against him. And his hands slipped from her shoulders, down her breasts to rest on her belly. Her eyes, dark and still, watched him from the mirror.

'Don't be afraid,' he said.

'I'm not afraid.'

'Good.' Still he held his hands firm on her womb.

'My belly's teeming with your children,' she said, turning to face the man himself. Holding her face in his hands, he looked deep into her.

'First things first,' he said.

PART THREE
Spring 1882

CHAPTER TWENTY FOUR

The sun, finding a chink in the blind, glanced on the diamond, which, prism like, shot out the refracted rays into a festival of rainbows, festooning the walls of the room. The baby in the cradle began to cry. The woman stirred, stretched out, and yawned. Time for another feed. Her breasts ached from the weight of the milk in them. She was sleepy, warm, and content. But the baby cried. So she pulled herself up in the bed, and reached over to the cradle, easing the child from under its blanket, and gently raising it, its mouth pushed against her breast.

'Come on, then. I thought you said you were hungry!' The woman watched as the tiny mouth dribbled open and blind eyes searched for the nipple, then the gums closed upon it, and the baby began to suckle. Outside, the coalman's horse clattered up the cobbled lane. Women cursed, taking down the washing, strewn on lines across its way. Edie shouted up the stairs to Harriet.

'You've got a customer and Ellen's wet herself again!'

Harriet, banging doors, thumped down to the shop. But in her room, Jane brooded in silent, powerful contentment. Though storms might rage on the surface, in the deep waters of her peace, nothing stirred her. She was become too strong for that, and the child at her breast drew contentment from her.

Dismissing the customer with her tulips, Harriet swept up the four year old, and roughly took down her knickers to reveal the sordid truth.

'You're a disgrace, our Ellen!' Ellen began to bawl, aware of her shame, made worse by the public exhibition. Edie glanced at the kitchen clock.

'Eeh, the missus'll be wanting her grub!'

'It won't matter for half an hour. I can't hold the fort in the shop *and* see to this little madam at the same time!'

'The master doesn't like it to be late. Every three hours on the dot. That's what he said!'

'Huh! She'll blow up if you ask me!' The soiled knickers were dropped into a pail ready for boiling, and the chubby bottom, washed and wiped was covered in fresh drawers. Ellen's red eyes reproached her assailant ferociously.

'Look at her!' Harriet complained. 'You'd think she'd be grateful!' And the shop bell went again. 'No peace for the wicked!'

'Where's the master?'

'It's Tuesday.'

'Oh aye.'

And Harriet departed into the shop.

'Howway, pet. How about toasting this bit of bread for your Mam, eh?' Pleased to be useful, Ellen fixed the bread precariously onto the prongs of the toasting fork, and held it up before the fire, while Edie got on with heating the milk. 'Eeh I bet you're glad you've got a little sister, eh?' The child ignored the maid's attempts at making conversation. 'Eh?' Edie insisted. The bread dropped onto the red coals, and the child leant forward to retrieve it. 'Leave it be! I'll give you another'n. We don't want you burning yourself now.' This time Edie fixed on the bread herself, and set the fork in the right position for Ellen to hold. 'That's better!'

'I'd rather've had a brother,' the child suddenly declared.

'What for? They're all rough, and they're all daft! Take my word for it. You're far better off with a sister.'

'Lads play football.'

'Exactly!'

'I like football!'

'Ooh, you! Ellen Beattie, you'll come to no good! See if you don't!'

'Huh!' The toast began to singe, and Edie left the simmering milk to turn it over to its second side. 'I like lads better than girls,' the child insisted.

'Shush!' Edie admonished her, just in time, as the father breezed in from his council meeting.

'It's nearly ready, Mr Beattie!' Edie quickly fended off criticism, as George checked his watch and waited till the tray was set, so he could take it upstairs to his wife.

'Eeh.' Edie shook her head in pleased wonder. 'They're like a pair of newly weds. Eeh!' She would have begun to cry, but Ellen, reaching for the jug of milk, spilled it, all over herself and the kitchen floor, where Scallywag waited, expecting the proverbial crumbs, and finding himself, instead, in the land of plenty. 'Huh! I'm glad somebody's pleased!' Ellen observed, as the pink tongue lapped, and the tail wagged.

'You spoil me, George!' Jane's voice wrapped itself like honey round his heart, and the figures from the treasurer's annual report went clean out of George's head.

'What a picture!' he said, delightedly, as he sat on the edge of the bed, watching his baby at his wife's breast. Jane smiled, her cheeks dimpling, then frowned as she looked at the tray in his hands.

'Not again!' she said.

'Get it down you!' George passed her the glass, insistently. 'Top of the milk. Drink it up!'

'And what's that?' Jane looked in disgust at the mess in the bowl.

'Yoghurt and royal jelly!'

'Yuk!'

'It's good for you!'

'It's not if it makes me sick!'

'Don't be so soft. You've got a child to suckle!'

'I'll just have the buttered toast thank you very much!'

'You'll eat this yoghurt, if I've got to spoon it down you myself!' George commanded. 'It's got bacteria in it!'

351

'Bac what?'

'Never mind. It's good for you! The Afghans eat it.'

'I'm not Afghan. I'm Geordie!'

'No need to split hairs! They live for a hundred years.'

'Fancy!' And Jane knew she would have to eat it. He would sit and wait till Kingdom come, if necessary!

Still, it was nice to be loved. Yes, *and* have somebody to clean up after you! Harriet thought, as she cleared away the flowers and struggled down the cellar steps with them at the end of the day.

'They take me for granted, Edie. That's the top and bottom of it!' Tears formed in Harriet's eyes as she peeled the onions.

'Oh, I'm sure they don't. No. It's *me* that gets taken for granted round here, if anybody does!'

'Don't be so daft! How can you be taken for granted? You're not even family! You get paid, don't you?'

'A pittance.'

'Rubbish! What about me? I'm sick to me back teeth of having to ask for everything.'

'Ask and ye shall be given,' Edie intoned.

'Oh shurrup! You're as bad as him!'

'Huh! I'd swop with you any day of the week.' Edie's eye took in the lace collar on Harriet's pretty dress, and the gold bangle on her wrist.

'You don't know you're born, you!'

Scallywag yelped as a hot coal fell out of the fire. His ancient legs shot him out of its way in double quick time.

'Eeh! Look at him!' Edie shovelled the smoking coal back onto the range, and Ellen laughed. 'You'd think he was still a puppy!' And so the competition for 'worst off' in the Beattie household came to an end.

But the resentment continued to brew, and from the depths of her contentment, Jane felt the first, faint ripples. What a pity! She would have to shake herself, get back down to the shop and the kitchen, and referee the household as usual. She sighed, and turned over. Tomorrow, tomorrow. She listened to the baby breathing, tiny breaths, so quick, so slight. How could one of those end up as big as George? It hardly seemed possible. And yet, he must have been a baby once! Idly, Jane considered the possibility. Had anyone ever seen George as a baby! Were there any witnesses? How many pounds did he weigh at birth? Or was he born, fully grown, Mayor of Shields, with his chain of office round his neck? She was giggling into the bedclothes, as Ellen, half asleep, in her nightie, wandered into the room.

'Mam, I want to come in with you . . . !' came the plaintive cry.

'Why?'

'Me knee hurts.'

'Tut. Well, what were you doing wheeling barrows about? You might've known it'd fall on top of you!'

'I like doing things.' Jane sighed. 'Please, Mam!'

'All right. Come on then. But don't tell your Dad.' And Ellen climbed into the warm, dark cosiness of her mother's bed, to fall asleep in her arms. She was a funny child. She should have been a boy. She was always scrambling up rubbish heaps, playing with marbles, kicking people. A proper little rough and tumble she was. George would have liked a boy. For a moment, Jane felt a twinge of sadness, which evaporated almost immediately. Better luck next time, eh? The thought was barely formed, when George entered the room.

'Are you asleep?'

'If I was, it'd be a pity!' Jane said.

'Sorry. Shall I put on the light?'

George turned to the new gas mantles he had installed in the rest of the house, when he had had the safe put in.

'No . . . I'm sleepy.'

'Oh. Can I come in beside you?' he asked. Suddenly Jane laughed.

'I've heard that somewhere before.'

'Come on, love. I miss you. It's hard getting into a cold, lonely bed.'

'Ellen has to.'

'Aye well. That's different.'

'Why?' she teased him. He was getting undressed by the moon-light, which filtered through the blind.

'Don't ask silly questions, woman!' Jane laughed, and, cursing, George crept in beside her.

'By God your feet are cold!' she objected, as he planted them

353

on her. His hands reached round her, and he moaned seductively.

'Now then!' But he had stopped already.

'Jane! Your hands've shrunk!'

Suddenly Jane giggled. 'Sh! You'll wake her up!'

'Two's company!'

'Not when I'm recovering from childbirth, it's not, you great rampant beast!'

'Speak for yourself, Mrs Beattie!' Then he groaned, and resigned his place in the bed, 'I know when I'm beaten!'

'It is a pity, though . . . '

'That's not fair!' He threw a pillow at her, which she fielded nicely away from the sleeping infant. Their laughter faded into longing, as they looked, through the moonlight into one another's eyes.

'Roll on next month,' she said.

'Amen to that!'

'George Beattie!' With that, the husband crept up to the spare room in the attic, leaving Jane to soothe the waking child. She sighed. She was so lucky! How could she have deserved such happiness? Dear, dear George!

Dandy fairly gloated over the announcement in the paper. 'To His Worship, George Beattie, Mayor of South Shields, and to his wife, Jane, née Ridley, a girl. The Borough offers its congratulations and best wishes for the future.'

' "The Borough!" Eeh!' Dandy beamed. 'Isn't that wonderful!'

'Aha.' Fanny pretended not to be impressed. 'Pity they didn't make as much fuss about the first one. There were no announcements about her!'

'Aye well, he wasn't Mayor then, was he? He wasn't in the limelight, like. I mean, they can hardly offer congratulations to every Tom, Dick and Harry that gets born, can they?'

'Depends who they get born to.'

'Exactly. Mind . . . ' Dandy said thoughtfully. 'It's a pity this one isn't a son, like. I mean, to carry on the business.'

'That's true.' Fanny nodded her agreement. 'Who's going to take it over when he's gone?' Dandy and Fanny looked at Eddie,

354

through the kitchen window. He was playing with some wooden boxes, salvaged from the Groyne.

'He'll be a pilot, like his dad!' Dandy said loudly. 'And don't you go getting ideas above your station, my lass!' Chastised, Fanny sulked her way upstairs, and took a bottle from beneath the bed. The cork squeaked as she wrenched it out. Why was it their Jane always fell on her feet? Living in the lap of luxury, money and to spare, a position in society. All Fanny had for society was the kids, the stray dogs on the quay, and the drabs in the pub. Taking a pull from the bottle, Fanny made her way to the washstand, and looked in the mirror. She studied her face carefully. There was no point denying it. She was ugly. Her skin was pot holed, and she looked old, old before her time. No wonder Dandy'd gone off her. No wonder. She sighed. But then, what could Fanny do about it, when all was said and done? It would take nothing short of a miracle to make Fanny attractive again. A miracle, and money for fancy clothes. Clothes like Jane's. She sighed and took another pull. She still looked miserable. Perhaps one more would do it. A long gulp of whisky sent the colour to the cheeks, the sparkle to the eye, and a smile to the lips, and Fanny was ready for the world again.

But standing in the kitchen at 18, Victoria Terrace, stirring a panful of toffee, Jane felt less than equal to her world.

'Tell me a "tory",' demanded the little girl who was making up posies of violets at the table.

'Our Ellen! You've had three today already!'

'I want another'n.' Jane sighed, and stirred on.

'How about . . . "The Princess and the Pea"?'

'Not that one.'

'I know. Once upon a time, there was a princess, with very beautiful, very long hair . . . '

'Not Rapunzel!'

Jane took the pan from the stove. 'Out of my way!' she commanded, as she scurried to the table, and poured the bubbling, dark liquid into the trays.

'Yuk,' said Ellen.

'You don't say "Yuk" when it's gone hard, and you want to eat it,' Jane snapped.

'Tell me a . . . '

'All right! All right! Wait a minute.' Jane sighed and sat in the rocking chair, taking the little girl onto her knee. 'I know. Once upon a time in the far off country of China . . . '

'Not Aladdin!'

'Then what *do* you want?'

'A new one. One I've not heard.'

'I very much doubt if there *is* one you haven't heard.'

'One with animals in it.'

'Animals. Now let's see . . . ' Slowly Jane began to smile.

'Can you think of one?'

'Maybe.' Faces round an oil lamp, and her Dad. his seaman's husky voice, "Once upon a time . . . " '

'Mam!' Ellen, impatient at her mother's mood of reverie, took hold of her apron straps with her fists and shook her.

'Stop it!' Jane reprimanded her.

'You were thinking again! You're always thinking!'

'No I'm not.'

'Yes you are. What were you thinking about?'

'I was thinking of your grandad if you must know, you little nosey parker.'

'I've not got one.'

It was true. Bob Ridley was dead two years since, when Ellen was only two. For some time, he had been working on the tugs, preferring to stay close to home, now he was getting older. It was safer, he said. He slept in his own bed at nights, and he ate good food, prepared by Fanny. He'd got himself onto the quoits team at 'The Globe' and one way or another, working on the tugs suited him. He was crewing the *Flying Huntsman*, when it had happened. It was a bad night, in late October. The *Isis*, the *Johanna* and the *Harry Clem* had all gone aground on the Pier and the South Sands. Ma Tully and Fanny'd gone down to watch, joining the group of women already gathered south of the Brigade House, where they had a good view of the vessels in trouble. Dandy'd gone out in the lifeboat, but there was more work than they could cope with. For two other vessels were also in trouble, on the river itself. A trawler and a steam tug had capsized. The tug was the *Flying Huntsman*. News of this second disaster reached the women on the sands, and Ma and Fanny were turning to go, when suddenly, the gully on the south side of

356

the pier was flooded, and finding themselves surrounded by sea, the women panicked. Many lost their lives, suffocating in the shallow water, as the crowd knocked them to the ground, stampeding over them. The next morning, bruised and shaken, Fanny took Dandy down to the site of the disaster. There, Fanny found her lost bonnet amongst the debris on the beach while the body of Dandy's mother lay stranded like a whale, trapped in the deep gulley, her three chins bobbing on the tide. Bob's body came up by the Mill Dam, two days later. Poor Fanny. She really went to pieces. To lose them both at once! Dandy had not the heart to refuse her her comfort, and all the work of the previous two years was undone in a matter of weeks. Fanny was a drunkard, and Dandy, too weak to battle against her, let her get on with it.

Faces round the oil lamp. Jane, Robert, Fanny, Josh and Dad. Jane shook her head sadly. So much had happened. Two were lost . . . three if you counted poor Fanny. And where in the world was Robert? Last heard of, he had been in Argentina, she must wait for another letter, and then send on the newspaper, announcing Maisie's birth. Maisie. She liked the name . . . Maisie . . .

'Mam!' Furious, Ellen tugged at Jane's hair.

'Get off!' Jane commanded.

'Tell me a . . .'

'All right. All right. Now then. Where was I? "Once upon a time, there was a little baby elephant".'

'What's one of them?'

'An elephant, is a large animal . . . wait a minute, I've got a picture of one, in my chest of drawers. Come on. Let's go and find it.' Jumping from her knee, Ellen tackled the stairs with great energy, arriving at her mother's bedroom door before her, and her hands were on the doorknob turning it, as Jane came to help. She found the old drawing underneath her stockings. She drew it out, smiling as she looked at it. 'There you are! That, Ellen, is an elephant!' Ellen frowned.

'Is a hephalant big?'

'Yes.'

'Big as a mouse, or big as a horse?'

'Oh, bigger than a horse.'

357

'Honest?'

'Honest.'

'Bigger than a house?'

'No. Not so big as a house. Sort of in between a horse and a house.'

'Oh. Get on with the "tory".'

'Please!'

'Please.'

'Once upon a time, there was a little baby elephant. It lived far away, on the other side of the world . . . ' As she retold the story of the elephant and the crocodile, Jane saw again in her child's eyes, her own amazement, at the elephant and its struggle against the enemy. She remembered Fanny, and the abortion. She remembered Ronnie and Jack. So much had happened since she had first heard the tale from her father. Ellen, eyes huge with wonder, watched her face as the story came to an end. 'And our elephant, growing old and wise, was soon watching over a family of his own, playing happily in the forests, unaware of the dangers around them.' There was a long silence.

'I don't believe in hephalants,' Ellen said at last.

'What do you mean, you don't believe in them?'

'Well . . . you made them up.'

'Me?'

'Well, somebody did, then!'

'No. Elephants are quite real,' Jane said firmly. 'I should know. I've seen one!'

'What? A real hephalant?' Jane nodded. 'I don't believe you!'

'Don't be so cheeky!' Ellen pouted. 'I *have* seen one. So there, our Ellen. I've even ridden on the back of one!' And now the child's eyes were round with amazement.

'Cross your heart and hope to die?'

'Cross my heart.'

'Where? Was it in the jungle?'

Jane laughed. 'Not exactly. No. It was down The Bents. There was a circus. They had a whole herd of elephants.'

'A family of them?'

'I suppose so. Yes.'

'What's a circus?' But Maisie was crying, and Jane had to put

Ellen down to tend to her, promising to tell her little girl all about it, some other time. Dissatisfied, Ellen kicked at the table legs and received a sharp look from Edie for doing so.

But the child continued pestering. If only George was at home, he could have dealt with her. Ellen needed a father's strict discipline, or she would run wild. Jane, tired from suckling her newborn, tired from working morning till night for the business, found the constant demands of her eldest too much to bear. Then, one day, when Maisie was three months old, little Ellen disappeared. Pangs of guilt and fear pained Jane's heart, as she and Edie searched the house for her. But she was nowhere to be found. Edie was sent over the road to the nurseries, to see if the child had ventured across there. Jane went round to the grocer's, next door, to see if she had gone to play with their little boy, while Harriet continued to hold the fort in the shop. It was a Saturday, and customers came in droves for flowers, seeds, plants, and the other commodities supplied by Beattie's store. They lined up at the counter, poked about amongst the tubs of flowers, and when they grew tired of waiting, complained, or even walked out, accusing Harriet of poor service. It wasn't fair. As she stood in the shop, outwardly calm, taking all they threw at her, inside her fury grew. It was true. They *did* take her for granted! She was a maid of all work. She was a fool to herself to let them do it to her! Wasn't her own mother George's first wife? Hadn't she, Harriet May Lovely, lived and worked at Beattie's before Madam Jane and her terrible brood had so much as been heard of! She was twenty-three years old, almost on the shelf, and she had no life of her own. None at all! The threads of resentment tightened inside her. They formed chains and knots that bound her. And the more they bound her, the more furious she became. She had to break free of this prison. She had to do something to show them what for!

When Mr James from the village came in to collect the basket of flowers he had ordered for his wife's birthday, Harriet had no option but to leave him and the other customers alone in the shop. Early that morning, she had made up the order - a beautiful basket of arum lilies and pink roses, over which she had taken a great deal of time and trouble. After all, Mr James was a valued customer, and the flowers he had ordered were extremely expensive. She had taken them down to the cellar, where the cold dampness would help to keep them fresh, before opening up. She was tired. She was overworked. And now as she scurried out the back, and into the kitchen, Harriet's nerves were close to breaking point.

But the baby had begun to cry. Where was Jane? Why had she not come back? Harriet stopped to pick up Maisie, and soothe her. She was wet. She smelt. Disgusted, Harriet put her back in her cradle, and cursed her, closing her ears to the bawling, as she wrenched open the cellar door, and lighting a candle went down into the darkness for her basket of flowers. Halfway down the stairs, she stopped dead. There was someone down there. A rustling sound, followed by a moan startled her. Her heart beat fast. What could it be? She raised the candle high, so that its feeble light burned through the pitch dark.

'Who is it?' she whispered.

'Me . . . Auntie Harriet.' Harriet clenched her teeth and stared into the corner, where the child sat, hunched up and tearful, beside an upturned basket of flowers, pink roses scattering the stone flags around her. The big eyes pleaded for mercy out of the gloom. 'You little brat!' Harriet screeched. With one hand, she grasped the child's collar, and dragged her, screaming, up the stair. In the shop, Mr James stood horrified, as he heard the sharp crack of leather belt, the hard clunk of metal clasp, and the terrified cries of the child.

'I'll teach you! I'll show you, you little hellcat!'

Rushing across the road with Edie and George, Jane saw the women pouring out of the shop, shocked expressions on their faces. George began to run, and Jane, close on his heels, barged into the shop, and out the back, after him. Ellen was crawling across the kitchen floor, her buttocks bared and bleeding, gasping out little cries of distress. Harriet, white with fury, stood, arms braced behind her, held by Mr James.

'Ellen!' Jane swept up the infant to soothe and comfort her.

'Let me go!' Harriet yelled. George nodded to Mr James, who, reluctantly let go of his charge. 'How dare you!' she spat at him.

'Harriet! Go to your room!' George commanded her. For a long moment, Harriet stood her ground, staring back at him, but finally, to the background of a crying baby, and a whimpering toddler, Harriet turned haughtily and left the kitchen.

'Mr James . . .' George began.

'No. Don't say anything, Beattie. The business will go no further.' He shook hands with the mayor, and left without his offering of flowers. 'The business will go no further,' he had said. But how could Mr James vouch for that? The droves of horrified women leaving the shop would see to it that news of this disgrace would be reported from one end of the town to the other. Turning the notice on the door to 'CLOSED', George knew he would have to do something about it.

The fright of the child hung in the air, tangible as scorched grass after lightning. The dog, coming in from the yard, was pulled up short at the door, and, warily skirting the edges of the room, suddenly fled up the stairs, out of harm's way, only to pause, alarmed outside the parlour door, listening to the raised voices within.

'I'm sorry, George. I can't forgive her. Not for this.' Jane's face, blotched with tears, was stiff with resentment. She could not look at Harriet, who leant against a chairback, shaking.

'It's her own fault. She's been goading me to it for ages.'

'How dare you!'

'A body can only take so much!'

'I work as long hours as you, but I don't raise a hand to anyone!'

'That's the trouble! That's how that little madam's got out of hand! Somebody should have leathered her ages ago!'

'You're cruel.'

'You've got to be cruel to be kind.'

'Rubbish!' George spoke for the first time, his eyes darting fire at his stepdaughter.

'I never got much kindness from you!' Harriet snapped back.

'I took you in. I provided for you!'

'You never liked me!' Suddenly George looked tired, and dejected.

Impatiently, Jane turned on both of them.

'What's all this got to do with anything?'

'A great deal,' George growled.

361

'You see!' Harriet was triumphant. 'The sins of the fathers shall be visited on the children!'

'And what right have you to be God's avenging angel, I should like to know?' George challenged her.

'Who has a better right?' Jane, bemused, looked from one to the other, tears starting into her eyes.

'Little Ellen's been forgotten, hasn't she? Doesn't anybody care about *her*?' She wanted to shake them. What were they on about, when her little girl lay, shocked and broken, in the nursery, watched over by the maid. George put his arm round her, and Harriet May's lip curled in distaste as she saw it.

'Of course I care,' George said, 'she's my little girl too, you know.' Harriet snorted, biting back bitter tears. He darted her a look, then sighed. 'I'm sorry, Harriet. I don't see how I can let you keep on living here, after this.'

'You're sorry!' Jane screamed. 'It's her that should be sorry!'

'You'll miss me when I've gone,' Harriet said in a tight hard voice. 'You'll learn how much work I do round here. You'll not get anybody to fill my place.'

'Shop assistants are ten a penny!' Jane sneered back.

'You'll see,' Harriet warned. 'The sins of the fathers, George Beattie. Mark my words.' Harriet turned and left the room, leaving the mother and father shocked and silent.

'What did she mean, George?' Jane asked. George shook his head, and sighed.

'She's right in a way. I neglected her, I suppose. I never liked her. You know that. Now she's paying me back.'

'But what's Ellen done?'

'Nothing,' he shrugged, 'she's innocent. No doubt. Like Harriet said, the sins of the father . . . '

'I don't understand.'

'You don't have to. But she does. Harriet does.'

'I felt . . . threatened somehow . . . '

'It's all right,' George took his wife in his arms, 'you've committed no sin. You've nothing to blame yourself for. Don't trouble yourself about it. I'll find a place for Harriet somewhere far away from Shields . . . I'll do my best for her.'

'After what she's done?'

'Jane, if you don't forgive her, you're not forgiving me either.

You see, it's my fault she's like this. It's my neglect that caused her bitterness.' Jane was silent. She didn't want to admit the truth of George's words, and yet, in her heart, she knew he was right. Once again, she would have to soften her heart, and forgive her, and every time it was more difficult. It had been bad enough when she herself had been the butt of Harriet's emnity, but now her children were involved, she had to fight against the primitive instincts of hate, in order to forgive. 'Can you forgive *me*, Jane?' George asked. Jane frowned. He was the father of her child. His heart was her heart. If she did not forgive him, she could not forgive herself. And so the whole thing came full circle, and Jane knew she would have to forgive Harriet. George, Harriet, Jane, and the children, were all inextricably entwined. Like one body, the cells could not fight against each other, they could only learn to tolerate, and accept one another's place in the scheme of things.

The cab, piled high with boxes, waited outside the shop. Dr Mrs Fletcher, coming for her eggs, saw it and hesitated on the other side of the road, before crossing. 'And a good thing too,' she thought, as Harriet May Lovely, dolled up in her best hat, issued from the shop, and got into the carriage. Mr and Mrs Beattie stood watching silently as the cab lurched and went on its way to the railway station. George saw Mrs Fletcher, with some satisfaction. She would see to it that the news would spread around the town. Justice had been done, and all was right with the world. Or, at least, all would appear to be right with the world. His own conscience weighed heavy, and he looked to his wife for comfort.

He was so big a man, so grand a personality, it was hard for Jane to see him humbled. Her arms reached out to him, and she loved him, healing him with her touch, sending the shivers of desire through him, to make the blood course, and the life throb and her woman's body melted for him. And he knew she loved all of him with all of herself. There was nothing left outside their union. She accepted all and gave all, gladly. So that his seed, joining with her, grew inside her again, and her belly swelled with him, and seeing it, he was proud, content. Their love had found new depths. The man was no longer afraid to show his wife his weaknesses, because he knew she would not whip him with them; she would only love and cherish him the more.

But the work was hard in the shop. Harriet's words echoed harshly. 'You'll learn how much of the work I do round here. You'll not get anybody to fill my place.' Girls came and went, and every time Jane had to train them up, arranging flowers, wiring in the wreaths, delivering, serving. There was the catering side, and then there were the children to see to. It was too much. George had his responsibilities in the town hall and was often away, sometimes late into the evening. So that, as her pregnancy advanced, Jane became weary and lonely, and her heart ached, as she cashed up the till, checked the books, and packed the flowers into their tubs, ready to take down to the cellar. Edie was upstairs, telling stories to the children. Jane sighed. She loved putting them to bed, but Edie couldn't be trusted with the adding up. She couldn't add up her own wage packet! And George was so particular about the flowers; better Jane saw to them herself. She picked up the tub of chrysanthemums and dragged it out into the kitchen, setting it down by the cellar door. She was so tired. Her back ached. She pulled open the door, and setting a candle on the ledge, to lighten her way, she took up the tub again and began to descend the stair.

The light, shining from above, sent dark shadows round her feet. Her arms trembled with the weight of the tub, and the chrysanthemums were pressed against her face. Their warm sweet smell reeled in her brain. Something scurried. Was it underneath the stairs? She hesitated, listened, but her arms ached, so she set her foot on the next step. It buckled at once. Something soft and warm gave under it, moving, throwing her, and it squealed loudly, and she screamed, as the weight of the tub pulled her down, and she twisted, falling down the steps, over the side, crashing to the hard flags beneath.

A sharp twinge brought her to her senses. A burning pain shot through her leg, up her hip, and her belly heaved. She felt sick. In the darkness, Jane retched. The sweet smell of flowers sickened her. What had Harriet said? She hated flowers. Flowers, flowers, flowers. Damn the flowers. They'd be the death of her. Yes. Jane hated flowers too. They made her feel sick, ill. George's flowers. Damn George. Where was he? Why was he not here to carry the heavy tubs down the cellar steps, where it was dark and full of unseen danger? A light showed through the door at the top of the stair. It grew brighter. Edie had come down from the nursery and had lit the gas.

'Help!' Jane called. 'Help me! Edie, please, help me!'

When George came home, it was all over. It had been a boy. Jane was suffering from shock; she had wrenched her back, and had a broken leg. The doctor wanted her transferred to the Ingham, but George would not hear of it. He had lost one wife there, he wanted this one at home, where he could keep an eye on her. Or so he said; and the doctor believed him. So Fanny was brought in to help nurse Jane, leaving her children, as usual, in the care of neighbours. Better Fanny than Harriet, Jane thought, as she lay back against her pillows, her nerves shattered, and her mind filled with thoughts of death. She had nightmares, in which the perfume of flowers overpowered her, dragging her down into darkness, and her own pain bore a sweet smell, like the odour of chrysanthemums, sweet and musty. Then she would wake gasping for breath, and believed she was suffocating, pressed down by the weight of the flowers. Fanny gave her laudanum, rocking her in her arms, like a child, as though for her own comfort; so the two sisters wept together. Then when Jane slept again, Fanny reached for her own medicine, her hand shaking as she brought the bottle to her lips, and drank.

And Fanny was clever. She cleaned Jane's room herself, so Edie had no need to go in, except to fetch and carry the trays of food. George, busy in the shop, blaming himself for Jane's accident, did not come near. He told himself that Jane needed peace and quiet. No excitement, the doctor said. No more shocks. Better George kept away. He would not be able to hide his distress when he saw her. She was so changed! He had to keep that from her, till she was strong enough to take it. So George excused his absence from the sick room and Fanny held sway at her sister's bedside, while Jane pined, feeling the desertion, but too drowsy, too feeble to question anything. And the dreams continued. But now Fanny began to appear in them. Fanny wore a black dress, and round her waist was a chain belt festooned with keys, like a chatelaine. She took Jane in her arms, bound her, and gagged her, taking her down to a deep, dark cellar, where there were rats, and cockroaches, and she left her there, locking her in, barring the door. Jane was her prisoner. Wet and shaking, Jane woke to find Fanny lying on the bed beside her. She was out cold. Drunk. Edie was at the bedroom door, knocking. Painfully, Jane raised herself, but waves of nausea swept over her, and she was sick over her sister, who lay motionless on the bed.

'Help me, Edie!' Jane gasped.

'Missus! Are you awake? Mrs Tully?'

'Edie!' Jane's voice found its way out of the blankets of depression which engulfed her.

'Missus?' Edie rattled the door. It was locked. 'Where's Mrs Tully? She's locked the door!' Jane searched her sister's dress, and finding the key in her skirt pocket, she lurched to the floor. Then, falling to her knees, she crawled, key in hand, to the door. Outside, Edie waited, heart pounding. She heard Jane panting, gasping, as she struggled with the lock. Then finally she heard it turn, and the missus fall back down to the floor, and Edie was in the room.

Darkness and despair. No days. Only nights. Fanny had been sent back to Hexham. Harriet, between situations, looked after the shop with George, while Edie nursed her mistress, till the shaking, shivering cold fevers had stopped. And daylight slowly returned. Jane began to put on flesh again. Her leg mended. She longed for George. She longed to see her children. She would have them in her room for tea today! She was sure her nerves were strong enough to stand their chattering and noise! Edie would tidy her hair for her and wash her face. They would have a little celebration, and perhaps George would join them, and sit down to a proper cup of tea with her, instead of just poking his head through the door for once!

There was jelly and paste sandwiches and angel cake. The children could hardly wait to see their mummy again and barged in, before Jane was out of bed and dressed.

'Come in my darlings!' Her arms opened wide for them, but they stopped in the doorway, uncertain. Ellen's head cocked to one side, and she said, 'Mummy, why're you an old lady?'

'Sh! What did I tell you!' Edie bustling in after them, too late, saw the damage had been done.

'Is there a mirror, Edie?' Jane's voice was firm. Edie sighed, and went to the dressing table, where she picked up the little silver hand mirror Jane always kept there. 'Give it to me, please.' Edie silently gave her mistress the mirror. Jane looked. Her hand rose slowly to touch her hair. Then her fingers tore at it, pulling it free from the plait. The hair fell about her shoulders and Jane lay back sobbing against her pillows.

CHAPTER TWENTY FIVE

Jane yawned and stretched comfortably, reaching out her arm to the place beside her. It was empty. She opened her eyes. In the pale light of the morning her white hair lay like snow across her husband's pillow. So he had not come home. Again. She sighed. Her eyes stung from last night's tears. She could hear Edie on the stair, and Ellen at her side, chattering gaily as the maid brought up her mistress's tray.

'Eeh but it's a lovely day!' she said, as she set the tray on the bedside table. The diamond ring fell to the floor. 'Oops! Sorry.' She bent and picked it up. Jane took it from her, placing it back on her finger as Ellen crawled into the warm bed.

'Hallo, pet . . . how's Maisie today, eh?'

'She's eating porridge, Missus. Well I say "eating" but throwing it round the room would be more like it. Scallywag's got a job to keep up with her, mopping up the bits.' Ellen burst out laughing. 'And you need laugh, Miss. You should have seen what *she* did with her fried bread today. She tried to plug her ears with it.'

'You disgusting little . . . scallywag!' Jane said at last, searching her daughter's ears for crumbs. 'You'll do yourself a mischief, see if you don't.' But the child shied away from her like a wild pony, and began jumping up and down on the bed. 'Stop it! You'll spill my tea!' The child stopped and reached across to the tray.

'There's some letters for you.' Jane peered at the envelopes, which Edie handed to her. 'There's one from Cromer.'

'Cromer?' Ellen asked. 'Who's that from?'

'Your Auntie Harriet.'

'Oh her!'

'Now don't be rude!'

'And there's one from New York!'

'New York!' Jane scrambled to tear open the envelope and pulled out a very long letter.

'Who's it from?' Ellen asked curiously.

'Your Uncle Robert, I expect.'

'Who's Uncle Robert?'

'My brother! You know, the one that's a sailor, and travels a lot!'

'Oh yes.'

'You've forgotten him! Huh! I thought he'd forgotten *us*!'

'Naughty Uncle Robert!'

'Yes!'

'Interesting, though! Read it aloud!' Jane frowned. Precocious child. What *was* she hoping to hear?

'In a minute,' Jane said. She'd better glance through it herself first. 'Naughty Uncle Robert' indeed! Heaven knew what her dear brother might have to report after so long! 'Practise your reading on Aunt Harriet's letter!'

'Yuk!'

'Yuk to you too!' And then, Jane began to read.

> May 21st 1888.
> New York City

'Dear Jane,

Your newspaper finally reached me in the Florida Keys, four years later! Eureka! Another chip off the old block, eh? Sorry to have been so long in offering my congrats and all that! I've been rather busy since then. And so have you, by the sound of it! Perhaps by now there's yet another offspring to add to the Beattie brood! Anyway! Well done, canny lass! I've almost forgotten how to speak Geordie, it's been so long. I've been up the Mississippi, working on a steamboat. What do you think of that? And why, you may ask, did your everloving brother do such a thing? Well, to tell you the truth old thing, I had to disappear for a while. There was this Argentinian lady called Juanita . . . '

Jane raised her eyebrows, and glanced at her little daughter. 'Interesting' was hardly the word for her uncle's activities! But the child was deeply engrossed in Harriet's writing; Jane hugged Robert's letter close, so that Ellen couldn't see. 'I can't wait to visit you, and tell you all my adventures . . . ' Jane sighed. There was he, travelling the globe, women at his beck and call, while she . . . She glanced over to the empty place beside her. Well, what would George want with a white-haired old lady? Not that she looked old . . . she was only twenty-eight and some said her white hair was quite becoming. Her skin was smooth and glowed with youthful health. Her mirror told her she was still beautiful, even striking! So, why? George had made his bed in the attics. Most of his time was spent in the shop, doing his books, or on council business. 'The world is too much with us.' In her heart, she knew George needed a public outlet for his talents and energies. She knew he was public spirited, and genuinely wanted to help the community. So he swanked! So he boasted! He deserved some credit for all he did! She didn't begrudge him that. He was like a little boy sometimes, but it only made her love him all the more. So, why could he not love her? After the accident, Jane had tried. But the doors of her husband's heart were firmly closed against her. If she dressed to please him, he refused to see. If she cooked a special meal, it went unnoticed. If she suggested they read poetry, he included little Ellen, and what spare time he had he gave to her. He was a good teacher, patient, and kind. Even Maisie managed to learn her two times table with his help. There was nothing left for Jane. Nothing at all. Not even bed. The doctor said she could have other children. There was nothing wrong with her. But for four years, or was it five, he had not touched her. Why? The hurt was buried deep, but the love lingered, and she felt she would wither away, if her love remained without expression. The thought caught at her

370

breath. A slight wheeze brought her attention back to the letter, and she read on.

'I've been in New York for a month now. I'm working a deal for Roper's. They want to freight paper over to England. It's a big contract. So wish me luck. If I pull it off, I shall soon be home for a bit of leave!' Suddenly the colour rushed into Jane's cheeks. Could it be true?

'He's coming home!' she shrieked. Ellen, puzzling through her aunt's fancy loops and twirls, looked up in astonishment.

'Uncle Robert?'

'Yes!' Jane leapt out of bed, upsetting her tea onto the floor, and began dressing.

'When?' Jane stopped dressing and frowned. She picked up the letter again, and looked right through it. 'He doesn't say.' She sighed. 'But soon . . . if he pulls off this deal.'

'Huh!' She might well say 'huh', thought Jane. This week, next week, some time, never! That was the way of it. Ah well.

'What does your Aunt Harriet have to say?'

'She's coming home too.' Jane's face fell.

'When?'

'Slurpaday.'

'Don't be silly.'

'That's what it looks like.'

Jane took the letter and Ellen pointed out the place.

'Saturday, you idiot!' But Jane was laughing. Ellen was no idiot. Not quite ten, she could read, write, and was already learning French thanks to George, whereas poor little Maisie . . . She hurried down to the kitchen, to tell Edie the news.

Maisie was sitting in a special chair, which George had had made for her. It was a high chair, and she was belted in to hold her back straight. They'd tried everything. Jane had bathed her daily in sea water, she had massaged her, strapped her up with seaweed, the lot, but there was still a twist to her spine. She was going to have a hump back.

'All right, pet?' Jane kissed her youngest on the cheek, and received a dollop of porridge on her chin. 'What a greeting!' she said, wiping it off.

'Hallo Mama. Hallo Dada,' was the reply.

'What do you mean, "hallo Dada"? Where is he?' She was smiling, but Edie avoided her eye. She and the missus might suspect the truth but, so long as it remained unspoken, it had no reality. So the household continued to function, on the basis of 'Don't rock the boat'. 'I expect he was caught late at a session of the planning committee,' Jane said indulgently.

'I expect so, Missus,' Edie agreed.

Preparations for Harriet's visit were well underway. Maisie was to sleep with Jane, and Ellen with Edie, so the big bed could be put up in Harriet's old room, now the nursery. Jane tried to make the room look as it had done before. Though there wasn't much she could do about the drawings Ellen had crayoned on the wallpaper. She was not an artistic child! And apart from the odd cat, games of noughts and crosses decorated the corner where she slept. Jane shook her head, and tried to cover the marks by hanging a drape of curtain material over the wall. It should suit Harriet's taste. It was exotic. It made the room look like a sultan's harem. George would not approve, so Harriet was bound to! And Jane rather enjoyed going against her husband's will. In little ways, she had begun to get her own back on George for his neglect. It gave her satisfaction to cross him where she could, without the inconvenience of creating ructions.

Harriet had got on well in Cromer. She was now a lady's maid and companion to Georgina Rowse, the middle-aged daughter of a Norfolk nobleman. She relished her position. And she relished the cast-off clothes her employer gave her even more. As usual, Harriet May had fallen on her feet. She swanned in, leaving a trail of feather boa. Ellen watched the tiny pieces as they escaped from the rest, and fluttered behind her. She caught one in her hands, and slowly, carefully, tore it to pieces, as though dissecting it.

'Do you like my boa?' Harriet asked, smiling benignly.

'I never knew snakes had feathers,' Ellen stated.

'Snakes? What have snakes to do with anything?'

'That thing round your neck. It's a snake.' Harriet shuddered.

'It is no such thing!'

'You said it was a boa.'

'So it is.'

'A boa's a kind of snake. I've seen pictures of them. They look like that, only they don't usually have feathers on them.' Jane laughed.

'You're thinking of a boa constrictor, dear,' she told her.

'Yes. Like what Aunt Harriet's got round her neck. It suits her!' Thoroughly discomfitted, Harriet tore off the offending article and laid it over the back of a chair, where it dangled dangerously close to her young niece.

As Harriet jabbered on, about the gay social life in Norfolk, and the wags who came up from London, Ellen watched the dangling boa. She was sure it was a snake. Underneath those feathers, it probably was. If she just were to pull off one or two of them she might perhaps see the skin of the animal underneath. Carefully, she reached forwards, and drew the boa down towards her. It slinked onto the floor and then the dissection began in earnest.

'Where is George?' Harriet was asking.

'At a meeting, I believe.'

'On a Saturday? Huh! More fool you, if you believe that!'

'What are you implying, Harriet?' Immediately Jane regretted her question.

'Same old excuse!'

'What do you mean?'

'God knows how often he used it with Adeline! Still, at least he never tried anything with *my* mother!'

'What are you talking about, Harriet?'

'Well if you want to hide your head in the sand, dear . . . ' At that moment, Edie saw the feathers drifting about the floor.

'Eeeeeh!' she screamed. Harriet and Jane stared at her, as she stood hands in front of her mouth, eyes bulging. Then Edie pointed silently to Ellen, who sat, surrounded by feathers, a long piece of string in her hands.

'OooooowWWWH,' Harriet yelled, grabbing the string from her. 'She's shredded it!' Suddenly Edie and Jane laughed, as Harriet sat, a piece of string round her neck, cheeks pink and bulging, the picture of righteous indignation.

'You naughty girl!' Jane laughed, and swept her off to her bedroom, to hide her own giggles.

It was insult to injury. Later that night, as the family sat in the parlour, and listened to the offending child reciting poetry, Harriet considered how she might get her own back.

My heart leaps up when I behold
A rainbow in the sky:
So was it when my life began;
So is it now I am a man . . .
So be it when I shall grow old,
Or let me die!
The child is father of the man;
And I could wish my days to be
Bound each to each by natural piety.

Butter wouldn't melt in the mouth! She'd seen it all before! Like mother like daughter. Now the infant scrambled over her father's knee, and he smiled on her dotingly. Yes. Harriet *had* seen it all before and it sickened her.

'That was very good.' George was thrilled with his little daughter. She was clever. She took after him! 'I think . . . I think . . . somebody deserves a treat just for being so clever!' Ellen shrieked with glee.

'You shouldn't spoil her, George.' But Jane was pleased. She liked to see her child at the receiving end of George's affection even if she was not.

'It doesn't hurt from time to time.'

'Huh! You've changed your tune!' Harriet couldn't help herself. But she shut her mouth again, as George darted her a warning look.

'Now what would my little girl like for a treat? Think hard now.'

Ellen frowned, racking her brains. 'I'd like a picnic . . . at the seaside.'

'Oh yes, George. That would be nice!'

'All right . . . suppose we close the shop, Monday afternoon . . . ' Jane and Harriet were equally astonished. George close the shop? Lose business? It was unheard of! 'I think we could all do with a little holiday. Especially as your Auntie Harriet's here.'

'Yes, but it's *my* treat.'

'Now Ellen, you won't mind if *we* all enjoy it too, will you?' prompted Jane.

'I suppose not. But it's my treat all the same.'

'Don't be so selfish!'

'She's only a bairn.' George was in an indulgent mood. 'We'll go down The Bents, eh?'

'No!' All eyes turned on the wild, dark eyes.

'Ellen! Behave yourself!' said Jane sharply.

'Well, if not The Bents, where would you like to go?' The father's patience stretched for his pride and joy.

'I want to go to Marsden.' There was a short silence. George stiffened visibly, and Jane had time to wonder why, before he gave in.

'All right. Why not? Marsden it is!'

At twelve-thirty precisely, the last customer was shooed from the shop, and the notice on the door turned to 'CLOSED'. Jane and Harriet had stayed to make up the picnic, while George went to market that morning, so all was ready. It made a change making up a hamper just for themselves. Jane even included some of the famous Beattie toffee for Ellen. It was a beautiful day. Jane's heart was light. She chatted gaily with Harriet and Edie in the back of the hired carriage, nursing little Maisie, while George and Ellen sat up front, driving the horses. Ellen was in her element. She would like to learn to ride. But the very idea frightened Jane. She was accident prone. She would be bound to fall off and hurt herself. And anyway, as George had pointed out, it was an expensive pastime. The clouds were wisps high in the deep blue sky, as they bowled along into the country, through Harton Village, down Harton Back Lane, and Redwell Lane. Then finally, they arrived at the cliff tops of Marsden.

'Don't go near the edge!' Jane called, as she and Harriet alighted from the carriage.

'I want to go down to the beach!'

'In a minute! Wait for us!' Jane shouted. George was taking the carriage back down the road to Redwell Lane, where he would pay a man to look after the horses. Jane had Maisie, while Edie and Harriet took the hamper between them. The wooden steps down to the grotto beneath were steep and dangerous. Jane's heart was in her mouth as the little girl skipped lightly down, peering over the edge, at the views beyond. You could see for miles, over the Velvet Beds, on to Shields harbour, and Tynemouth Priory. A mist hung on the horizon. The air was still and heavy, as they descended into the shelter of the cliffs, where the afternoon sun beat down. Jane guarded her eyes, seeking Ellen, when they reached the bottom. But she, shoes and stockings scattered on the sand, was already kicking in the waves, running in and out of the caves, which burrowed beneath the big rock. It stood alone, separate from the cliff, on the edge of beach and sea. Jane had loved to play there as a child. She remembered a day when she and Robert . . . it was before Fanny had got married, and they had gone looking for flowers for a wedding posy. Memories crowded in, and drowned out the present. Leaving Edie to set the picnic out, Jane rested on the sand, mind drifting, till the sound of the flocking gulls, screeching to and fro from the cliffs, paled into unreality, and she was asleep.

A shiver of sand fell on her face, and woke her. The sea swished into her awareness and children screamed. She screwed up her eyes against the sun. Her head ached. She should have gone with Harriet and sat in the shade of the cliff. Where was Ellen? She peered into the heat haze at the sea's edge, and saw the children playing. They had a bat and ball. Four children there were, the youngest barely able to walk. He was a little boy, and Ellen kept going to him, to pick him up, and take him to safety, away from the water's edge, for the tide was coming in. His sturdy little legs tottered, then he ran back after her, and Ellen stood again, hands on hips, ready to tell him off. Jane laughed. Ellen would have liked a little brother. She would have been good with him. Reassured, Jane rose, to move back into the shade of the rocks and wait for George.

The warmth, the comfort, the peace, were luxurious. She felt quite content. They needed more days like this. Days together, away from the business, to restore themselves. He was a long time. But then, it was quite a walk along the beach from the lane. She put her hand over her eyes, and looked into the sun, along the stretch of sand. Families with buckets and spades, chairs, and parasols, sat bunched in little groups, scattered along the length of the beach. A dog played in the water. What a pity they had not brought Scallywag with them, Jane thought. A woman was throwing driftwood into the sea, for her dog. He bounced onto the water, and swam courageously into the waves, to fetch it for her.

'Good dog!' Jane heard her call. And then, the dog saw someone he knew. He ran off to shake himself all over a man, coming towards them along the beach. But the toddler, the little boy, ran after the dog, and Ellen chased him, ready to pick him up and bring him back to safety. Jane watched the drama from the shade of the cliff. The wet dog was jumping up and down. The man, silhouetted against the sun, held his arms high, trying to ward him off.

'Down boy! Down boy!' he ordered. Jane switched her attention to Ellen. She was getting too far away. Jane got up and ran to follow her. 'Down boy!' the man commanded. Jane had almost caught up with Ellen, whose arms opened wide to snatch up the little boy. Then the boy, seeing the man, cried out, 'Daddy!' And Jane looked up to see the man was George.

Ellen stopped, as though shot by a bullet. George froze. The dog continued leaping, and the woman called him off, picking up her boy, shouting to the other three to follow, as she made her way up the beach, silhouetted against the sun, buckets and spades left behind. George, Jane and Ellen stood amongst the debris of the scattered family. The sun turned cold.

The great rock cast its long shadow across the waters, as the tide, coming in closer and closer, slapped the rocks at the base of the cliffs. Cold and grey the sea. Steel the sky. Red the sun and pale the rising moon. Realities, while all the rest was confusion. So, George sat on alone. Pain engulfed his world. He saw it in the eyes of his wife. He saw it in the eyes of his little girl. He saw it in the eyes of his mistress, and he knew it, as an old friend, in his breast. Friend? No, pain was his master. If Jane, Jane his first wife had not died . . . if Adeline had had the strength to bear his love . . . if there had been no passion in him . . . What then? Would he have been a man at all? 'If' . . . useless word. But if . . . if he had had no conscience . . . Useless. Yes. Jane. His third wife. His beloved angel, golden hair turned to silver. Beautiful, adorable Jane. He had loved her from the first. The day in his shop . . . He could see her now, twirling with delight, as she smelt the herbs in the drawers, looked at the flowers, face shining, glad to be alive! He had envied her that life. He had longed for it. She was just a child, and he was married. But his mind strayed. And he was besieged by guilt.

I asked a thief to steal me a peach:

What could he do? To protect the child, to save his wife from further pregnancies, to save himself from going out of his mind?

As soon as I went
An angel came.

He had told Jane he was no angel. Even then. He had told her. But Alice Minto had been willing, glad of his help, lonely, starved of comfort and affection. And so it had begun. Poor Adeline.

And without one word . . .

But Alice had saved Adeline. Or so George reasoned. And then Adeline had come to him again, and he had dropped Alice Minto, as he had found her. Poor Alice. His guilt had switched. It seemed he could not do right by one woman without doing wrong by the other. And all the time, George loved Jane Ridley. Jane who was growing up, who saw him as a father, who was innocent. The sun sank below the horizon. The moon hung in the deep blue sky like a milky breast . . .

Jane had made him young again. Their marriage was a marriage of two souls, two hearts, two minds, two bodies, two into one. The past was over. He could not believe his luck. Alice was nearly forgotten, a mere twinge in his conscience, like rheumatism in damp weather. He had continued to support her, to send her little gifts of money; salve to his conscience. If only he had had no conscience . . . 'If'. Useless word. His gifts of money to Alice Minto had left him short, and he could not afford to pay proper wages for a girl's help in the shop, so they had kept on leaving and Jane had worked too hard, so she had lost their child. Mea culpa. George had to punish himself for that! He had killed his son, had almost killed his third wife, just as he had killed the others. He would not risk it again. No! Jane whom he loved. She would not die! No! He would leave her alone! History repeating itself. In his misery he had left her to Fanny, unable to bear the sight of her, and he had been in the wrong again. Wrong! Wrong! Wrong! Whatever he did it was surely wrong! George took up a stone and threw it at the moon. It fell, spattering, into a rock pool at his feet.

And there was a second moon. When the rings of motion ceased, and the pool was still, George saw it, but which was the reflection? Which the reality? Water gushed at his feet. Full tide at last. The moon looked down, as though in judgement, and the moon looked up. And George stood, searching for a way out. The high cliff towered behind him. The sea danced around him. Too late. He would have to sit it out. He would have to wait, till the tide turned again, and freed him, in its own good time.

Jane could have envied Harriet May Lovely. She was free. She was independent. She had seen her off, the next day, at the railway station, back to the comfort of her companion/mistress. At least you knew where you were with a woman. You could trust a woman. Men were different. They lied. They hid things from you, and pretended it was all for your own good. 'What the heart doesn't know, the heart doesn't grieve over,' they said. But they were wrong. The heart can grieve, without knowing why. The heart senses its neglect. The heart bleeds, even when it cannot see the dagger thrust into it. But now she had seen the dagger. Now she understood. No good George crawling back to her. How could she love him now? How could she respect him? How could she ever trust him again? She could not. And the only way to stop her pain was to remove George from her heart. He was the dagger. She would therefore exclude him. Her heart would turn to ice, and he would find no way into it. And the pain stopped. Cold and numb, Jane went about the business of the shop. Mechanically, she saw to the cooking. Only with her children could she open, like a flower, the petals of her heart unfurling, revealing the soft, warm centre of her being. And then, at the sound of her husband's step, the petals clamped back, closing tight, locked against him.

And her children needed her. Ellen, she clasped close to her bosom, taking her into her bed at night to comfort her when she cried, remembering the little boy who had claimed her Daddy. How could Jane forgive George for that? Harriet had merely wounded the child's flesh. George had hurt her spirit. Together, mother and child rocked themselves to sleep, leaving the husband/father to do what he would. And where no words were said, the eyes spoke. Dark with reproach, sharp with pain, two pairs of eyes tore at him like fish hooks, and he, caught in an agony of his own, might wriggle and struggle to be free, but in the end, the woman and the child were master of him. Only they could show him mercy. And they would not. Silently the war waged. And the children, caught between, fought on the mother's side, the web of love drawing threads about them that grew tighter every day.

And every day, Jane looked for news of her brother. She needed him. Why didn't he come? Letters came from Harriet, and she left them half read, while Edie devoured them wholesale; stories of nobility, parties, famous people, dresses, long menus. And then, a letter came, post marked Phoenix, Arizona. Jane tore it open, at the breakfast table, watched by the silent husband and the clamouring infants.

'It's from Robert!' But it wasn't from Robert. It wasn't his handwriting. This was ill-formed, childish, as though the person who had penned it did not know his letters. She turned the page to check the name at the end. 'Joshua Ridley' it said. Jane gasped. Her face went white. George looked up.

'What's wrong?'

'Nothing. Nothing. It's from Josh.'

'Who's he?'

'My younger brother. We thought he was dead.' George took the letter from her, and tried to decipher it. Jane watched, annoyed. The letter was addressed to her. It was from her own brother. What right had George to read it? She reached out her hand. He looked at her, and then, a strange smile on his face, he gave her back the letter, and got on with reading his newspaper.

Was this really Josh? He who had played cowboys and Indians on the Lawe Top, writing to them from Arizona?

'I have not had much luck panning for gold. But I know I will make my fortune one day, in spite of you all. All I ask for, is what is really mine. My money. I worked hard for that money, foyboating on the river, doing odd jobs. Now I want it. And I know who stole it from me too. Our Robert! So, Jane, seeing as you are now in the money, and married to a mayor and everything, I do think you might send me it. Think of the scandal if I let it be known that my own brother stole from me. This address will always find me. I expect to hear from you soon, if not earlier.

P.S. If you are wondering how I found your address, it is a long story. But I read your news in a paper, and went from there. Does that ring any bells?

Your brother,
Joshua Ridley Esquire'

Out of the corner of his eye, George saw Jane tremble. So then! Her precious brother Robert was a thief! He was no angel, either!

'It *will* be interesting to hear what Robert has to say about the affair,' he remarked. 'If he ever *does* come back.'

'He will, George. Oh he will. And then the whole matter will be cleared up to your satisfaction. I promise you.'

'You show such touching faith.'

'Yes!' Jane snapped. 'Don't I!'

'This week, next week, sometime, never.' And then 'sometime' finally came, and Robert Ridley, carrying his sailor's hold-all on his back, came in at the back door, arms wide; crying with relief Jane fell into them, her children hanging onto her skirts, glad she was happy.

'Uncle Robert, tell us a "tory",' Ellen insisted, as he took the two girls on his knee.

'Story not "tory",' Jane told her. 'You can pronounce your "s's", so why don't you?'

'I can do better than that!' Robert said, winking at his sister.

'Better than a "tory"?'

'Story!'

'Mmmhumph! I'm going to take you to a circus!'

Jane looked up sharply, and frowned. 'Didn't you know?

381

They're coming to The Bents next week.' Jane said nothing, but the children clamoured, as Robert told them all about the lions, and the tigers, and the horses, and the performing dogs, and the clowns, and . . . the elephants.

'Mama's ridden on a hephalant,' Ellen declared.

'So she has. I remember her telling me.' Robert looked at his sister.

'It's a long time ago, Robert,' she said quietly. He smiled and nodded.

'You don't mind?'

'No. I don't mind. In fact I think it might lay a ghost, if I go with you!'

'Do they have ghosts at circuses as well?' Ellen asked, round eyed. Robert and Jane laughed, and tried to explain that no, ghosts were not another kind of animal.

Late that night, when the children were in bed, and Edie had gone up to her room, brother and sister sat alone by the kitchen fire, warming their toes. In the companionable silence which followed the first interchange of news, Jane's toes reached out to touch Robert's, wriggling and tickling them underneath. He pulled his feet back, laughing.

'Get off!'

'Shan't!'

'Shall!'

'Shan't.' And they grinned at one another, perfectly at ease again. 'Oh, isn't this lovely!' Jane sighed. Robert grunted a drowsy 'yes'. 'I hope George *doesn't* come home tonight!'

'Why? Might he not?'

Jane snorted. 'My husband has two families.' Suddenly Robert was awake. 'It seems he always has. At least, since Adeline's day. The "lady" is called Alice Minto. She has borne my husband a son, something I, unfortunately failed to do.' Robert stared at his sister. Her voice was hard, like steel. 'It seems he prefers her to me. He hasn't been near my bed for years.' Robert sat staring at Jane in silence. She would not look at him. Her eyes were fixed on the red coals in the grate, and her body, so relaxed a moment ago, was now rigid as the poker beside her.

'Jane, is there something you aren't telling me?'

'What!'

'I don't know. Maybe . . . you don't like . . . you know . . . '
'Don't be ridiculous!'
'All right! All right! Some women don't, you know . . . '
Robert watched her. There was something. He knew there was.
He stretched out his foot to touch hers again. She glanced down,
surprised. His foot held still against her. It felt warm. Suddenly
Jane began to cry. 'Tell me . . . what is it?' She shook her head.
'Please, Jane.'
    'I hate her!'
    'Who?'
    'Alice Minto!'
    'That's hardly surprising.' But still, she wouldn't look at him.
'Have you met her?' Jane glanced up, a frightened look in her
eyes.
    'What makes you say that?' Robert shook his head, and she
looked away again, towards the door, towards the window, back
to the fire. Was she looking for escape? She caught his eye, and
tried to smile, then dropped her gaze to their feet. Robert moved,
to come to her, but she stopped him.
    'No, please, leave your foot where it is. I know it sounds silly,
but it's so comforting. I never realised how lonely my feet were!'
She was laughing and crying at the same time, and he laughed
too. But laughter died and the silence between them was
haunted. Alice Minto, at the graveside, dressed in black; eyes
exchanging messages; she wanted George. 'Forgive us our
trespasses . . . ' Well, she had him now! Jane sobbed. The third
Mrs Beattie had deserved all she'd got. If it had been anyone but
Alice . . . some stranger, Jane might've forgiven. But, how could
she forgive her own victim? She had ground the woman under
her foot. She had stolen her man. She could not begin to forgive
her, because she had never forgiven herself. As Jane's sobbing
increased, Robert's foot stroked hers, soothing her. 'Oh! It feels
like you were stroking my heart!' she cried, and her voice pleaded
for more. He drew her down beside him on the floor, where he
could hold her tightly in his arms and comfort her. 'Oh, I *have*
missed you so!'
    'Sh . . . ' he whispered. 'Robert's home now. Everything's
going to be all right.'

★ ★ ★

383

The white hair shone with violet oil. It was like silver.

'I don't know why you don't like it, Jane,' Robert told her, 'I think it's beautiful.' Jane smiled at her brother's reflection in the mirror, as he stood behind her, the brush poised in his hand, head and shoulders above her. She reached up and gripped his fingers in her own, gratefully.

'I don't know. I've lost all my confidence, Robert. That's what it is. I feel plain. I feel somehow less than a woman.'

'That's silly.'

'But I do!' she turned to face the man. 'You can't know what it means to me, to hear you say I'm beautiful.'

'Even if I *am* only your brother?'

'Yes,' she smiled.

'He's got a lot to answer for, George Beattie!'

'It's not his fault I fell down the stairs!'

'Isn't it? What was a pregnant woman doing lifting heavy great tubs of flowers in the first place?' Jane was silent.

'Best not say anything, Robert,' she said sadly.

'Why not? You're my sister. I've got to look after you!' Jane hesitated. Then she drew Josh's letter out of the dressing table drawer.

'This will come as a surprise to you.' Robert took it from her, and began deciphering the childish hand. 'George read it. I'm sorry.' Suddenly Robert sat down on the edge of the bed.

'Our Josh! But . . . are you sure it's really him?'

'You mean, you think it might be somebody having a joke?' Robert frowned, then shook his head. No-one else would have known about that tin box and the money.

'No. No. It's Josh all right,' he whistled softly, 'who'd've thought it!'

Jane looked uncertainly at her brother. 'What does he mean, about the money?' she asked. Robert sighed, and put down the letter.

'Do you remember when I'd sold some of my drawings, and saved up?' Jane nodded. 'I was going to use the money for college. But Dad took it to help pay for a new coble for the foyboatman?'

'I remember.'

'Well . . . I didn't sell any drawings at all. That money was

Josh's. He'd kept it under the bed. But I didn't steal it, Jane! He'd already disappeared, dead we all thought, and suddenly Fanny produced the box, and told Dad it was mine. And I . . . well . . . I suppose I should've said something, put her right, but . . . well, I didn't. I let everybody go on thinking I'd earned it with my drawing. I hoped it would make Dad see there was a future in it. It never did. I didn't mean any harm, Jane . . . ' he shrugged.

'You must write to Josh and tell him what happened. We can send him his money. Then everything'll be fine again.'

'Yes. I suppose so,' Robert sighed. 'What's that proverb, about webs, something "weave, when first we try to deceive . . . " ' Jane stared vacantly into the green reflections of the mirror, and saw a web, high in a corner of an attic room, years ago. She shivered. The fine threads reached out forever, from the green depths of the past, into the green depths of the future. Who knew where it would all end? Once said, a single word, a single action, began a train of events which nothing, and no-one, could break. Not even God himself. She, George, Josh, Robert, Alice Minto, the children . . . on and on and on forever and ever, Amen. She shivered, and struggled to grasp the tiny thread which Robert had held out to her.

'But this is nothing, Robert! It's not a crime! You were very young, and you . . . just didn't let on, that's all. It wasn't a deliberate lie. No! We mustn't make mountains out of molehills. We'll send Josh the money, and that'll be an end of it!' Robert smiled, reassured. Deep down, he was glad the thing had come out into the open. It had always nagged at him. Yes, as Jane said, now they could make an end of it, and let bygones be bygones. Their Josh alive! What a turn up! They had something to celebrate, didn't they? And they *were* going to celebrate, Jane, Robert and the kids! They were going to the circus!

CHAPTER TWENTY SIX

Potter's Circus seemed small to her now. The Big Top was shabby, in the afternoon sun, and the costumes of the acrobats, as they passed among the caravans, had seen better days. But the children did not notice. To them the whole thing was a miracle, as Ellen led them in a dance through all the tents and cages, behind the show tent.

'Come back! You aren't supposed to go in there!' Robert shouted. Jane ran with him, after her brood.

'You'll get eaten by the lions, mind!' she yelled. But to no avail. They had disappeared. Jane was beside herself. 'Maisie's so little!'

'Look, you try that way. I'll try this. Right?'

'Yes. Good idea.' So they split, and Robert went off to search amongst the performers' living quarters, while Jane went towards the animal cages. There was a cacophony of strange noises. None of them what it seemed. The braying of an ass turned out to be a huge camel, snarling, restive, a bag of fodder round its neck. She skirted it, hurrying on, past the horses, to the roar of the cat house. A man with a barrowload of raw meat, dirty and bleeding, wheeled past her. He stopped by the great barred door.

'You're not going to open that, are you?' she asked, dismayed.

'How else am I to get inside, I should like to know?' he said.
'You're very brave.' The man shrugged.
'Meat goes first. I go last.' He put down the barrow, and took out his key. 'Stand back, lady.' Jane took a step back. There was a huge tiger in the shadows of the cage. Seeing the man, the tiger slowly, lazily rose to his feet, the muscles of his flesh rippling under the great bold stripes. Slowly, master of his time, the beast moved towards the bars of the cage.
'He looks half asleep,' Jane remarked.
'Don't be taken in by that!' She felt the tension rise, as he turned the lock in the gate. And the beast waited. Jane watched, sensing the power, the brute strength, that waited, poised. And the gate opened. The tiger crept close to the ground. But the keeper's eyes never left the beast. And the beast moved one paw. The keeper stood. The tiger stood. The paw, suspended in mid air, ready to strike, ready to fall back, waited. The barrowload of dead flesh stood between them. The man's foot moved back. The paw fell to earth. The next paw quickly raised and the body of the brute slunk low across the ground towards the man. The arc of energy between them cracked; the man sprang: the beast sprang, and the gate shut between. Behind bars, caged by the man, the wild beast raged.

Jane shook. She sat on a bale of straw, watching, as the tiger ate the flesh, and the man walked. Over the circus sounds she could hear the distant roar of a heavy sea. Black clouds scudded in from the north, purple black. Threatening. But the sun still shone. She saw it bright on the iron bars of the cage. The flesh of the cat, loose on its bones, moved voluptuously, as he gnawed, and rent, and took of the meat. He was handsome. He was fine. He was dangerous. She could not tear her eyes away.

Tyger! Tyger! burning bright
In the forests of the night,
What immortal hand or eye
Could frame thy fearful symmetry?

Ellen's childish voice piped like a skylark high overhead on a summer's day; light and cool, it hovered over the heavy air, trapped between the cages where Jane sat. She turned her head to try the direction of the sound, and saw, bearing down on her, a huge, grey elephant, its ears flapping at the flies. Crouched on its back, Ellen and Maisie sat, laughing and giggling, as their mother finally looked up and saw them, mouth gaping in surprise.

'I've been looking for you everywhere!' The urbanity of the remark embarrassed Jane, but the man leading the elephant, smiled.

'Are these two your'sns?'

'I'm afraid so! Get down at once! Both of you!'

'Ma!' the girls complained vociferously.

'They're not doing any harm. Leave 'em be. They're safe enough with me.'

But the elephant was restive. He began to sway from side to side, and his eyes rolled.

'All right, Jumbo. He's locked up. He can't get out of there.'

'Jumbo.' Could it be the same 'Jumbo' she had ridden all those years ago? How long did elephants live? A long time. A very long time. A low growl from the caged animal, teeth locked in dead flesh, set their nerves juddering. Jumbo moved on, Jane's children laughing gaily on his back, and Jane followed. Blake's poem echoed through her brain like thunder, as she looked back over her shoulder at the red hot eyes of the wild cat, its jaws running blood down the bars of the cage.

When the stars threw down their spears,
And water'd heaven with their tears,
Did he smile his work to see?
Did he who made the Lamb make thee?

The sun, its rays like arrows through the dark, purple clouds, pierced the stone on her finger, igniting its fire. The furnace of light blinded her eye, stopped her thought. Fire fighting fire. George's heart.

'With this ring, I give my heart into your keeping.'

'And I shall be its faithful guardian . . . '

George. His heart no longer burned for her. It was cold. The stone lied. He had turned her body into a desert, and she was guardian of nothing.

* * *

388

'The same, but different,' described Potter's circus of 1888. The camels were new, the clowns had a different act, and the lions had been replaced by tigers. But everything else was more or less the same. True, the elephant man's little girl had grown up, but he wore the same sequinned suit, and the elephants were festooned with the same flowers, made of red crêpe. Only now, the elephants preceded the tigers, who were to come on last.

There were twelve elephants. Sweetly, gently, they did their tricks. Patiently, Jumbo held his great foot in the air, above the girl, forebearing to crush her, lovingly, raising her up with his trunk. They stood on stools, they got off stools, they twined trunks in tails, and circled the arena, veering round, dancing a dignified minuet, to the music of the little band. And the audience loved them. To Jane now, they seemed so friendly, so familiar, so safe. She was glad she had come. She laughed at herself for her sentimentality. Harking back to childhood, that's what it was. It brought tears to her eyes! Yes. Jane still loved the elephants, and Jumbo had a special place in her heart. She waved like mad, with the children, when they filed out of the Big Top, and Jumbo gave a last blast of a trumpet to say 'goodbye'.

Yes, she was glad she had come. She smiled at Robert, who was pleased to see her enjoying herself. He grasped her hand in his, as the clowns came on, while behind them, the arena was transformed for the next act. The clowns tumbled, fell on banana skins, over their own great feet, dropped buckets of whitewash over one another, slipped, fell again, and waves of laughter roared round the arena, egging on the men in the ring, and, they, timing their rough and tumble artfully, caught the waves on the turn, and sent them back again, crashing into more laughter, till bellies ached, and eyes ran, and the pitch of the excitement could rise no higher. Then the clowns left the arena, and the spectators, intoxicated with mirth, sat, faced with the great bars of the huge, empty cage.

From far off came the low snarl of an approaching beast. The brass sounded a fanfare. A man, a lone man, dressed in black and gold, walked into the cage, whip in hand. And then, the drums rolled. The snarl came closer. And the first beast slouched into the ring. Jane's hand gripped Robert's, as the animal skirted its iron prison, flesh rippling against the bars. Then the whip cracked, and the brute's fangs rent the air with a savage hiss; claws stretched, ears back, it cowered away to its corner, waiting, watching. The drums rolled again. And the second beast crawled down the dark tunnel into the light; then a third, and a fourth. And now, a predator poised at every corner, encircled the man at the centre of the ring. And the whip lashed! Wheeling through the air, it whirred and whizzed, it whistled and spat, sending the invaders that dared to threaten the space where the man reigned, cowering back, each to his corner. And so the brutes obeyed. Scourged, they dared not attack. Untameable, the man controlled them with his wits, with his supreme authority. And Jane was with him, in the centre of the ring.

Ellen gasped, eyes huge, and Maisie began to cry. Jane took her in her arms, and nursed her, holding her face away from the ring, and covering her ears with her hands. But Jane's eyes were fixed on the spectacle. Her body was rigid with excitement. Ellen too jumped up and down in her seat, screaming, as a tiger dared the space between him and the man with outstretched claw. And Jane knew why the man did it. Death; life; side by side in the ring. Both had their fascination; both had their attraction. The beast that would prey on the man was magnificent indeed. Her heart reached out to the brutes. Fierce with anger against the man, she longed for the cat to pounce. She desired it. She willed it. And watching her, Robert smiled, taking her fevered flush for joy, missing the darkness in her eyes.

How could he stay away so long? His sweet sister. All the women of the world fell short of her. Innocent as the infant in her lap; he loved her. He squeezed her hand. The show was over. The tigers left the ring. They left the ring, but not her heart.

As Jane's eyes turned blinking on the ordinary world, she was dismayed to see the greyness of it. The drab faces. The shrill voices. The feeble rhythm of the life around her. Pitter patter went the collective heart of the town, while hers pounded out a jungle beat, hard, insistent, loud. It made demands. Could no-one else hear it, as she put the girls to bed, as she made the tea, as she laid the table, as she spoke to Edie? Could no-one else see the Jane imprisoned in her life, clamouring to be out? Her unspent, surging passion for life threatened all around her. 'Let me out, before I die!' her soul cried out. The years with George had turned into a desert and she was withering in it.

When the children were in bed and Edie had gone to read up in her room, Jane sat with her brother by the kitchen fire. Tears of anger and frustration stung her eyes. Robert's heart was still, caught in the magnetic field of her desire. His foot reached out to touch hers, and she jumped, her eyes like starbursts on him.

'Sorry!'

'No! It's me! I'm a bit jumpy. That's all.'

'Why?'

'I don't know . . . it was . . . this afternoon . . . I felt . . . it was as though I'd come alive again,' suddenly Jane was crying hard, painful tears, scorching her throat, 'and I don't want to lose that! Robert? Do you hear me? I don't want to lose that!'

'Why should you?'

'I'm dying here, Robert. Slowly dying!' Robert shook his head, amazed and a little afraid. 'I can't go on living like this. I've got to get out. I should never have come to this shop. I should never have listened to you all. I should have done what I wanted. I should have gone on the stage, been an actress! At least I would have lived!'

'It's not all it's cracked up to be . . . '

'You can say that, Robert! Look at you! It's not fair. You've got everything I ever wanted! You've seen the whole wide world, and the farthest I've even been is Newcastle! Hah! Newcastle!'

'You've got a secure home, a husband, children . . . '

'I've got nothing!'

'Jane!'

'Oh, I love my children. But I'm dying inside! My whole life is spent supplying the needs of others. No-one thinks of my needs. And I do have them, even though I *am* only a woman!' Robert was silent, as he looked on the tear streaked face of the woman who was his sister. 'Help me, Robert.' Dumbly he stared on. Then he shook his head.

'How can *I* help you?'

'Help me get away.' Robert frowned.

'You mean, you want to leave George?' Jane nodded sharply.

' . . . what about Ellen, and Maisie . . . ?'

391

'I don't want to leave them behind . . . if there was a way . . . '
Her body began to shake, the pent up feelings of the years racked
her frame, the temple too weak to hold the spirit.

'Where would you go?'

'I want to go to India . . . '
A moment's stillness crept between the pounding drumbeats of
her heart. A promise of fulfilment, of peace which was not death,
but the culmination of her most passionate seeking.

'Why?' Robert asked, shaking his head, 'why?'

'I don't know why!' she shouted, 'I just know I must!'

'Well, women do live there . . . white women, I mean. I
suppose . . . ' Hope sprang into Jane's eyes.

'Then so can I! Robert, you must help me! You must!'

'I don't know . . . '

'You must.' Her strength was too much for him. His eyes
wavered, and he looked away. 'Where are you bound next?'

'I don't know. Wherever Roper's send me, I suppose. Where
there's a cargo to be shipped . . . maybe South Africa.'

'Maybe India?'

'Maybe.'

'But you will go to India some time?'

'Probably.'

'And you'll see Chandrika?'

'Yes.'

'Then there *is* a way!' Robert waited.

'I have a plan . . . you, me, maybe even the children, we could
all go!'

'What about George?'

'George? What *about* George?! He doesn't love me!'

'He loves the children.'

'He has his son! Isn't one family enough for him, without me
and mine?'

'I suppose that's fair . . . '

'Fair? Nothing's fair!' Jane spoke through bared teeth, her
voice rasping. 'I want to start a new life, Robert, before it's too
late! Will you help me?' It was a challenge to his very manhood.

'Yes.' Robert smiled, and the hands of brother and sister
reached out to one another, grasping firm. A new excitement

392

surged in the man. 'You know, I'm really looking forward to it! I can't wait to show you India. There's some amazing places. You wouldn't believe . . . !'

'Oh Robert!' Crying with joy, Jane jumped out of her chair, and took her brother in her arms, 'I do love you!'

'I love you too, little'n!' He hugged her close, then stood back to look at her. 'Not so little now. You're a fine woman.'

'Am I?'

'Yes.'

'George is a fool.'

'Why worry about George?'

'He doesn't know what he's got.'

'Then it's time he learnt,' her hands clawed down her brother's back, 'I'll show him!'

In the darkness, the elephants were restive. One by one, they rose, cumbersome, to their feet. Silently, ears pricked, the adults formed a circle round the young, safe at the centre. Something prowled. Something deadly. The great heart of the elder pounded. His foot pulled on his chain. It rattled in the silence. A pause. Listening. Then great feet shuffled, closing the circle, and Jumbo raised his trunk. Danger smelt. It burned across the heavy air, like the crackle of lightning. His foot pulled on the chain. Sharp. Then again. Sharp. Then again. And the chain snapped, dragging after him, out of the circle, to stand alone. And the sea swelled, heaving onto the shore, stamping, beating the sand in the dark night. And the elephant looked up out of the compound, searching the black sky for the moon. Had it fallen from the sky? Had it deserted him in his time of need? Would it leave him without light? The whisper of danger spread its claws. It felt its way towards him. Primitive. Darker than the night. Known on the sixth sense. Ancient enemy, dredged from the unconscious, the elephant knew him yet. Knew him and feared him. And then, fiery, the burning eyes blazed. And the elephant saw. And the circle closed. Jumbo stood outside, guardian, ready to defend. The cat sprang, powerhouse spearing the air, landing, lancing the back of the elephant, slashing the thick grey hide. And the blasting trumpets blared, angry, red hot the sound which woke the keepers. And they ran, nets, sticks, guns ready. But the tiger and the elephant, locked in passionate embrace, let no-one, nothing near; only the dust of the ground, which swirled about them, as though the gravity of earth itself had entered into combat. The world was chaos. Blood rained. Savagery curdled the air with the discordant howlings of the terror of death. And the tiger, thrown high, turned, a catherine wheel, falling beyond the perimeter of the compound, at the keeper's feet, curling, rolling, into the net. And the elephant stood dark, in the darkness. And when the moon came up, the keeper saw the blood, and he took his gun, and he aimed, and he shot. The elephant stood, aged beyond time. There was silence. All watched. Then the elephant sagged, fell to his knees. And the keeper raised his gun again, and he shot. But the elephant rose slowly to his feet. Ancient. Proud. And the keeper raised his gun for the third time. And he fired. The agony of the elephant jarred through his frame. The legs behind buckled under. His head raised in one last trumpet blast. Like a huge rock, he seemed to tower. Then the great beast crashed to earth. Dead. And the rain began. And the dark blood oozed, seeping into the clay, through the cracks, deep down to the centre of the earth.

George stared at the gaping door of the safe. There had been a thief in the night. Everything had gone. A moment of disbelief, rage following close on its heels, and George knew his man. Robert Ridley! Stalking from the parlour, he ran down to the shop.

'Where is he?' His wife turned from the customer, and coolly looked at him.

'Who?'

'Your precious brother!'

The customer, sensing the impending storm, made her excuses and left.

'If you had been here yesterday, you would have known. Robert received a sudden order to sail. He left in the early hours of this morning!' George growled. His fist crashed down on the counter. But Jane stood firm.

'You're lying!'

'How dare you!'

A woman entered the shop, leaving at once as she sensed the

mood. Roused by the clanging bell, George went to the door, locked it, and turned back on his wife.

'Upstairs!' Jane stood still, intent on disobedience. But George made a move towards her, and she scurried from behind the counter, up the steps, to the balcony above the shop, where George now waited beside the open parlour door. 'Inside!' Mustering her dignity, Jane walked into the room, and stood before the gaping safe. There was a long silence. She felt his hands fall, heavy, on her shoulders, and he spun her round to face him. 'Look me in the face!' he commanded. Rebellious, the burning eyes looked back at him.

'Tell me the truth!'

'I did it! I gave Robert the money.' George searched Jane's eyes, and saw a barrier in her heart.

'Liar!' The wife's fury increased, but she said nothing. Frenzied with frustration, George shook her hard. 'Once a liar always a liar! Robert stole it!'

'No!'

'I know he did!'

'Then you know more than *I* do!'

'You're a liar, and he's a thief.'

'It's not true!'

'Then why did he run away?' Jane dropped her eyes. Again he shook her, till her head hurt. 'If you *gave* him the money, why would he run away?' Still, she said nothing. 'He stole it, didn't he? The man's a thief. He stole from his own brother, and now he's stolen from me!'

'No!' His hand, high above her, fell, stinging, on her face. 'Don't you dare touch me!' she screamed at him.

'It's my right!'

'You have none over me!'

'You're my wife, damn you!'

'I hate you!' She backed from him, making for the door, but he was too quick. Like a whip, his arm reached out, and pulled her back. A startled cry escaped from her, as he held her, pinioned to his chest. 'You don't own me, George Beattie!' she hissed into his face. But he stopped her mouth with his hand, pushing her head back.

'Don't I?' he roared. Her hand reached up, clenching his wrist, wrenching at it, to free herself. And there was no ring on her finger. He stopped. Jane waited, then pulled away. But again he caught at her, dragging her down to the floor at his feet. 'Where's your ring? Your diamond ring? Where is it?'

'I gave it to Robert.' Her voice was dark. It dared him. He had no choice. She had thrown him a challenge and his manhood rose to it. He threw her body backwards, sprawling on the floor, helpless, as his weight crushed her. His hands, holding hers, pinioned to her side, his teeth tearing at her clothes, he raised her, crashed her back to the ground, till she was sobbing for mercy. And he had none. He took her. On the floor before the gaping safe, George Beattie raped his wife.

CHAPTER TWENTY SEVEN

The God was dancing. One foot stood on the mouse, the other, raised high, was bent in towards the groin, the great belly protruding over it. The first arm pointed to the ground, finger raised in curse, or blessing. The second, on the left side, carried sweetmeats, the third held a lotus flower, high in the air, and the fourth, on the right held an axe. The head, with its huge flapping ears, looked straight before, and the graceful trunk curled to the left side.

The great hall was full. Smoke from the oil lamps, the central fire, the fumes of incense, curled around the guests, as the priest chanted salutations to the God Ganesha, elephant headed Lord of innocence, remover of obstacles. May He bless this marriage.

SumukaschAikadantascha Kapilo Gajakarnakah
Lambodarscha Vikato Vighnanasho Ganadhipa
Dhoomraketur Ganadyaksho Bhalachandro Gajananah

Behind the bridal veil, dark lashes lowered, and almond eyes turned to look sidelong at the bridegroom. And he was red, like her father, like the guests, like the fire, like the Great God, through the scarlet veil. Ushas, seventeen years old, shyly looked away as the groom, feeling her gaze, turned towards her.

Dwadshaitani namaniyah pathet shrunu yadapi
Vidyarambhe vivahecha praveshe nirgame tatha
Sangrame sankate chaiva vighnastasye na jayate

And he smiled, content, his heart filled with gratitude for the man who, today, was to become his father. White-haired Chandrika sat with his wife, while the Rahki sister, Kunti, sat some way off with the other women, to watch the ceremony of Robert's wedding. This was now his family. He had none other. But Chandrika was remembering another wedding day, another daughter he had given away, not in a red sari, but a white dress, pink roses, a garland round her golden hair. He had a duty to Jane too. *Her* daughter was getting married. Surely, there was something he could send . . .

But there was not much time. Three months gone by the boy next door, the grocer's lad! And George was furious with her! Poor Ellen felt his anger like a cloud, as she let out the seams of her wedding dress.

'It doesn't show, though, Mam, does it?' Jane looked up from the bridesmaids' gowns, and cast a critical eye on the tiny bump.

'We'd better make up some roses to trail down one side. That'll camouflage it.' She sighed, shaking her head. 'I'm not sure you should be wearing white at all!' Ellen said nothing. Pursing her lips, she pulled off the dress and began to sew.

'Will Dad ever speak to me again?' she said.

'I hope he doesn't!'

'Hester!' Jane reprimanded her youngest, a little girl of eight, who swung her legs, kicking, as she sat on the dressing table stool. 'Don't be so mean!'

'She's mean to me!'

'I am not!'

'Be quiet, Ellen! I shall be glad when you're safely out of the way in a home of your own. There's no peace in this house!'

'Huh! Don't blame me!' Ellen snapped. 'You'll learn who the troublemaker was soon enough. It's Maisie I'm sorry for.'

'Where is Maisie?'

'Went to make the tea for Da.'

'Let's hope she sweet talks him into a good temper, then. He was like a bear with a sore head this morning.' Jane pricked her finger, and sucked the blood from it. Hester tore the dress out of her hands.

'You'll get blood on it!' she shouted at her mother.

'As it happens, Hester, that's Maisie's dress, not yours.'

'I want to try mine on!'

'Later!' She looked at the wounded finger, holding it up in the air. A tiny globule of blood oozed out, and she sucked it again. Hester impatiently jumped off the dressing table stool, to search for her own dress, and knocked the table. The three mirrors, balanced on their supports, shook dangerously. 'Watch my mirrors!' Jane called out. 'It's seven years' bad luck, if you break one of them! Not to mention a good hiding!'

The flames leapt in the air. Ushas, tied to him, by a scarf, led Robert round the fire. Seven steps. One vow made, and with their feet, they knocked down one of the piles of rice.

Maisie came up with a tray for the ladies, closely followed by George.

'Are you all decent?' he called out, before coming in.

'Yes! Come on, dear,' Jane shouted, and George, cup and saucer in hand, walked into the room.

'What are you holding your left index finger up to heaven for? Are you beseeching your God?'

'I stabbed it with the needle. Satisfied?'

'Quite,' George sat amongst the threads and frayed ends on the bed. 'I feel neglected,' he said.

'Don't sulk, dear. It's not every day your daughter gets married.'

'It's just as well. It's costing me a fortune. I don't know how other men manage!'

'Ah yes, but of course, you have extra overheads.' Jane's voice had a sharp edge to it, and George darted her a warning look. Quick as a flash, Hester caught it.

'What?' she asked archly, hugging her own bridesmaid's dress close.

'Never you mind. It's business,' her mother said, frowning.

* * *

399

Robert followed Ushas round the fire, for the second time. Seven steps, another vow made, and the second pile of rice toppled under their feet.

'What business?'

'None of yours!' her father shouted. Hester pouted, and fiddled with a powder bowl on the table.

'Leave that alone!' her mother ordered. Hester jumped and upset the bowl, spilling pink powder onto her new dress. Jane tore it from her, and held it up, groaning.

'You clumsy fool!'

'Sorry, Mam.'

'Sorry, my foot!' her father said. 'You did it on purpose.'

'No I didn't!' And now the child was crying.

'Never mind, I expect it'll wash out.'

'You shouldn't be so soft on her, Jane!' George said sharply.

'I'm *not* soft! She's only a child!'

George looked at his youngest, but the eyes evaded him, slyly turning to the spilt powder on the dressing table. Ellen shrugged.

'See what I mean? Now who's the troublemaker?' she said triumphantly to her mother.

The third pile of rice toppled, and Robert now led his bride around the fire, seven steps, and the fourth vow made, and the fourth pile of rice demolished under their feet.

In the parlour, George ploughed through the bills. In the kitchen, Jane's hands, blistered with holding the piper, iced the cake. It had three tiers.

'Do you want bells or horse shoes or what?' she asked Ellen.

'Both.'

'You can't have both. It would look far too much.'

'Horse shoes, then.'

'All right.'

'It's the nearest I've ever got to riding!'

'Don't let your father hear you complaining, our Ellen. He'll have your guts for garters!'

'Well, he's mean to me!'

'He is not! Look what he's paying for this wedding! And you know how he feels about it!'

'I wanted the Queen's Hall.'

'I wanted Buckingham Palace, but I never got it!' She heard steps on the stairs. George was coming down. 'Sh!' The father came in, bowed down by bills, looking for his supper, but found instead icing and marzipan everywhere.

'Ellen says she thinks you're mean,' Hester told him.

Again, Robert led. The fifth vow, seven steps, and the fifth pile of rice fell. Behind him, Ushas giggled softly, his steps were so huge, she had trouble keeping up with him, and the scarf pulled at her. Robert looked back and smiled apologetically. But she didn't mind. He was her husband. Her loving Lord. Whatever he did was right and proper in her eyes. 'Where you lead, I will follow . . . as quickly as I can!' her teasing look said. But being a loving Lord, he adjusted his step to suit her, and the seven steps of the sixth vow were completed, amidst the laughter of the company.

'Mean! Mean!' George raged. 'Me mean? I tell you one thing, Ellen, you're the only one in this family who's going to get a send off like this, now I know what it costs!'

Maisie, deep in the washing up water, suddenly threw her apron over her face, and rushed out into the yard, sobbing.

'George! Now look what you've done!'

'Give me strength!' George put his hand to his head. 'I thought Edie was bad enough, but our Maisie . . . !'

'*I* want a proper wedding!' the little voice in the corner insisted, 'with cake, and flowers and veils and millions of people and everything!' George turned on his youngest child.

'You!' he shouted. 'You! Hah! That's what you think, my girl!'

'I'm just going next door to see the Lidells.' Making her excuses, Ellen sidled out unnoticed to escape the storm.

'George, stop it!'

'You'll be lucky if you get married at all!'

Hester began to cry. 'George . . . !'

'In fact, you'd do *better* not to marry, if you ask me! "Hie thee to a nunnery!" That's what I say!'

401

'Don't be so melodramatic, dear.'

'You're always cross with me!' Hester whimpered pitifully.

'You never do anything to please me!'

'I do! Honest I do!'

'She does try, George!'

'All this talk of marriage!'

'It's only natural, dear with all this going on . . . ' Jane surveyed the table with the cake ornaments of silver bells, and horse shoes. 'She's bound to think of when *she* grows up.'

'When she grows up, she should join a religious order! Never marry at all! No man would put up with her!'

'George!'

Howling like a banshee, the little girl ran into the shop, and began throwing flowers everywhere.

Seven more steps, Ushas following Robert round the flames, the final vow was made, and the last pile of rice was overturned. The scarlet veil was thrown back, and Robert looked upon the face of his lovely bride. Tears came to the eyes of the mother, and Chandrika's heart was full, as the guests clapped, and cried out in jubilation.

'Nobody's going to want to marry me!' Crouched at his daughter's feet in the yard midden, George tried to comfort her.

'Now then, Maisie. You're a nice girl. And one day . . . '

'I'm ugly.'

'Handsome is as handsome does.' His hand reached out to comfort the humped back of his second daughter, 'I'm sorry I said what I did. Just a fit of temper, that's all. I'm disappointed in our Ellen. It's upset me.'

Maisie sniffed back her tears, ready to comfort her comforter.

'I promise I'll be a good girl,' Maisie said softly.

'Yes. I know *you'll* be good.' Maisie's face suddenly creased again.

'Because nobody's likely to ask me to be wicked!' she wailed. George raised his eyes to heaven. 'God give me strength!' he prayed, 'daughters!'

Music and singing ended the long ceremony in Bombay. Robert, at his ease, sat cross-legged on the floor beside his bride, and called out, 'Wah! Wah!' as the musicians rose to greater and greater heights of inspiration. There was darkness outside, but in the hall, the oil lamps flickered. Hundreds of tiny flames glowed in the faces of the wedding guests. But no face was more radiant than Robert's. Leaning over to Ushas, he whispered into her ear, 'I love you.' She smiled, and bit her bottom lip, trying not to laugh, but unable to stop herself, she giggled, bringing the attention of the company on the bridal pair. Robert was surprised to find he was blushing, as fingers pointed, and faces grinned at the new couple. Accepted by the world in which he lived, his marriage sanctioned by his new religion, it only remained for Robert to express his gratitude.

'Put out the light.' George opened one eye as Jane appeared in her dressing gown. She turned to the mantle on the wall, and the light faded at her touch. 'On second thoughts . . . ' George smiled slowly, 'leave it on, very low.' Jane laughed, and in the dim glow of the gaslight, she slipped out of her gown to get into bed beside her husband. 'Come here, old lady.'

'Speak for yourself!'

'You have got white hair!'

'Doesn't mean a thing!'

'My angel!' George groaned as he nibbled at her ear.

'Huh! I'm no angel!'

'Mmmm . . . I suppose . . . ' he lay back against the pillows, 'I suppose I'm rather relieved really. It makes you easier to live with . . . '

'Hah! You mean if I'm not perfect I can't expect *you* to be either!'

'Exactly.'

Jane curled in to her husband's side. 'I hope Alice Minto isn't coming to this wedding . . . '

'Hah!'

'What does that mean?'

'Don't be so soft!'

'Good. Because if she did . . . '

'What would you do?'

'I'd tear her eyes out.'

'No you wouldn't. You'll have to forgive the poor woman, Jane. It's not her fault.'

'Who's is it then? Mine?'

George was surprised at the defensive tone in Jane's voice.

'Does it have to be somebody's?'

'Yes.'

George considered the matter.

'I don't think it does. That's simply how it is now. What's the point in apportioning blame? What's done is done. It can't be undone.' There was a long silence.

'No.'

George turned to his wife. He tried to look at her face, close to his own on the pillow. But she turned her head away. George frowned. This wasn't like Jane. His hand reached out and touched her cheek. It was wet.

'Jane!' He pulled her close to him, and comforted her gently. 'What is it, eh?' Jane sniffed, and blurted out,

'You're far too hard on Hester.'

'It's for her own good.'

'If you say so.'

'I do.'

'She really tries to please you.'

'I know. But I worry for her. Look what's happened to Ellen, and we had such hopes of her!'

'Ellen's all right. Stop fretting, George!'

That was more like it. Better than tears anyway! She was probably getting upset about losing a daughter . . . women! He felt her rounded hip with his hand.

'Mmmmmm.'

Jane laughed. 'I love it when you say "Mmmmmm", like that.'

'Mmmmmm,' he repeated and Jane lay back to look at the moonlight as it fell through the window.

'I haven't drawn the blind.'

'What are you suggesting . . . ?'

'Nothing!'

'Pity.' His hand reached round her hip.

'Now who's suggesting . . . ?' She moaned softly.

'Leave the blind. Put out the light, though. It'll be better by moonlight.' Jane smiled and got out of bed again, fading the gaslight down to nothing.

'Better?' she stood at the window, looking up at the moon. The same moon that shines on India . . . She sighed.

'What's wrong?'

'Nothing.'

'Come to bed.'

The crescent of the moon lay on its back, and the scarlet silk was draped lovingly over the carved chair. The past was dead. Long live the present. Robert's heart burst with love. If only Jane could find such happiness, he thought, as he looked on the pale and sultry face of his lovely wife.

'I love you,' she whispered, and her arms opened to him. Yes. The past was dead. Long live the present.

Jane turned from the window, and crept into the bed beside George.

'What were you thinking?' he asked her.

'Nothing.'

'Hah!' The subject was forbidden. He had forbidden it. How could he blame her then, if she would not admit she was thinking of her brother? So many years ago . . . if he had forgiven her, then equally, all should be forgotten. But had he forgiven her? Had she forgiven herself? Or would the ghosts always haunt them?

'What are *you* thinking about?' Jane's hand touched her husband's beard.

'Nothing!' he turned on her, kissing her violently.

'Help!' she cried weakly.

'I love you. Always have, Jane.' In the mirror of the dressing table, the moon reflected its pale light.

All that remained was for Robert to show his gratitude. In the Laxshmi Temples of Bombay, he took off his shoes, leaving them with the attendant at the gate; then he bought his garlands of marigolds, his baskets of flowers, and took them to the shrine of Lord Ganesh. Humbly bowing before the priest Robert made his offering, and then prostrated himself, before the image of the God.

'Forgive me,' he whispered. He looked up into the face of The Lord of Innocence, and prayed, with the full desire of his heart, that his union with Ushas would be blessed; that they would have a long, contented life together, their joy spilling out to everyone. The priest marked his brow with red dye, and placed one of the garlands round his neck. The deity had been propitiated. Robert could now begin to propitiate humankind.

18, Victoria Terrace was in a state of total bedlam. In the kitchen, Jane was putting the finishing touches to the bride's bouquet, while George himself saw to the button holes for the men. The cake, the sandwiches, and the trifle had all been sent ahead to the Town Hall in the market square, where George had booked a room for the wedding breakfast. Upstairs, Harriet had arrived, and was helping Ellen into her dress, while, in Jane's room, the bridesmaids struggled into theirs. And meanwhile, guests kept on arriving. Would they be ready in time? George took out his pocket watch, and stormed at his wife,

'Late as usual!'

'Oh stop it, George!'

'She'd be late for her own funeral,' he informed Mr Lidell, who quailed in the corner with a glass of cooking sherry.

'Well,' George turned to the groom's father, 'this day marks a truly dynastic occasion,' he intoned. Jane gave him a look, but not to be quashed, George continued, 'the union of our two businesses, Lidell's grocery, and Beattie's florists. May they prosper.' Uncertainly, Mr Lidell raised his glass and drank. Would the mayor take him over? Was he not so much gaining a daughter, as losing a business? It made him quake in his shoes even to look at his grand neighbour, sometimes. Oh dear! What a coward he was. And he knew very well there was nothing George Beattie detested more than a coward.

'Take no notice, Mr Lidell,' Jane reassured him. 'He just likes the sound of his own voice!' She laughed, and George could not be angry. 'Give him his buttonhole now, and shut up!' Obediently, George produced the red carnation, and gave it to his neighbour.

'We've got to look on the bright side,' he told him. George meant well, but the groom's father, wondering what lay beneath the remark, resumed an anxious look.

Upstairs, Maisie had been called in to assist Harriet with Ellen's dress.

'She's bursting out of it!' Harriet shouted, so the entire household could hear.

'Sh!' Ellen whispered desperately.

'We'll have to let out this dart.' Harriet showed Maisie the place.

'There's no time to sew it. It'll have to be pinned, that's all.'

'I can't get married with pins in my dress!' Ellen shrieked in alarm.

'Stop complaining!' Harriet ordered. 'It's your own fault you're in this state in the first place. Be thankful we're here to help you out at all.' Disconsolate, Ellen suffered her aunt's prodding and pulling.

'Ow!' she yelled. She always knew she was an old witch, but there was no need to stick pins in her!

In Jane's bedroom, Hester twirled in her bridesmaid's frock. It was so pretty. She liked it better since her mother had washed it. It was stiff before, but now it hung in soft, wispy frills about her slight frame. She was like a fairy. She was like one of the fairies that was invited to Sleeping Beauty's christening. One of the nice fairies, of course, not the bad one that brings the curse with her! She could be the Lilac Fairy, except her frock wasn't purple. But there was something wrong. She cocked her head to one side and pulled a face. Fairies didn't wear their hair in plaits! It was supposed to fall like wisps of spun gold about your shoulders. She sighed. Her mother had spent ages doing it up this morning. Her eye strayed to the dressing table. The brush and comb sat invitingly on it. Why not? Quick as a flash, before she could have time to regret her decision, Hester flew across the room, and sat on the stool before the triple mirrors. Pulling and tugging at one ribbon, she loosened it, then tore her hair out of its braid. She brushed it quickly, and admired the waving sheen. She turned her head, this way and that, marvelling at how the mirror reflected the lovely fall of her hair, so many times, she could not count. She went on forever in the reflecting glass. That was better! Much better! A satisfied smile came to her face. And it was no use anybody being angry with her either, because there wouldn't be time to plait it all up again! They would just have to like it or lump it! She was going to have her own way! Now for the other one! Hester put down the brush, and struggled with the ribbon. She pulled the wrong way, and the knot tightened. Her jaw set, and her brow furrowed. Her determination was reflected to infinity. She would just have to pull the ribbon off, that was all! Holding the plait with one hand, she heaved mightily with the other. The ribbon stuck, gave, stuck again. One last effort, and the ribbon flew off the end of the slippery hair, sending her hand crashing into the mirror. It tottered dangerously, then smashed forwards over the table, pinning Hester's arm under it. Blood spurted, covering the glass scarlet, on both sides, clouding the image of the child between, whose screams of terror brought the household running.

Harriet, first on the scene, applied a bandage, and the doctor, supping sherry in the kitchen, hurried up the stair to sew the wound. Hester cried pathetically. Everyone was angry with her. It had been her own fault. She was vain, wilful, stupid. No-one was sorry for her. Look at the mess she'd made! Frightening them all half to death, ruining her frock. Look at it! Spattered with blood, it had to be discarded.

'That dress was fated!' her mother said, as she sponged the matted blood out of her daughter's hair.

'It's a bad omen!' Ellen wept, shaking in her wedding dress.

'It's no such thing!' Jane snapped. 'You didn't look at the broken mirror, did you?' Ellen shook her head. 'There you are, then. If it's a bad omen for anyone, it's for our Hester!'

And then Hester moaned again. 'I'm always getting wrong!'

'That's because you so often *are* wrong!' Harriet scolded her. Red-eyed, pale and tired, Hester had to be put to bed. Harriet would stay behind to look after her. To Ellen's relief, 'that bloody child' was not to be a bridesmaid after all.

Frantic, Jane arrived at the chapel just ahead of the bride. She panted as she sidled into her pew, using sign language to indicate to the groom that all was more or less well. What a day! Her hat must be lopsided, her cheeks red, what a fright she must look!

But then the organ struck up the wedding march, and Ellen, leaning on George's arm, began the long walk down the aisle.

Harriet took off her tight shoes, and loosened her skirt. She hated weddings anyway! Her employer sneered at the chains women put on so willingly. No, marriage was not at all the done thing in the Bohemian set. And Harriet liked to think she was part of it. The 'lady's maid' aspect of her work was glossed over, and she considered herself primarily a companion to her erudite mistress. Of course, as far as the family were concerned, her staying behind to look after the child was a huge sacrifice. Harriet May would play the part of martyr to the full. But meanwhile, she would simply put her feet up, and have a nice glass of that sherry the men had been hogging!

There was someone rattling at the front door. Couldn't they read? The notice was clear enough. Hooking up her skirt, Harriet stalked through the shop, to stand arms akimbo, looking at the two men outside. They pointed at a huge parcel on the ground between them. Harriet frowned, and unlocked the door. The parcel was addressed to 'Beattie's'. It had foreign stamps all over it, and 'Port of Bombay' written on the side. What on earth could it be? Sighing at the inconvenience, Harriet signed the necessary papers, dismissed the men, and locked the door again. And now the child was crying for her! What next! She hurried up the stairs, to find Hester in her blue party frock, a silver horseshoe in her hands.

'I was supposed to give it to Ellen, after the service!' she whimpered, fists in eyes. Harriet sighed loudly. Was there no peace for the wicked? Very well! If that's how she wanted it! Harriet, martyred again, squeezed into her shoes, pinned on her hat, and half-carried, half-dragged the crying child down the back streets to Chapel Row.

Looking over her shoulder, over the heads of Dandy O and Eddie, Jane saw them creeping into the back rows. Alice Minto and her four children. The youngest, a boy of fourteen or fifteen, stood awkwardly, cap in hand, at his mother's side. Jane's heart missed a beat, as she turned back to face the altar. How could she? How could George? How dare they? Today of all days! The

409

shame! The humiliation! Jane could never forgive either of them for this! Never!

'I require and charge you both, as ye will answer at the dreadful day of judgement when the secrets of all hearts shall be disclosed, that if either of you know any impediment, why ye may not be lawfully joined together in matrimony, ye do now confess it. For be ye well assured that so many as are coupled together otherwise than God's word doth allow are not joined together by God; neither is their matrimony lawful.' A dreadful silence followed the words of the preacher. Why was it, that no matter how innocent the parties, those words invoked such dread? A sudden flurry at the back sent all heads turning. Hester, in her blue dress, led by Aunt Harriet came into the church. Jane frowned. The child looked pale and ill. It was the height of folly to bring her here! She turned back to the preacher, who was now continuing with the service.

The vows were taken, and Ellen Beattie became Ellen Lidell. The first fledgling had left the nest. Jane felt unaccountably upset. So much had happened in her life. So many faces had passed away. Her father, Rattler, Ma, Fanny and her little girl, dear Ronnie, Josh, who nursed a grievance against her and Robert, the dogs, Gormless, Scallywag. Edie, who'd got married and gone to live in Hull of all places! Adeline, and Robert . . . lost to her. George, raising his eyes to heaven in sweet relief, turned to his wife and grinned. But his face fell as he caught sight of Alice Minto. Men! They were so callous! But Jane was grateful for the little attention to herself, and comforted, she knelt to say 'The Lord's Prayer'.

'Our Father, which art in heaven, Hallowed by thy name. Thy kingdom come. Thy will be done, in earth as it is in heaven. Give us this day our daily bread. And forgive us our trespasses . . . ' If she forgave, would the ghosts leave her alone? She had forgiven Harriet. She had forgiven Jack. She had forgiven herself over Ronnie. But Alice still haunted her . . . 'Forgive us our trespasses . . . ' It had all begun with Alice, all her troubles . . . She had wronged her, standing at Adeline's graveside. She had wronged Alice Minto. At last, facing the cross itself, Jane admitted it. 'I'm sorry,' she whispered. 'Forgive me . . . everything.'

Maisie was showering the newly weds with confetti. Hester, pushing to the front, pale and grim with determination, shoved the silver horseshoe at her sister.

'How are you, my pet?' Ellen asked in unusually affectionate terms, as she took the offering. Quickly Jane turned the horseshoe the other way about.

'It was upside down,' she said. 'It should be a rainbow shape, not a "U". If it's like that it lets all the luck out!'

'Superstitious drivel,' Harriet snapped, but Ellen took care to keep the horseshoe the right way up. 'My heart leaps up when I behold a rainbow in the sky.' She remembered the little poem her father had taught her and feeling like a child again, she wept, laying her head on her husband's shoulder, as they made their long, slow way to Market Square and the wedding breakfast.

Alice faded, as she had appeared, unnoticed by all but Jane, George and Harriet May. The bride and groom sent off for their one night honeymoon to Newcastle, the family repaired to Fowler Street. Mellow and nostalgic, they were ripe for a cosy sit down by the fire, and a nice cup of tea. George turned the key in the lock, and pushed the shop door. Something stopped it. He pushed harder, and he heard the slither of something heavy moving across the floor. He sidled into the shop and, raising the blinds, saw the great parcel with its foreign marks. 'What's this? It's addressed to me!' he said. Jane looked, and her heart leapt into her throat. She shook her head. 'It says "Beattie's" not "Mr Beattie",' she pointed out. 'Don't split hairs, woman!' Taking a knife, George ripped the casing open. Inside the huge wooden box was a carving made out of sandalwood. 'Just smell it!' Harriet exclaimed. 'Eeh, I don't know what it is, but it's exotic, all right!' Jane pursed her lips. Harriet could be so silly! Holding her breath, she watched, as George heaved the great carving out, and placed it gingerly on the floor, amongst the tubs of flowers. Jane stared at the statue. It was huge, coming up to her waist. What could it be? Some strange and primitive idol no doubt. It had an elephant's trunk, of all things, which curled to the left side. And it had huge flapping ears. George was fishing about in the bottom of the box, and came up triumphantly with a piece of paper. He held it to the light and read it.

' "From Chandrika. On the auspicious occasion of a wedding." '

And that was all. 'Who's Chandrika when he's at home?' George asked, puzzled.

'Don't you remember? He was that Indian friend of my father's!'

'What's he want to go giving expensive presents like this for?' George demanded, 'it's not right!'

'I don't see why! He gave me away at *my* wedding. So he's a bit like a sort of father to me really. And that makes Ellen a sort of granddaughter. I think it's very nice of him.'

'Oh yes!' Vaguely, George recalled the quiet man who had stood at his bride's side. 'I suppose that's all right, then.' So persuaded, George took out his red carnation and rubbed his hands. 'How about a cup of tea then?' Carelessly dropping the flower on the floor, he turned to go into the kitchen. Jane frowned and bent to pick up the discarded buttonhole. A single red flower. Memories came in waves. Ronnie. Saint George. A single red rose, earth smattering upon it. Tears rained down her face. 'Forgive us our trespasses.'

'Jane! I want my tea!' George called from the kitchen. Leaving the flower where it was, at the foot of the idol, Jane dried her tears and went into the kitchen.

As she undressed for bed, thoughts of the day drifted through her mind. There had been such a tumult of emotion to get through. What with Hester, safely tucked up in bed by now, Ellen's dress, Alice turning up . . . my, but her youngest had the look of George about him . . . As though stung by her thought, George glanced at his wife, and said guiltily, 'I didn't invite her, Jane. Believe me.'

'No, George. I'm sure you didn't.'

'You said you'd tear her eyes out if she showed her face.'

'Did I?' Jane smiled to herself. 'It wouldn't have helped matters, would it?' George was amazed. Women! He'd never understand them in a million years! And what about that statue? That was a funny thing. He didn't like it. He didn't know why, but he just didn't like it! He'd got the impression that Indian was a poor man! How could he have afforded such a thing? It must have cost a fortune! The shipping alone . . .

'What are you thinking?'

George started, as he lay back against the pillow, deep in thought.

'How beautiful you look.'

'Hah! Liar!'

'No. It's true.'

'Thank you, George. You can be very sweet sometimes.'

She pulled back the covers and got in beside him.

'So can you.'

'I love you.' George looked into his wife's eyes, and he knew it was true. There were no barriers there. She was his wife. And she was glad to be his wife.

'I love you too.'

'I know, George. It's just . . . sometimes you have a funny way of showing it!'

'I'm human.'

'To err is human, to forgive divine.'

'I've forgiven. Have you?'

'Yes. And I'll keep on forgiving, George.'

'Till Kingdom come. It's the only way.'

'Love me. Only love me.'

'Of course, my dear.'

Downstairs, amongst the tubs of flowers, the God was dancing. One foot stood on the mouse, the other, raised high, was bent in toward the groin, the great belly protruding over it. The first arm, pointed to the ground, finger raised, in curse, or blessing.